A hunt through the Scottish Highlands for a hidden cache of gold draws in three passionate couples—who discover that love is the greatest treasure of all—in the thrilling new trilogy from *New York Times* bestselling author

CANDACE CAMP
Secrets of the Loch

❧

"*Treasured* demonstrates Candace Camp's ability to draw her readers in with strong, well-drawn characters. A legend of hidden treasure, a man who hides behind many façades, and a woman who fights for her birthright form the tapestry of this poignant, sensual, and emotion-packed romance."
— *RT Book Reviews* (Top Pick)

❧

And praise for Candace Camp's acclaimed trilogy
Legend of St. Dwynwen

THE MARRYING SEASON
A SUMMER SEDUCTION
A WINTER SCANDAL

"Sensuality, intrigue, and Camp's trademark romantic sparring. . . . Delightful."
— *Publishers Weekly*

"A charming courtship. . . . Readers will be captivated."
— *Booklist* (starred review)

"Sexy and sweet! Beautifully written, with just the right touch of mystery and a generous helping of a scandalous romance."
— *Coffee Time Romance*

❧

Be sure to read Candace Camp's dazzling Willowmere novels. . . . Critics adore this breathtaking Regency trilogy of the unforgettable Bascombe sisters!

AN AFFAIR WITHOUT END

"Delightful romantic mystery. . . . With clever and witty banter, sharp attention to detail, and utterly likable characters, Camp is at the top of her game."
— *Publishers Weekly* (starred review)

"Sprightly dialogue . . . [and] a simmering sensuality that adds just enough spice to this fast-paced, well-rendered love story." —*RT Book Reviews* (4½ stars)

A GENTLEMAN ALWAYS REMEMBERS

"Intensely passionate and sexually charged. . . . A well-crafted, delightful read." —*Romantic Times* (4 stars)

"A delightful romp. . . . Camp has a way with truly likable characters who become like friends." —*Romance Junkies*

"Where the Bascombe sisters go, things are never dull. Candace Camp delivers another witty, heartwarming, and fast-paced novel." —*A Romance Review*

A LADY NEVER TELLS

"This steamy romp . . . will entertain readers."
—*Publishers Weekly*

"Well-crafted and enchanting."
—*Romantic Times* (4½ stars)

"Superbly written and well paced, *A Lady Never Tells* thoroughly entertains as it follows the escapades of the Bascombe 'bouquet' of Marigold, Rose, Camellia, and Lily in the endeavor to make their way in upper-crust London society."
—*Romance Reviews Today*

"One of those rare finds you don't want to put down. . . . Candace Camp brings a refreshing voice to the romance genre."
—*Winter Haven News Chief*

"Filled with humor and charm. . . . Fine writing."
—*A Romance Review* (4 roses)

A PERFECT
Gentleman

Pocket Books

New York   London   Toronto   Sydney   New Delhi

Pocket Books
An Imprint of Simon & Schuster, Inc.
1230 Avenue of the Americas
New York, NY 10020

This book is a work of fiction. Any references to historical events, real people, or real places are used fictitiously. Other names, characters, places, and events are products of the author's imagination, and any resemblance to actual events or places or persons, living or dead, is entirely coincidental.

First Pocket Books paperback edition April 2017

POCKET and colophon are registered trademarks of Simon & Schuster, Inc.

For information about special discounts for bulk purchases, please contact Simon & Schuster Special Sales at 1-866-506-1949 or business@simonandschuster.com.

The Simon & Schuster Speakers Bureau can bring authors to your live event. For more information or to book an event, contact the Simon & Schuster Speakers Bureau at 1-866-248-3049 or visit our website at www.simonspeakers.com.

Interior design by Carly Loman

Manufactured in the United States of America

10 9 8 7 6 5 4 3 2 1

ISBN 978-1-5011-4157-7
ISBN 978-1-5011-4158-4 (ebook)

For my favorite Abby, who keeps these books on track and has an answer for every question

prologue

1871

Abby tucked her hand into Graeme's arm, and they started up the stairs. Everyone was watching them. Afraid she might stumble or do something equally embarrassing in front of them all, she was grateful for his support. She cast a shy glance up at the man beside her and was struck all over again by how handsome Graeme was—the clean-cut profile and firm masculine chin, the full mouth that could curve up in a smile that made her heart lift in her chest, the blue eyes rimmed by sinfully thick lashes a shade darker than his brown hair. More amazing still, he was hers.

She ducked her head to hide the little smile of pleasure. She was Mrs. Graeme Parr now—no, Lady Montclair. No, that couldn't be right, either, for he would not be Lord Montclair until his father died. All the names and titles were confusing. It was best to avoid the subject altogether—Abigail had found that in London, the wisest course of action was to keep one's mouth shut.

Not that Graeme was ever unkind. He was a perfect gentleman, the sort hostesses relied on to dance with the wallflowers or spend a few minutes talking to the old ladies. Unfailingly pleasant and polite, he treated her, as he did everyone, with quiet courtesy. He had not once gotten that supercilious look on his face that other English people did when she said a name wrong—how could anyone expect Worcester to be pronounced like that!—and he kept a polite expression on his face the few times she did say something, no matter how banal it was.

He did not love her, of course. Abby was well aware that her attraction lay in her father's fortune, not her face and figure. And, in truth, between the chaperones and social activities, the two of them hadn't been alone enough to become more than acquainted. But Graeme would be good to her. Kind. And she would earn his love; Abby was certain of that. She was now a married woman, out from under her father's thumb, with a husband who would not scold or try to rule her every movement.

She stole another look at her groom. Deep lines bracketed his mouth, and he had shadows beneath his eyes. Like her, she thought, he had been unable to sleep well recently. How could one, with the myriad of things to do before a wedding? All the running about, meeting so many people it made her head swim . . . the nerves that would not quiet.

Still, the set look on his face seemed too grim for mere weariness. Was he angry? Only minutes ago she had noticed him talking to her father. Thurston Price had a way of infuriating people, snapping out orders as if one must scurry to do his bidding. Of course, most people did. Including her.

But it didn't matter. She was free of her father now. *They* were free of him. Tomorrow they'd be off on a monthlong tour of the Continent. Alone. Just as they would be tonight. Her fingers tightened on his arm. For the first time, she would be truly alone with her husband. The thought was intoxicating . . . and a little frightening. She was decidedly uncertain of the details; no one would say anything clear about what went on. Even her maid, Molly, on whom she could usually rely, was little help, having been a spinster all her life.

"Just trust in his lordship," was Molly's best advice. "He seems like a gentleman even if he is British." Molly, whose mother hailed from Glasgow, had an inbred distrust of all things English.

Molly was right, of course. Graeme was a perfect gentleman. Unlike her father, he would not roar at her over a mistake. Still, she could not help but wish that this night was over, that it was tomorrow morning and they were starting out on their life together.

Abigail had looped the train of her wedding dress over her arm to make certain she did not trip over it, and it was beginning to weigh on her arm. The long veil and the intricate hairstyle beneath it were heavy as well, and her corset, fastened more tightly than normal to create the perfect wasp waist, made it impossible to draw a full breath.

Leaving the stairs, they started down the long hallway to their suite. It seemed to Abby that Graeme's pace picked up, and she wondered if it was eagerness or merely the same excess of nerves she felt. Her heart was pounding as he opened the door and stepped back, politely ushering her into the room. She walked inside, hearing the door close heavily behind them.

She wasn't sure what to do, much less what to say. Her cheeks flushed as the silence stretched, and finally, curiosity overcoming her shyness, she turned to look at him. He stood facing her, that same tense look on his face. The nerves in Abigail's stomach tightened.

"What—" she began, not even sure what she was asking. "Are you—is something wrong?"

He let out a short, humorless huff of a laugh. "What isn't wrong?"

The blood drained from her face, and a buzzing began in her ears, so loud she could not make out his words. She clenched her hands, drawing a deep breath, willing herself not to faint.

". . . but I'm not dancing to his tune," Graeme was saying when her ears cleared. His eyes were hard in a way she'd never seen them. "Or yours."

"Excuse me?" Her voice came out barely more than a whisper.

"Your father may have bought you a husband, but he did not buy a puppet."

"I—I don't understand."

"Then I shall make it as clear as I possibly can." He took a long stride toward her, his eyes implacable. "The two of you have the title you wanted so much, the name you coveted. But that is all you acquired. I am not here to provide him with future earls carrying his bloodline. I made this bargain to save my family, not to stand at stud for the Prices."

Abigail drew in a sharp breath, as stunned as if he had slapped her.

"That surprises you? Are you so incapable of human feeling?" His words came out fast and furious, raining down like stones on her bruised heart. "Did you honestly think, knowing I loved another, that I would just slide into your bed? That I would be your lapdog? You'd best think again. I will never be a husband to you in anything but name."

Abby could not speak, could not move, could only stare at him in bleak horror. It took every ounce of will to keep her trembling knees from collapsing under her. Graeme despised her. This perfect gentleman, this kind husband who she had thought would be her lifelong shelter, in fact wanted nothing to do with her. He loved someone else.

Graeme paused, watching her as if he expected a reply. Pain and loss and fury swirled inside Abby, almost choking her. "I see."

His mouth twisted. "I thought you would."

Turning on his heel, he strode to the door. He tossed the hotel room key onto the lamp table and walked out of the room.

Abigail continued to stand, gazing at the blank expanse of the door, still too stunned to move. Her legs began to tremble until they could not hold her any longer, and she sank to her knees, a low cry escaping her. Reaching up, she wrenched the delicate veil from her head and, at last, she gave way to sobs.

chapter 1

1881

There was someone in his room.

Graeme's eyes flew open, and he found himself staring at a massive square head on a level with his eyes. The dog regarded him unblinkingly, its graying forehead creased as if in deep concern. Graeme, muscles instinctively tensed, relaxed, letting out a sigh.

"Good Lord. James . . ." Graeme turned his gaze toward the man in the doorway, shoulder carelessly braced against the frame. "A fellow could have a heart attack, waking up with that beast staring at one. And what the devil are you doing in my room at the crack of dawn?"

"Hardly the crack of dawn, cousin." The lean, dark man snorted and strolled farther into the bedroom, his gray eyes reflecting an icy amusement. "We've already eaten breakfast and driven over from Grace Hill. Even my mother is up and about, and you know Tessa is never seen before noon."

Graeme sat up, wincing, and raised a hand to his head. "I had trouble going to sleep last night."

"Too much brandy, eh?" James crossed to the window and thrust aside the draperies, letting in a shaft of light that stabbed straight into Graeme's eyes.

Graeme turned his head away, but with a sigh swung his legs out of bed and stood up. "I thought you were in London."

"We returned yesterday." James picked up the dressing gown lying on the back of the chair and tossed it to Graeme.

"That doesn't explain what you're doing in my house." He pulled on the robe, adding darkly, "Or why Fletcher let you come up to roust me out of bed."

"Oh, he tried to stop me." James tugged at the tasseled cord to summon Graeme's valet. "Surely you don't think I listened."

"Of course not." Graeme rubbed his hands over his face, trying to pull his scattered thoughts together. "You say Aunt Tessa is here, too?"

"Indeed."

"But why?" Was it possible he had so overslept? He had consumed a good deal of brandy last night. He had been somewhat at loose ends—well, he might as well admit it, he had been crushingly bored. But surely he could hold his liquor better than that. Graeme glanced toward the clock. "It's barely ten. I've never known Aunt Tessa to venture out before noon."

"Ah, but we have been charged by the dowager countess to deliver a message to you. Mother would never miss that opportunity, even if she had to rise at your proverbial crack of dawn. Gossip, after all, is her métier."

"Gossip? What are you talking about?"

"Get dressed and come downstairs, and I'll tell you in detail." James strolled to the door, slapping his hand against his thigh to summon the gigantic mastiff, which had grown bored with the talk and was now stretched out on the floor, taking up what looked to be a third of the room. "Your mother is, of course, insisting on laying out a second breakfast for us all."

"James . . ." Graeme said through clenched teeth, letting his words drop one by one like stones. "What in the bloody hell is going on?"

"Lady Montclair is in London."

"My grandmother?" Graeme frowned in confusion. "But—well, of course she's in London; you just said she'd given you—"

"I'm not talking about the dowager countess. I meant the other Lady Montclair."

"My mother? But she's—"

"I *meant*," James said with heavy emphasis, "the third Lady Montclair. Your wife."

With that parting shot, Graeme's cousin turned and walked out, the mastiff padding at his heels.

Graeme stared after him, frozen. His wife! He sat down hard on the ottoman in front of the chair. The pounding in his head increased its beat. *His wife*.

He tried to summon up an image of the woman he had married ten years ago. Tall, thin, and drab, her black hair a stark contrast to pale skin. Quiet and always dressed in white, she had faded into the background. He had paid little attention to her looks, other than to see she was nothing like Laura. She had large eyes. He could not recall their color, but he remembered them fixed on him, watching, measuring. He'd had no idea what was in her head; in truth, he hadn't cared to know. She had, he thought now, sat like a spider in her web, waiting while her father pulled him in.

Resentment and anger, long buried, stirred in him. They had wanted a title, Abigail Price and her father, and they'd had the money to pay for it. And if their fortune was not enough to secure it, they had other means.

Graeme had known he had to marry wealth to save the estate. He'd been prepared to do his duty, even if it meant giving up Laura, the woman he loved. What he hadn't expected was that they would blackmail him into it. But Thurston Price was not the sort to leave anything to chance.

Grimly, Graeme rose and began to dress, not bothering to wait for his valet. What had possessed the woman to come back? His life had been . . . well, maybe not happy, but *comfortable* with her far away in New York. It was not the cozy future he had once envisioned with the woman he loved—raising their children, growing old together— but at least he was spared the daily presence of the wife he'd never wanted. There had been a bit of a scandal, of course, what with his bride fleeing on their wedding night. And one couldn't explain to everyone that he was happy to see her gone. But the family had weathered that. He had kept the estate intact. He had concealed the stain on the family name. And he had his solitude, his undisturbed peace.

What could Abigail Price want from him now? He had given her the name she and her father had so desperately coveted. She had the life she wanted in the far-off city where she belonged.

It had been something of a shock ten years ago when he returned to her hotel suite the day after their wedding, armed with an apology for his blunt, even rude, assessment of their marriage the night before, as well as a proposal for living politely apart, only to be informed that his wife had checked out that morning. His astonishment was quickly replaced by relief that, just as he'd thought, Abigail had been interested only in acquiring a title. Having obtained that, she has raced back to her own country.

She had remained there for ten years, apparently as content as he to live without the burden of a spouse. He had heard, now and then, rumors of how she reigned in splendor in New York society, her parties the most elegant, her invitations the most sought-after, but, in truth, he had little interest in what she did . . . as long as she did it an ocean away from him.

When he strode into the dining room downstairs a few minutes later, he found the others waiting for him, James standing at the window a few feet apart from the two middle-aged women seated side by side at the table. The sweet-faced woman in black, her brown hair liberally sprinkled with white, was his mother, and she looked up at him with her usual smile. She was a softened, slightly faded, and pleasingly plump version of the woman beside her, whose thick dark hair, startlingly silver eyes, and lush curves still brought men clustering around her.

"Mother." He went around the table and bent to kiss his mother's cheek. "Aunt Tessa. How kind of you to visit." Graeme smiled. One could not help but smile at his aunt.

Aunt Tessa, of course, rose as he turned to her and flung her arms around him. "Graeme! My favorite nephew." She stepped back, hands on his arms, and tilted her head, studying him. "Handsome as ever, I see."

"Your only nephew," he reminded her. "And you are as radiant as ever."

"Flatterer." Tessa smiled in her impish way. "Just what I like in a man."

"Mother, must you flirt with every man you see?" James joined them.

"Don't be such a stodgy old man." Tessa turned the same fetching grin on her son. "One has to practice one's art when one can, you know."

"Mm. So I've noticed." James sat down beside her, nodding toward Graeme. "Better get yourself a cup of tea, coz. You'll need it. A dollop of whiskey might help."

Graeme sat down, accepting the cup of tea the butler poured. He took a sip and gave a nod to Fletcher, who discreetly melted away, closing the door behind him. "Very well. I am braced for the worst. What is going on, and why did Grandmother send you?"

"I told you. Your absent and very unlamented wife has returned to London."

"Really, James," Tessa protested. "You haven't the faintest idea how to tell a story properly." She turned to her nephew, eyes sparkling. "She appeared last Tuesday at Lady Rochester's soiree. No one had the least idea who she was. She was wearing this marvelous satin gown of midnight blue, with the most wonderful lace draped—"

"I don't think Graeme is concerned with the style ball gown she wore," James interrupted drily.

"Mirabelle and I are." Tessa addressed her sister, "It was just divine, Mira; you should have seen the satin roses over the bustle. It was made by Worth or I know nothing of fashion."

"No one would dispute your eye for clothes, Aunt Tessa," Graeme said with more amiability than Tessa's son. "But why is Abigail here?"

"I haven't the faintest idea." Tessa gave a careless shrug. "Neither has anyone else. But of course, everyone is guessing like mad. Lady Crowley is certain she's come to confront you—but you know Lady Crowley, she is always so dramatic."

Graeme shot a laughing glance at his cousin at the prospect of Aunt Tessa's deeming anyone dramatic. "But what would she confront me about?"

"That is why everyone is so interested, darling boy."

"Surely she could not be angry with Graeme." Mirabelle frowned. "It was she who left him, after all." She sighed. "And she seemed such an unexceptionable girl. I rather liked her."

"You like everyone, Mirabelle." Tessa took up her tale again. "The most popular theory is that she has come to act as a matchmaker."

"Matchmaker! What are you talking about?" A sizzle of alarm ran up Graeme's spine.

"For wealthy American girls, dear. They say she will use her British connections to find noblemen in desperate need of an infusion of cash and match them up with American heiresses. After all, she did it for herself."

"What connections?" Graeme asked. "She has no British connections."

"There's you," James pointed out.

"*I'm* not going to help her find her victims," Graeme said in an affronted voice.

"You know that, but does she?" James retorted. "Personally, I think you should help her if it means she'll leave the city."

"Of course, there are those who believe she simply wants to flaunt her, um, *friend* in your face."

"Friend?" Graeme's voice iced over. "What friend?"

"There's an American who dances attendance on her," James said. "Apparently he's a business associate of her father's."

"Business associate?" Graeme's lip curled. "Fellow crook is more like it. Is her father here, as well?"

"No," James told him. "Thurston's still in America, no doubt perpetrating stock swindles on other unsuspecting souls."

"At least there's some relief in that."

"I don't know how that dreadful man can do such things," Mirabelle said, her eyes suddenly glinting with tears. "Poor Reginald. He had no idea . . ."

"No, of course not, Mother."

"It's my opinion Thurston Price should have gone to gaol, enticing innocent people to invest in something just so he could make an enormous profit, then leaving them to crash." Mirabelle pulled a handkerchief from her pocket and dabbed at her eyes.

Her sister reached over and patted her hand. "Reggie always was inclined to great optimism."

"Yes, he was, wasn't he?" Mirabelle gave her a tremulous smile. "It was one of the many things everyone loved about him."

Everyone had loved his father altogether too much, Graeme thought, but he said only, "Unfortunately, what Mr. Price did was not illegal."

"Hmph. Only wicked." Mirabelle sniffed.

"Yes, wicked indeed. But that is long past. It has nothing to do with why Miss Pri— I mean, Lady Montclair, is here. Is she having—" He glanced at the women. "I beg your pardon, Mother, Aunt Tessa. This is not a fit topic for ladies."

"Good heavens, Graeme, don't stop just when you're getting to the interesting part," Tessa exclaimed. "One can be too polite, you know."

Graeme looked at James, whose eyes were brimming

with laughter. "Oh, very well. Is she having an affair with this American chap?"

"I have no idea." James shrugged. "The thought doesn't seem to disturb you."

"I don't care what she does. If she thinks to hurt me with an affair, she's fair and far off."

"But, Graeme, dear," his mother said in a soft voice. "What about the heir? What if she . . . you know . . . bore another man's son? What would you do?"

"It would be a dreadful scandal," Tessa agreed, her voice threaded with excitement. "Even if she doesn't have a child, it makes for titillating gossip. Merely by appearing in London again, it has stirred up all the old gossip. Everyone is rehashing the wedding—"

"Oh! That ostentatious display!" Mirabelle shook her head.

"Perhaps more importantly," James added, "there was the matter of the new bride taking to her heels the following morning."

"Yes, really, Graeme, couldn't you have held on to her for longer than a night?" Tessa asked.

His mother whirled on her sister. "Tessa! It wasn't Graeme's fault! He could hardly have kept her prisoner. I am sure leaving is what she had in mind all along."

"Well." Tessa turned up her hands in an eloquently questioning manner. "There were all those rumors . . ."

"Could we please not discuss the details of my wedding night?" Graeme ran his hand back through his hair. "You said Grandmother sent you with a message for me. What is it?"

"She wants you to come back to London and deal with your wife," James said tersely. "It's Lady Eugenia's opinion you should bring her to the estate, where she can't create any more talk."

"Bring her here? To Lydcombe Hall?" Graeme straightened. "You can't be serious. She wants me to live with Abigail?"

"Men have been known to live with their wives," James offered mildly.

"I won't. I refuse to have her here, to subject my mother to—"

"Oh, no, dear, I won't mind." Mirabelle leaned across the table and patted his hand. "Truly. I am sure she cannot be that disagreeable. It's a large house. No doubt we could all rub along well enough for a while, at least until the scandal dies down. Maybe she regrets running off like that years ago. It could have been a momentary impulse, just a fit of nerves, you know, and now she would like another chance."

"Speaking of great optimism," Graeme said in an exasperated voice. He sighed and squeezed his mother's hand gently. "No. I don't think the Prices are given to fits of nerves. I don't know what she wants, but I feel sure it is nothing good. And Grandmother is right, as always. I shall have to go to London to settle the matter."

"Will you bring her back here?" Mirabelle asked. "What room, I wonder, should I make up for her?"

"Don't bother, Mother. I don't intend to bring Abigail home. I am going to make sure she leaves."

chapter 2

Two hours later, Graeme was on the road in James's carriage, rolling toward London.

"The train would have been faster," Graeme remarked, twitching aside the curtain to gaze out.

"I've found that other passengers tend to resent having Dem on board." James nodded toward the brindle mastiff lying sprawled across the floor of the carriage. The dog responded with a thump of his tail against the door.

"Can't imagine why. After all, he does leave a few inches open where one can place one's feet."

The corner of James's mouth twitched in something that might have been a smile. "Buck up, coz, it doesn't take long. Even my mother managed it."

"*That* would have been something worth seeing." Graeme tried to imagine his luxuriously dressed aunt in close proximity to the animal.

"Mm. There was a bit of a contretemps over his drooling on a ruffle."

"One would think you're more attached to that dog than you are to your own brothers."

James shrugged. "Well, you've met my brothers."

"Point taken." After a moment, he went on, "You didn't

need to haul me back to the city, you know. I would have gone anyway."

"Ah, but I have a direct order from the dowager countess. I wouldn't dare do otherwise. It doesn't matter—I would have returned in a day or two anyway. My cousin Maurice has graced us with a visit; over a day in his company, and I would likely be jailed for homicide." He cast a sideways glance at Graeme. "I saw a letter from Miss Hinsdale on the entry table."

Beside him Graeme tightened. "She has kept up a correspondence with Mother. Her late mother was my mother's friend, you know. Don't worry. I have no correspondence with her."

James quirked an eyebrow. "You think I care if you write her? That my morals would be offended?"

"No. You simply were—and always are—the voice of cool reason."

"It comes in handy now and again."

"I rarely see Laura. Only sometimes at a party when she comes to London to visit her aunt and cousin. I don't pursue her." Seeing her now and then was difficult enough—her slim, serene blond beauty awakened far too many thoughts it was better to keep buried, reminding him all over again how much he had lost. "I wouldn't cast any doubt on her honor. No doubt that strikes you as laughable."

"No. Unfamiliar, perhaps." James studied the other man for a moment. "You still . . . feel the same about Miss Hinsdale?"

"Do I still love her? Yes, of course. Did you think I would just forget her? Like a lost toy?"

"It's been ten *years*, Graeme. Even widows move into half mourning eventually."

"Love doesn't die just because time passes," Graeme shot back. "But that is something you wouldn't know about." He stopped abruptly, and the temper that had flared in his eyes died. "I'm sorry, James, I shouldn't have said that."

"Why not? It's common knowledge that I am unacquainted with the gentler emotions. As I remember, you told me the same thing after my, um . . . conversation with Miss Hinsdale."

"I stopped laying the blame for that at your door long ago. I know you had the best of intentions when you convinced Laura not to marry me. You did it for the family's sake."

James snorted. "To hell with the family. If you think I gave a farthing for your dragon of a grandmother or the Parr name or that beloved land of yours, you're mad as a hatter. I spoke to Miss Hinsdale to keep *you* from making a foolish, lovesick mistake." James turned his gaze to his cuffs, tugging them into perfect alignment. "Besides, if I'd let you follow your love into poverty, I would have had you and your beautiful lady turning up on my doorstep as well. It's bad enough having to support my siblings."

"Ah, of course." A faint smile hovered on Graeme's lips. "Well, you needn't be concerned, cousin. I assure you that I do not weep into my pillow every night or spend my days bemoaning my fate. I am well content with my books and managing my 'beloved land' and the occasional foray into London for a bit of recreation."

Graeme saw no reason to mention the ennui that seemed to tighten its hold on him almost daily or the loneliness that would settle on him in the evening. He would not reveal the way his heart sped up when he happened to see Laura at a party or how eagerly he went forward to take her hand in greeting. How he would stand across the room, drinking in the way she looked, so that he could take out the memory later and savor it. Least of all would he tell James of the emptiness that dwelt deep inside him, a hollow space that neither duty nor brandy nor even the soft, warm body of an occasional mistress could fill.

⤫

"There." Molly settled the decorative pin in her mistress's curls and stepped back to admire her handiwork. "There won't be a lady there who can hold a candle to you, Miss Abby."

"Thanks to you." Abby smiled into the mirror at her maid. Molly was not what anyone would consider a proper lady's maid. She had been Abigail's nurse as a child and had simply grown into the role as Abigail got older. Though Molly had proved to have a surprisingly adept hand at creating coiffures, she often seemed as much mother as employee to Abigail, readily scolding or cosseting or giving Abigail the benefit of her advice.

"Och, without that bonny face of yours, wouldn't anyone notice the way your hair's arranged." Her voice carried a faint trace of her Scottish ancestry. "What jewels will you be wearing tonight, then?" She eyed the delicate dragonfly of diamonds and silver wire that she had just secured in Abigail's dark hair. "Diamonds?"

"No, the jet necklace, I think, to accent the dress." Abby glanced over at the creation that lay across the bed. An underskirt of rich black satin was overlain by a shimmering silk overskirt, pulled back and pinned to fall in extravagant folds over the bustle and into the short train. The front of the silver bodice and overskirt were marked with a few bold black chevrons, the finishing touch a delicate black strip of lace lining the edge of the heart-shaped neckline. "The dress itself is the real jewel."

"Aye, that it is, and cost as much, too, I'd say."

Abby smiled faintly. "But well worth it."

"Everyone will be looking at you tonight," Molly agreed, setting the jewelry chest down on the vanity table before Abigail. "He'll see you, sure enough, if he's there."

"I am told he will be." Abby picked through the drawers of the chest until she found the necklace of faceted jet beads and handed it to the other woman. "And if he isn't, well . . ." She shrugged. "There will be another time. He won't stay away long; after all, it's his duty to his family."

"I hope you know what you're doing," Molly grumbled, settling the string of beads around Abigail's slender throat. "If you want my opinion, which you dinna, that man is the last thing you ought to wish back in your life."

"It's been ten years. Don't you think he might have changed? I know I have."

"Aye, well, you've become the lovely woman you were always meant to be. I dinna know what that Sassenach devil's become."

"To be fair, he was in love with someone else. He didn't want to marry me."

"Aye, well, then, he should have married her, not you."

"He had to marry me in order to save his estate. I can't fault him for doing his duty to his family. I am sure my father pushed him, as well. You know how he is."

"Aye, well enough."

"I was just too young and foolish to see how it was. I assumed Lord Montclair was content enough to marry me. I took his behavior as British reserve, gentlemanly restraint, not resistance. Indeed, I think I didn't want to know the truth. He was . . ." She tilted her head to the side, remembering, and her eyes softened. "He was so handsome, so refined. Not at all rough or consumed with making money like my father and his friends. Not wild and extravagant like their sons."

"He had a bonny look to him," Molly admitted.

"Yes, he did, didn't he?" Abby smiled and met her maid's gaze in the mirror. "I wonder if he still does."

Molly snorted. "If he got his just desserts, he's balding and has a paunch."

Abigail chuckled, standing up and taking off her robe. "It's been a decade, not two or three."

"Och, well, dissipated living can do much to a man."

"He didn't seem 'dissipated.' More upright than anything else."

"I suppose." Molly was reluctant to give up her vision of the man. Picking up the whalebone corset, she wrapped it around Abigail. "Breathe in now." As she pulled in the ties, she went on, "I canna see why you don't set your sights on someone better suited for you. Mr. Prescott would do anything for you. Look at the way he came to London with you."

Abby waited until the ribbons were fastened to let out her breath and speak. "I believe Mr. Prescott had business to attend to here, as well." Molly gave an eloquent shrug, and Abigail continued, "And Mr. Prescott is not my husband."

Molly sighed. "I know. That's the devil of it, isn't it?"

They continued the dressing ritual, pulling on her petticoats and fastening the bustle attachment. Then, finally, Molly stepped up on a stool and carefully lowered the magnificent Worth creation over Abigail's head without disturbing her coiffure. She fastened the buttons up the back and gently adjusted the train that cascaded over the bustle and flowed out a few inches onto the floor behind Abigail.

Together they studied the results of their efforts in the mirror. Molly let out an appreciative sigh. "Ah, Miss Abby, you're a picture. If that man doesn't go down on his knees and beg your forgiveness, he's a fool."

Abigail laughed. "Well, that would certainly enliven Lady Pengrave's ball, wouldn't it?" She picked up her fan and gloves and paused to let her maid settle the gossamer silk wrap around her shoulders. "Whatever Montclair does, I am quite looking forward to it."

∞

"Are you sure she's here?" Graeme asked, scanning the crowded ballroom. "I don't see her."

"How could you hope to spot anyone in this crush?" his grandmother retorted. The place was stuffed with people, with only the dance floor relatively clear—and that was being encroached upon by the minute.

Graeme turned back to his grandmother. The dowager countess, square and stout in her usual purple, was a formidable woman. She was not tall, but she was as immovable as a wall, and there were few who dared cross her. Even James did his best to avoid her. Everything about her, from her haughty expression to her firmly corseted form, seemed carved from granite.

"She will be here," Lady Eugenia decreed.

"Everyone comes to Lady Pengrave's ball," added the countess's companion, who stood just beyond her. Mrs. Ponsonby's statement was delivered in a soft, die-away voice, as one would expect from her. A small, frail woman, Mrs. Ponsonby was as unlike the countess as it was possible to be. Quiet and soft-spoken, she rarely offered an opinion unless it was to agree with the countess. Living on Lady Montclair's generosity since her husband's death, she did her best to be as unobtrusive as possible. It was, Graeme thought, probably the wisest course to take with his grandmother.

"It makes it deuced difficult to find anyone."

"Don't swear, Graeme. Now, give me your arm, and let's stroll about."

This sort of meaningless social round was exactly the reason he usually spent his time at the estate instead of the London house. He could not refuse to escort his grandmother to parties—courtesy had been too much bred into him for that—but in general he found them a complete bore. However, he had committed himself to this path, so Graeme offered the countess his arm and they began their slow procession about the room, Mrs. Ponsonby trailing along behind them.

"Look for a knot of gentlemen," the countess instructed him. "Most likely she's in the center of it."

"Why? There's little reason for fortune hunters to hang about a married woman."

Lady Eugenia sent him a wry look. "There are other reasons for men to hang about a woman."

"But it's not as if she's—"

His grandmother rapped her fan against his arm. "There she is."

He looked in the direction she indicated. "—beautiful." His last word came out as little more than a whisper.

Abigail Price had been thin and pale and drab. Abigail Parr, Lady Montclair, was . . . well, stunning.

"Don't gape," his grandmother said crisply. "The American mouse has changed."

"So I see."

She was still slender, still pale, her hair still black, but there was nothing drab about her now. She wasn't beautiful, not exactly. Her mouth was a little too wide and her cheekbones more sharp than soft, and she was altogether too tall. But when one saw her, it was hard to look away. Her thick hair, black as night, was swept up into a fashionable pompadour style that looked as if it might tumble down at any moment. Her large eyes sparkled, her mouth curved, and color bloomed along her cheeks. Even her dress drew the eye—a silver concoction with dramatic black chevrons decorating the front and a neckline that showcased her perfect white shoulders.

It was utterly irritating that the first thing he felt when he saw the woman was a swift, sharp stab of lust. Clearly, he thought, casting a jaundiced eye at the men around her, a number of other males felt the same way.

"Excuse me, Grandmother. Mrs. Ponsonby." Giving them a short nod, he strode over to the knot of men, stopping at the edge. "Lady Montclair."

The men turned toward him, more than one eyebrow lifting, and Graeme realized how short and sharp his words had come out. Abigail's gaze went to him as well. One of the men started to speak, but Abigail cut him off.

"Lord Montclair." To his surprise, she smiled, her eyes dancing, as if she found the moment amusing. She was enjoying this, he realized with equal parts irritation and disbelief. Abigail turned her smile on the men around her. "Gentlemen, you must excuse me. My husband has first claim to a waltz with me."

The last thing Graeme wanted was to dance with the woman, but she had caught him neatly. To refute her words would only make him look foolish or churlish, probably both. He forced a tight smile and stood rigidly, watching her as she walked toward him. She moved at an unhurried pace, making no effort to be seductive, but clearly confident in her ability to hold his gaze.

He nodded to the other men, unable to repress a certain sense of satisfaction at the envious expressions on their faces. "Gentlemen."

Graeme extended his arm, and she slipped her hand into the crook of his elbow. He started toward the dance floor, very aware of the warmth of her body beside him and the faintly exotic, supremely tantalizing scent of her perfume. He glanced at her and found her watching the dancers; apparently she felt none of the same vibrating awareness of him. He noticed that nestled in the thick black hair atop her head was a small diamond dragonfly. His fingers itched to reach out and touch it. Farther down, a stray bit of hair had slipped from the puffed roll and lay along the nape of her neck. And that led his thoughts to stray to other places he should not go.

Sternly he pulled his mind back to reality. Now that the moment was upon him, he found himself curiously tongue-tied. Why hadn't he considered what he should say to her?

"No doubt they are placing bets on whether we shall create a scene here at the ball," she said, obviously suffering none of his uncertainty, either. She turned her head toward him. "How would you place the odds on it?"

It was an unusual—and somehow intriguing—sensation to look into a woman's face mere inches below his own. "*I* have no intention of causing a scene."

"Of course not; it would be most ungentlemanly. Needless to say, you have no such confidence in me," she went on in that same light way, as if she found him faintly amusing.

No doubt she did—a scene was probably precisely what she hoped to provoke.

"I don't know what to expect from you," he told her flatly. "I haven't the least idea what you plan to do here."

The music had stopped, and couples were drifting onto and off the dance floor. She turned to face him, smiling. "Why, at the moment, I am going to dance."

She held up her hand, and he could do nothing but take it. He stepped closer, settling his other hand at her waist. It seemed to take an age for the orchestra to strike up again. He was intensely aware of her hand in his, even through the glove; of the slick satin of her dress beneath his other hand. Sweet heavens, but there was something dizzying in her perfume, and it was all he could do to keep his eyes from straying down to where the lace-edged neckline skimmed over the soft mounds of her breasts.

"I meant in more general terms," he snapped. "Why the devil did you come back to London?"

"Surely it isn't unusual for a wife to visit her husband," she tossed back, widening her eyes a little in faux surprise.

How could he have forgotten the color of her eyes? They were green as new leaves, the pupils ringed with golden starbursts. They disconcerted him as much as the lightly teasing, almost flirtatious way she was speaking to him. Did she think he did not remember what had happened after all this time? That he would overlook the fact that they had blackmailed him into marrying her? That she could smile beckoningly and smell delightful and he would fall in with whatever she wanted?

She might have turned from a wallflower into a seductress, but he'd be damned if he had become such an easy mark. The music finally started, and he swung her into the waltz with rather more vigor than was necessary. It gave him a petty satisfaction to see the surprise flash across her face. Her hand tightened on his shoulder.

"I would find it a trifle unusual," he responded to her earlier question, "if that wife had not visited her husband in the previous ten years."

Her eyes sparked with an answering anger, and that, too, gave him a little fillip of satisfaction. "My absence was at your request."

"Yes. And I would prefer it to continue."

"I know this will come as a shock to you, but you cannot control who does or doesn't come to London."

"Perhaps not, but my wife *is* under my control."

She did not answer for a long moment, simply regarded him in a cool, level way that made him feel suddenly foolish and embarrassed. "You gave up your role as my husband long ago, as I remember it."

He felt a flush rising in his cheeks, which only increased his irritation. "I will not allow you to insinuate yourself into my life. You will not sweep in and take over my home."

"I would never presume to enter your sacred ancestral home. I am staying at the Langham Hotel." She held his gaze, her eyes and voice as cool as his were heated.

"It will only cause more talk for you to live in a hotel instead of Montclair House."

"Really, my lord, you cannot have it both ways," she said in the tone of one humoring a madman. "I must stay at one place or another."

"What you can do is leave the city."

"Oh, I will." Once again her lips curved up in that delicious way. "When I'm ready."

chapter 3

It was clear she was trying to goad him. No doubt she hoped to provoke some intemperate response. The only way to counter her was to tamp down even more firmly on his temper. Taking a deep breath, he went on in a lowered voice, "I could not care less where you go or what you do. But I will not stand idly by while you bring scandal to this family."

"Perhaps you might have considered that before you decided to add me to your family."

"I can assure you, I did so through no desire of my own."

"I am well aware of that." She looked away, and for the first time the lightness leached from her voice.

"I apologize. That was rude." Guilt snaked through his irritation. Reminding himself that her father, too, had been a master manipulator, he forged on. "Rumor has it you are looking to become a matchmaker."

"A matchmaker?" She sent him an incredulous look.

"Yes. To find impoverished British nobles to wed American heiresses."

Her laughter was brittle. "I hardly think my experience in that regard would be any recommendation. Few brides are looking for a husband, aristocratic or otherwise, who will repudiate them on their wedding night."

"I didn't—you know very well it wasn't like that! You were the one—" He stopped suddenly, realizing that his voice had risen.

Abigail quirked a brow. "I thought your purpose here was to avoid a scandal, not precipitate one."

Graeme clenched his jaw, swallowing the hot words that bubbled up in his throat. "At least before, you weren't so bloody infuriating," he muttered.

To his surprise, she began to laugh. And when she laughed, he discovered, her face was entrancing. Graeme could not even begin to identify the feelings roiling inside him. It was all he could do to shove them back down before they tumbled out.

Fortunately the orchestra blared into its last soaring notes and stopped. Graeme dropped her hand as if it burned and took a half step back. He had a cowardly impulse to just walk away, but of course one could not leave one's partner stranded on the dance floor. Sketching a bow, he offered his arm. She took it, though with such a knowing look in her eyes that he wanted to grab her shoulders and shake her or—well, best not to delve into that.

As they crossed the floor, he kept his lips firmly clamped shut and his eyes turned away from her. It was rather more difficult to ignore the feel of her hand curved around his arm. He wondered where to take her—it was tempting to think of thrusting her on his grandmother and walking away.

A man angled toward them, clearly intent on intercepting them. This, Graeme thought, must be the American with whom his aunt had said Abigail kept company. Something about his carriage marked him as not British, but it was the proprietary, even combative look in his eyes that made Graeme certain the stranger had an interest in Abigail.

Graeme slowed and stopped, regarding the man coolly. He was much older than Abigail, at least forty; his dark reddish hair was graying at the temples. Shorter than Graeme, he was built solidly, and his square face had an equally implacable look.

"Abby?" The man's eyes went immediately to her. "Are you all right?"

"You are an acquaintance of my wife's?" Graeme asked before Abigail could open her mouth. Four hundred years of aristocracy colored his voice.

"Yes." Abigail dropped her hand from Graeme's arm, shooting him an arrow glance before favoring the other man with a smile. "I'm quite all right, David, thank you." Americans were, Graeme thought, terribly free with given names. "Allow me to introduce you to the Earl of Montclair. Lord Montclair, this is Mr. David Prescott."

Prescott gave him a greeting as chilly as his glance, and Graeme replied in kind. "You're visiting London?"

"Yes, Mr. Prescott was kind enough to escort me on the trip," Abigail explained.

"Ah, I see." Graeme shifted, subtly positioning himself between Abigail and the other man. "Then I must give you my thanks for watching over my wife."

Prescott met his eyes levelly. "I thought someone should."

"I beg your pardon?" Graeme's eyebrows soared.

Without the least degree of subtlety, Abigail latched hold of Graeme's arm and squeezed. She flashed a brilliant smile at both men. "Mr. Prescott also had business in London."

"Indeed? You are an associate of Lady Montclair's father?"

"I used to work for him." His tone was as blunt as the look in his reddish-brown eyes. "But I would say I am more a friend to Lady Montclair now."

"Are you." Graeme bared his teeth in something like a smile. Naturally the man *would* come from Thurston Price's camp. The insinuation in Prescott's words was obvious, an insult that made him itch to take the fellow outside. But, of course, that would result in exactly the sort of scandal he was trying to avoid.

It was, he reflected sourly, probably what Abigail was hoping for. And it didn't matter, not really. He did not care where Abigail might choose to give her favors; indeed, the man was quite welcome to her. It was the insult that annoyed him, the reflection on his name. He was not jealous.

Abruptly Graeme stepped back. "Then I will take my leave so that you may pursue . . . your friendship." Sketching a bow to the other two, he turned and walked away.

∞

Abigail watched Graeme's retreating figure, feeling suddenly drained. Prescott studied her with a frown. "Are you all right, really? Shall I escort you back to the hotel?"

She summoned up a smile for the man. It wasn't his fault that seeing Graeme had left her shaky. "That would be most kind of you. I believe I am a little tired."

"Of course. I'll fetch your wrap."

They left the ballroom. Abigail carefully avoided glancing in the direction Graeme had gone. She refused to let him see that she was looking for him. She had gotten through it; that was the main thing. She had not let him see how the nerves had danced inside her from the moment she saw him standing there.

He was more handsome than she remembered. She wasn't sure if her memory was faulty or if maturity had honed his looks into a sharper, more vivid image of himself. He had been only twenty-three when she married him, not that much older than she. His form had filled out into the more powerful one of a man in his prime. The square jaw and firm chin were a trifle harder, the even features tempered by time and experience into something deeper than mere attractiveness. He looked, she thought, like a man in whom one could put one's trust.

But that, of course, was an absurd thought. Experience had taught her how little she could entrust any of her feelings or hopes to him. She knew Graeme was a man of his word, for he had never wavered in the slightest regarding his vow to stay away from her. No doubt those he loved could rely on him. But someone like her, someone whom he held in disdain, would be a fool to let down her guard.

"Could we walk?" she suggested as they left the house. "It's a lovely night and not all that far."

"Of course, if you wish." Prescott fell in beside her, and she took his arm with easy familiarity.

"I'm glad you came with me," she went on. "I know I told you I could handle it all without help—and I could have—but it is nice to see a friendly face."

"Was it very hard meeting him again?"

Abby shrugged. It was impossible to describe the wild mixture of emotions that had flooded her at the sight of Graeme. The rush of excitement and the downward tug of dread, the swift, mindless attraction to his face and form, the effort to keep up the light, unemotional role she had decided to adopt.

"It was . . . odd," she admitted.

"You don't have to do this, Abby." He stopped and faced her, taking both her hands in his. "You needn't face Montclair."

Abigail smiled fondly at him. "No. I do need to." She gave his fingers a gentle squeeze, then let go and started walking again. "I have to go forward with my life. I cannot continue in this limbo forever."

"I hate that you should have to have anything to do with him. I'm not sure what you hope to accomplish by all this."

"Frankly, I sometimes wonder myself."

"I was here before when you fled London in tears. I know your devastation at Montclair's cruelty and how long it took you to recover. I don't want that to happen to you again."

"It won't. I'm not the naïve dreamer I was then. I did recover—and more than that. I built a new life for myself. I am a realist now. I don't fancy myself in love with Lord Montclair. I don't expect moonlight and roses and waltzes at midnight. Just a chance at a new life. Of having some part, at least, of what I wanted."

"You know, I hope, that there are any number of men who would be happy to love you. To have a life with you. Myself included."

"I know." She tucked her hand into his arm again. "And don't think I don't appreciate the offer. But you are too good a friend, I think, to risk losing you."

He stifled a sigh. "I would never wish to risk that. You have been a better friend to me than anyone in my life. Without your help I would never have gotten free of your father."

Abigail smiled. "It wasn't charity; I made a very good investment with that loan."

"I've done my best to see to that. But still, I will always be grateful to you. And whether it is with me or some other man, I want you to make a good life. Away from Montclair."

"I could choose someone other than him, it's true. But it wouldn't be making a life. It would only be having an affair. I am married to Lord Montclair."

"Unless you obtain a divorce."

"I know." Abigail sighed. "But one marries for life." She looked up at him, her eyes great pools of sorrow. "At least, that is what I believe."

Prescott let out a long sigh, too, and patted her hand on his arm. "Ah, Abigail, I fear you are still a dreamer, after all."

They soon reached the hotel, its entrance brightly illuminated, and Abigail made her way up to her suite. She turned on the gaslight, reflecting that she rather preferred its gentler glow to the much-touted electric lights in front of the hotel. They had not been installed last time she stayed here.

But she didn't want to think about that time.

She should ring for her maid; it was almost impossible to get out of her corset single-handedly. But she did not do so; she needed a moment to herself before she faced questions from Molly.

The truth was, she wouldn't know what to tell Molly any more than she had known what to say to David Prescott. Perhaps they were right in their gloomy predictions for a future with Graeme. Certainly there had been nothing in his manner tonight to give her encouragement. However he might have changed in the past ten years, his antipathy toward her remained unswerving.

Abby started across the room. Something crackled beneath her feet, and she looked down. A small square envelope lay on the floor. Molly or one of the hotel servants could have brought it in while she was gone, but they would not have tossed it on the floor. Someone must have slipped it beneath the door.

Curious, she picked up the white square. It was sealed and addressed to "Lady Montclair." Opening it, she found a single sheet of paper. The message was short and simple: "Do you want to know the truth behind your marriage?"

She stared at the paper blankly. The truth behind her marriage? The words made little sense to her, and she read them over again. What did it mean? What truth? That Graeme did not love her? That was amply clear and had been so since her wedding night. Surely no one could think that would be a revelation to her. That he had married her solely because he needed money? She had known that, too, even before he'd told her how little he wanted to be her husband.

Abby refolded the letter. Why would anyone have sent such a missive to her? And who would have done so?

The secrecy of it—the lack of signature, the hinting without really revealing anything, the way it had turned up on her floor—indicated a certain malevolence, she thought. As the daughter of a wealthy, powerful, and ruthless man, she was not unaccustomed to being the object of jealousy and dislike. But she knew hardly anyone in London, really.

Though she had received numerous introductions and invitations, it was merely because people were curious about the American heiress Lord Montclair had tossed aside. They hoped Abby might provide some titillating entertainment for a party or give them a bit of gossip to pass along. She doubted any of them actually liked her, but she wouldn't have thought they disliked her enough to try to hurt her.

Except her husband, of course. But she could not believe this letter was from Montclair. It simply wasn't something he would do. He had been straightforward in his dislike of her. He wasn't the sort to send mysterious letters suggesting dark secrets.

Besides, it hardly served his purpose. He wanted her to leave London as soon as possible. This note was the sort of thing that would arouse her curiosity. It was more likely to make her stay here than to flee.

Perhaps it was simply a matter of money, someone who knew or thought they knew something Abby would pay to find out. Or it could be a friend of Graeme's—someone who wanted to punish her because they believed Abby had ruined Montclair's life.

Or maybe someone who felt her own life had been ruined. The woman whom Graeme had been in love with, for instance. Now, *that* idea made some sense. Abigail stood at the window, staring sightlessly out at the lights of London, thinking.

She could imagine the dislike a woman could harbor for someone who had taken the man she loved away from her. However much Graeme had not given his heart to Abigail, the fact was that he had married her and was thus lost to the woman he loved. A woman in that position might very well despise Abigail enough to torment her in any way possible, even with something as small as a note that disturbed her evening.

Abigail sighed. Unfolding the little square of paper, she methodically tore it in half and then again, tossing the pieces into the trash. She could not as easily dismiss her thoughts.

She didn't know the name of the woman Graeme had loved, only that he had preferred her to Abigail. At the time, Abby had not really cared. When she decided to return to London, she had thought that Graeme's love for the unknown woman had probably died over the years. But what if it had not? Perhaps he had been having an affair with her all these years.

What if Molly and David were right and there was nothing for Abby here? She could not help but wonder if it had been foolhardy to come back. Perhaps she should be content with the life she lived in New York and not risk more heartache.

Abigail looked across the room at the elegant woman reflected in the mirror over the vanity table. She drew closer, studying her hair and face, her dress, her carriage. She was not, she thought firmly, the tongue-tied, dreamy-eyed girl who had walked blindly into marriage ten years ago.

After the fiasco of her wedding night, she had fled to the Continent, miserable and alone. When her father tracked her down and sent Prescott to bring her back, David had convinced her to return—not to her sheltered life in her father's house, but to take her place in society on her own. And she had done it. Abby had faced her fears, weathered the storm of scandal, and set herself up in her own household, no longer her father's pawn, but a married woman of substance.

She had remade herself into a confident, attractive woman, one who was not afraid to speak up, who dared to do what she wanted, who made her own decisions. Abigail lifted her chin, giving her image a disdainful smile. The life she had in New York was one she had built. She could do the same again here.

She had come here with a purpose. She was not about to slide back into the quicksand of fear and doubt. Abigail Price might have been a timid sort whose heart was easily bruised, but Abigail Parr, the Countess of Montclair, was a woman who could handle whatever came along.

Nothing that Graeme or any mysterious letter-writer could do would stop her.

chapter 4

The woman was haunting him. It seemed as if everywhere he went, Abigail was there. He saw her at the opera, sitting in the Havertons' box, chatting and laughing with their thoroughly dissolute son. She was at Mrs. Battleham's soiree the next night with that upstart American Prescott in tow. Last night he spotted her at the Hammersmiths' dinner party, this time seated next to and madly flirting with Lord Cargaron, a man old enough to be her father and married, as well—not to mention reputed to also maintain a mistress. No doubt he hoped to work Abigail into his sexual juggling act.

It was nothing to Graeme, of course, with whom Abigail flirted or what man was standing beside her, sneaking glances down the front of her gown. But any scandal she brewed now would stain his name. That was his only concern.

She was too free and familiar in her speech. Her gowns were—well, they were not lewd, of course; his grandmother assured him they were from Worth or another elegant designer. It was just that they all looked so . . . so delectable on her. A pale pink satin that looked as if Abigail were layered in rich pink frosting, or a vivid gold velvet that changed the color of her eyes to a bewitching shade of tarnished copper. Even a simple black silk frock drew one's eyes inexorably to the contrasting creamy white skin of her breasts and shoulders.

He never saw Abigail in the same dress twice, and he heard the envious murmurs among other ladies as they studied her attire. Lady Montclair's ball gowns, the dowager countess assured Graeme, occupied a large space in the conversations of every afternoon call. Graeme was not entirely certain whether his grandmother deplored the idea or was proud of it. He could not help but wonder how Abigail could afford so many luxurious dresses. He gave her a very generous allowance out of the estate, of course, but still . . . he wouldn't have thought it extended to a seemingly limitless wardrobe of Parisian gowns.

Graeme had never paid attention to women's dresses. He had admired one or two on Laura, but he had never noticed them as he did now. No doubt Laura had dressed more conservatively, not trying to bring attention to herself. Laura had always been a perfect lady.

Abigail, on the other hand . . . It would not be fair to say that she did not act like a lady. He had not seen her do anything untoward or inappropriate. It was more that wherever she was, whatever she did, she drew everyone's eyes. When she smiled, she sparkled; she moved her hands expressively as she talked; when she was amused, she laughed aloud. There was nothing demure about her, nothing reserved. He remembered the silent wisp of a girl he had married and he wondered where she had gone.

Had she purposely deceived him? She might have thought he would be more agreeable to tying himself to her if she pretended to be a proper lady. If so, she had certainly done an excellent acting job. He admitted that his eyes had been too full of Laura to really see any other woman. But he couldn't have been that blind, that mistaken. Abigail must have been manipulating him, just as her father had. It made him wonder what she was trying to maneuver him into now.

Whatever it was, he refused to fall in with her schemes. Despite his grandmother's prodding, he avoided Abigail. He did not try to speak to her. In fact, if he found himself anywhere near her, he immediately left. No matter how inescapable her presence seemed to be, he refused to acknowledge it. The irritating thing, of course, was that avoiding her meant that he had to keep an eye on her. He saw her conversations, her dances, her laughter. Even more annoying was that when she was not at a party, he still looked for her, wondering where she was and with whom.

"Why don't you just go talk to her?" his grandmother asked him now. "I don't know what you hope to prove by standing here watching her."

"I'm not watching her. I happened to glance over."

"Hmph."

"And what I am proving is that she cannot goad me into action. She wants to stir up trouble, to provoke me into doing something."

"Doing what?" Lady Eugenia asked.

"I don't know. I have no intention of finding out."

"This seems a most peculiar plan, I must say."

"If I refuse to respond to her as she wishes, if I ignore her, eventually she will realize I am not going to rise to the bait, and she'll stop."

"Stop what?"

"Bothering me." He glanced over at Lady Eugenia. Her

expression reminded him forcibly of the time he was eight and had knocked over her favorite Waterford vase.

"Graeme Edward Charles Parr, it is time you stop shilly-shallying about and take that woman with you to the estate."

"I have no intention of taking her home." Graeme set his jaw. "I don't know why you think that is any sort of solution to the problem."

"It is a solution that will keep her out of London. A result, I might add, that folding your arms and glowering at her every night has not brought about."

"At least she does not have that American fellow with her," Mrs. Ponsonby offered in her soft voice.

"That is little consolation, Philomena," Lady Eugenia told her.

"No, of course not." Mrs. Ponsonby nodded.

The dowager countess heaved a sigh. "Well, if you have no intention of doing anything constructive, Montclair, take me home. It's deadly dull, as Mrs. Wellersby's parties always are, and listening to that old fool Danforth gave me a headache. I don't know why we came in the first place."

Since there was nothing he wanted so much as to leave, Graeme was not so impolite as to remind his grandmother that they had come because she insisted on it. He escorted the dowager countess home, then went to his study to settle down with a brandy. But he was too restless to settle down . . . just as he had been the entire time in London, it seemed.

He began to pace. His grandmother was right; he was accomplishing nothing by ignoring Abigail. Apparently Abigail did not even notice his absence. He wished he knew what scheme she had in mind. He was certain there was one—there had been that mischievous glint in her eyes when she bantered with him, that teasing smile. He could deal with it if only he had some idea what she had in mind. Perhaps that was what she intended—to drive him mad waiting and wondering.

Letting out a disgusted noise, he set down the glass with a thunk and left the house. His steps turned toward White's. James might be there. His cousin would doubtlessly laugh at him and point out that Graeme was a fool, but at least he could be counted on to listen and advise without emotion coloring his answer. If not James, there was bound to be someone else he knew, some conversation to take his mind off its tedious circular path.

As luck would have it, though, Graeme had barely stepped inside the door when his eye fell on David Prescott, chatting with Egmont Burrows and Manning's son. What the devil was that American doing here? His jaw tightened as he watched the man, sipping some brown liquid—probably that ghastly bourbon Americans seemed to love—and chatting with Burrows. This brought up another issue: What was Prescott's connection to Abigail? Was he her lover or merely one of her father's business associates? Graeme suspected that if Prescott was not her lover, he would like to be; he had a decidedly possessive way of hanging about her.

But whatever he was or hoped to be, it seemed clear to Graeme that the man was in Abigail's confidence. If anyone knew what she was about, it would be he. As if he felt Graeme's gaze on him, Prescott glanced up and saw Graeme. Prescott held his gaze for a moment, direct and almost challenging.

Graeme strode forward. Egmont Burrows saw him approaching. "Ah, Montclair!"

"Burrows. Manning."

"I'm sure you already know Mr. Prescott," Manning's son offered in his languid way, his eyes amused. No doubt he hoped for fireworks between Graeme and his wife's friend.

"Indeed." Graeme smiled tightly, determined not to provide the show the others hoped for. "I came here to speak with Mr. Prescott." His eyes went to Prescott, carrying their own challenge.

"Of course. My pleasure." Prescott nodded toward the other two men. "Gentlemen, if you will excuse us . . ."

Graeme made his way to a corner of the room where two wingback chairs were set at right angles for a cozy conversation. Prescott settled into one of them and cocked an eyebrow at Graeme.

"Well? I presume you have a reason for this conversation."

"I do. I want to know exactly what you and Lady Montclair are doing here. What is she planning?" Graeme had intended to keep his tone cool, even disinterested, but the edginess he'd felt for days rose in him, making it difficult to remain aloof. "Does she intend to create a scandal? Embarrass my family in some way? I warn you, I will not allow her to hurt my mother and grandmother."

"I don't see that Abby's plans, whatever they may be, are any of your business."

The man's use of her first name, especially the casual nickname, and the intimacy that implied, grated on Graeme's nerves. "I'd say it's very much my business since *Lady Montclair* is my wife."

Prescott let out a short, humorless laugh. "So it's 'my wife' now, is it? I was under the impression that you tossed her aside ten years ago. I'd say that doesn't make her yours anymore."

"I didn't 'toss her aside.'" Graeme scowled.

"That is generally what is meant when one abandons his bride on their wedding night."

"I didn't abandon her." The years-old tendrils of guilt teased at him. "Is that the tale she put out?"

"She didn't put out any tale at all. It was clear to everyone."

"Did they expect me to welcome a bride who had coerced me into marriage by ruining my father? Price encouraged him to invest in that scheme with the object of destroying my father financially, making it impossible to do anything but accept his bargain." Everyone knew this much. Graeme wasn't about to reveal the full extent of Thurston Price's threats.

"That was Thurston, not his daughter. She was blameless."

"The apple doesn't fall far from the tree, I've found." Graeme's voice was thick with scorn. "She wanted to be a countess. That was all she was interested in—as evidenced by the fact that she left the country as soon as she acquired the title."

"Do you really think any woman with an ounce of pride would have stayed after the things you said to her?" Prescott surged to his feet.

Graeme rose to face him, a flush edging his cheekbones. "I spoke hastily, in anger, I admit. I came to apologize to her for my rudeness the next—"

"For your rudeness?" Prescott took a step closer. "Is that what you call trampling all over a young girl's feelings? Abigail knew nothing about her father's schemes. Surely you aren't so foolish as to think Thurston Price would have taken an eighteen-year-old girl into his confidence? He told no one. I worked for the man. He knew I had invested my savings in the stock, too, but he didn't breathe a word of warning to me. He sure as hell wouldn't have let his daughter in on his secrets."

"You're the one who's foolish," Graeme shot back. "I told her exactly why I had no intention of living with her, and she didn't deny a word of it. It was clear that what I said came as no surprise."

"I doubt she was surprised to find out her father had been engaged in underhanded activities. She knew what he was like—she had to live with the man, after all. But I can promise you she didn't know his plans to maneuver Lord Montclair into bankruptcy. Abigail is nothing like her father, which you would know if you had ever taken the trouble to become acquainted with her. She is kind and generous to a fault. When I left Thurston's employ, she was the one who helped me."

"All that proves is that you have reason to be thankful to her. It means nothing to me."

"I'm sure it does not, since clearly no one matters to you except yourself. Abigail was not privy to her father's machinations; she certainly did not participate in them. Nor did she give a damn about your sacred title. She had to put up with Thurston Price her entire life, ashamed of the things he did and bullied by him like everyone else. She was hopeful and innocent and desperate to get away from the man. Her only fault was in mistaking you for a knight in shining armor. She thought marrying you was the answer to her prayers. Instead, you repudiated her on her wedding night."

"Stop saying that!" Anger bubbled up in Graeme, the frustration of the past few days mingling with memories of the fury and pain he had felt on his wedding night. "I didn't—"

Prescott overrode his words. "*And*, as if humiliating her in front of two continents was not enough, you completed the devastation by throwing in her face that you loved another woman. You doomed her to a loveless, bitter future. Abigail was eighteen and alone in a foreign country, too young and foolish and starry-eyed to realize that a British 'gentleman' is all courtesy and no kindness."

"Damn it, you're in love with her, aren't you?" Graeme flared, too furious to care that their voices had risen until all conversation around them had ceased as everyone turned to stare.

"What if I am? What difference does it make? She's married to you."

"Then take her! With my blessing. Take her and leave London. I don't care if she has an affair with you or any man. I just want her gone."

Prescott's fist shot out, catching Graeme on the mouth and sending him staggering back.

chapter 5

Graeme slammed into the wall and came back swinging. His fist connected with Prescott's chin, snapping his head back, but it didn't knock him down. Prescott launched himself at Graeme, and they crashed into a small table, knocking it and the decanter of whiskey it held onto the floor. The two men rolled across the floor punching and wrestling as voices rose around them.

"Oh, for God's sake." A disgusted voice finally sliced through the others, and someone hooked his hand in the neck of Graeme's shirt, hauling him up. Prescott came after him, but the gold-knobbed end of a gentleman's cane in the center of his chest held Prescott off until two other men grabbed his arms.

Graeme turned to look into his cousin's cool gray eyes, all his momentary fury draining out of him. He was humiliatingly aware of the fact that he was standing, bloodied and disheveled, in the middle of his club, with a circle of gentlemen gaping at him. "Bloody hell."

"Just so," Sir James de Vere agreed, and the corner of his mouth twitched. "Cousin, you are turning into a veritable fountain of scandal."

With something like a snarl, Graeme jerked out of his cousin's grasp and stalked off.

When James caught up with him on the front steps, Graeme didn't even turn his head. "Go away."

"You can't seriously think I am going to allow you to walk off with nothing more than that."

"I don't see why not. It's not your concern."

"It will be when the dowager countess calls me into her drawing room tomorrow afternoon to account for this little brawl." He matched his long stride to Graeme's. "So tell me why I walked into White's to find you grappling on the floor like a schoolboy. With an American, no less."

Graeme related the entire conversation to him.

"Ah," James said when he finished. "I suppose that puts a different slant on one's view of your spouse."

"If you believe him," Graeme said grudgingly. "Well, he does believe it, clearly. It's whether you believe *her*."

"And you don't?"

"I don't know!" Graeme scowled. Blood trickled down beside his eye, and he wiped it away. "I was sure she knew all about Thurston. When I told her, she didn't say a word of protest. No denials, no apologies. Then she hied off to New York, didn't even wait for an apology. Does that sound like a naïve, helpless, innocent girl to you?"

"I try to have as little acquaintance with naïve, helpless, innocent girls as possible."

Graeme ignored James's comment, deep in his own thoughts. "I shouldn't have spoken so harshly to Abigail. I went round the next morning to apologize."

"Of course you did."

"Damn it," Graeme said a little sulkily. "I'm not accustomed to being in the wrong."

His cousin chuckled. "Oh, one becomes used to it after a while."

After a moment, Graeme said abruptly, "It was what he said to me."

"What who said? Prescott?"

"No. Thurston Price. Her father. After he had humiliated Father, ruined him and brought me to heel. Gotten everything he wanted. That evening, after the first waltz, Price pulled me aside." Graeme's mouth twisted. "And he said to me—in this complacent, oh-so-jovial voice, as if we were boon companions sharing a smutty jest—'Now, go on, son, take her upstairs and get to work on producing my grandson.' As if I were his possession, bought and paid for. Of course I was, but that only made it more infuriating. I thought, I'll be damned if I let his bloodline into the Parr family."

They walked on in silence for a moment. Graeme sighed. "Before that, I hadn't intended to be so sharp with her. So blunt. I would have phrased it differently."

"Instead you were honest." James shrugged. "It's not a crime."

"Not terribly gentlemanly." Graeme smiled faintly, then winced as it sent a stab of pain through his split lip. "And as you can see, I am always a gentleman."

"Mm. Clearly. So, to sum up, you were less than a perfect gentleman. She was a naïve fool who knew nothing about her father's plans. Or she wasn't. Now, after a ten-year absence, she is in London again. And her reason for being here, her expectations, her plans—in short, everything about her—is unknown."

"Yes. And as her husband, however reluctantly, I will be accountable for whatever she does."

"It seems to me it might behoove you to speak to Lady Montclair again."

"Yes. I know." Graeme considered the idea gloomily.

They had reached a corner and James paused, then nodded up the street. "Do you want to come back to my house to clean your wounds? Lady Eugenia will not approve of your condition."

"No. Grandmother hopefully has gone to bed. But I think I'd like to walk a bit." Graeme shrugged and discovered that he had hurt his shoulder as well.

His cousin departed and Graeme walked on alone, too sunk in thought to pay attention to the time or the direction of his steps. It was with some surprise that he glanced up and found himself in front of the Langham Hotel. He started toward the brightly lit entrance before he remembered the condition he was in. He'd stormed out of the club without his hat or gloves. A button or two had popped off his waistcoat in the struggle, and his ascot was askew. The pocket that housed his watch had been torn half off, so that his watch dangled loosely on its chain. Not to mention his split lip or the cut above his eyebrow.

He whipped around to leave just as Abigail stepped down from a carriage, her hand in the helping hand of a well-dressed gentleman. For an instant Graeme thought wildly of fleeing, but Abigail glanced over and saw him. Her eyes widened, and she started toward him, her escort trailing uncertainly in her wake.

"Graeme! What happened? Are you all right?" Her green-gold eyes were filled with a concern that he found strangely satisfying.

"Yes, um . . . bit of a dustup." He shoved back his hair and tugged at his lapels in a futile attempt to bring himself into order. "I beg your pardon for appearing here like this."

"Lady Montclair, is this man bothering you?" Her companion came up beside Abigail, gazing down the length of his nose at Graeme. His voice was tinged with a foreign accent.

Abigail started to answer, but Graeme jumped in before she could. "This man is her husband. And I assure you, your assistance is not required." He fixed a stony gaze on the man.

Her escort looked nonplussed. Abigail's concern changed to irritation. "Honestly, Gra— Montclair. What would your grandmother say about your lack of manners?" Graeme started to speak, but she effectively ignored him, turning to the other man with a smile. "It's perfectly all right, Monsieur Benoit. You need not worry. I'll be fine. Thank you for escorting me tonight."

Graeme watched sourly as she took her leave of the Frenchman, which involved a great deal of smiling and gesturing and bowing over her hand before the fellow finally left and she turned back to Graeme.

"So you're bringing them in from France now?"

"What?" Abigail looked at him blankly.

"Your swains." He nodded toward the back of the retreating Benoit. "All the men always dangling around you. I wondered where the devil they came from."

Her eyes took on a twinkle and she pressed her lips together firmly. "Oh, of course! Those hundreds of men who have escorted me to the theater or a party." She was laughing at him. It was no wonder, really. He was acting a fool. She went on. "No doubt it would have been more appropriate if I had attended them alone."

He scowled. They both knew that would have caused gossip. "Oh, devil take it."

Graeme started to swing away, but Abigail laughed and hooked her hand around his arm. "Come, Lord Montclair, I think we'd better get you cleaned up."

She smelled delicious, he realized. He would have to bend his head only a little to kiss her. "I don't remember you being this tall." Good Gad, what was wrong with him, blurting out things like that? He was beginning to think that Prescott's blows must have knocked something loose in his head.

Abigail, however, seemed to take no offense, for she only laughed again in her easy way. He had noticed her laugh several times the past week—light and infectious, without self-consciousness. "Well, I haven't grown, I assure you."

"Of course not. I beg your pardon—silly thing to say."

"Not really. The difference is my shoes, I imagine." They had reached the lift and paused. Abigail lifted her skirts a little, sticking out one foot to show her slipper and turning it this way and that. The shoe matched the deep emerald of her dress and had a raised heel, but Graeme found the sight of her ankle far more interesting.

He pulled his gaze away and saw that the young man operating the lift found the sight riveting, as well. Graeme cleared his throat, and the man jumped, hurrying to open the gate for them. As the lift rose—a sensation Graeme had not yet grown accustomed to, though he'd been in one a few times before—Abigail continued. "I used to wear flat slippers—I was so tall, you see, and I tried to hide it as best I could. But one day I decided, what did it matter? If a lovely shoe had a heel, there was no reason not to wear it."

"No. I suppose not." It was a peculiar conversation.

Graeme glanced over at the operator of the lift, who was sneaking surreptitious glances at him. Graeme almost laughed. No doubt their conversation or even Abigail exposing her ankle paled in comparison to the battered state of Graeme's face.

"Now," Abigail said when they stepped out of the lift and started down the corridor, "I have to wonder, what have you been up to since you left the party? It couldn't have been much more than an hour since I saw you."

"Oh." It seemed an age ago. "Yes, well, I, um." He shoved his hand back through his hair. "I beg your pardon for my appearance. I'm not usually so—"

"Bloody and bruised?"

"Well . . . yes." He tried once again to bring his jacket and waistcoat and shirt into order. It was hopeless. Finally he unfastened the dangling watch and chain and stuck them into the pocket of his jacket. "It's, uh, not my usual custom."

"Getting into fights?" She lifted an eyebrow. "I am relieved to hear it."

She stopped in front of a door and took a key from her reticule. Graeme reached out, expecting her to hand it to him to open the door, but she ignored him, inserting the key and turning it. He followed her into the suite. It felt odd, vaguely illicit, to be standing alone with her in a hotel room. It was not inappropriate, of course; they were married. But she was in every way a stranger to him. Only steps away, through the other doorway, was her bedroom. A low light glowed from within it, and he could glimpse the corner of the bed.

Abigail peeled off her gloves and tossed them aside, discarding her wrap as well. Casually she kicked off her slippers, tossing a grin over her shoulder. "They're beautiful, but my feet are rebelling."

His belly tightened. There was an intimacy to her gesture that heightened his vaguely sinful feeling. They stood only feet apart in the soft glow of the gaslight. If he stretched out his hand, he would touch her bare arm. He had a very good notion how it would feel beneath his fingers—the softness, the warmth . . .

The illusion of intimacy was shattered as a short, stocky woman bustled out of the bedroom. "There you are, M—" She stopped, seeing Graeme. "Are you all right, Miss Abby?" Her eyes flickered to Abigail, then back to Graeme, filled with suspicion. "What's happened?" She drew closer to Abigail, her voice dropping to a whisper. "Has he hurt you?"

Graeme's eyebrows shot up. "Hurt her! You think I would—"

"No," Abigail cut through his words, smiling reassuringly at the maid. "I rather think it was Lord Montclair who suffered some damage. Fetch water and a rag for me, would you, Molly? Oh, and ice, iodine . . ." She paused thoughtfully. "Ring for some brandy, as well. Lord Montclair would probably appreciate a drink."

Molly set her jaw stubbornly, but said only, "Aye, miss, if you want it." She cast another look of ill will at Graeme and left the room.

Graeme gazed after her in astonishment. "She, um . . . You have an unusual maid."

"Molly's much more than a maid." Abigail smiled. "She was my nurse when I was young, as well. She is rather protective."

"I saw." He hesitated. "Surely you do not think that I would hurt you?"

"No, of course not. You would never physically harm a woman."

He noticed the distinction of physical harm, and once again guilt and doubt twined through him. Abigail seemed so pleasant now, her earlier sharp teasing dropped, so open and candid. So subtly alluring.

Molly popped back into the room, carrying a pitcher of water, small towels draped over her arm. "Here you are, miss." She set down her burden. "I've sent for ice and brandy and some nice hot chocolate for you." She half turned toward Graeme. "Shall I—"

"No, Molly, that's fine. You can go back to your room now. I'll handle this."

"I'll wait in there." The older woman nodded toward the bedroom. "You'll be needing help with your things later."

"No," Abigail replied firmly. "I'll send for you when I'm ready to retire."

"Very well." The woman shot another warning look at Graeme, but she left the suite.

Abigail wet the cloth and walked over to him. Taking his chin firmly in her hand, she began to clean the blood from the side of his face. She worked in a businesslike way, and Graeme was embarrassed to feel his body respond to her nearness. Her scent went straight to his head, making it difficult to think, and the feel of her fingers on his chin was alarmingly stirring. Even the gentle stroke of the washcloth across his cheek affected him like a caress.

She brushed his hair back from his forehead, and though she was only clearing it from the cut above his eye, the soft intimacy of the gesture shook him. He sought to control his breath, hoping she could not feel the sudden heat in his skin. She went up on her toes to inspect the cut more closely, and he thought of her bare feet, the way she had casually kicked off her slippers. How could that be so seductive?

She was only inches from him, those intriguing gold-green eyes focused on the cut above his eyebrow so that he was looking straight into them. It was deeply disturbing that just being with her had the power to arouse him. Had he been wrong all those years ago? Had he unforgivably wounded a delicate young woman? And why had he never noticed how soft and plump her lower lip was?

The cloth touched the cut directly, and he drew his breath in with a small hiss. Abigail stopped, her eyes going to his. "I'm sorry. But I must clean it."

"Of course."

"It's not deep, fortunately." She finished cleaning the cut and pulled her hand away. Her knuckles brushed over his cheekbone. "I think you're going to have a shiner there."

"A, um, a what?"

"A shiner. You know, a black eye. A bruise."

"Ah, yes, no doubt."

"You don't seem like the kind to get into fistfights." Now she began to dab at the cut on his lip, and a tremor ran through him, the little dart of pain tangling with a sudden pulsing hunger. He wanted to feel her lips against his, the pain be damned. He wanted her mouth to open beneath his, to slide his tongue inside the warm, wet cave . . .

Graeme jerked back. "I don't normally. Get into fights, I mean."

She released his chin, looking a little surprised and something else. . . . Was that chagrin in her eyes? And what did that mean?

"Naturally." Her voice was bright and faintly brittle. She

turned away to pick up the bottle of iodine and splash it on the cloth. "What was this all about? Who hit you?"

She held the iodine-soaked rag to the cut on his brow.

"Well, um . . ." He felt a flush spreading up his neck. "Actually, ah . . . it was Prescott."

She stared at him. "David?"

"Yes." His embarrassment was replaced by irritation. "Your good friend David."

"David hit you?" she said, as if she could not take it in. "Why? What did you do?"

"I don't know why you should suppose it was I who started it."

"Don't turn all lordly," she told him, folding her arms. "I don't know you, but I do know David Prescott. He isn't the sort to go about hitting people without reason."

Graeme would have liked to argue, but it struck him how utterly, irredeemably foolish he was being. He had not set out to call on Abigail, but he knew why his steps had turned without volition to the Langham. Whether Prescott was right in saying Abigail was innocent of her father's scheme, Graeme was duty-bound to admit his own fault in the matter. Arguing with her over David Prescott was not going to accomplish that.

He straightened his shoulders. "It was not without reason. I—Mr. Prescott took me to task for my behavior after our wedding. I am sorry for what I said to you and how I acted. I did not behave as a gentleman should, and I must beg your pardon."

chapter 6

Abigail gaped at him. If Graeme's intent had been to render her speechless, he had certainly accomplished it. She wasn't sure what she had expected from him when she saw him dawdling in front of the hotel this evening. Her first thought had been only a swift concern that he had been hurt. The last thing that would have occurred to her was that he had come to offer her an apology.

It was not precisely the apology she would have hoped for. His words had been as stiff as his posture, and there had been more regret over his failure to act as a gentleman than there had been over hurting her. Still, it was the first time he had ever unbent toward her, and Abigail felt a tender shoot of warmth start to uncurl in her chest.

Graeme continued. "I was angry and . . . frustrated at my own powerlessness in the situation. But that is no excuse. However I felt, whatever had happened, I should not have been so blunt or unkind, so lacking in courtesy to a young woman—especially one whom I had just sworn to protect."

So he was not saying he had been wrong about her.

"I should have handled it differently. I should have made arrangements for us to live separately without exposing you to gossip."

Not that he regretted parting from her.

"I see." Abby stepped back, tossing the cloth onto a table. "Arrangements—like hiding me away in some manor house in the country where I wouldn't be seen. Where I would be no embarrassment to you." She flashed him a smile so bright it was a weapon. "No, thank you. I prefer the life I have."

He frowned. "I didn't mean—you weren't—"

A knock on the door interrupted whatever explanation he was scrabbling for. Abigail seized the opportunity to turn away from Graeme and opened the door. A footman entered, carrying the ice and the brandy she had ordered, and set the tray down on the table next to the bottle of anti-septic.

After his departure, the room was heavy with silence. Abby focused on bundling the ice into a towel and tying its corners together, then thrust it at Graeme. "Here, hold this against your cheek; it will reduce the swelling. Brandy?"

"What? No, I—it doesn't matter. What I was trying to say . . ."

She poured him a glass despite his words and handed that to him as well. Crossing her arms across her chest, she regarded him steadily. "Please, you need not apologize fur-ther. I am aware of your normally impeccable courtesy. But at least you were honest in stating your feelings and your intentions toward me, which was an improvement over the fortune hunters to whom I was accustomed. Indeed, hon-esty was not a commodity I encountered with my father, either. It was a new experience. So what you said stunned me a bit."

Graeme started to speak, but she forestalled him, raising her hand. "No, please, hear me out. What happened that evening, what you said was . . ." She drew a little breath, hoping he could not hear the shakiness in it. "It was good. It forced me to face reality. I realized that my life would be whatever *I* could make of it. I could not while away my time, waiting for a fairy-tale prince to ride in and rescue me. I had to take charge of myself and of my future."

"A lady should not have to do so."

"She must if she is to be her own person. I'm glad I built a life free and independent from the rule of a man. I am my own woman, and I'm happy to be so. Proud. I don't need a husband. And I don't need your apology."

Graeme set the glass of brandy down on the table with a thud. "Well, you have it, anyway. You also have a husband, however much you choose to act as if you did not. And as your husband, what you do concerns me. You're Lady Montclair now, not Abigail Price, and—"

Abigail managed an imitation of laughter, saying lightly, "Is that why you are so alarmed about my presence in London? You're afraid I'll do something in my boorish American way that will embarrass you?"

"I didn't say that. Stop putting words in my mouth."

"You needn't worry. I *am* aware of which fork to use. I bought my clothes in Paris last month, so I shan't look provincial. I am careful not to wear more diamonds than British ladies. Perhaps the people who invite me to their parties do so in hopes of obtaining gossip. Perhaps the aristocracy all laugh at me behind my back. You would know about that better than I, since you are one of them. But if they do, they won't blame you for my failings. They'll pity you for your misfortune."

Abigail shrugged, as if none of this mattered. It was true that the English nobility's barely concealed disdain no longer burned. It had been foolish to let it bother her so much ten years ago. "But none of them will dare snub me. They're hopeful that through my connections they can sell *their* sons to American heiresses."

Graeme's lips tightened, and she saw that her barb had found its home. "I realize that you hold me in contempt for marrying you as I did."

"No," Abigail replied honestly. "I thought you were rather noble, actually, for making the sacrifice. Saving your family estate and all that." She made a self-deprecating moue. "I was hopelessly romantic then, as only an eighteen-year-old girl can be."

His eyes narrowed. "You knew, then . . ."

"That you did not love me? Yes, of course. I wasn't so deluded as to believe you married me for anything other than my father's money. However, I was not aware that you had already pledged your heart to another woman. I didn't realize you were giving up all hope of happiness." It was difficult to keep her smile from wobbling, but she managed it. "I would not have agreed to my father's wishes if I had known how you felt."

Graeme studied her for a long moment, then offered a ghost of a smile. "I must be thankful that you did not, or I would have truly been in the basket."

Abigail relaxed, and her answering smile was, for the first time, natural. She saw that he still held the small bundle of ice in his hand, and she stepped forward, taking it from him. "Here, you better put this on, or you'll be even more sore tomorrow."

She moved in closer, raising it to gently lay it against his split lip. He reached up, his hand covering hers, and for a long, breathless moment, they stood that way, her eyes unwaveringly on his. Then a soft noise came from behind him, and Abigail quickly pulled back her hand, turning toward the door. A square envelope like the one she had found the other night lay on the floor. Someone had slid it beneath her door.

Graeme went to pick up the envelope. Abigail hurried after him, and as he turned to hand it to her, she almost snatched it from his hand. He looked startled, but she ignored him, rushing to open the door. She stepped out into the hall and peered up and down the corridor. There was no one. She turned back and found Graeme watching her.

"Is something wrong?" he asked.

"What? Oh." She glanced down at the envelope. The writing on the front was the same. She forced a little laugh. "No. Just another invitation, I'm sure." She crossed to the small spindly-legged desk and slid the missive into the shallow drawer. In this moment of tenuous truce between them, the last thing she wanted was to introduce a mysterious note purporting to offer her the "truth" about their marriage. "Well . . ."

"Yes. Um . . ." He glanced around vaguely. Silence stretched between them. "I'm glad everything is straight between us now."

"Is it?" Abigail asked lightly. She wasn't sure why she continued to tease him, like a child who wanted to provoke a response, any response, to get one's notice.

"Thank you . . . for, um . . ." He waggled the bundle of ice, then set it down on the table.

"You're welcome. But perhaps you should keep it."

"Oh. Thank you." He picked it up again. "I suppose I couldn't look any more foolish than I already do. And thank you for the brandy."

"You didn't even have any."

"That's true." He picked up the glass and downed it.

Abigail laughed. "I didn't mean that you must."

He shrugged. "Mustn't let good brandy go to waste." He paused again. "I should go now. You were most kind to tend to my wounds. I'm sorry for making a shambles of your evening."

"I didn't mind."

"Well . . ." He nodded to her. "Good-bye, then. I suppose I won't see you again."

"I wouldn't say that." She smiled and sailed over to open the door. "Good night."

He hesitated, the frown returning, and she thought for a moment he was going to question her statement, but he only sketched a bow to her and strode from the room.

Abigail closed the door, leaning back against it. Her knees were suddenly trembling and her heart pounding. Silly to fall to pieces now she had gotten through the scene relatively unscathed. She had concealed her alarm at his bruised and bloody state; it would not do to let him glimpse any weakness. She had managed to keep her manner light and dispassionate even after he began to talk about their wedding night.

He couldn't have guessed from her tone how crushed she had been at his rejection, how she had crawled into a hiding hole like a wounded animal. It was the impression she must give him; indeed, it was what she must *feel*. What she wanted would not work unless she could remain free of emotion.

It had surprised her a bit to feel the old pain and anger welling up in her as she talked. She had believed herself rid of them years ago. But she didn't think her resentment had showed through her words . . . or at least only a little. She *had* meant to prick his pride with that remark about the nobility selling their sons to American heiresses. Abigail smiled to herself. No doubt it was wicked to feel satisfaction at the expression on his face.

All in all, it had worked out well. Graeme had come to her. He had apologized. She had handled it with apparent sangfroid . . . at least until that blasted note had been shoved under the door. The way she had snatched the letter from him had not been calm and controlled.

Abigail went to the dainty desk and pulled the envelope out of the drawer. Opening it, she read,

> *If you want to know the truth about your marriage,*
> *come to the corner of Pinksey Lane and Harburton at the*
> *old wall. Nine tomorrow evening. Come alone or you will*
> *learn nothing.*

It was absurd. Like something from a melodrama. She knew the truth about her marriage. Didn't she? What more could there be than that her husband loved another and hated having to marry Abigail instead? What could be worse than knowing her father had been the cause of Graeme's financial dilemma?

Still . . . what if there was more? How could she walk away and not find out if there was?

Stepping into her slippers, she hurried down the corridor and, eschewing the slower lift, trotted down the stairs. The clerk behind the imposing mahogany counter smiled ingratiatingly at her approach.

"Lady Montclair. May I help you? I trust there isn't a problem."

"No, no problem. But I hope you can help me." She held

up the envelope for him to see. "This note was pushed under my door. Did you receive this letter? Did one of your employers bring it up?"

"Under your door?" The clerk looked horrified. "Oh, no, my lady, I assure you. We would never leave a letter for you like that. If a message for you was brought to me, I would have put it in the box for your room." He gestured toward the set of cubbyholes behind him. "If someone had handed it to one of the other employees, he would have brought it to me. Even if one of them had taken it upon himself to deliver it to you"—his frown did not bode well for such impertinence from an employee—"he would have knocked and given it to you, not shoved it beneath your door. I will question the employees, but I doubt it was brought by any of them."

Even if they had done so, Abigail thought, none of them would be likely to confess it, given the desk clerk's thunderous look. She nodded. "Thank you."

"I do hope the note did not upset you," he went on anxiously. "I assure you we keep a careful eye on any strangers who come in our lobby. The Langham has a reputation for—"

"Yes, I'm sure. Don't worry. I'm not upset. I simply wanted to find out who had brought it. There was no name on it, you see."

"Most irregular." The clerk seemed put out by the sender's breach of etiquette. "I will question everyone thoroughly, I promise you, and if any of them saw a person enter with the letter, I will bring him to you to question."

"Thank you. I appreciate it." Abigail turned away. She had little hope of learning anything from the man's underlings. She stood for a moment, thinking, then strode outside. The doorman pulled the door open for her with a grand gesture.

"I wondered if perhaps you had seen someone enter the hotel tonight carrying an envelope like this?" Abigail smiled encouragingly at him. The doorman would see everyone who came through.

"An envelope?" He looked doubtfully at the item in question. "No, ma'am, I can't say as I have. This evening?"

"Yes, just a few minutes ago, in fact."

He shook his head. "No, ma'am. There have been people in and out the last hour, but I didn't see one carrying a letter. I'm sorry."

"Thank you. Do you know where the corner of Pinksey Lane and Harburton is? It's by an old wall."

"Well, that'd be the old city wall." He frowned, thinking. "I'm not sure exactly where Pinksey Lane is. But I know Harburton, and that's not an area a lady would have anything to do with."

"Mm. I don't know that it's supposed to be a lady's sort of place." She started to leave, then turned back. "Please have a hansom waiting for me here tomorrow night. A little before nine?"

"My lady!" His eyes widened in alarm. "You're not thinking of going there! It wouldn't be safe. Really. That's not a place you should go."

"I am sure I'll be fine. Just have the carriage here. Thank you."

In truth, she was a good deal less than sure that it would be either safe or wise to keep the mysterious appointment. But she knew that she could not stay away, either. She would always wonder about it and wish she had found out this "truth," whatever it was.

She thought about asking David Prescott to accompany her. But the note had said to come alone, so she feared a companion would frighten the letter-writer away. Besides, she didn't want anyone, even a friend, to know some horrible fact about her marriage, if it did indeed turn out that the man had viable information to offer.

The invitation sounded to her as if the fellow was after money in exchange for his information. This would no doubt be a preliminary meeting to establish good faith on both sides. He would tell her something to indicate that he had information worth selling, and they would haggle over price. The man would have no reason to harm her; in fact, he'd have every reason to keep her safe, at least until she could get the money he wanted.

There was more she could do to protect herself. She'd take that handy little weapon Mrs. Carson had given her when she had started visiting the settlement home. It, too, had been in a disreputable part of town and even with her coachman taking her there, the founder of the settlement home had insisted she have a weapon on her person as well. Abby had never had to use it, but she was certain she could if need be. And she would have the driver of the carriage wait for her discreetly down the block so that she could leave quickly.

It would be perfectly safe.

∞

Abigail was less inclined to feel that way the following evening when the hansom she was riding in turned down ever narrower and seedier streets. She had dressed in her plainest brown dress, without a bustle and with only one petticoat, and despite the mild summer evening, she had pulled on a hooded cloak, which hid her entire body from top to bottom. Tall as she was and with her skirts melting into the shadows, perhaps any watcher would assume she was a man.

But, peeking around the curtain in the window, she wondered if even a man was in danger of attack here. The best thing that could be said about the place was that it seemed largely made up of small shops and was deserted at this time of night.

The carriage rolled to a stop, and the driver turned around to say, "'Ere you are, miss. You said to stop before I got to it. Pinksey Lane's that little lane ahead."

He pointed with his whip, and Abigail peered down the dark street. At least a hundred feet away, there was a small break in the buildings—an alley more than a lane, she would have said. It was almost black outside, the nearest gaslight some distance behind them. The buildings rising around them cut out all trace of moonlight, and the scene was made even eerier by the drifting wisps of fog.

Abigail swallowed, tempted to remain in the carriage and return to the hotel. But, reminding herself that she had long ago left behind the timid girl she had once been, she handed the driver his money and climbed out of the cab.

"Remember, wait for me. I'll pay you extra when I return."

He looked at her as if he thought she was a lunatic, but nodded his head. "Aye. I'll wait. For a bit, mind you."

"I won't take long."

She curled her fingers tightly around the small leather-wrapped truncheon in her hand and started down the cobblestone street. Instinctively she drew closer to the protection of the buildings, though it was even darker there. Making her stride as long and confident as she could, she moved forward, hoping that she would not step in anything disgusting. It certainly smelled as if there might be refuse lying everywhere around here.

When she reached the small lane, there was, thankfully, another lamppost, though the feeble light it cast barely penetrated the wisps of fog. Abigail suspected that the light served more to illuminate herself than to show her what lay ahead. A figure, darker than the night around it, moved in a doorway down the lane. She started toward it. Suddenly, the figure darted from the doorway and took to its heels.

"No! Wait!" Abigail ran after the fleeing form, but she lost her footing on the slick, uneven cobblestones and fell to the ground. She scrambled up onto her hands and knees, her shoe catching in the hem of her cloak and impeding her. She peered up the street. The figure had disappeared. "Curse it!"

Suddenly a hand lashed out from behind her and clamped around her arm.

chapter 7

Fear lanced through Abby, and as he hauled her to her feet, she twisted and struck out at her attacker. The short cudgel in her hand slammed into his side, and he let out a startled "oomph." In the next instant she saw that her "attacker" was her husband.

"Bloody hell!" Graeme grabbed her wrist, holding it up to examine the heavy leather-wrapped object in her hand. "What the devil did you hit me with?"

Abigail drew in a shaky breath. "I believe it's called a cosh."

"You carry this around with you?"

"Not all the time. But I thought this might be the sort of place I should have a weapon."

"I should bloody well think so! What in heaven's name are you doing here?"

Abigail lifted her chin. "I might ask you the same thing."

"That's easy—I was following you." He released her and stepped back.

"Why? How did you know—"

"I asked the doorman."

"The doorman! That traitor!" Her eyes narrowed. "I'm going to have a few words with him—telling everyone my plans."

"You mustn't blame him. He assumed your husband had a right to know what idiocy you had up your sleeve."

"Well, he assumed wrong." Abby whipped around and stalked away.

"Just a minute." Graeme caught up with her in two quick strides. "You're not going anywhere until I get some answers."

"Really?" She raised an eyebrow. "What do you intend to do? Hold me prisoner?"

"Hopefully it won't come to that," he said through clenched teeth, taking her arm and steering her toward the carriage. "What are you doing? Why did you come here?"

"It's none of your business." That wasn't strictly correct, since the matter concerned the "truth" about her marriage, but Abby was not about to give in to his high-handed manner. Besides, this person, whoever it was, had approached her, not Graeme; perhaps there had been a reason for that. What if he knew something her spouse didn't want her to learn? However trustworthy and upright Graeme might seem, she didn't really know him. She had discovered that ten years ago.

"Not my business? You're my wife."

"Not so one would notice."

"Blast!" Abigail thought she might actually hear his teeth grinding together. "However little joy we may get out of it, legally we are married. I am responsible for you. You are Lady Montclair."

"Please." She rolled her eyes. "Are you about to go on again about creating a scandal?"

They had reached her hansom, and as the driver watched in interest, Graeme handed Abby up into the vehicle with a good deal more energy than was necessary, in her opinion. He climbed in behind her and swiveled to face her. She glared at him.

"You almost had me fooled," Graeme told her bitterly. "Between you and your champion Prescott, you had me believing you were an innocent whom I had misjudged and mistreated years ago. Until that note was shoved under your door."

"What does that have to do with anything?"

"I don't know. That's what I'm trying to find out. It was obvious you were hiding it from me."

"Am I obliged to show you my correspondence? I must say, your view of a husband is more like a warden."

"Of course not! I don't give a farthing who writes you or what they say. It was your secrecy! If it were perfectly innocent, why did you immediately stick it away in a drawer? Why did you rush into the hall and look around? Why did you say you didn't know what it was when it was clear from the look on your face that you recognized it? You snatched it out of my hand—why would you be so alarmed that I might see it?"

"You read a good deal into my putting away a letter."

"I told myself I was refining too much on a simple matter. So when I left, I sat down in the lobby to consider what had happened. The next thing I knew, you came flying down the stairs and over to the desk, where you showed the note to the clerk and talked to him at great length. Then you hustled out to speak to the doorman. After you left, I paid him a visit. He told me you were asking about someone bringing that envelope into the hotel. He also said that you showed him an address in a decidedly unlikely area for you to visit and ordered a cab for this evening."

"Congratulations. You found out a great deal. Perhaps

you should join the police force." She set her jaw mulishly.

"You are involved in something, just as I suspected from the beginning. I have asked you time and again, but you have never given me your reason for returning to London. What are you planning?"

"I don't have any nefarious plans."

"Whom did you go there to meet?"

"I don't know."

He made an exasperated noise and turned from her, visibly pulling the remnants of his control around him. After a long moment, he said tersely, "What do you want?"

"I beg your pardon?"

"What will it take to make you leave? What are you after? Do you want me to increase your living expenses? I've always given you a generous amount, I thought, but—"

Abigail let out a humorless laugh. "Are you offering to pay *me* money? From the money my father gives you?"

"I don't receive money from him. I have managed your dowry well and brought the estate back into order. It now makes a profit. The remainder of the funds I have invested in—"

"Please, I don't need an accounting." Abby sighed. Why had she ever thought this would work? "You are welcome to increase my allowance. I am sure the settlement home would appreciate it."

"The what? What are you talking about?"

"It's a place where they help the women and children from the tenements. They offer food and aid and even housing. I give them the money you send me. Returning the payments to you got tiresome after a few months, so I started passing them on to a charity instead."

He stared at her blankly. "But how do you live? Did you

go back to your father's house? Do you think to shame me by living on his charity, as if I don't support you?"

"Of course not. I don't have to live with one or the other of you. It isn't scandalous to set up my own household; I'm a married woman. I have my own house; I have my own money. I am not beholden to any man."

"But that's impossible. I don't understand. The moment we married, your money became mine under law."

She cocked an eyebrow. "Under British law. I don't live in Britain. In New York a married woman can have property; we are, you see, somewhat more forward-thinking. Your arrangement with my father involved a chunk of *his* money. I receive income from a family trust on my mother's side—Thurston is nouveau riche, but my mother's ancestors have been stockpiling cash since the *Mayflower*. My father settled an endowed trust on me, as well, when I married. He didn't trust you to support me in the proper style. That is no slight on you; my father doesn't trust anyone. In any case, I have made investments on my own. Mr. Prescott has been kind enough to advise me on financial matters."

Graeme snorted. "I'm sure he has."

She glanced out the window and saw that they had arrived at the Langham. "So you see, I don't need your money. I don't want your title or your position or even your public embarrassment, for that matter." Abigail reached out to turn the door handle.

He caught her wrist. "What the devil do you want, then?"

She looked at him. "A baby."

∽

Had Abby been in a lighter mood, she might have laughed at the stunned expression on Graeme's face. His hand fell away from hers. She climbed out of the carriage and strode toward the hotel door. Let him pay the hansom driver; it served him right for taking over her carriage—and her meeting.

She didn't bother to send the doorman a hard look. What did the man's disloyalty to her matter when she doubted she would be here for long? Graeme had forced her hand. She had hoped to spend enough time with him to overcome his initial dislike, even perhaps to arouse some modicum of desire, so that he might agree to her offer.

But it was clear he was determined to believe the worst of her, even about something as insignificant as this letter. Abigail had no chance of softening him to the idea. All she could do was throw out the bald truth and see if Graeme would be reasonable about the whole thing. She feared there was little chance of that. His enmity seemed unshakable.

Inside her suite, she ripped off her cloak and gloves, tossing them onto a chair. Going to the sideboard, she poured herself a glass from the decanter of brandy and took a drink, grimacing at the heat that seared her throat.

Her head ached. She pulled the pins from her hair, letting the heavy mass tumble down, and began to massage her scalp with her fingertips. She felt close to tears—she wasn't sure whether from disappointment or anger—but she refused to cry. She had vowed years ago never to shed another tear over Graeme Parr. Not that it was about him. The loss looming before her was larger than that.

She was jerked from her thoughts by a loud knock at the door. Hope rose in her chest, and she started forward. She made herself stop and draw a calming breath, before she opened the door.

It came as no surprise to see Graeme standing in the

doorway. Whatever he had been about to say died on his lips as his eyes went to her hair, falling over her shoulders. No doubt he found it reprehensible of her to answer the door in such dishabille. She lifted her chin and sent him a challenging gaze.

He cleared his throat. "May I come in?"

Abigail shrugged and walked away, leaving him to step inside and close the door. She swung back around to face him, crossing her arms.

"You cannot simply drop that on a man and walk away," he told her. "What the devil are you talking about?"

She raised her brows. "Surely you don't need me to explain how I would acquire a baby."

His mouth tightened. "Of course not. But why did you come to me about it?"

Anger rushed through her. "You think I'm the sort of woman who would cuckold you instead?"

"I didn't think anything. I never considered the matter."

"Naturally. You wouldn't have cared what I did." Abigail could not keep the touch of bitterness from her voice.

"I didn't say that."

"You didn't have to. You've made it perfectly clear. I understand how you feel. I even understand why you feel that way. However, I cannot change the things that have happened. I have to make the best I can of my situation. This last year I came to realize that despite all my wealth, all the parties, the title, the multitude of things that others might envy me for, I do not have a life. You and my father, you see, got what you wanted from our marriage. My father has the connection to aristocracy that he craved. And you, even though it was at the expense of sacrificing your heart, received the money you needed to rescue your estate. What did I get? An empty marriage, an empty house. An empty life. I want more than an endless round of shopping and parties. I want a child."

"I—I see." Graeme glanced around uncomfortably, then picked up the glass of brandy she had set down and slugged it back. "You want a real marriage."

"No. I can live without a husband. I no longer expect to have romantic love. I don't need to be sheltered or supported or have companionship. But I do want the fulfillment of a child. I want to have someone to love and—well, there's no need to explain my reasons. Suffice it to say that I intend to have a baby, and since I am married to you, you seemed the logical choice for a father."

He avoided her eyes as he poured himself another drink.

"I could, of course, take a lover," Abby went on. "But whatever you think of me, I am not the sort of woman who breaks her wedding vows. And it seems wrong to present you with an heir that is another man's child. I presume that is something that would bother you as well."

His gaze flew to her then, and he said in a strangled voice, "Yes, I mean no, I shouldn't want that." He cleared his throat. "But don't you think that this is, ah, a trifle . . . cold-blooded?"

"Yes, it is, isn't it?" Abby gave him a bright smile. "I believe I'm getting the hang of being a noblewoman."

"Is this a jest to you?"

"No. It is no jest. I want a child. Don't you? You need an heir. That's the way it is with the nobility, isn't it?" Abby took a step toward him. "Come now, you always do what a gentleman should, make whatever sacrifice is necessary for the family. It would only be one more."

"It is hardly that simple."

Abby knew she was going about it wrong. She could not argue him into it; he was obviously far too stubborn for that. And this was too important to lose. Pulling on whatever acting skills she had, she summoned up an arch tone. "I understand that it may be . . . difficult for you to perform your, um, duty. Since you love another woman, I mean."

A dull flush reddened his cheeks. "I realize that you find me an object of ridicule."

"Nonsense. I find it admirable, rather, that you have stayed true to your love these many years. Not many men would have remained celibate all this time." He shifted uncomfortably, and Abby pressed her point. "Most men would have found . . . other outlets, shall we say?"

"This is hardly a fit topic of conversation." His color deepened.

She ignored his words. "A willing widow, say, or, perhaps a business arrangement. Yet you—"

"You know bloody good and well I didn't—" he burst out. "I mean, of course there were—I did sometimes avail myself of, um . . ." He faltered to a stop.

"Prostitutes?" Abigail suggested brightly.

"Yes!" he snapped.

"So you have had other women despite your love for the woman you could not have."

"It's been ten years!" he ground out. "What the devil would you expect me to do?"

"I expected precisely that. I was merely pointing out that you have in the past—"

"Blast it, that was different! I wasn't—it was just business."

"Perhaps you could pay me, then, and that would make it all right."

He slammed the glass down on the table. "This conversation is absurd."

Energy and hope drained from her. "No doubt you're right." Tears burned behind her eyes, but Abby sternly suppressed them. "That's the end of it, then."

"I'm sorry." He sent her an abashed glance. "But you must see that it's impossible."

"I do." Abigail nodded. "I was indulging in a fantasy." She wanted nothing more at the moment than to be alone, to sink down on the bed and weep with disappointment. But she refused to allow herself to be weak. She would not allow this man or anyone else to rule her life. "I shall return home and file for divorce."

"What!" Graeme stiffened. "No. You cannot."

"I must. It isn't what I want. I believed my marriage was for life. But there is no other way."

"No. It's impossible." Graeme's expression was implacable. "It would take an act of Parliament and I will not—"

"I'll remind you again: I don't live in England." Abigail faced him. She would not back down, not even before his anger. "It is still somewhat difficult to obtain a divorce in New York, but it's an easy enough matter to move to Ohio and sue for divorce there. I am sure I would have ample grounds. Desertion, for one thing."

"I didn't desert you. *You* were the one who left."

"Adultery, then. I can hire someone to follow you when you visit your prostitutes. Or perhaps it's good enough cause that you have refused to perform your 'marital duties.' I'll have my lawyer look it up."

"No, damn it!" He took two quick steps forward, his eyes blazing. "I will not allow you to subject my family to scandal. It would be a stain on the Parr name for generations."

"I don't care!" Abigail cried, her arms rigid at her side. "I am not throwing away the rest of my life for the sake of your stupid infernal name!"

"So that is it, then—if I don't give in to you, you will drag my family's name through the muck. You plan to coerce me into doing what you want. You *are* just like your father."

"I'm not forcing you to do anything. But I refuse to sacrifice all hope of happiness."

"Happiness?" He loomed over her, so close she could feel the heat of his body. "You think you will enjoy forcing a man who despises you into your bed? You want to be taken without pleasure? Without love? That is nothing but rutting."

"Women have been doing that for centuries," she shot back. "I am sure I can endure it."

"Endure it?" he growled. "Really?" He grabbed her arms and jerked her flush against his body. His mouth came down on hers, hard and hungry. He turned, walking her back until they came up hard against the wall, his mouth locked to hers. Finally he raised his head, his eyes bright, his breath coming in hard, fast pants. "This? This is what you are ready to endure?"

Abigail stared up into his hot, furious gaze. Her entire body thrummed. She smiled at him, a slow, triumphant, beckoning smile. "Let's find out."

His eyes widened, and, with a low groan, his mouth returned to hers.

chapter 8

It would be a lie to say that Abby had not wondered what her wedding night would have been like if Graeme had not stormed out ten years ago. She had more than once imagined how his lips would have felt upon hers, how his arms would have enveloped her. But never in any of her daydreams had she imagined this.

He pressed his body into hers, imprinting her with the hard lines of muscle and bone. His mouth consumed hers, hot and drugging. Abigail kissed him back, imitating the movement of his lips and tongue. He clenched his hands in her hair, making a soft noise deep in his throat that threatened to melt her very flesh.

It had never occurred to her that her whole body could ache and yearn like this, that a deep insistent throbbing would spring to life between her legs, that she would find herself trembling and scarcely able to breathe . . . and yet wanting more and more. She heard a soft whimper and realized in some amazement that it had come from her.

Graeme rubbed his body over hers, and the ache inside her grew, pleasure and hunger flowing together. His hands slid down her, touching her in shocking places that made her shiver with delight. He cupped one of her breasts, dragging his thumb across the cloth and awakening the nipple beneath. With wonder, she felt her flesh harden beneath his touch, his thumb circling and circling until she thought she would have cried out if his mouth had not been clamped on hers.

His lips went to her cheeks, her ears, her throat. She heard the harsh rasp of his breath, and, like the searing heat of his skin, this evidence of his desire multiplied her own. She had to fight back a moan. She wanted him; she wanted . . . something. Wanted it so badly that she dug her fingers into the cloth of his jacket as if she could pull it out of him.

His fingers fumbled at the buttons of her dress, opening it, and he slid his hand beneath the cloth. The feel of his fingertips on her skin shocked her, thrilled her, and the yearning between her legs blossomed. He roamed over the soft flesh of her breast and delved beneath the lace edging of her chemise. He nipped gently at her neck, circling with his tongue, as his fingers found the hard bud of her nipple. And now she did moan, the sound soft and helpless, and she felt his body shudder against hers in response.

Abby breathed his name, her hand caressing his hair. He raised his head and his eyes locked with hers. His heat surrounded her; his scent filled her nostrils; his hard, rapid breaths brushed her skin. She saw only him, felt only him. And nothing had ever been so right.

"Oh, God." He let his head drop, and she felt his muscles tighten. He levered himself away from the wall, away from her. He sent her a single fevered look, a volatile mix of anger and desire that should have made her shrink from him but only made her want to pull him back to her.

Graeme swung away, slamming his hand flat against the wall. He strode out of the room, thudding the door closed behind him. Abigail remained where she was, leaning against the wall, her heart racing, breath rushing in and out. Slowly she slid down to sit on the floor, unsure whether to laugh or cry—and knowing what she wanted most was to run after him.

❦

Graeme stretched his legs out in front of him, a glass of whiskey dangling from his fingertips, and contemplated the coals glowing on the grate. That woman, he thought with great bitterness, had driven him insane. After he charged out of her hotel suite, he'd walked so long and aimlessly through the streets that he had wound up hopelessly lost. He had been fortunate to find a hansom cab to take him home—and even more fortunate, probably, that some footpad hadn't seen him, deep in his fog, and decided he was perfect prey.

That would have been all he needed, to be bashed over the head and acquire a large knot to go along with the cuts and bruises from his round of fisticuffs with the American—not to mention the large purplish oval on his ribs from the cosh wielded by his wife. It was no coincidence that she was also an American; there was something decidedly bellicose about those people.

Worse, they seemed to have an extraordinary ability to turn him into someone who was just as mad as they were. Never in his life had he acted as he had the other night with Abigail. If anyone had told him he could be eaten up with hunger that way for a woman whom he disliked with equal intensity, he would have scoffed at the idea.

He was a reasonable man. An even-tempered, polite sort ruled by logic and duty and practicality. He was not unemotional. He felt everything from love to pity to despair and hatred, but not to such excess . . . and not all at the same time! Yet there he had been, pawing her like some lecher, kissing her as if he would consume her—and, Lord, but he had wanted to do exactly that. He wanted to be inside her, over her, around her, driving into her with all the desperation in his soul. Her, of all people—a woman whom he held in contempt. A woman whom he never wanted to see again.

Yet he could not get her out of his mind.

It had been two days since he'd left Abigail, and he had done nothing but think about her. He should apologize; he'd behaved like a lout. Graeme had never handled a woman roughly in his life—though, God knew, it hadn't seemed to bother her any. Perhaps she was used to men who shoved her against a wall and kissed her wildly, who thrust their hands down the front of her dress. Graeme sighed. He wasn't sure which he felt more when he thought about his actions, guilt or arousal. The truth was, much as he knew he should apologize to her, he was frankly uneasy at the thought of calling on her. He wasn't sure what he might do if he was alone with her again.

She was damnably seductive, though he wasn't sure what she did to lure him. It might have been her laugh, or, no, it was more the teasing way she spoke to him, as if goading him into something outrageous. Perhaps it was that mouth that quirked up at the corners, not quite a smile, but clearly an invitation.

Abigail was no innocent, he was sure of that. A woman who went about making bold proposals as she had, who reacted as she did to his kiss, was a woman of experience. For all her proclamations of unwillingness to get a baby off some other man, she obviously must have had a lover.

Lovers. He wondered if the man normally in her bed was Prescott.

His jaw clenched. He should have hit the fellow harder.

"Montclair?" The dowager countess's voice cut through his gloomy thoughts. "Honestly, child, what are you doing in the dark?" She turned on the wall sconces.

"Sorry, Grandmother." Graeme squinted in the sudden light.

"You have been acting most peculiarly." She swept over to stare down at him. "You haven't been outside this house for days."

Suppressing a sigh, Graeme rose to his feet with ingrained courtesy. "I apologize if I have worried you."

"Your grandfather was a moody man. I do hope you aren't turning out to be like him."

"A momentary aberration, I assure you. I shall doubtless be sunny again soon."

"No need for impertinence." She frowned. "Obviously you don't wish to talk about whatever is troubling you, at least not to me."

"Grandmother . . ."

"I know. I know. There are things a gentleman cannot speak of with ladies. Indeed, I am sure I would not wish to hear it. Why don't you visit your cousin?"

"James?"

"Yes, of course James. The rest of that lot is useless, just like their mother. But James at least is levelheaded."

"There's nothing to talk about, really." He could well imagine how James would react if Graeme started pouring out this welter of emotions to him.

Lady Eugenia sniffed. "It's up to you, of course, if you

choose to act like a bear with a sore paw, snapping at every-one."

"I haven't—"

"Or mope about like Hamlet on the castle wall."

"Grandmother . . ."

"However, I do expect you to escort me to the theater tomorrow night."

With an effort, Graeme refrained from grinding his teeth. "Of course. I shall be happy to."

"Well, that's a lie, and we both know it," she said with a flash of a smile that surprised them both. She reached out and patted his arm awkwardly. "But I shall hold you to it. Good night, dear, and don't stay up too long, brooding."

"I won't." He sank down into his chair. He would jolly well brood if he wanted to.

Lord, now he was beginning to sound like a seven-year-old.

Graeme surged back up to his feet and began to pace. His grandmother was right—as she so often and irritat-ingly proved to be. He should get out of the house, clear his head. Why not talk to James? He would doubtless snicker at Graeme's dilemma, but after thirty-three years, Graeme was accustomed to that. James was the least emotional per-son Graeme knew; if anyone could cut through the tangle inside Graeme, it would be he. Besides, Graeme was thor-oughly sick of his own company. He might as well inflict it on James.

James was home, and though his dog lifted his great head from the rug and glowered at the interruption of his sleep, James was unruffled by the late visit. "Cousin! Come in. Out brawling with Americans again?"

Graeme grimaced. "None other than my wife. She hit me with a cosh the other night." He flopped down in one of the chairs before the fireplace.

James's eyebrows vaulted up. "Probably best not to ask why."

"She thought I was someone else."

"Now you really have roused my curiosity. Who, pray tell, did she think you were?"

"I don't know. A footpad, I suppose; she was wandering about in an abysmal area. Or perhaps someone she went to meet. I followed her."

"Cousin . . . whatever is going on? Your life has become something of a melodrama lately."

"It's a thorough mess. Abigail is up to something, and she won't tell me what. Well, she did tell me, but I don't see how that would explain why she's hiding messages and sneaking out to meet people in dark streets."

"I think this tale calls for a drink. Brandy?"

"I started out with whiskey tonight; best stick to that."

James went to the sideboard and poured two drinks. Handing one to Graeme, he settled down in his chair. The mastiff hauled himself to his feet and leaned against James's knee. Absently James scratched Dem's head as he sipped his drink. "There. I am armed. Tell away."

"She wants a baby." It gave Graeme some satisfaction to see his usually unflappable cousin gape at him.

"I beg your pardon?"

"She's decided she wants to have a child."

"And she's chosen you as the, um . . . provider of this service?"

"Well, I *am* her husband—and if you say, 'Not so anyone can tell,' I swear I will thrash you."

James raised a hand pacifically. "Go on."

Graeme shrugged. "That's it, I suppose."

James looked at him for a long moment. "So, to sum up, the woman offered to sleep with you, correct?" The corner of his mouth twitched. "How dastardly of her."

"It's not that simple."

"It seems rather simple to me."

"She threatened to divorce me if I refused—apparently in America they all run about divorcing one another. She's holding the scandal over me like a club. It's coercion. She's just like her father—controlling, deceitful. I know she has something else in mind. She's plotting some devious plan."

"Such as?"

"I don't know! The other night, after Prescott told me Abigail knew nothing about what her father did, I began to believe him. Believe her. I thought I'd been unfair to her before. But then she got this message slipped beneath her door . . ." He described Abigail's peculiar actions and his own investigation. "So the next night I followed her. That's when she hit me—with this little cosh that she apparently carries about with her. She says a woman at some almshouse or other gave it to her for protection when she goes traipsing around the slums of New York. That's another thing—she's been giving the money I send her to this almshouse. It seems she doesn't want anything from me."

"I wouldn't say that," James murmured, taking a sip of his drink.

Graeme sent him a dark look. "Except for *that*."

"Who was it Lady Montclair went to meet?"

"I don't know. She refused to tell me. She was bloody secretive about it, and when I demanded to know what the devil she was up to and what she wanted from me, that's when she said, 'A baby.' Why would that cause her to be creeping around dark streets and meeting people she won't name? I know she must have something more in mind. Some scandal she'll create to ruin the family."

"How? What scandal?"

"I don't know. I haven't a devious mind—maybe *you* could figure it out."

"Ooh, cousin!" James grinned. "A direct hit."

"Sorry. I'm lashing out at everyone, it seems. Grandmother told me tonight I was acting like a bear."

"Who wouldn't if they had to live with the dowager countess?"

Graeme smiled faintly, then sighed. "Maybe Abigail just intends to have my child, then use him to punish me. Go back to New York and take him with her. Turn him against me. I don't know."

"Why?"

"That's obvious—for revenge. I told you how harsh I was to her ten years ago. I didn't think about it at the time; I was so furious, I wouldn't have cared, frankly. But it wasn't just that. It exposed her to ridicule, not just here but in her own society, as well. You recall the gossip—when she left, it made the split very public. She was humiliated."

James shrugged. "She wouldn't have been if she hadn't taken off like a rabbit."

"I doubt she looks at it like that." Graeme sipped his drink, falling into silence.

"Graeme, I realize that you don't want to dance to this woman's tune . . ."

"I will not be coerced," Graeme said fiercely, leaning forward. "I had to marry her, but I bloody well don't have to sleep with her. She's manipulative and . . . it's damned cold and calculating, isn't it? She has no interest in me; she just wants a baby."

"Women always want babies, Graeme. It's God's little favor to men."

Graeme made a disgusted noise. "Can't you see? It isn't just sex."

"No? What is it?"

"It's not as if she's any woman, someone I can see a few times and leave with a diamond necklace. She's my wife. To sleep with her, to have a child with her—that's an intimacy I don't want to share with Abigail. It's a betrayal. . . ."

"Of Laura Hinsdale? Good Lord, Graeme . . ."

"I know you think I'm a romantic ass, but—"

"You *are* a romantic ass. Miss Hinsdale is a pretty girl, but she could not be that remarkable. One woman is much like another, I find."

"You don't understand. You've never been in love."

"No, thank God." James sighed, causing the mastiff to raise his head and look worriedly at him. James gave Dem a reassuring pat. "I will accept that you still pine for the fetching Miss Hinsdale even though you haven't touched her in ten years—have you?"

"I didn't touch her then. I wouldn't have compromised her. And I certainly haven't done so since."

"Of course not. But, for pity's sake, be sensible. You must have an heir unless you want to leave everything to your second cousin once removed or whatever Randall is."

"I'm willing to do that."

"Very well, then. How would you like to be presented with an heir fathered by another man? Would you be happy with that, too? What if she decides it would be easier to have an affair than to get a divorce? Are you going to accept her lover's child? Watch him grow up year after year, the proverbial cuckoo in your nest. Or would you refuse to acknowledge him? That would be a certain way to produce the scandal you say you want to avoid."

"I don't want any of that! Of course I don't."

"All you have to do is bed the woman. It shouldn't be too onerous a task. From what I've heard, she's eminently beddable."

A white-hot fire licked through Graeme's chest, and he was aware of a strong desire to yank his cousin out of his chair and pummel him. He was turning into a maniac. An absolute lunatic. He shoved his hands in his pockets and regarded James stonily.

"And if you're lucky," James went on, ignoring the expression on Graeme's face, "she will get pregnant, die in childbirth, and you will have an heir, a fortune, and no inconvenient wife."

"Good Gad, James!" Graeme stared, shocked out of his ill humor. "I never know whether you actually believe the things you say or just wish to enhance your reputation for coldness." When James only quirked an eyebrow at him, he went on. "For pity's sake, I don't wish harm on the woman; I just want her to go away."

"I have to say, this bothers you a good deal more than would seem warranted. Is it really so burdensome? Surely you are capable of going to bed with a woman without loving her. Is your Abigail so repellent to you?"

"She's not 'my' Abigail. And she's not repellent. Far from it," he added beneath his breath.

"Ah." James nodded, his eyes glinting silver in the lamplight. "Now I understand."

"I am glad to hear it. I wish *I* did."

"The only reason you don't understand is because you don't want to. You're not reluctant because you don't want her. You're afraid you will like it too much."

Graeme narrowed his eyes. "Don't be a fool."

"I'm not the fool here. Grow up, Graeme. Stop mooning about like some adolescent Romeo. You aren't married to Laura; you're married to Abigail. Living with the woman you love is not one of your choices. If you intend to have an heir, it must be with your wife. What do you plan to do? Make the sacrifices you have made, put in the effort it took to bring your estate back into prosperity, all to leave it to Randall bloody Parr or some other man's child? Spend the remainder of your days in short, meaningless affairs with women for whom you care nothing?"

"That's what *you* do," Graeme shot back.

James let out a dry bark of laughter. "And is that what you want?" He settled back in his chair, with a long, level look at Graeme. "Do you really want to become me?"

chapter 9

Two days passed without any word from Graeme, and Abby was beginning to think she had gambled everything and lost. At first her spirits had been buoyed by Graeme's kisses. She had never felt anything like the sensations that poured through her at his kiss, his touch. It was enough to make her blush even to think about it. Surely his reaction meant that he desired her, too, however little he might like her.

After all, she didn't require affection from him; she had done perfectly well for years without it. Her goal was to have a baby, not a love affair. What she needed was Graeme's cooperation—and to that end, whatever lust she aroused in him was her ally.

But as the hours, then days, went by, doubt pushed its way in. Perhaps his passion had been nothing but anger. It seemed strange that fury alone could make a man grab her and kiss her so hungrily, but she was inexperienced in that regard. What few kisses she had received had been stolen in haste by some opportunist who hoped to lure her into adultery. None of them had tempted her in the slightest. She was, Abby suspected, the only married woman who was as untutored as a maiden.

She would see him again. But what if he merely looked

at her coldly—or, even worse, with disgust? He already thought her wicked. Perhaps her fervent response to his kisses had lowered his opinion of her even more.

Abigail found it difficult to enjoy the ballet tonight. She left early, pleading a headache, and returned to her hotel. She walked from the lift down the corridor to her room, so lost in thought that she did not even glance down the dark intersecting hall as she walked past it.

A hand lashed out and grabbed her arm, jerking her into the shadows of the side corridor. His arm went around her waist, pulling her back against him, and he clamped his other hand over her mouth.

"Don't scream. I'm not here to hurt you." Abby kicked out behind her, connecting with his shin. "Ow! Stop it! I just want to talk to you. Why didn't you come alone like I told you?"

It was the man who had sent her the letters. Abigail went still.

"If I take my hand away, you mustn't scream." He sounded shaky, she thought, as if he, too, was frightened. "I just want to talk," he repeated. "Understand?"

She nodded emphatically, and he moved his hand so that it still hovered in front of her mouth, ready to stop any attempt to cry out.

"I didn't know he was there," Abby told him in a low voice, matching his tone. "He followed me."

"Montclair?"

"Yes. I came alone as you asked. He tricked me. Please, tell me what you wanted to then."

"It'll cost you."

She nodded, feeling on firmer ground now. "I presumed so. How much do you want?"

"Five hundred pounds."

"Five hundred! Are you mad? That is a great deal of money."

"What I know is worth a great deal," he responded. "And this time make sure Montclair isn't with you. You don't want him to hear this."

"Why not? Really, you cannot expect me to simply hand over that much money without any idea what I'm paying for."

"Don't you think it's worth it to find out about his father's embezzling money? And Thurston Price's involvement in it?"

Abigail froze. "What? What are you talking about?"

"No, that's all you'll get until you pay me. Bring the money tomorrow night to the Crimson Pirate."

"The Crimson Pirate?"

"It's a tavern. Any hack will know where it is. I'll meet you outside it. Same time—nine o'clock."

"No. Wait. That's impossible."

"You better make it possible."

"I can't. I haven't that large a sum of money simply lying about my room. I have to make arrangements at the bank. It will take a couple of days, and they will be closed Sunday, of course. I cannot possibly have it before Monday evening." In fact, Abby was certain she would be able to withdraw the sum the next morning, but she had to take control of this issue. She could not let him dictate all the terms. It was always better to give oneself time to think, and besides, she wasn't about to change her plans for tomorrow night.

He hesitated before giving in. "Very well, Monday night, then. The Crimson Pirate. Nine o'clock."

"I'll be there."

"You better." He released her, pushing her at the same time so that she stumbled forward and had to catch herself against the wall.

Abigail whipped around, but he was already almost to the end of the corridor. All she could see was the back of a medium-size man in a hat, and then he was gone down the stairs at the end. She stood there, one hand against the wall, struggling to bring her whirling thoughts back into order.

Graeme's father? Embezzling money? The idea was mind-boggling. She had met the man only a few times and in the most formal of circumstances, but he had seemed like an older version of Graeme—handsome, polite, and honorable. Still, she supposed that desperation over losing his family fortune could have driven him to commit a crime.

It was, sadly, far easier to believe that her own father had been involved. She had never heard of Thurston Price doing anything that was outright illegal, but his legal activities often skirted the edges of the law—and definitely went over that line morally. He would be careful to keep himself out of trouble, but he would be unlikely to show the same concern for Graeme's father.

Frowning, Abby continued to her room and unlocked the door, her fingers shaky on the key. Did Graeme know about his father's embezzlement? She doubted it. She imagined his father would have gone to great efforts to hide the secret from his loved ones.

She planned to do the same. Graeme was so proud, so concerned about his family's name, so dutiful and honorable that she feared it would devastate him to learn that his father had stolen money. And, selfishly, she couldn't bear for him to discover that her father had had anything to do with it. Graeme already despised Thurston and was apt to tar her with the same brush. It made her quail to think how Graeme would feel about her if he found out her father had led Lord Reginald to do something dishonorable.

Abigail began to pace. David Prescott might know the truth; he had worked for her father at the time. She wished she could ask him about the matter, but she couldn't take that risk. It was likely David was unaware of the embezzlement—her father was not a man to share his plans—which meant she would only reveal Reginald's misdeeds to David. The two men already disliked each other. David was the last person Graeme would want privy to a scandalous family secret.

Abby thought back to her encounter. She had been too frightened at the time to pay attention, but looking back on it now, she realized that she had learned some details about the man. For one thing, he was not any taller than she was. His voice had been right behind her ear. The glimpse she had had of him as he ran away had confirmed that he was not large.

He had not spoken in the rounded, crystal-clear tones of the upper crust, but his speech had indicated an educated man. He had worn a suit and hat much like Graeme or David or other gentlemen wore, marking him as one who if he worked did so with his wits, not his hands.

A clerk or lawyer or teacher or journalist. He could be an enterprising reporter who had somehow dug up the facts. Or a clerk who worked in the business from which the money had been embezzled. An attorney who dealt with that business or with Reginald . . . although it seemed a little absurd to think of one of those dignified fellows in a robe and wig going about blackmailing people.

Unfortunately, the information she had managed to glean didn't really help her. Even if she could figure out the man's identity, it wouldn't stop him from telling everyone what Graeme's father—and hers—had done. She could not allow that to happen.

Obviously he wanted money in payment for not revealing the damning information. She could provide that. It likely would be only the first of many more demands. But she would find some way to deal with that later. Tomorrow she would be visiting the bank.

∞

Graeme offered his arm politely to his grandmother and started up the wide stone steps to the theater. He was certain the evening would prove to be a tremendous bore. He was not in the mood for a farce. His life already provided enough of that.

He wondered if Abigail would be here this evening. It would be annoying and distracting, making it even harder to keep his mind on the play. He glanced around the lobby. It was filled with the usual crowd, women in glittering jewels and elegant gowns, men in starkly formal black-and-white. Everyone came to the theater more to be seen than to watch the performance.

There was no sign of Abigail. Which was, of course, a relief. It should be a relief.

He glanced up the stairs, and his breath caught in his throat. Abigail stood at the top of the grand staircase, watching the lobby below. Topazes gleamed at her throat and ears. She wore a golden-brown dress, and a gold wrap of the sheerest material lay across her bare arms, shimmering on the skin beneath. The skirt was made from some crinkly material that twisted cunningly to the side and was caught by the bustle, so that she looked as if she were encased in meringue.

Graeme started toward the stairs, only belatedly remembering that his grandmother was with him. Fortunately, she made no objection. Abigail watched them ascend, her mouth curved up in a smile. Graeme's pulse hammered in his ears.

"Montclair. Lady Montclair," Abigail greeted them.

His grandmother nodded regally. "I'm so glad you were able to join us."

"What?" Graeme, in the midst of making his bow, was brought up short. He glanced toward his grandmother, then back at Abigail.

"It was so kind of you to invite me," Abigail replied to his grandmother. She turned her expressive green eyes to Graeme. "I hope you do not mind."

"Mind? No, of course not." His stomach felt as if he'd just taken a step off a cliff. Two hours or more of being enclosed with Abigail in a tiny theater box, watching her, breathing in her bewitching perfume, only inches from touching her. "My pleasure." That, at least, was not a lie. He did not add that it would be a nerve-racking pleasure.

He escorted the two ladies to the box and was irritated to find that several gentlemen of his acquaintance intercepted them, obviously angling for an introduction. He introduced them each time somewhat tersely. "You know the dowager countess, of course. And Lady Montclair, my *wife*."

"Goodness," Abigail commented as the fourth such man walked away. "You seem to know everyone here."

"A great many more than I care to."

She cast a laughing glance up at him, and he had the uneasy feeling she suspected exactly why he was disgruntled.

"Arthur Dexter is scarcely anyone with whom you'd want to advance an acquaintance," his grandmother told Abigail firmly. "Jumped-up little mushroom. His grandfather was in trade."

"Shocking," Abigail agreed with such a twinkle in her eye that Graeme had to hide a smile.

The countess sent her a sharp look. "In general his mother's line is respectable, but there was always something a bit off about her uncle."

"Scarcely Arthur's fault, surely," Graeme put in.

Lady Eugenia shrugged. "I suppose not, though I must say it gives him little reason to put on such airs."

"Perhaps he is proud of what he has accomplished rather than his family," Abigail offered.

"What a very American thing to say."

Graeme suppressed a groan. It was shaping up to be a long evening. In addition to his own turmoil, he would have to intercede between the two women. What had possessed his grandmother to invite Abigail? He cast about for something to stave off a battle between his companions, but to his surprise Abigail merely laughed.

"Yes, I suppose it is," she agreed. "It's difficult for some people to transcend their upbringing."

"Precisely." His grandmother nodded. Graeme wasn't sure whether she had caught the subtle message in Abigail's words. He suspected not; Lady Eugenia did not deal in subtleties.

He glanced over at Abigail. She returned his gaze with a wide-eyed blandness that convinced him she had intended the little dig at his grandmother's prejudices. Again he found himself wanting to smile.

Why did it have to be so bloody easy to like this woman? He knew she was manipulating him, trying to bend him to her will. Just as her father had. She interspersed her threats with charm and allure, but the result was the same. She meant to control him. However reasonable James had made the matter sound last night, Graeme knew that the seemingly easy path Abigail offered was a quagmire.

He had intended to seat his grandmother between him and Abigail, but Lady Eugenia ignored his maneuvering and sat down at the end of the row, forcing Graeme to take his place between the two women. He resigned himself to an evening spent deflecting their sniping at one another.

They took it up immediately, of course. "I am looking forward to Mr. Wilde's play. I have seen it in New York," Abigail began pleasantly.

"Ah, well, you will find this superior," the countess replied. "Americans have difficulty, I've found, comprehending the niceties of British society."

"Yes, we tend to place more importance on substance than appearance."

"Hopefully this evening will be enjoyable even though you have seen it before." Graeme jumped into the breach before the dowager countess could respond. "Fortunately Mr. Wilde's words are worth repetition."

"Indeed." Abigail cast him a knowing glance, but fell in with his conversational deflection. "Have you seen this actor before? I've heard he is excellent."

They continued the conversation in this manner, lurching from stilted pleasantries to hidden (and sometimes not so hidden) barbs, with Graeme struggling to maneuver a safe path between. Graeme wondered more and more why his grandmother had invited Abigail. Lady Eugenia was acting rather high-handed even by her standards. It put him in the position of having to defend Abigail—though, in truth, she did not seem to need any help.

It was a relief when the curtain went up. Of course, the dim quiet brought a problem of its own, for now his mind was free to wander wherever it wanted—and where it wanted was Abigail. There was the constant temptation of her perfume and the white swell of her bosom above her dress, the soft upsweep of her hair, so heavy and insubstantially pinned it seemed likely to tumble down at any moment.

Graeme thought of the other night, Abigail's hair falling down all over her shoulders. He remembered the passion that had pulsed in him, mingling with anger and frustration into an explosive mix. He must apologize for that kiss, for the way he had handled her with such familiarity and so little gentleness. Impossible to do so, of course, with his grandmother sitting beside them. And if he didn't stop thinking about it soon, he would be in a sorry state, indeed.

Eventually the evening passed. Graeme got through the intermission by rushing out to procure refreshments for them. Of course, when he returned, it seemed half the crowd was in his box. It made it easier, for Abigail's attention was taken up by others, but somehow that irritated him as well. The play crept by, though he followed it in the most disjointed fashion, having to pull his attention back time and again to the stage.

At last it was over, and Graeme sprang to his feet in relief. But when he escorted the ladies outside, he learned that Abigail intended to take a hansom cab home. Predictably Lady Eugenia reacted with horror to the idea, and Graeme had to agree with his grandmother.

"Go home unescorted? No, I cannot allow it. You must ride with us," he told her.

"I will be perfectly safe," Abigail assured him. "I have trespassed on your good nature long enough already."

The polite social bickering continued until finally he won out, and Graeme handed Abigail up into the carriage after the dowager countess. He politely took the backward-facing seat opposite the women, frankly grateful that courtesy allowed him to thus separate himself from their conversation. With the sound of the carriage wheels on the pavement and the various noises from outside, he could hear only snatches of their discussion. At least it seemed amiable enough, as the dowager countess dissected the in-génue's performance, with Abigail spiritedly insisting that the blame lay more on the older actress who repeatedly upstaged her.

Watching Abigail laugh at something Lady Eugenia said and his grandmother manage a tiny smile in response, he had to marvel at Abigail's ability to hold her own. Many women, including his own mother—perhaps he should say *especially* his own mother—wilted under the dowager countess's sharp tongue.

When they reached the hotel, Graeme stepped out to give Abigail his hand in descending, then offered her his arm.

"You don't have to escort me inside," she told him, though she took the proffered arm. "I am quite safe here, I believe. Your doorman, after all, would rush to defend your wife."

"He's not my—" He gritted his teeth. "I will see you to your door."

As they walked through the lobby, Graeme rehearsed in his head what he must say to her. As soon as they stepped from the lift, he began. "I wanted to speak with you. I could not with my grandmother there, of course, but I have been remiss. I should have come to see you immediately. The other evening, when you proposed that we—that I—that is to say, that we alter the arrangements of our marriage . . ."

"You mean sleep together?" Abigail suggested.

He gave her a pained look. "Are you always so blunt?"

"I don't know." She grinned, mischief lighting her eyes. "I have never discussed the matter with anyone before, you see."

"Good Gad, I should hope not." He sounded, he realized, like a pompous old fogy, and he could feel heat rising up the back of his neck. How did he always wind up feeling awkward and embarrassed around Abigail? He cleared his throat and plowed ahead. "What I mean to say is that I acted inappropriately. I was angry. I should never have—I am not in the habit of forcing my attentions upon a woman, and I must apologi—"

"Stop it!" Abigail jerked her hand from his arm and whirled to face him. The color was high on her cheeks, and her eyes flashed. "Just stop it." She reached out and dug her hands into the lapels of his jacket, crumpling them, and stared straight into his eyes. "Don't you dare apologize for kissing me."

Still holding the front of his jacket with a death grip, she stepped in closer and went up on her toes and kissed him. Graeme stood still, too stunned by her action to move, as her mouth closed soft and warm on his. A quiver ran down through him.

She pulled back, her breath coming as swiftly as his, heat shimmering between them. "You kissed me the other night because you wanted to." She moved in again, and this time he seized her waist and pulled her up into him.

Their lips met, hungry and fierce, and she let out a satisfied little sigh that swamped him with heat. Her hands slid up his chest and neck, sinking into his hair, and every movement made his flesh tingle. He was immediately, achingly hard. When at last she pulled back, it took all his strength of will to relax his arms and release her.

"You wanted to kiss me," she whispered. "And you want more than that. Can't you for once stop playing the gentleman and tell the truth? At least ten years ago you were honest."

Abigail whirled and walked rapidly away. He watched, his mind a jumble, as she opened her door, then turned to him. "I'll be here tomorrow evening if you want to accept my offer."

She stepped inside and closed the door.

chapter 10

Graeme ran a shaky hand back through his mussed hair and glanced around. He was relieved to find the hallway empty. His hat had wound up on the floor. He bent over to pick it up and absently brushed a piece of lint from it.

She had finally driven him to madness. Kissing her right in the middle of the hotel corridor, where anyone might have come along and seen them. Bizarrely, the thought sent another sizzle of arousal through him.

He took the stairs down, unwilling to face the lift operator, and paused for a moment to gather his wits before leaving the hotel. Hoping that nothing of what he'd just done showed on his face—the dowager countess had eyes like an eagle—he smoothed his hands down the front of his jacket and set his mind to think of anything other than that moment in the hall outside Abigail's room.

"Goodness, Montclair, you've left me sitting here an age," his grandmother greeted him. "You might have a little more consideration."

"You might have had a little more consideration than to invite Abigail to join us," he shot back, his nerves too ragged for courtesy.

Lady Eugenia raised her eyebrows. "I was unaware I needed your permission to invite a guest."

"You needn't put on that look of wounded innocence. You know perfectly well I have never limited you—would never limit you—regarding guests or anything else. But I would hope you might give a thought to how I would feel about it. Couldn't you have warned me?"

"I was afraid you might balk if you knew."

He snorted. "At least that's honest."

"I prefer not to lie unless it's absolutely necessary."

"Then tell me the truth again—why in the name of all that's holy did you invite her?"

"Because, my boy, you don't seem to be accomplishing much on your own."

Graeme stared, the silence in the carriage as thick and brittle as glass. His grandmother returned his gaze with an air of calm expectation.

"You're in on it with her!" His voice slid upward in amazement. "Good heavens, Grandmother. How did she talk you into it?"

"Please." The countess sniffed. "She didn't talk me into anything. I wrote to her, suggesting she visit England and attempt a reconciliation."

"*You* suggested it?" He had not thought he could be any more astonished, but clearly he was wrong. "Why? I find it hard to believe that you took a sudden liking to Abigail."

"Of course I don't like the woman." She looked at Graeme as if she found him deficient in reason. "But you must have an heir, and your wife lived on the other side of the Atlantic. Clearly someone had to do something. I want grandchildren, and I will never have any if I leave the matter up to you."

His jaw dropped. "Good Lord. I don't love the woman. I don't even like her. Hell, I don't even *know* her. And you expect me to . . . to . . ." He sputtered to a stop, unable to say in front of his grandmother any of the words that came to his mind.

"I *expect* you to do your duty," she returned with asperity. "You are your father's son, after all. Surely you are capable of bedding a woman without loving her."

"'*Et tu, Brute?*'" Graeme murmured.

"There's no need to bring Shakespeare into this." The countess turned on him the gimlet gaze that was usually guaranteed to bring any recalcitrant relative into line. "It's not as if I'm asking you to jump off a cliff or face a horde of savages."

"I am bloody well tired of playing the pawn in someone else's game."

"Don't swear."

"*That*'s what concerns you?"

"What concerns me is this family." Lady Eugenia leaned forward, her expression implacable. "Stop emoting like a tragedian and be Lord Montclair."

∽

His own grandmother. It was unbelievable. It was no surprise for James to be cavalier about it, but for the dowager countess, the stickler for propriety, upholder of aristocratic values to urge him to—well, it was outrageous! Infuriating. Why were they so insistent on pushing him into Abigail's arms?

For that matter, why was he so damned insistent on *not* doing something that he wanted quite urgently to do?

Kissing Abigail had set him afire. Why not take what she eagerly offered? She asked for no emotional entanglements. Abigail was being coolly logical; he was the one twitching around like some coy maiden. It was no wonder James laughed at him.

But there was nothing wrong in having some pride, surely. Abigail was manipulating him—on the one hand using the hammer of divorce, on the other the sweet enticement of her kisses. Nor was it just pride or stubbornness or even principle. No one seemed to understand that taking her into his bed, living with her, would mean an acceptance of his marriage. Of her.

His grandmother spoke of duty. But hadn't he already given up enough for duty? The name would survive and so would the title without Graeme taking a woman he distrusted into the very center of his life.

It was easy for James to treat it as a casual thing, a few encounters. But it wasn't that simple. Abigail would be the mother of his child. He would have to live with her unless he let his child go off to live with her alone, something he would never allow. He would have to honor and respect her, treat her as his wife.

Maintaining a mistress or visiting a lady of the night had never struck him as wrong when Abigail was his wife in name only. But if Abigail was his wife in truth, such dalliances would be an insult. He refused to be the philandering sort of husband his father had been.

But then he would be trapped indeed. God knew, he would enjoy coupling with Abigail now. But passion faded. When he no longer felt this surge of hunger for her, what would be left for him? Lovemaking without passion or love, merely to satisfy a need, held little appeal, like eating just to survive. A lifetime of celibacy held even less allure.

Or, worse—what if he came to care for her?

His father had been weak where women were concerned.

Graeme knew that in many ways he was the same, though he exercised more control over his desires. A woman's tears, her smile, her softness, undid him. How many times had he done something just to please his mother or his grand-mother? Even Aunt Tessa had only to look at him with her huge eyes sparkling with tears and he would weaken and give her the money that her less-susceptible son would not.

Abigail was an expert at deception. After all, until he'd found her going out in the night to secret meetings and threatening him with divorce, she had convinced him that she knew nothing of her father's machinations.

She was already determined to make him dance to her tune. How much would she be able to twist and turn him to her will if she was able to reach his emotions? She could turn him into nothing more than a puppet.

But surely he was not so weak a man that he would allow her to control him. Could he not maintain his reserve and wariness where she was concerned?

Yes, she was attractive and he felt a certain amount of desire for her—very well, a large amount of desire for her—but at some point passion would fade. Then they could settle into a distant relationship, maintain a formal civility. It wasn't as if he were spineless. He knew better by now than to trust her. He would not allow her to worm her way into his affections.

He had hurt her pride when he'd rejected her. The bit-terness in her tone, despite her light words, made that clear. And he was sorry for that, no matter what he thought of her character. He could understand why she thought he owed her something.

Perhaps he did. It was scarcely fair to deny a woman a child, the thing most women longed for. She was as tied to him as he was to her. He sometimes thought with regret about not having children. How much more so would a woman?

It would have been easy enough for her to saddle him with another man's child, so it spoke well for her that she had not.

If she was able to go into an affair with such cold practicality, surely he could also. They could establish rules—a contract of sorts, as if it were a business arrangement. Which, he supposed, in a way it was. Yes, he would be giving in to her coercion, which galled him. But it would be foolish, surely, to stubbornly refuse to do something that was in his own best interest to do.

He would call on her the following evening, as she had suggested, and they could discuss the matter, agree to certain ground rules, lay out the various aspects of their agreement. It would all be very civilized, very cut-and-dried, not a repetition of what had happened between them the last two times they had broached the matter. It was the sensible thing to do.

Still, as he went to bed, he could not help but wonder if, rather than being reasonable, he had merely talked himself into jumping into quicksand.

∽

Abby spent a good deal of time on her bath and toilette. She could not rely on Graeme calling upon her this evening. Their heated kiss the night before had given her hope, but she was coming to discover just how stubborn a man he was. Molly, aware that Abby was expecting a visit from Graeme, glowered at her in the mirror as she brushed out Abby's hair and helped her into an elegant blue satin dressing gown. Abby ignored her.

It was more difficult to ignore her own nerves, especially after she dismissed the maid. Her stomach was too twisted to eat anything and her nerves too jumpy to sit down, so she spent her time pacing and checking and rechecking to make sure every detail was just right. The lighting was appropriately low and rendered faintly exotic by the gauzy red scarf thrown over the lampshade; the wine and two glasses sat ready on the table in front of the sofa; the door to the bedroom was invitingly ajar but not boldly open, and a mellow glow came from the lamp within.

Her appearance, of course, was the centerpiece of her plan, and she had accomplished all she could there. She could not, after all, magically become a delicate slip of a girl. But her dressing gown was perfect—as elegant as a dress, it was unencumbered by the excesses of fashion, so that there was no bustle, no corset, no yards of material, no petticoats.

Designed to resemble a kimono, the sky-blue satin was patterned with clouds and trees in a Japanese style. The long sleeves were slit at the elbow and hung almost to the hem of the robe, showing the red satin lining inside them. A very wide sash emphasized her waist and the lack of a stiff corset beneath. Lacy frills of her nightgown showed above the waist and below the cut sleeves and flashed into view between the sides of the skirts as she walked.

Modest but subtly provocative, it was the perfect attire for a lady's boudoir. Her hair was arranged in a casual coil atop her head and anchored with two red-lacquered chopsticks. She remembered the way Graeme's eyes kept going to her unbound hair the other night.

She had done everything she possibly could. Now she just had to wait.

A knock sounded on the door, startling her even though she had been hoping for it. Her heart began to hammer in her chest. Her future hung in the balance. What if she could not bring it off?

"Abigail."

Graeme said her name in the way only he did: so formal and crisp and English. It broke her from her momentary paralysis. She could do this. She *would* do it. She refused to accept any other possibility.

Abby opened the door. "Graeme—or perhaps I am presuming. Should I call you Montclair? I confess I haven't yet gotten the British way with names."

"Graeme. Yes. Of course," he said distractedly as his eyes took in her attire. "I'm sorry. Do I have the time wrong? I—" He glanced back toward the hall as if he might leave.

"No." Abby curled her arm through his and pulled him into the room, closing the door behind them. "This is the right time." She guided him toward the sofa. "I'm glad you decided to accept my invitation."

"Well, I—I thought we should clarify a few things, lay some groundwork, so to speak—if that is, we are to do this thing."

"Then you are amenable to . . . this thing?"

Graeme cleared his throat and glanced away from her, turning his hat brim around and around in his hands. "I have taken it under advisement."

He looked so ill at ease that Abby almost smiled. "Very well."

She reached out and slipped his hat from his grasp, hanging it on the coatrack. Graeme trailed over to the window, aimlessly touching the back of a chair, the closed draperies, a decorative vase on the table. He glanced toward the lamp, softly glowing beneath the gauzy scarf, then reached out to brush his fingertips across the material. He quickly pulled his hand back.

Graeme turned back to face her, his face carefully remote. "Little as I wish to give in to your threat of divorce, I must admit you have a point regarding my, ah, need for an heir. It is understandable that you should want a child. I—it is scarcely fair of me to deny you the, um, joys of motherhood. I fear I had not considered that aspect of the situation."

"Then you are agreeable. I'm glad."

"There are certain things that must be made clear, however." His eyes ran down the front of her dressing gown. "Perhaps you should . . . Don't you think you might prefer to change into something more—I mean, perhaps we should talk about this in a more . . . formal setting."

"A formal setting? You mean—at an attorney's office? You intend to make a contract?"

"No. No, no, of course not. I just thought . . . perhaps someplace else."

"I think this is the sort of conversation that would be better served in an intimate setting. Don't you?" She slipped her hand in his and led him back to the sofa. "Why don't we sit down and you can tell me your stipulations? Would you care for a glass of wine?"

"What?" He tore his eyes away from her bosom and looked at the carafe and glasses. "Oh, no. That's perfectly all right. Well, perhaps."

She sat and leaned forward to pour the wine. Picking up her own glass, she settled back and faced him. "Now . . . what is it you want to make clear?"

"If we have a child, he—"

"Or she," she interjected.

"Yes, of course, or she—or they."

"They? Then you are thinking of more than one?"

"Well, I do need an heir." Color began to rise in his face. "And one cannot be certain . . ."

Abigail smiled. "I see. Then you're saying we should keep at it until we have a boy?"

His color deepened. Perversely, Abigail felt herself growing more relaxed with each expression of Graeme's nerves.

"I didn't mean—I don't know." He picked up the glass of wine and took a gulp.

"Well, we can deal with that when the time comes. What else?"

"He—she—must be raised here."

"In London?"

"In England. I will not allow you to take my child away, to whisk him back to America with you and raise him there."

"I agree. Your heir should grow up here, where he will inherit the title. I wouldn't want him to be a foreigner to his heritage, after all."

"Then . . . then you will continue to live here?" He kept his eyes on the glass in his hand rather than on her.

Cold pierced her chest. She pushed that feeling aside. She had to remain calm and rational. "I will live with my child, of course. However, you need not worry that I shall try to interject myself into your life. I am well aware that our arrangement is a temporary thing. I shall maintain my own household."

His eyes flew to hers, stony now. "I will not be a stranger to my child."

"Of course not. There is no question of that. I'm sure we can arrange it so we both can be with the child but not in each other's company. You have your estate and your home here in London. I might buy a retreat—like the Vanderbilts' summer home in the mountains. Perhaps in Scotland. It will be easy enough for us to avoid one another."

"I didn't say that we must avoid each other." Graeme frowned.

"There's no need to explain. You must not worry about tact. My feelings are armored to insults, I assure you," she lied smoothly. "I have no interest in anything permanent. We are simply two people in a difficult situation—rather stuck with each other."

"Yes, well . . ." He took another sip of wine, still looking troubled.

"Graeme . . ." Abigail leaned forward to lay her hand on his arm. "I do not want to cause you distress or . . . or inflict something abhorrent on you."

"No," he said hastily. "Nothing abhorrent, I assure you. You are obviously quite . . . beautiful. Any man would be honored."

Abigail raised her finger to his lips, stopping him. "I am not asking for compliments. Least of all lies. I know how little you desired this. I want to make it easy for you." She reached up and pulled out the lacquered sticks anchoring her hair, letting it uncoil and slide silkily to her shoulders.

chapter 11

Graeme could do nothing but gaze at Abigail, his mouth suddenly dry as dust. From the moment she opened the door, he had been struggling with a throbbing, insistent arousal. To his astonishment, Abigail wore a dressing gown, as if ready for bed—and not only a dressing gown but one that was lush and exotic, with slashed sleeves that invited a man's hands to slide up her arms. White lace peeked out between the lapels and showed in glimpses as she walked, a continual reminder that she wore only a nightgown beneath the robe.

He felt an intense need to caress the lush blue satin, to trace the embroidered figures with his fingers, to slide his hands along the wide sash that delineated her waist. Everything about her was soft and rich and inviting. Even her hair was twisted around the crown of her head in a fashion so precarious it seemed it might come tumbling down at any moment. His fingers itched to pluck those absurd shiny red sticks from the knot and watch it fall. When she had done exactly that, it had taken his breath away.

He knew he must have sounded like a bumbling rustic every time he opened his mouth. It was a wonder he had been able to speak with any coherence at all. Everywhere he looked, soft sensuality teased at his senses. The low glow of the lamps, tinged with the warmth of the gossamer scarf thrown over one, the door standing slightly ajar so that he could look into her bedroom without really seeing anything at all, the touch of her fingers on his arm. It was easy to get lost in watching the movement of her lips. Even the sound of her voice set something thrumming inside him.

"You're trying to seduce me," he said, and the smile she sent him made him feel both foolish and hungry.

"I am," she agreed, unembarrassed. "I understand your reservations. Your scruples. Whatever you may think of me, the truth is I don't want to harm you or make you do something you dislike." She reached out to take his glass and refill it. "I have heard that alcohol will make one more amorous."

He made a noncommittal noise and took a drink, watching her with a curious combination of wariness and eagerness. Whatever else this woman was, she excited him. Abigail slid closer.

"I know it must be difficult for you since you don't want this. Don't want me." She laid her hand lightly on his chest. It might have been a burning brand, the way it felt.

"Abigail . . . you needn't—" he began, his voice thick.

"No, I have given it a great deal of thought." He missed the words that followed, because she slid her hand across his chest and all thought left his brain. The next thing he heard was, "Don't think about me. Pretend I am someone else."

Little likelihood of that. Right now she was the only person he could think of—or see or feel or smell. And sweet heaven, but she smelled delightful. He circled her wrist with one hand, sliding it up over the lace and silk of her gown.

She edged nearer, her hand gliding over his shoulder, her voice soft. He could feel the brush of her breath against his skin as she leaned toward him. "Clearly you are able to separate your emotions from your desires when you go to, um, 'professional' women. So I thought perhaps you could pretend that I was one."

"What? Pretend you are a . . ." It was ludicrous. Demeaning. It sent the blood roaring through his veins.

Abigail nodded. "Your mistress. Or a woman you bought for the night. From a bordello, say."

"Abigail, no." He shifted in his seat. He must stop; there were things they had to agree on, rules to establish. He should move away. Or at least stop stroking his hand over her arm. And he definitely should not move his other hand to the wide satin sash at her waist. "What you're saying is absurd. Wrong." Almost unbearably arousing.

"What would you do there?" She trailed her forefinger up the side of his neck, and he could not control a tremor. He closed his eyes, not sure what she might see in them. "You would relax, wouldn't you? Take off your jacket?" She went up on her knees and reached across him to grasp the other side of his jacket and ease it back off his shoulders.

He moved forward to let her pull the jacket back and down his arms. He opened his eyes and looked into hers. There was no longer any question of ending this. The only thing on his mind now was what she would do next.

He saw her eyes spark as if she had read his thoughts, and the faintest smile curved her lips. "Then this, perhaps?" Her fingers went to his ascot, unfastening the stickpin and sliding the folds apart with a whisper of silk.

"And surely your waistcoat would be unfastened." She began on the buttons.

His eyes locked to hers, Graeme laid his hands on either side of her waist, spreading out his fingers and sliding them up the wide sash until they were tantalizingly close to her breasts. When his hands curled around those luscious orbs, she drew in a sharp little breath that almost undid him.

Graeme glided his thumbs over the sleek satin of her dressing gown, stroking the nipples beneath it. The buds tightened, pressing against the cloth, and Abigail's eyes fluttered closed, her fingers digging into the cloth of his waistcoat.

Heat speared him, and with a little groan that was part hunger, part surrender, he pulled her into his lap and kissed her.

∞

Abby had thought she knew what to expect, but now she found that she had not, could not have, prepared herself for the rush of sensations pouring through her. His mouth, his hands, his heat . . . the raw need that suddenly blossomed low inside her, aching for something unknown, but with the deep certainty that only he could provide it.

Graeme's arm was hard around her. She was not sure she could have stayed upright if not for that, for every part of her body seemed to be melting, consumed by the fire he caused in her. What would have been alarming, if she had been able to form a rational thought, was that she was happy, even eager to be lost in him.

She wrapped her arms around his neck, holding on in the torrent of pleasure. His kiss went on forever, and when at last he pulled his mouth from hers, she started to protest. But then his mouth was finding such interesting places to explore, roving over her neck and down to the swell of her breasts, that all that came from her lips was a sigh of sat-isfaction.

His hand roamed down her front, sliding between the sides of her dressing gown and nudging it open. He curved over her breasts and down onto her stomach, his skin searing through the thin cloth of her gown. His fingertips traced the circles of her nipples and moved to the shallow well of her navel. Slid even lower.

Abby drew in her breath sharply as he delved into the crevice between her legs. It was startling and embarrassing . . . and so very delightful that she found her-self opening to him, hoping he would do more. Graeme's breath rasped against the soft flesh of her throat as he aroused her with teeth and lips and tongue, and farther down, his fingers caressed and teased until she felt almost desperate. She turned her face into his shoulder, sinking her teeth into him.

She felt the tiny jerk in his body and heard the low sound he made, and she feared she had done something wrong. He would pull back. Leave her. Instead, he surged up from the sofa with her in his arms and carried her into the bedroom. Settling her onto the bed, he untied the sash of her dressing gown and spread the sides apart.

Leaning over Abby, one hand braced against the bed, he ran his hand slowly down the length of her body, his gaze following the path of his fingers. His face was slack, his eyes dark and hungry. When he reached the hem, he slipped his fingers beneath the material and started back up her leg, his skin like fire against hers. The cloth pooled before him as he moved upward, exposing the long line of her legs.

Abigail suspected she ought to feel embarrassed—and

perhaps she did, a bit—but far more than that, desire flowered in her at the touch of his eyes, and she knew that what she wanted was to be completely naked before him, to see the passion rising in him at the sight of her. To know in the most elemental, clearest way that he wanted her.

Graeme pulled the dressing gown down from her shoulders. She sat up to make it easier, and as he turned to toss the robe away, she pulled her nightgown up and off. Graeme turned back and saw her, his eyelids drooping lower as he studied her.

"Abigail . . ." He sat down on the bed beside her, tracing the line of her collarbone with his fingers. "You are so beautiful." He bent and kissed her lips, her cheeks, her ears, her throat, his lips velvet soft and lingering.

She trembled beneath his touch, her senses filled with him. His mouth moved lower, exploring the hard center line of her chest, the contrasting softness of her breasts, and all the while his hand trailed over her stomach, her hips, her thighs, arousing her with a feather-light touch.

Abigail twined her fingers through his hair, stirred by the soft glide of it over her skin. She wanted more, and experimentally she ran her hands down the sides of his neck, rewarded by the surge of heat in him. She caressed his shoulders and back. Frustrated by the cloth that lay between her fingers and his skin, she went to the buttons of his shirt.

He stood up, his eyes never leaving her as he stripped off his clothes, cursing softly when his hasty fingers slipped on the fastenings. Then he was naked, long and lean and fully aroused, but she hardly had time to take in the sight of him before he was on the bed beside her, his mouth on hers, his arms around her, pressing her into him.

He was hard and hungry, and his questing fingers found the hot damp center of her. Abigail moved against his hand, instinctively seeking release, but what he was doing only increased the need inside her. His breath labored in his throat and she could feel the hard length of him pressing against her hip, throbbing and insistent.

Murmuring her name, he moved between her legs. Slipping his hands beneath her buttocks, he lifted her slightly and pushed into her. Abigail tightened at the sudden pressure and pain. This wasn't going to work, she thought, panicked. Graeme stopped abruptly, his eyes flying to hers.

"Abigail! You're . . . why didn't you say?" He started to move back, and she flung her arms around his neck, holding on.

"No! No, please, don't stop. It will be all right, won't it? I'm not—there's nothing wrong with me, is there?"

"No." He braced himself on his arms on either side of her head, bending down to kiss her lips. "There's nothing wrong with you." She could feel his smile against her cheek as he kissed his way lightly across her face and down her neck. "You're perfect. Lovely." He drew a shaky breath. "I shouldn't have rushed." He nuzzled into her neck. "Just relax."

She could feel the tension in his arms, hear it in his breath, but his voice was soft and soothing, his lips tender on her skin. She gave way, her body responding to the gentle coaxing of his mouth, the soft brush of his fingers down her side. He moved into her slowly, and again she felt the pressure, followed by a sharp swift pain.

Then he was inside her, filling her. It felt so strange and yet so right that she wanted to laugh or cry or perhaps shout out loud, she wasn't sure what, but she only turned her head and pressed her lips against his arm where it lay beside her head.

He let out a low groan and buried his face in her hair. He began to move inside her, and Abby realized with a start that yet more pleasure was possible. Now she did let out a breathy laugh that slid into a moan as the sweet sensations intensified. Sinking her hands into Graeme's hair, she moved with him. He murmured her name as he thrust with harder, swifter strokes. "Abigail . . . Abby . . ."

The sound of it on his lips stirred her almost as much as his movements. Need built within her; she felt as if she were racing and reaching and what she sought was just beyond her grasp.

Then it exploded within her, flooding out all over her in great waves, startling her so that she cried out. Graeme shuddered against her, groaning, as he rode out the cataclysm.

chapter 12

Abby awoke in the wash of pale morning light, huddled against a firm warmth. She realized in the next instant that the source of the heat was Graeme. He lay naked, his back to her, his breathing soft and steady, indicating he still slept. She did not open her eyes, but simply lay there, luxuriating in the moment.

It would not last, of course. Graeme would awaken and reality would return. They would once again be strangers, poised somewhere between enmity and intimacy. But for a bit, right now, he was her husband, the man who had evoked such passion and pleasure in her last night and who had, for an instant, been joined to her in a shattering union.

Slowly, almost reluctantly, Abby opened her eyes. She inched away from Graeme. Theirs was a mutually beneficial arrangement, a rational and impersonal relationship, and if by some stroke of luck there had been passion between them, that was not love or even affection. There was no reason to cuddle up to him. It wouldn't do to cross a line or break a "rule" of their arrangement. She tried to recall exactly what Graeme's stipulations had been but could not. She hadn't been paying much attention to his words.

Her movement must have disturbed him, for Graeme rolled over in his sleep and onto his side, one arm falling over her. His eyes opened hazily and he frowned. She could see recognition awaken in his eyes. "Abigail."

"Good morning." She had the annoying feeling that she was blushing.

Abigail expected Graeme to pull back, but he only reached up and smoothed his hand over her cheek, brushing her hair from her face. "Good morning. Are you all right? I mean—why did you not tell me?"

"Tell you what?"

"That you were untouched. That you hadn't been with a man before."

"I thought that was a given," she responded tartly, and she was the one who slid several inches away. "Since I am your wife and you have never touched me. I didn't realize you believed me a wanton."

"No. I didn't—it's just—" He rose up on his elbow to look at her. "It's been ten years, after all, and we were apart."

"So you assumed I slept with other men." It was satisfying to see him squirm a bit.

"I am sure there were a number of men who were eager candidates. Besides, the way you acted last night—what else was I supposed to think? You were the one seducing me. 'Wouldn't you do this?' and 'Let's take off that.' How did you know those things?"

His expression was so puzzled, his tone so aggrieved, that Abigail had to laugh. "One doesn't have to have *do* something to learn *how* to do it. I thought you would be more . . . comfortable if I approached it like a professional. So I asked a professional."

He stared. "You went to a prostitute?"

"A high-class one, of course. I assumed that was the sort you would be accustomed to."

"Abigail. My God." He sat up. "How did you find her?"

"I have found that one can learn almost anything if she's willing to pay for it. I asked the man who operates the lift which was the finest bordello in London."

"The man in the lift!"

"Yes. I thought about it a good deal. I couldn't very well ask you, and it would have embarrassed David if I had asked him. I was sure Lord Cargaron would know—"

"Good God."

"—but it would have caused gossip if I had asked him or, really, anyone in society. I thought someone who worked in a nice hotel where a number of gentlemen stay would probably have such information. He seemed the likeliest choice, as one sees him every time one goes up or down."

"And he told you?" His voice hovered somewhere between dismay and fascination.

"He appeared somewhat taken aback," Abigail admitted.

"Imagine that."

"But when I opened my purse, he was happy to provide the names of several brothels. He assured me they were the best."

"Please don't tell me you went there."

"Of course not. It would have caused a great deal of scandal if anyone found out, and since it is the sort of place aristocratic gentlemen frequent, it seemed all too likely I might run into someone I know." She ignored the choked noise Graeme made. "I sent a note to the establishment, offering to pay the best rate if the woman came here to the hotel. She came cloaked; it was all very sub rosa."

"What did she—what did you ask her?"

"Oh, all sorts of things. She was quite agreeable . . . once she got over her astonishment. She had expected a man. One would, I suppose."

"Mm."

"But when I explained what I wanted, she was happy to help me. I asked her how a visit would proceed and what she would do to . . . to encourage a man." Heat flared in Graeme's eyes, and Abby stopped, suddenly off-balance. She cleared her throat. "Fortunately, those things weren't really necessary, for some of them were rather embarrassing."

"Abigail . . ." His eyes dropped to her mouth, then down to the swell of her bosom above the blanket. He skimmed a finger along the blanket's edge, his eyes darkening.

He was going to kiss her, Abby thought, her body tensing in anticipation. It seemed different here in the light of day, somehow more real. More genuine.

A knock sounded on the suite door. Graeme froze.

"Molly!" Abigail leaped out of bed, too alarmed to be concerned about revealing a glimpse of her naked body. She grabbed her dressing gown and wrapped it around her as she walked out. Pulling the bedroom door shut behind her, she hurried to the hall door, hastily tying her sash and running her hands back through her hair. A blush rose up her neck. Molly had been aware Abby was meeting Graeme here last night. As soon as she saw Abby, she would guess what had happened.

And though Molly was Abby's maid, she was also the closest thing Abigail had ever had to a mother. It was embarrassing—and made even more so by the fact that Molly knew Graeme's reluctance to consummate their marriage.

However much Abby pretended to Graeme that she was matter-of-fact, she was not blasé about any of it, including talking to the woman from the brothel yesterday. In fact, if she let herself think about it, she would probably feel humiliated. And that was why she shoved it aside, as she had learned to do with many things for the past ten years.

She opened the door a few inches, blocking it. Molly stood there, looking grim, holding a tray in front of her as if it were a weapon.

"Molly, what are you doing here? I told you I would call you this morning when I was ready to dress."

"I brought you breakfast." Molly peered into her face. "I wanted to make sure you were all right."

"I'm fine." With a sigh, Abigail opened the door and grasped the tray, practically pulling it from her maid's hands. "I'll send for you when I need you."

She closed the door before Molly could come up with any reasons to stay. Setting the tray of food down on the table, Abby returned to the bedroom. There she was disappointed to see that Graeme had gotten up and pulled on his trousers and shirt and was now in the process of putting on his socks and shoes. The intimate interlude of a few minutes earlier was gone.

Abigail paused, ill at ease now in her dressing gown, her hair doubtless a rat's nest from sleeping. She pushed the heavy mass back over her shoulders. "Um, Molly brought some breakfast."

"Oh." He glanced up, then quickly back down at his shoes. "Thank you, that sounds very nice. But I should leave." Graeme stood up, as armored in courtesy as ever. "It is no doubt late."

"Yes. Of course." She hid her disappointment with the

small practiced smile that covered any number of social occasions. It would be better if he left, really. She still had a few things to do before she met her mysterious informant tonight, and the current situation was awkward. What was one to say in a moment like this? Thank you? Shall we make another appointment?

It was suddenly dispiritingly tawdry. Abby turned away, occupying herself with drawing back the draperies. Behind her she heard Graeme walk toward the door, then stop.

"Perhaps . . . that is, I thought that we . . ." Abby turned to face him, and he finished hurriedly, "I wasn't sure if you had a social engagement this evening. I could escort you."

Abby froze. Naturally he would offer to escort her tonight, the one evening she absolutely could not have him with her. "I—ah, that is—I wasn't really planning to—I've already promised to attend a—a—" She couldn't very well tell Graeme she was meeting a man who was going to reveal his father's embezzlement. She was seized with inspiration. "A dinner! So you can see it would not do to arrive with an escort. It would throw the numbers off."

"Ah. Of course." His expression turned even more remote. "Very well."

"And I have to go," she went on, thinking he would wonder why she didn't send her regrets and spend the evening with him instead. It was precisely what she would have done had the situation actually existed. "I wouldn't want to be rude to . . . Mrs. Brown. The American ambassador's wife." That would be someone he wouldn't know. "She would feel snubbed, you see. She is a little ill at ease . . . the British . . ." She realized she was explaining too much. She willed herself to stop.

A faint frown had replaced the aloof expression on his face. "Yes. No doubt. Another time, perhaps."

"Yes!" She started to suggest the following evening, then thought that would be too forward. He already thought her far too pushy. She didn't want to do anything to make him dislike her more.

He lingered. "Well, good day, then."

"Good-bye." She trailed after him into the other room, hoping she didn't sound as forlorn to him as she did to herself. Graeme picked up his jacket from the chair where she had tossed it the night before and glanced back at her. Abby began to blush, remembering her former boldness.

Graeme hesitated, then nodded and was gone. Abby sighed as she watched the door shut behind him. It was silly to feel lonely now. She had spent the last ten years without Graeme Parr. One night with him did not make him indispensable.

It was useless to wish they were nestled on the sofa, sipping their coffee and talking, smiling, maybe now and then pausing for a kiss. That wasn't the sort of life Abby could have with Graeme.

She couldn't afford to spend the time it would have taken, anyway. It was late, and there were a number of things she had left to do today, chief among them visiting a gunsmith.

Meeting her informant outside a tavern sounded even less savory than their first meeting place. The weapon she carried last time had done well enough, she supposed, but it would be far safer to carry a pistol. She had decided to purchase a small gun that would fit into her pocket. Doing that and learning how to shoot it would take up most of her afternoon.

There was no time to waste mooning about over a man like some lovestruck girl. With that firmly in mind, she settled down on the sofa to eat her solitary breakfast.

◦◦

Ten hours later, Abby stuck her head out the window of the cab and glanced up and down the dark street. The only streetlamp hung at the corner of the Crimson Pirate, faintly illuminating the weathered sign over the door. Cracked and fading, the color of the figure on it might once have been red; it was more difficult to identify the form as a pirate. The rest of the street lay in shadows of varying degrees. Nothing moved, but there was no way of telling what might be waiting in the darkness.

Abby closed her hand around the derringer in the pocket of her cloak. Stepping out of the carriage, she looked up at the driver. "Stay here. If you do, there'll be five pounds in it for you."

"Aye, I'll wait," the rough voice above her said. "But I tell you, best you get back in and I'll take you back to the 'otel. Ain't no place for a lady."

"No doubt you're right. Still, this is where I have to go. If you'll just stay here, I'm sure I shall be fine."

The coachman shrugged and settled back in his seat. Abby started briskly toward the tavern. One thing she had learned over the years was that one could not afford to look afraid. Confidence—or the appearance of it—had carried many a day.

She paused at the edge of the light, reluctant to expose herself to full view, and glanced around. The hack was still there, waiting. The river must be nearby; she could hear the lap of water. The rank smell of it was almost overpowering.

Skirting the arc of light, she drew near the tavern. The

sound of the water was louder. Glancing down, she saw that only a low rock wall separated the street from the river's edge. A shoe scraped on the pavement. Abigail peered into the darkness.

A shadow separated from the side of the building and a man came forward, stopping too far away for her to make out his features. "No Montclair this time, eh?"

"I came alone as you instructed. I must say, you have chosen an even more disreputable area than last time. If you expect to conduct business with me, I insist you find a better meeting place."

There was a muffled snort, which she realized was amusement. "I can see you've got Price's fierceness; for your sake, I hope you're not as heartless."

"You know my father?"

"I met him. I worked for Lord Reginald. That's how I know about the money he 'borrowed' from the soldiers."

"The soldiers?" She frowned. "What soldiers?"

"The wounded and infirm. The charity he sponsored. The tale is he took it from their funds, meaning to pay it back after he made a fortune buying that stock of your father's. It was going to be a windfall—well, it *was* a windfall for Price when he sold out and sent it crashing. But not for Montclair or that fund."

"Do you have any proof of this story?"

"Did you bring the money?"

"Yes, I have it right here. But this is very little information. Do you know anything worth buying? Did my father know Lord Reginald had embezzled the money?"

"Know?" He had moved forward as they talked, so that now he stepped into the dim edge of the light. His lips drew back in a humorless grin. "Oh, Price knew, right enough. He was the one who suggested that it be done."

Abigail felt the blood drain from her face. "He encouraged the theft?"

"Yes, he said how easy it would be—no one would know what Montclair had done; he'd double the money and have it back before anyone knew, right and tight."

"Oh God, no." Abigail pressed her hand to her stomach. This was worse than she had suspected. Thurston had urged him to take the money, knowing that he would lose it all and be disgraced. He was responsible for everything that had happened. "And I presume you're suggesting I pay you to keep silent."

"I'm no blackmailer!" The man's voice rose in indignation. "What you'll pay me for is to learn the rest of it. That story is what it *appeared* to be. But I know what really happened."

"What do you mean? Are you saying the story is false?"

"Oh, your father did what I just said, right enough. And the money disappeared. But maybe it wasn't Lord Montclair that took it."

"What?"

"If you want to hear the rest of the story, you're going to have to hand over the money." He held out his palm.

Abigail nodded and reached into the pocket inside her cloak. A sharp pop sounded in the night, startling her, and she swung around. But as she did so, out of the corner of her eye, she saw her companion jerk and crumple to the ground. She ran to where he lay beside the low stone wall. Just as she dropped down to her knees beside him, another pop sounded behind her.

"Are you all right? What happened?" The dark stain spreading across his shirt answered both her frantic questions. He had been shot. She grabbed the bottom of her cloak and pressed it against his wound, trying to stem the bleeding.

The man made a horrible bubbling sound. Abby's attention was on him, so she was only vaguely aware of the sounds of panicked horses behind her and the clatter of feet running across the street. Someone slammed into her from behind, knocking her against the wall. She toppled over the wall into the darkness. She landed on muddy ground, but her momentum carried her down the sharp slope. An instant later she hit cold, black water.

chapter 13

Graeme toyed with his dessert spoon, the pudding before him untouched. He cast a surreptitious glance toward the clock on the mantel. He wondered where Abigail was. And what was she doing? She had been suspiciously evasive with her answers this morning.

"Do you have an appointment, Montclair?" Lady Eugenia asked. "That is the fourth time you have checked the clock in the past ten minutes."

"No. I beg your pardon; I was unaware."

"Are you seeing Lady Montclair this evening?"

"I think not."

The dowager countess was unaffected by the repressive tone of his answer. "I had hoped things had improved in that regard. Norton tells me you did not return home until this morning."

"Grandmother, I have no intention of discussing the details of my marriage with you."

"I have no desire to hear them, I assure you."

He was tempted to ask why she was interrogating him about it, then, but courtesy was too ingrained in him. He merely inclined his head. "What are your plans for the evening?"

From years of experience, Graeme kept an expression of mild interest on his face without actually listening as Lady Eugenia related the reasons she was not attending any of a large number of parties available to her. His mind returned to the problem of Abigail.

He had begun the day bathed in a warm glow of satisfaction. There had been some awkwardness, of course, in waking up with his arms full of his wife's soft, warm body and realizing passion was stirring in him again. But the conversation that followed had been absurd, and Abigail's tale of tracking down and interrogating one of the denizens of a bordello had been appalling, really.

It doubtless said something equally appalling about him that he found the story amusing and titillating, as well. He had spent a good portion of his day wondering exactly what Abigail had learned from the woman. If only that blasted maid hadn't chosen that moment to knock on the door, he might have found out.

Then Abigail had turned down his offer to escort her this evening. That rankled a bit. It wasn't that he was so eager for her company (although he would admit that last night was well worth repeating). Still, one would think that now he'd agreed to her bargain, she would be more interested in getting on with it. Perhaps all she wanted was the victory. Or she had no interest in his presence in her life outside of the bedchamber. The idea wasn't complimentary, but there was no reason to brood over it. That was what he preferred, as well.

There was no reason to feel offended. Or to wish that she had not turned him down. But what was she doing? And with whom? The likeliest answer was that she had plans with Prescott. But why hadn't she said so? He would not have protested. Graeme didn't like the man, but he wasn't jealous of him. There was no reason to be jealous—he had learned last night in the clearest way that Prescott had never been Abigail's lover.

"Graeme, why are you smiling? Are you listening to me?"

He started. "What? Of course. You were discussing . . . um . . ."

"Mrs. Ponsonby's ill health."

"Yes, of course. I, um, wasn't smiling." He cast about for some plausible excuse.

"Oh, I am sure Lord Montclair was just trying to lift my spirits," Mrs. Ponsonby hastened to say. His grandmother's companion cast a timid smile at Graeme. "So good of him."

"What nonsense, Philomena. The boy is obviously champing at the bit to go somewhere, and we are delaying him." Lady Eugenia arose regally from her chair.

Graeme started to deny it, then stopped. What was the point in clinging to courtesy when the truth was he was itching to leave? Abigail was right; there was something freeing in candor. He stood up and bowed to his grandmother as she left the room, trailed by Mrs. Ponsonby, who paused to give him a small, apologetic curtsey.

The butler carried in a bottle of port, but Graeme waved him away. "Not tonight, Norton. I'm going out."

"Very well, my lord. Shall I send round for your carriage?"

"No, I'll walk. Clear my head."

There was no reason to turn his steps toward the Langham. Wherever Abigail was going and whoever's company she would rather keep, it was nothing to him. He was glad she was undemanding; it would make their arrangement far easier.

It was just that she had so obviously lied about her plans—the stumbling answers, the way her gaze shifted from his—the same way she had lied about the note slipped under her door a few nights ago. That incident had been the impetus to her slipping out secretly to meet someone in an unsavory part of town, which, by the way, she had never adequately explained. What if she was doing it again? And why the devil was she determined to keep it a secret? It was enough to make anyone suspicious.

Just because he had thoroughly enjoyed last night didn't mean he could turn a blind eye to Abigail's scheming. No matter how exciting and enticing she was, he would be a fool to trust her. It would be even more foolish not to make clear to Abigail that she had not deceived him.

The doorman at the Langham greeted Graeme with a smile; it turned even brighter when Graeme handed him a gold coin. "How can I help you, guv'nor?"

"Has Lady Montclair left the hotel yet?"

"Yessir, you just missed her."

"Where was she going?"

The man's face fell. "Sorry, sir, 'fraid I don't know. She won't tell me anymore." He sent an accusatory look at Graeme.

"Ah. Sorry." Graeme gave the man a rueful smile and headed inside. It took him only moments to wangle a key to his wife's suite from the manager. When he opened the door, his wife's maid jumped up from a chair as if she'd been shot, the petticoat she was mending falling to the floor.

"Oh. It's you." Molly scowled. "What are you doing, coming into Miss Abby's room like that?"

"Are all American servants like you?" he asked, returning her frown.

She crossed her arms. "We're not afraid of a man just because he's got a 'lord' in front of his name, if that's what you mean."

"Actually, rude was more what I was thinking. Where is your mistress?"

Molly's frown deepened, but there was now as much worry as dislike in her expression.

"What?" he asked sharply, taking a step forward. "What do you know? You're afraid of something; I can see it."

"Not of you."

He sighed. "That's hardly remarkable, since I have no intention of hurting you. Nor Abigail. Why are you worried?"

"Because she's not safe!" Molly burst out. "I told her that little popgun wasn't enough to—"

"She has a gun now? Good Gad, the woman's a walking arsenal. Where has she gone? Why does she need a gun?"

Molly looked at him, torn. He waited. Finally the words rushed out of her. "The Crimson Pirate."

"The what?"

"It's a tavern. By the Thames."

"The docks?" His voice rose. "She's gone to a dockside tavern?"

Molly nodded. "That's where he said to meet him."

"Who? Who is she meeting?"

"I don't know." She set her chin mutinously, and Graeme knew he had gotten all he could from her.

It didn't matter. It was enough. He hurried from the room. His steps grew ever faster as he walked down the hall, and he took the stairs almost at a run. What in the world could have possessed Abigail to meet someone by the river? One didn't have to be from London to know that would be a dangerous place.

She must have been desperate to do that. But why? What did she hope to do? What could be worth the risk? Anger and worry warred for dominance within him as he strode out of the hotel and hailed a cab. The driver sent him an askance look when Graeme named his destination.

"I'll double your fare if you get there quickly," Graeme added.

The man took him at his word. It was only minutes before the hansom was rolling down a narrow street that ended at the split and faded sign of the Crimson Pirate. A muted pool of light illuminated a scene that sent Graeme's heart into his throat. Two figures stood facing each other at the edge of the light, with the dark void of the river beyond them.

A shot rang out, and one of the forms fell to the ground, followed almost immediately by another bang, and the second form sank to its knees.

"Abigail!" Graeme flung open the door as the driver pulled his horse to a halt. He jumped down from the carriage before it completely stopped rolling. Behind him the driver let out a shout, but Graeme took off at a run, ignoring him. He was aware of nothing but the cloaked figure kneeling over the fallen one. Not shot, then, just tending to the other. It was her; it must be. It couldn't be Abigail lying on the ground.

Graeme saw a figure race out from beside a building and dart straight at the fallen pair. The dark form slammed into the person kneeling beside the body, knocking her over the low wall. There was a splash as she hit the water.

Graeme let out a roar and raced forward.

A quick glance at the prostrate figure on the ground assured him it was not Abigail. He turned to the low wall. It was black as pitch beyond it. "Abigail!"

He heard her cry, cut short, and a great deal of splashing. Cursing the darkness, he kicked off his shoes and started over the wall. A door swung open behind the building beside him, and light cut an arc across the water, enabling him to see the river below him. There, struggling against the current, Graeme saw a flash of white. He dove into the water.

He put out of his mind how easy it would be to lose sight of her in the dark and how much her soaked skirts and cloak would drag her down. He concentrated only on slicing through the water in the direction he had seen her. Suddenly more light arrived on the wall behind him, enabling him to see.

He caught a glimpse of her only feet away from him, just as her head slipped below the water. He gave a furious kick, diving beneath the surface, and found her. Wrapping his arms around Abigail, he surged upward. When they broke the surface of the water, she let out a low, wordless cry and her arms clamped around him, clinging.

It was awkward, swimming with only one arm, and the current tugged at him, her water-logged clothes weighing them down. But Abigail, after the first frantic thrashing, had the presence of mind not to struggle, just to cling to him, kicking her legs to help propel them forward.

They wallowed through the water to the wall. The driver of his cab stood there, holding up a lantern. His was the illumination that had shown him Abigail. Other figures joined the driver, and as Graeme drew closer, one of them reached out, extending a long wooden stick. Graeme wrapped his hand around it, and the men pulled them the rest of the way. Hands reached down to lift Abigail from the water. For a moment she clung stubbornly to Graeme before she let go and allowed them to pull her up. Two other men grabbed Graeme and helped him as he heaved himself out of the water.

Abigail was slumped on the ground, coughing, Graeme's driver and another man bending over her. A few feet away, several other people were crouched over the still and silent body.

"Abigail." Water streaming from him, Graeme went to her. She was frighteningly pale in the light of the lanterns. "Get the cab." Graeme pulled her to her feet and swept her up into his arms. She shivered convulsively. "I'm taking her home."

The crowd gave way before him, though one protested, "'Ere. Wait! Wot about 'im? 'Oo's this? 'Oo shot him?"

"I haven't the faintest idea."

Graeme lifted Abigail into the carriage. She was still shivering and far too ashen. He held her on his lap, wrapping his arms around her to warm her, though he suspected his own wet, chilled body would be of little help. "Hold on. We'll be home soon, and you'll be warm and dry."

"I was so scared," she whispered, so softly he could barely make out her words.

"I know. But you're safe now." His arms tightened around her. "What the devil were you thinking, going to the docks?" Relief suddenly swelled into anger. "Have you no sense? Why didn't you tell me?"

She made no answer, just shook her head and burrowed into him. The gesture only added to the turbulent confusion of emotions inside him. He wanted to hit something, to shout at her, and at the same time to cradle her in his arms.

"Was it worth risking your life? Who in the hell did you go there to meet? Who killed him?"

"I don't know!"

He made a noise of disbelief, and Abigail struggled to sit up and face him. He clamped his arms around her even more tightly, holding her against him. She glared at him, which perversely made him feel on safer footing.

"That's the truth," she insisted. "I don't know his name. He wouldn't tell me."

"Why would you go down there to meet someone you don't even know?"

"He said he had information I'd want."

"Information?" He stared. "Information about what?"

"About . . . about . . . my father." She was shaking so hard her teeth were chattering.

Graeme subsided. He would have liked to ask her what she'd learned and why someone in England would know anything about Thurston Price, but his anger had fizzled out as rapidly as it had come, and he felt a brute for interrogating a woman who had almost drowned.

"I'm sorry. I shouldn't plague you." He rubbed his hand up and down her arms and back, trying to bring some heat to them.

The ride home seemed to take forever, though the rattle of the carriage on the street told him that the driver was setting as fast a pace as Graeme had told him to. When they reached Montclair House, Graeme jumped out of the cab and reached back to lift Abigail down.

The front door was flung open and the butler himself hustled out. "My lord! What—" His eyebrows shot up. "You're wet!"

"Yes. Pay the man, Norton, whatever he says." He strode into the house and headed for the stairs, snapping out orders to the gaping servants. "Build a fire in my room. Get me blankets. Brandy. Draw a warm bath. Now."

As they scattered to do his bidding, he rushed up the stairs toward his bedroom. His grandmother, swathed in a dressing gown, her hair enveloped in a puffy white nightcap, flung open her door as he passed.

"Graeme!" She trailed out into the hall after him. "What is the meaning of this? You're getting water all over the floor."

"Not now. I'll explain later."

"Well!" the countess said in an affronted tone, but she did not follow him.

He laid Abigail down on the rug in front of the fireplace. One of the maids bustled in to stir up the fire and add coal to it, followed by two more carrying blankets and brandy.

"Libby's drawing a bath now, sir."

He merely nodded as he knelt beside Abigail, struggling to untie the sodden knot that fastened her cloak, his fingers rendered clumsy by haste and cold.

"Sir!" His valet burst into the room and halted, staring in shock. "You're wet!"

"I am well aware of that fact, Siddings. I don't know why everyone finds it necessary to notify me of it."

"Beg your pardon, sir. But—"

"Pour me some of that brandy if you want to be useful. Hah! There." The stubborn ties finally parted beneath Graeme's fingers, and he pulled the cloak off Abigail, tossing it aside on the floor. It landed with a thud as well as a splat. No doubt it contained her supply of weaponry.

Siddings returned with a glass of brandy. Graeme curled

his arm around Abigail's back, lifting her to a sitting position. "Here." He held the glass to her lips. "Drink this." He gave her a little shake. "Abigail, blast it, drink this."

He tilted the glass, and though some liquid spilled down her front, she swallowed. Her eyes flew open and she turned her head away.

"Thank God. I was beginning to think you wouldn't wake up. Take another drink." He held the glass to her lips again, and though she frowned, she sipped at it. She gasped, feebly pushing at his hand, and began to cough.

"Good." Graeme drained the rest of the glass himself and handed it back to his valet.

"My lord, you must get out of these garments," Siddings said, setting the glass aside.

"Later." Graeme laid Abigail back down, and her eyes closed again, but he thought this time her color was better.

"But, sir, you'll catch cold." Siddings plucked at his shoulders.

"Oh, the devil." Graeme shrugged out of his jacket. "There! Now go away. And close the door behind you." Graeme turned back to Abigail and started on the buttons of her dress. Lord, there must be a hundred of them, and they were all the size of a pea. "I cannot imagine why you bought this dress. It's the very devil to unfasten."

In frustration, he jerked at one recalcitrant button, and it popped off. He eyed the little thing rattling across the floor, then grasped either side of her dress and yanked, sending more tiny buttons flying.

That roused her to open her eyes. "Graeme? What are you doing?"

"Trying to get you out of these damned clothes before you catch pneumonia." Graeme pulled the bodice down and was faced with the armor of a corset. With a curse, he rose and went to his dresser, returning with a pocketknife. Flipping it open, he slid it beneath the top of the laces and cut them all the way down the center.

"You're de-destroying . . . my clothes." Abigail pushed feebly at his hands.

"Sorry." He looked down at her. With a stab of shame, he realized that ripping open her clothes had sent a wave of primitive arousal through him. The sides of her corset fell away, exposing the camisole beneath. Soaked as it was, the thin garment was almost transparent, and it clung to her flesh, revealing the lush curves of her breasts and the darker circle of her nipples, pressing against the cloth.

It was inappropriate. Wrong. Animalistic. But he knew that the tremor in his fingers as he untied the ribbon of her undergarment had only a little to do with the chill in his fingers. Doing his best to keep his movements calm and detached, he tugged the camisole off over her head.

"Here." His voice came out husky, and he kept his eyes firmly turned away as he reached over and grabbed up a towel, wrapping it around her shoulders.

She made a pleased noise at the warmth, pulling the towel tightly around her, and a long shudder ran through her. And that, too, Graeme found, stoked the fire in his veins. He kept his eyes on his hands working on the ties of her petticoats, but sliding those down her legs provided an equal amount of temptation. He could not keep his mind from straying to the way her long, slender legs had felt wrapped around him last night, how achingly sweet it had been to slide between them and bury himself inside her.

He hoped she could not feel the surge of heat in his hands. Hastily, he laid a blanket over her. Perhaps it was all right to leave the pantalets; they were, God knew, thin enough to dry quickly. Graeme turned his back to her and settled down to work on the elegant leather boots. For a moment he was tempted to pick up his knife again and use them on the long crisscrossing laces, but he refrained. Perhaps the tedious task of unlacing the myriad of aglets would cool his blood.

Lord, but he was becoming a lecher. Abigail had been inches away from a man who was shot to death; she'd been pushed into the river and almost drowned. And he couldn't keep his mind off making love to her again.

The knock on the door came as a relief. The housekeeper swept in, carrying a tray. "Here we are, sir. I've brought you each a cup of nice hot soup." She cast a disapproving look down at Graeme. "You ought to put on something dry, if you don't mind my saying so."

"And if I did mind?" A smile tugged at the corner of his mouth. Mrs. Burbage had been the housekeeper since he was a lad, and she ran everything and everyone in the place, servant or earl, with the same cheerful domination.

"I'd say it anyway, I expect." Her dark eyes twinkled as she thrust a cup into his hand.

The soup was too warm and enticing to protest. He stood up as the gray-haired woman bustled about, pulling Abigail up and wrapping her blanket around her with an efficiency Graeme knew he could not hope to match. She settled Abigail onto a low stool directly in front of the fire and pushed the cup of soup into Abigail's hands.

"Drink up, dear, and you'll feel better in no time. Now." Mrs. Burbage swung back to Graeme, pointing a stern forefinger at him. "*You* go let Siddings get you cleaned up before the man has apoplexy. I'll take care of Lady Montclair."

Graeme turned to Abigail. Her mouth curved up a little, her eyes already regaining their glow. "Yes, well, clearly you will do that better than I." He winced inwardly at the almost sulky tone of his voice.

"Graeme." Abigail leaned forward, throwing out her hand to him. He took it and was startled when she raised his hand to her lips and kissed it, then pressed it to her cheek. "Thank you."

"Yes. Well." He shifted and glanced around vaguely, feeling at once warmed and embarrassed. He squeezed Abigail's hand. "Mrs. Burbage will take good care of you. I—I'll be close by. If you need me." He was strangely reluctant to leave.

Graeme glanced over at the housekeeper, who nodded at him, her face sympathetic. "Don't worry, she'll be fine. You go on now."

Graeme nodded, and with a last glance at Abigail, he left the room.

chapter 14

Now that he was no longer tending to Abigail, Graeme realized just how wet, cold, and dirty he was. It was a relief to bathe and put on fresh trousers and a shirt. Afterward, he returned to Abigail and was told by Mrs. Burbage that "Lady Montclair is soaking in a nice warm bath" and the housekeeper would let Graeme know "when Lady Montclair is ready" to see him. Interpreting this statement to mean his presence was both unnecessary and undesirable, Graeme sat down beside the fire in his study and, leaning his head back against his chair, let his mind drift.

He was, he thought, rather a failure as a husband. He had not succeeded in even the most basic of a husband's responsibilities, keeping his wife safe. Of course, his wife's refusal to inform him of what she was doing made the task somewhat difficult. He supposed a better husband would have known what she was up to.

What had sent Abigail down to the docks? Her vague explanation of an unknown person offering "information" about her father was flimsy, and her demeanor indicative of a lie, just as it had been this morning. Surely she must have known more about this "information" or the informer or she would not have risked going to as unsavory a place as a dockside tavern.

What did she hope to discover about her father—or, more likely, what did she hope to conceal? Thurston Price doubtless had done numerous things one wouldn't want bandied about, but that didn't explain why she wouldn't tell Graeme. It wasn't as if he had any illusions about her father's character. Perhaps the information wasn't about her father, or at least not solely. What if it was something about her she was hiding?

Graeme was roused from his reverie by Mrs. Burbage's entrance. He jumped to his feet. "How is she?"

"She's right as rain, sir, now don't you worry about that. It'd take more than a dip in the Thames to do her in."

He smiled faintly. "No doubt you're right."

"I'll set the maids to preparing a room for her, but in the meantime, I put her to bed in your bedroom. I hope you don't mind."

Graeme thought of Abigail tucked up in his bed, and lust stirred deep inside him. How could he desire a woman this much when he did not even trust her? "That's fine. No need to bother with that tonight."

"As you wish, sir." She turned to go.

"Mrs. Burbage?"

"Yes?" She swiveled back.

"Send someone to Lady Montclair's maid at the Langham. Molly's her name. Instruct her to pack up her ladyship's things tomorrow and bring them here."

"Of course, my lord."

As soon as Mrs. Burbage left, Graeme started toward his bedchamber. But before he could reach the stairs, he came upon the butler and a footman standing side by side at the front door, as if blocking entrance to the man and woman in the doorway. Voices rose, increasingly agitated, a mingling of Norton's plummy tones, an American accent, and another voice tinged with a faint flavor of Scotland.

Prescott and Abigail's maid. Graeme sighed.

"Out of the question," Norton was saying as Graeme came up behind him. "His lordship cannot be dist—"

"It's all right, Norton. I'll deal with the matter."

The butler turned, puffed up with outrage. "Sir. I am so sorry you were bothered. I told these—these—"

"I am sure you did. They are Lady Montclair's maid and her . . . friend. Molly will be staying with us now."

"I what?" Molly stared. A spasm of horror crossed his butler's features.

"I am sure that they are here out of concern for Lady Montclair," Graeme went on, ignoring both of them.

"Where is Abby?" Prescott demanded. "Do you have her? I insist on seeing her."

"*My wife* is asleep, Mr. Prescott, and I have no intention of disturbing her rest to satisfy your curiosity. Lady Montclair has had a rather . . . eventful evening." He turned to Molly, saying mildly, "I take it you did not trust me to find her."

Prescott answered before the maid could. "When Lady Montclair didn't return, Molly became concerned for her mistress's well-being, so she came to me for help."

"I assure you, there is no need to be concerned. Norton, send Timothy back to the Langham with Molly so that she can pack up her ladyship's things."

"I'm not doing any such thing." Molly crossed her arms mutinously. "Not till I hear it from Miss Abby's lips."

"Will you not? I suspect Lady Montclair will be distressed when she wakes up tomorrow and finds she has nothing to wear. But if you would rather not stay on with her, that is your decision, of course."

Molly's eyes widened. She looked about to burst into an angry speech, but after a moment, she set her chin and said, "All right. I'll bring her things back. But I don't need any help from them." She cast a mutinous glance at Norton and Timothy.

"Of course not. It seems to be a national trait. I will leave it to you, then, to settle the matter." He nodded toward Norton and swung toward Prescott. "Now, Mr. Prescott, if you will join me in my study, I have a few things to discuss with you."

Prescott shot him a frustrated, furious look, but he, too, seemed to realize how little he could do to challenge Abigail's lawful husband. With a short nod, he followed Graeme to his study.

"Have a seat." Graeme gestured toward the wingback chairs in front of the fireplace.

"I'd rather stand."

"As you wish." Graeme shrugged. "Now—"

"What happened? Why is Abigail here?"

"She is here because she was almost shot this evening."

"What?"

"After which she was pushed into the river and nearly drowned." His words apparently rendered the other man speechless, for Prescott continued to gape at him. "I brought her back here, where I could protect her."

"Protect her!" Prescott found his voice. "You sure as hell haven't done a very good job of it so far."

Graeme's mouth tightened. "Clearly not. Unfortunately, I was unaware of just how much protection Abigail required. But from now on I intend to make bloody well sure she's safe. I hope you have enough interest in her safety to help me do that. Tell me who she was meeting tonight. Why? Did she return to England to see him?"

"I didn't know she was meeting anyone tonight, much less who. I am not privy to Abby's plans." The bitterness in Prescott's voice convinced Graeme the man was telling the truth. "As for why she returned, she had the absurd idea she wanted to reconcile with you. I tried to tell her that being alone by yourself is better than being alone *with* someone, but she wouldn't believe me. You are the reason she's here. If she was attacked, I imagine that has to do with you as well."

"Me? I can assure you that until Abigail arrived in London I had not been subject to any attacks."

"I'm sure not. It's your inconvenient wife who is the victim."

"What the devil are you suggesting?"

"I am *saying* that when she was in New York, no one harmed Abby. But here someone has tried to shoot her and drown her. I wonder, who in this city would like to get rid of her? Who has told her to leave time after time?"

"You're accusing *me* of harming her?" Graeme took a quick step forward. "Are you mad? She is my wife."

"Exactly. A wife you would prefer not to have." Prescott did not back away.

"I would never hurt her. I wouldn't harm any woman, much less one I took a vow to protect."

"You made a number of vows that day," Prescott sneered. "You haven't kept the others. Why keep this one? We both know you have failed Abby in every way possible. I suppose you might not have been behind what happened to her tonight. But I doubt you'd shed any tears if she were gone. Forgive me if I am not reassured by the idea that you have locked her away in your house and are 'looking after' her."

Graeme clenched his fist, thinking how satisfying it would be to smash it into the man's face. "Lady Montclair is not a prisoner here. You are free to call on her tomorrow at a more reasonable time and see the state of her health for yourself."

"Oh, believe me, I will." Prescott's baring of his teeth could hardly be termed a smile. He stalked away, but at the door he stopped and turned back to Graeme. "Take damned good care of her, Montclair. You'll answer for it if you do not."

∞

Graeme swung around and began to pace, seething with anger. As if *he* would try to hurt Abigail! It was absurd, of course. Abigail would not think that; she was too reasonable. Oh, the devil, what was he talking about? He had no idea whether Abigail was reasonable or not; he scarcely knew the woman. All he really knew was the strong and inconvenient hunger for her that had taken up residence in him lately.

He felt like smashing something, but that would be childish. He took out some of his ill humor by jabbing the fire with the poker, then banging the poker back into its stand. What was most annoying was the fact that several of Prescott's arrows had struck too close to home, echoing his own thoughts earlier this evening. He *had* failed to protect her. Indeed, he had failed in any number of ways.

At least he could do something about safeguarding Abigail from now on. He had already taken the first step by moving her here, under his roof. It was clearly impossible to keep an adequate watch over her when she lived somewhere else. The next task was to untangle the mystery of tonight's rendezvous. He was certain that was the key to it all. Tomorrow he would find out the name of the man who had been shot tonight.

Right now he needed to see her. Despite Mrs. Burbage's assurance that Abigail was fine, he wanted to check for himself. As he climbed the stairs to his room, he realized that he also needed to sleep. His anger at Prescott had drained away, taking with it the remnants of his energy.

He thought of Abigail in his bed, of slipping beneath the covers with her. It had been nice—far more than nice, if he was truthful—to wake up beside her this morning. But it seemed an invasion of her privacy to lie down with her uninvited. Which was enormously foolish. He was her husband, after all; he had every right to be there. It was, in point of fact, his bed.

The only thing wrong about lying down with her was the fact that his need for sleep had nothing to do with it. He was already aroused, just thinking about her, but it would be base of him to importune her. Abigail had been through an ordeal tonight.

His bedchamber was dark save for the flicker of light in the fireplace, but that was enough to allow him to see Abigail's form in his bed. He walked over and stood for a moment, gazing down at her. She was nestled on her side, dark hair spread across his pillow. The covers had slipped down, and he could see that her shoulders were bare. She was naked beneath the sheet.

His body tightened, his mind filling with images of stripping her wet clothes from her this evening. Graeme thought about the way he had ripped her dress apart in frustration and sliced the laces of her corset. Predictably, now he was hard as a rock. He should turn away and let her sleep.

Graeme reached out to glide his hand across her hair. Abigail's eyes opened and she smiled sleepily.

"Sorry. I didn't mean to awaken you." And wasn't that an enormous lie?

"That's all right." Abigail turned over on her back, reaching out to take his hand, which sent the covers sliding perilously down the slope of her breast. To his disappointment, it stopped just above her nipples. "Come to bed." Her voice was soft, and she tugged at his hand.

His tongue stuck to the roof of his mouth. "I, um . . . You should sleep."

"I will." She smiled again, the curve of her lips slow and provocative. "We can both sleep here. It's quite large."

"You must be tired," he said thickly.

"So must you."

"Not at the moment."

She chuckled a little, her lips parting over her teeth, and all he could think of was how it would feel to have those teeth sink into his shoulder. Abigail slid over, flipping the corner of the covers back in invitation.

Graeme stripped off his clothes and climbed in beside her.

Abigail was, as he had guessed, deliciously naked, her flesh warm and pliant. He stroked his hand down her body, watching her eyes darken with desire. He bent to kiss her. Now, he knew, he could not stop. He kissed her over and over—long, drugging kisses as his fingers sought out the hidden places that made her tremble and moan.

Graeme was drunk on the taste of her, the feel of her.

Her skin was satin against his fingertips, and when his hand slipped between her legs and found the thick moisture of her arousal, it was all he could do not to let out an animal growl of hunger. Passion pounded in him, urgent, insistent, but he clamped down on it with merciless control, determined to take the time and care that he should have taken the night before.

Abigail writhed beneath him, her hands caressing his dampened skin, her breath coming in short, sharp pants. "Graeme . . . Graeme . . ." She threaded her fingers through his hair, and when she clenched her hands in his hair as a tremor ran through her, the prickle of pain only heightened his hunger.

At last he moved between her legs, sliding into her slowly. Desire was a deep, throbbing ache, a swelling pressure that pushed at the dam of his control as he thrust and retreated in a timeless rhythm. Abigail dug her heels into the bed, arching up against him, her relentless need building until with a thin cry she shuddered and clung to him. Then, at last, he released the reins of his control and rode, hard and fast, to a shattering climax.

Graeme collapsed against her, his flesh quivering and damp with sweat. And that, he thought with a deep satisfaction, was a husbandly duty done sufficiently.

chapter 15

Abby awakened in a strange bed in a strange room. Disoriented, she sat up. It was a man's room, the furniture heavy and dark, men's brushes on the dresser, a shaving stand across the room from her. Graeme's bedroom.

She remembered it all now—the blood running down that man's face, the hard shove in the back, the cold water closing over her head, the panic exploding in her as she fought not to breathe it in. And Graeme's arms closing around her, lifting her up and pulling her to safety.

After that, her memory was a trifle spotty—flashes of a speeding carriage ride, of Graeme saying her name, the warmth of the fire and Graeme's face looming over her, sharp with anxiety. She remembered, too, much later, when Graeme had joined her in this bed. A smile curved her lips. Yes, that she remembered quite well.

Abby glanced around, and there, as if by magic, was her dressing gown laid over the foot of the bed. She was tying it around her a moment later when the explanation for the robe's presence opened the door and craned her head around it.

"Molly." Abby smiled. "What are you doing here?"

Her maid came the rest of the way in. "*He* ordered me

to bring your things here." She sniffed her disdain. "But you just say the word, and I'll whisk them all back into the trunks and we'll be off."

"He did, did he?" Abby smiled. "No, I think we are fine right where we are."

"Hmph. I don't trust him, and that's a fact."

"I got that impression. Yet you told him where I was last night." When the older woman began to bristle, she added hastily, "I am very glad you did. I would have drowned if Montclair hadn't arrived in time. I'm merely surprised you entrusted him with the information."

"Well, the devil you know . . ." Molly shrugged. "They've made up a room for you in here." She went to a door in the side wall and opened it into another spacious chamber.

"Ah, the countess's bedroom, I take it." Abby surveyed the adjoining room. It was a much more feminine room. The furniture was still dark, but its lines were more graceful, less massive, and the wallpaper was an elegant blue-and-white pattern, the draperies a matching blue.

She would have liked a lighter wood, but no doubt it would be considered sacrilege to change anything. She would not be here long, in any case. Once she was pregnant, their goal reached, doubtless she would not be living with Graeme.

The thought lowered her mood, and Abby set it aside. There was no reason to spoil what she had with thoughts of what would come later. She dressed with Molly's help and made her way downstairs in search of food. She was, she discovered, ravenous.

Glancing around, she saw that she was alone in the corridor. She began to waltz, humming a tune, making her way down the wide hall in great, swooping circles, and as she danced she sang. She was still humming beneath her breath when she entered the dining room. Abby was disappointed to see that only the dowager countess and a small, dowdy woman were there.

"Was that singing I heard?" Lady Eugenia asked in astonished tones.

"Yes, I believe I was singing." Abby smiled as she took the seat the footman held out for her. "Good morning, Countess." She turned a little inquiringly toward the other woman.

"Mrs. Ponsonby," Lady Eugenia explained. "She is the widow of my late cousin. Philomena, allow me to introduce you to Montclair's wife."

"Oh, yes, we have met." The small woman smiled shyly and bobbed her head, reminding Abigail forcibly of a sparrow. "At your wedding, Lady Montclair."

"What nonsense, Philomena," the countess said. "That was ten years ago; I am sure she wouldn't remember meeting you."

"No, no, of course not." Philomena let out a little titter. "I wouldn't expect you to remember so small a thing."

Abby felt a twinge of sympathy for the woman. "Please, call me Abigail. I should remember meeting you. But I have forgotten most of what happened then."

Lady Eugenia gave her a narrow look, but apparently could not decide if there had been a barb in Abby's words. "You are looking well this morning, considering your adventure last night."

"Yes, I am quite recovered, thank you."

"You must have been terribly frightened," Mrs. Ponsonby said, her eyes wide. "I am sure I would have been."

"It was rather scary. I am very fortunate Graeme was

there." Abigail added casually, "I had thought I might see him here."

"Montclair left the house some time ago."

"Oh?" Abigail waited, but Lady Eugenia did not elaborate. "Where did he go?"

Graeme's grandmother looked pained. "I am sure I don't know. I never question a gentleman about his plans."

Abby suspected that was a thumper, but she said only, "Indeed? I'm afraid I'm far too curious for that."

"In my day, young ladies were taught to restrain their curiosity. No doubt it is different in America."

"No doubt."

"It is so nice that the weather has been pleasant while you are here," Mrs. Ponsonby offered. "Hardly any rain."

"The spring was terribly wet," Lady Eugenia added.

By the time Abigail finished eating, they had thoroughly explored all aspects of the weather, both in June and earlier months, not to mention in previous years. Abigail finished her cup of tea, which she had to doctor with large amounts of milk and sugar to make it palatable, and politely declined to join the other ladies in the dowager countess's sitting room upstairs.

Graeme had not returned, so she whiled away the rest of the morning exploring the house. That, too, soon palled. She was contemplating tracking down the butler to ask that coffee be added to the breakfast menu—she suspected both he and the countess would consider that bad form—when Norton appeared in the doorway to announce Mr. Prescott.

"David!" Abigail followed the butler into the entry to greet her friend—no doubt another social solecism. "It is so good to see you. How did you know I was here?" She tucked her hand in his arm as they returned to the drawing room.

"I came by last night. Didn't Montclair tell you?"

"No, I haven't seen him this morning. I slept rather late."

"Molly came to me for help last night."

"She notified you, too? I must say, she was certainly busy."

"When you didn't come back after she talked to Montclair, Molly grew very worried. And rightfully so. Did you really go down to the docks, Abby? What were you doing?"

"Well, it wasn't *my* choice of a meeting place. But that was where he told me to be."

"Who?"

"I don't know his name." Abby sighed. "Please don't lecture me, David; Graeme has already pointed out how foolish it was. I took precautions, and I was positive the man wouldn't hurt me. He wanted money, and injuring me would not have achieved that. I hadn't foreseen that someone would shoot him."

"And push you into the river, apparently."

"That was probably just an accident." Abby doubted it, but hopefully the idea would soothe her friend's worry. "He was running past me."

"Why didn't you tell me? I would have gone with you."

"He was very clear that I must come alone. Besides, I couldn't confide in you." She shook her head. "It involves someone else; it's not my secret to tell." He frowned, and she cast about for something to deflect his next question. "David . . . you were working for my father when we came here before."

"Your father?" His eyebrows shot up. "This is about Thurston? Good heavens, Abby, don't risk your life trying to help your father. If Price is in trouble, I am sure it is well-deserved and nothing to do with you."

"I'm not trying to help my father. I wondered if you knew Lord Montclair's man of business at that time."

"Lord Reginald's business man?" He looked surprised. "I suppose I might have. Let me think. . . . Yes, I believe I met him. I don't remember why."

"That's not important. What I want to know is his name."

"I have no idea what his name was. That was years ago, and he wasn't memorable. I can't even recall what he looked like. Why don't you ask Montclair?"

"Ask me what?" said a voice from the doorway.

Both Abby and Prescott whirled around to see Graeme standing in the door, his expression one of polite inquiry. Red flooded Abby's cheeks. How much of their conversation had Graeme heard? Her mind was suddenly, stubbornly empty of any answer to his question. She was sure she must look the very picture of guilt.

Fortunately, David was less at a loss. "Just a question about the British Museum. I had suggested we might go there one day, and Abby wondered if she would enjoy it."

"I am sure Lady Montclair would find it quite interesting." Graeme looked at her. "She has a great deal of curiosity about all sorts of things." He strolled farther into the room. "I see you decided to take me up on my invitation, Mr. Prescott. I trust you find Lady Montclair well."

"Yes." Prescott gave him a nod as stiff as Graeme's stance. "I was pleased to see her in good health after her ordeal."

"It sounds worse than it was," Abby said lightly. "All in all, I only swallowed a bit of nasty water."

"I'm sure there was a good deal more to it than that." David gave her a tight smile. "I shall take my leave of you now. You must not tax your strength." He directed a pleasant nod to her and a lesser inclination of the head to Graeme. "Good day."

Graeme watched the other man walk away, then pivoted slowly back to his wife. He regarded Abigail for a long moment, then said, "Now . . . why don't you tell me the real story about yesterday evening?"

The cold composure on his face, so unlike the warmth they had shared last night, took her aback. She had the uneasy feeling she had missed something, taken a wrong turn. "The real story? I already told you—"

"Lies are what you have told me. Or perhaps it's half-truths. Omissions. But I know you have not told me what you know." As she opened her mouth to speak, he held up a hand as if calling a halt. "And do *not* tell me it is none of my business. You are my wife; you say you want to be the mother of my child. Last night I had to pull you out of the Thames. Then I had to whisk you away from the scene of a crime before the police could find you there. I would say that makes it very much my business."

"Graeme!" His hard tone struck her like a blow. "Surely you don't think I was doing anything criminal!"

"I don't know what to think. Clearly you're involved in something that is worth killing a man over. It would have been two murders if I hadn't managed to chase you down in time." He whipped around and walked away, then strode back. "I needn't ask you the identity of the man you were meeting; I know that."

"You do?" Abigail gaped. "How?"

"I went to the police this morning. I told them it was I

who had gone to meet the fellow, arriving in time to see him shot and his killer flee. They had no trouble believing I was meeting him, you see, since he was my father's man of business."

"Oh." The blood drained from Abigail's face.

"Yes, the self-same person you were discussing with Mr. Prescott when I entered."

"I didn't know his name," Abby said quietly. "I told you the truth."

"About that. I want to hear the rest of it. Why were you meeting Milton Baker last night?"

"I told you. He said he had information for me."

"Information about what?" When Abigail hesitated, Graeme took a long step forward. "Don't lie to me. Or I promise you, this is the end of our 'arrangement.'"

"Graeme!"

"Don't you understand? How can I possibly be with you in any way if I cannot trust you? How could I allow you to raise my child? You said you were not like your father, that you are not engaged in underhanded schemes. Yet from the moment I saw you, you have kept things from me, received secret letters, crept out to clandestine meetings in the most unsavory parts of the city. I want the truth. What sort of scheme are you embroiled in? Why did you come back to England?"

"I came back to England for the reason I told you," Abigail snapped. "Your grandmother wrote me. She suggested I come here; she talked about all the years that had passed and how you must have an heir. I had already been thinking about my life and the changes I wanted—just as I told you. That's why I returned."

"How does Milton Baker come into it?"

"He doesn't have anything to do with my returning. I swear it. After I arrived—in fact, it was the very evening we met again—I found a note lying on the floor of my room. It had no signature. It said that I didn't know the truth behind my marriage."

"The truth behind your marriage?" Graeme frowned. "What truth is that?"

"I didn't know! Obviously this person believed he knew something I didn't, something I would pay money to find out."

"And did you?"

"I was going to. That evening you came to see me after your fight with Mr. Prescott, another note was slipped under my door, as you saw. He told me to meet him if I wanted to discover whatever this 'truth' was. So I went; that was when you followed me the first time. He was frightened away when he saw you."

"Instead you met him last night. He sent you another letter?"

"No. He was waiting for me in the hotel corridor near my room."

"Milton Baker?"

"I presume so. He didn't tell me his name. I didn't see his face, either. He came up behind me and grabbed me, and I couldn't—"

"He attacked you?"

Abigail took a step back, startled at the sudden fire in his eyes. "No—I mean, he wasn't trying to hurt me. He just hooked his arm around me so I couldn't turn around and see his face. At the end he turned and ran, and all I saw was his back."

"Yet still you went to meet him? By yourself? Haven't you any sense?"

"He said to come alone, and I didn't want to risk scaring him off again. Besides, it was clear he had no intention of harming me. He could easily have done so when in the hotel, but he didn't. He wanted money, and he wouldn't get any if I was dead. Anyway, who should I have taken with me? I thought of Mr. Prescott, but I didn't want him—or anyone—to hear some awful thing about my marriage."

"Prescott! What about me? Don't you think *I* might have some interest in the matter?"

"I didn't want you to know!"

"Why?" Graeme clamped his hand around her arm. "What did you want so much to hide from me?"

Abby jerked away. She glared at him, trapped. "I didn't want you to learn that your father was a thief! That's what."

chapter 16

"What?" Graeme's voice was quiet, his eyes fixed on hers.

"Mr. Baker told me your father embezzled money from a charity he was involved in. *That* is what I didn't want you to hear. I thought I could keep him silent by paying him, and there wouldn't be any scandal. You wouldn't have to find out what your father had done."

"You were trying to spare me embarrassment?"

"Yes, of course." Did he really distrust her so much he believed she wouldn't try to save him from pain? "I know how important your name is to you, how little you want scandal attached to it. I thought I could ward it off by paying him, and you would never have to know. Your memory of your father wouldn't be tarnished." She simply could not reveal the part her own father had played in it. If Graeme knew her father had encouraged Reginald to embezzle the money, he would be furious. She feared he would turn away from her forever, as he had threatened just now.

"Abigail . . ." He cupped her face in his hands. He gazed down at her, an odd look on his face. "I already knew."

"You did?" Now it was her turn to stare.

He nodded, his voice thoughtful. "So you didn't know . . ."

"No. I was aware your finances were poor and you were faced with losing the estate. And that matters were worse because your father had bought a lot of that stock my father sent crashing. But I had no idea Lord Reginald had taken the money from a charity. Obviously, it would have made your situation more desperate. You would have had to replace it immediately, before anyone found out. It's no wonder you felt imprisoned and angry." Her eyes filled with tears. "I'm so sorry."

"No, don't cry. It wasn't your fault." He pressed his lips to her forehead. "I apologize for accusing you of lying."

The tenderness in his gesture filled her with warmth. "Well, I *was* trying to hide it from you. But I promise, I never had any intention of harming you."

He kissed her with equal gentleness on her lips. When he lifted his head, there was a look in his eyes that turned the warmth inside her into a blaze. For a moment she thought he would kiss her again. He stepped back to a respectable distance, glancing toward the door. Graeme, of course, would never be so lacking in propriety as to kiss his wife in a room where anyone might walk in on them.

Abby suppressed a sigh and turned the conversation to a neutral topic. "It seems odd that someone would have shot that man. Why would anyone be harmed by my paying him to keep silent? *I* was the one who wanted to shut him up."

"I suspect that if Baker was trying to extort money from you, he might very well have been playing the same game with others. Maybe someone else was not so willing to pay as you."

"I suppose so. And maybe it *was* an accident that the man pushed me into the water. Or he feared I had seen his face—though I don't know how I could have."

"Perhaps. Still, I think you should be careful—promise me you will not leave the house alone."

"Very well. I won't." Her spirits rose a little at the note of concern in his voice. "Graeme . . . did Mr. Baker have a wife? A family?"

"I don't know him well. I used a different agent. But I believe he was married. Why?"

"I'd like to call on his wife. Do you know where he lived?"

"No, but I can find out." He looked at her quizzically. "You want to offer your condolences?"

"He was there because he was giving me information."

"You think you are to blame?"

"No, not to blame, but . . . I feel I owe him something. I was about to pay him when he was shot. I am sure his wife needs the money."

"No doubt."

"And he did give me information—not that there's much I can do with it, for he died before he could tell me the rest."

"The rest? What do you mean?"

"He was vague, so I fear it's useless. After he told me about the embezzlement, he said it was 'what everyone believed' or 'what it appeared to be.' Something like that. As if there was more to it or people were wrong. He said he would tell me when I gave him the money, but then he was shot."

"Are you thinking my father might not have embezzled the money?" He shook his head. "I fear Baker was simply saying what he hoped would cause you to give him more money. My father himself told me he had lost the fund's money and he had to replace it before anyone knew."

"Oh. Well, still, I want to give his wife the money. Her life will be harder now. And there might be a chance she knew what he meant. There may not be anything more to the story, but if there is, wouldn't you like to know it?"

"Yes. And I cannot but admire your generous heart." He moved closer. "You are very different from the person I imagined."

Her eyes twinkled up at him. "Given what you thought of me, I am glad to hear you say so."

"I have been wrong and unkind." Graeme brushed a curl back from her cheek. "I have not shown much of that same sort of heart."

"You came to my aid, not once but twice, however little you liked me. I think that says a great deal about your nature."

"I will take you to see her tomorrow." Graeme remained only inches from her, gazing into her eyes. "But right now, I think you should go to bed. After your ordeal, you need to rest." He circled her wrist with his hand, gliding it up her arm.

"Alone?"

"No, I think not. You are doubtless still weak." He turned, his hand on her arm propelling her forward, and leaned down to murmur in her ear, "You will require my assistance."

A breathless laugh escaped her. "I believe you are right."

They took the stairs at such a pace as to belie any claims of tiredness. Abigail started toward the bedroom Molly had shown her earlier, but Graeme whisked her into his room instead. "'Tis far too likely that my nemesis is in there. I'm not risking that."

Abby laughed. "Molly?"

"Yes, Molly. She's more Praetorian Guard than maid."

"But what shall I do without the services of a maid?" She turned to show the long line of buttons down the back of her dress, smiling archly at him over her shoulder.

"I shall be happy to serve you." Graeme nuzzled her neck, sending bright sparks shooting along her nerves. "In that way . . . or any other."

"I hope you are more careful than you were last night. I'd rather you not lay waste to all my clothes."

"I wouldn't mind." His low chuckle reverberated through her. "But I promise I will take the utmost care." He began to work his way down her back, his fingers brushing enticingly against her skin. "Though I cannot imagine why you choose dresses with so many buttons."

"Perhaps it's to challenge you." She felt the flare of heat in his hands at his words, and she smiled to herself. It was embarrassing to have him undress her; he was so much a stranger to her. Conversely, it filled her with a sizzling excitement.

"Mm," he said in a meditative voice as he stroked a finger down the length of her back. "It does that." He bent to press a kiss to the skin of her back where her dress now gaped open. His hands slid around her waist and up to cup her breasts. "But it's frightfully easy to get distracted from the task."

Abby closed her eyes, luxuriating in the sensations his hands and mouth aroused. "You'll never become proficient that way."

She felt his smile upon her flesh. "That depends on the area in which you want to be proficient."

His fingers circled her nipples slowly as his mouth explored the nape of her neck, the twin pleasures rippling through her. Somehow the soft barrier of cloth between his fingers and her own sensitive flesh made the sensation even more erotic. Abby let her head loll back, resting against him, exposing the side of her neck. Graeme was quick to take advantage, his lips moving down her neck and across to her shoulder. His mouth was hot and seductive, tightening the coil of desire in her.

He lifted his head and returned to the remaining buttons on her dress, and now his fingers were swift at the task. The dress slid farther down as the fastenings gave way, and Abby made no move to hold it, until it hung loosely from her wrists. Graeme slid his hands down her arms, sending her dress to the floor and igniting shivers wherever he touched her.

He went next to the top of her corset. "Hooks now, I see." His fingers were nimble. "You are well-armored. I feel as if I'm storming a castle."

Abby laughed, and he jerked the last hook free. The stiff form fell away as he ran his hands beneath it, caressing her. "Ah, this feels much better. You should leave that off always."

"None of my dresses would fit."

He pulled her chemise up and off over her head, and his finger went to the red creases left by the stays' ribs. "I don't like to see your skin marred."

Graeme turned her around, tracing the lines. His lids drooped lower as he studied her.

"Beautiful." His voice was thick. He cupped her breasts, thumbs gently stroking them to hardness. "I could look at you all day . . . if I did not want so much to taste you."

He pulled her to him, wrapping his arms around her, and kissed her. Slow. Deep. Hungry. He worked his lips against her, used teeth and tongue to arouse her. Abby felt him swell against her, hard and pulsing. When he raised his head, his eyes were dark and slumberous, his mouth softened.

"Abigail." He said her name as if trying it out to see how it felt. His hands moved slowly down her body. "Abby."

She leaned toward him, and he met her, his mouth hot and eager. He sank his fingers into her hair, popping pins loose and sending her tresses tumbling. He fumbled at the ties closing her undergarments, divesting her of bustle and petticoats. One tie knotted, and she felt his fingers clench in frustration, followed by a snap that meant the ribbon had been torn from its moorings. Abby didn't care. She loved the feel of his eagerness, his haste, just as she reveled in the heat radiating from his body and the faint tremor in his skin where she touched him.

He walked her back to the bed, his mouth roaming her face and throat. His arms beneath her buttocks, he lifted her, his mouth moving down to fasten on her breasts. Abby bent her head over his, her hair falling down around them like a curtain, as she caressed his shoulders. She tugged impatiently at his jacket, and he set her down to tear off his jacket and unfasten his clothes.

Abby helped by reaching down to the buttons of his trousers. She felt the muscles of his stomach jerk as her fingertips slid beneath the waistband, and she hesitated, thinking she had made a misstep, but he breathed, "No, don't stop. Don't stop."

His flesh pressed against the material as she moved down the line of buttons, and experimentally she delved inside, sliding her hand over the smooth, throbbing flesh. He let out a low noise, his hand reaching down to guide hers. She could hear his breath rasping in his throat, fast and hard. Emboldened, she moved farther, slipping between his legs and taking the heavy sac in her palm.

Graeme put his hands on either side of her face, raising it to his, and he kissed her deeply, shuddering as she stroked him. He pulled away, shoving down his hampering garments and kicking them free. Lifting her, he tumbled her back onto the bed and covered her with his body. Braced on his elbows, his hands cupping her head, he continued to kiss her.

He had managed to unbutton his shirt but hadn't gotten so far as to pull it off, so that it hung open and loose. The bared skin down the center of his chest was pressed against her; she felt the hard line of his bones, the firm padding of muscle, the tantalizing prickle of chest hair upon her flesh. Abby slipped her hands beneath the sides of his shirt, tracing his ribs and exploring his back. Everything she did seemed to heighten his passion.

Even lost in sensation as she was, another part of her mind was noting his reactions to the things she did and storing them up so that she could please him later. How was it that arousing him could give her so much pleasure?

Untouched as she had been, her ideas about what happened between men and women had been somewhat vague . . . at least until she had had that startling and informative conversation with the woman from the bordello. Certainly she had never dreamed that the whole thing would prove to be so enjoyable. She had wanted a child, but never had she thought that the act of getting one would turn out to be something she longed for as well.

Now, as Graeme kissed his way down her body, his hands awakening in her such sensations that she felt she must shatter with the delight, she could only wish that she had not waited so long to discover it. Then he was inside her, filling her, moving with long, languorous strokes, and Abigail ceased to think at all.

She moved with him, delighting in his strength, his power, so carefully leashed to please her. Tension coiled within her, but now, knowing the prize that awaited her, she was content to let it spin out until at last she reached the crest and tumbled over the edge. She heard his hoarse cry, felt his body shudder against hers, and she knew that he, too, had found his release.

He collapsed against her, his heavy weight an entirely different pleasure. Heat poured from Graeme, his skin damp with sweat, and his lungs labored for air. Abigail relished his reaction. She kissed his shoulder, and his skin trembled at her touch.

Graeme rolled over, taking her with him, so that she nestled in the crook of his shoulder. His arms were still wrapped around her, his leg anchoring hers to the bed. She felt the brush of his lips against her hair.

This, she thought, was what she had ached for for so long and not even known that she wanted. This, at long last, was happiness.

chapter 17

The following day Graeme and Abby called on Milton Baker's widow. Their coach carried them into an unprepossessing area, the streets becoming narrower and the buildings less well-tended the farther along they went. By the time they reached the address they sought, the road was so narrow that they had to leave the carriage to walk the last few yards. The driver looked uneasy, and Abby suspected that had it been a cab rather than their own vehicle, the coachman would not have waited for them.

The addresses were not marked, so they had to ask for directions from passersby, but eventually they found the right set of stairs. Graeme knocked, but it was a long time before anyone answered, even though the sound of coughing indicated someone was inside.

A woman opened the door, one hand on the doorjamb for support. She was small—Abby was uncertain whether she was actually short or just bent over so much she appeared that way. She was thin, though the loose hang of her dress hinted that she had not always been so. Shadowed eyes and sallow skin completed the look of ill health. The woman pressed a handkerchief to her mouth and turned away, coughing.

A pang of pity went through Abby. She glanced at Graeme, and he curled a hand around her waist as if she needed support, an entirely unnecessary gesture that somehow made her feel better.

"We are sorry to disturb you, Mrs. Baker," Graeme began. "We came to offer our condolences." The other woman looked at him dully. Graeme tried again. "I am Lord Montclair. Your husband worked for my father."

"I remember. But you didn't want him." She seemed more matter-of-fact about it than resentful.

"I already had a business agent."

"Milton expected it. He knew he'd have no chance with you after he had endorsed your father's investment. Excuse me, I must sit down. I'm not well."

There was no arguing with that. Mrs. Baker sank into a chair beside the small stove, burning despite the warmth of the day. It made the small room stifling, but Mrs. Baker huddled next to the stove as if chilled. She gestured toward a nearby chair, a spindly thing that looked as if it might collapse. Abigail sat down in it gingerly, and Graeme came to stand beside her.

"It was you, wasn't it?" Mrs. Baker looked at Abigail. "The woman he went to see."

"Yes. He told me he had information for me."

The other woman nodded. "He did that for me, you know. He wasn't that kind of man. It was hard for him after Lord Montclair lost the money. Everyone knew, you see, that Milton had been foolish enough to agree it was a good investment. Still, he was able to get a job as a clerk, at least, and we managed on that. Till I came down sick."

"I'm very sorry."

"He wasn't a bad man." The other woman's eyes filled

with tears. "It hurt him inside; he didn't like to frighten you. But it was all he could think to do." She peered intently at Abigail. "Were you there? Was he in pain?"

"No, he wasn't in pain." It seemed the only comfort she could offer the woman. "I don't think he even realized what had happened, it was so quick."

"That's good. I'd hate to think he suffered."

"Mrs. Baker, I wanted to give you the money he asked for." Abigail pulled the roll of bills from her purse and handed it to her.

The other woman stared at Abigail in amazement, but her fingers quickly curled around the money. "Thank you. I— You are a fine lady. I hope he told you what you wanted to know."

"He wasn't able to tell me all of it. Do you know what he planned to say?"

"I—I don't know." Mrs. Baker's hand clenched convulsively around the money as though she feared Abigail might snatch it back. "He knew something about what happened back then. With Lord Reginald and that charity." She cast a cautious glance at Graeme, and he nodded reassuringly. "It bothered him."

"What bothered him, Mrs. Baker?" Abby asked softly.

"Milton said he hadn't done it—Lord Montclair. He said it wasn't Montclair who took the money."

"What?" Graeme stared. "Are you certain?"

"Oh, yes." She nodded emphatically. "He—Milton took to drink for a while, and sometimes when he'd had too much, he'd talk. He'd say they were wrong; it wasn't Lord Reginald, and maybe he should have told someone. Then he'd scowl and say, 'But it served him right. Why should I lift a finger to help him?' He was angry, you see, because you didn't hire him on, sir. Milton expected it, but still he couldn't help but be angry because he'd only done what your father wanted. He felt guilty, too, though, because he said nothing. After Milton gave up the gin, he stopped talking about that time. Then I got sick, and we hadn't enough money, and he was desperate. He heard about you coming here, my lady, and that's when he decided he could get money for what he knew."

Abigail glanced at Graeme. His face was an odd blend of hope and disbelief. Since he seemed unwilling or unable to speak, she asked, "If Lord Montclair hadn't done it, why didn't Montclair himself speak up?"

"He was proud, you see, and it would have been a great scandal if anything was said. Better to just pay it back and keep it quiet."

"But, if he didn't do it, who did?"

"I don't know." Mrs. Baker shook her head. "Milton never told me that. He just said someone else took it. He said you'd pay to find out Lord Montclair's father wasn't a criminal. He didn't want to go to his lordship, you see." She glanced toward Graeme apologetically. "I'm sorry. That's all I know."

"Thank you." Abigail smiled at her. "I'm very glad you told us this. I—I hope the money helps."

"Yes, my lady. Thank you."

It was clear that the woman was starting to flag, so they took their leave. Abigail slipped her hand into Graeme's arm as they went down the stairs; it was hard as iron. His face was unreadable in the dimness of the stairwell. When they stepped outside, he took a deep breath, as if cleansing himself of something.

"She couldn't be right." The uncertainty in Graeme's eyes belied his words. "He told me himself he'd done it."

"What did he say exactly? Did he say he had taken it?"

"Of c—" He stopped, then sighed and shook his head. "Honestly? I'm not sure." He was deep in thought as they walked to the waiting carriage. When they climbed in and the carriage started rolling, he said, "I can't remember him actually saying he took the money. I think his words were, 'The foundation's money is gone, and it's my fault.' Or perhaps, 'I am responsible.'

"Father was obviously ashamed, and, frankly, I was so shocked that I didn't even question him about it. I think I asked what had happened or where it had gone, and he said it didn't matter. I was so furious I barely spoke to him for weeks afterward. I couldn't bear to be around him—or anyone, really. I was horrid." He had been staring blindly out the window as he talked, and now he cast a quick, abashed glance at Abigail. "You know what I was like. The truth is, things were never the same between my father and me after that. We talked; we were polite. But we were never . . . comfortable together. Then he died."

Seeing the bleakness on his face, Abigail reached over and slipped her hand into his. He glanced at her, surprised, and tightened his clasp. "I beg your pardon. I shouldn't burden you with this."

"Who else should you tell?" Abigail said reasonably. "I promise you, no one understands better than I feeling torn about one's father. I know the sort of man my father is; I've felt shamed by the things he's done. Angry. There were times when I hated him and wanted to be miles away from him. But still, he's my father, and deep down, I cannot help but love him."

"Of course you do." He rubbed his thumb across the back of her hand in a small gesture of comfort.

"In his own way, Thurston loves me," Abby went on. "His rules and restrictions, his insistence that I do this thing or that, until I thought I could not bear it anymore—to his way of thinking, he was protecting me, keeping me safe and sheltered. He was certain he knew what I should have, what would make me happy. He showered me with presents; he gave me everything I asked for and much more besides. He even bought me a husband." She flashed a teasing smile at him and was rewarded when his lips curled up ruefully in return.

"A rather disappointing present there."

"I wouldn't say that." Abby squeezed his hand again. "Just because you love someone, it doesn't mean you have to be blind to his faults or approve of everything he does. I'm sure your father knew you loved him even if you were rightfully upset at him."

"Perhaps." He was silent for a moment. "Everyone loved my father. Well, you met him; you know what he was like."

"He was a very handsome man," Abigail agreed. In truth, the main thing she remembered about him was that she thought to herself that this was how Graeme would look when he was older. "And quite pleasant."

"Yes. If you do not remember him well, my grandmother will be happy to expound on his charm. There was, apparently, none who could equal his manners or his expertise on the dance floor or his seat on a horse."

"I believe mothers often feel that way about their sons."

"Yes. But she is right. Ladies loved him—and he loved them in return. He wasn't faithful to my mother. A very minor fault in my grandmother's eyes—at least he was usually discreet. Most felt that way, I suppose. But I had seen how my mother cried over his 'indiscretions' and I could not be so forgiving. I swore I would never be like him.

"He was foolish and feckless, and he could not understand why I couldn't see that art and jewels and horses and elegance were more important than something so mundane as the state of our finances. He told me one would think I was in trade, the way I nattered on about his spending."

Abigail let out a mocking gasp. "A grievous insult!"

Graeme shrugged. "To him it was. As frivolous as he was about many things, the title was important to him. The Parr name. That was why I was so shocked by what he had done. He was careless about money and his wedding vows, but he was a man of his word, and he had a strong code of conduct. He would have called himself a man of honor. I could hardly believe he had done something so disgraceful."

"So you would not be surprised if he had *not* been the one to embezzle the money?"

"No. I would have firmly believed it was stolen by someone else if Father had not said what he did to me."

"Saying one is responsible is not precisely the same as saying he did it himself," Abby pointed out.

"That's true."

"Would he have taken the blame for someone else?"

"I wouldn't think so. For my mother, yes, or my grandmother, or even me, someone he felt he had a duty to protect. But one thing I am certain of is that none of us embezzled the money. On the other hand . . . he was in charge of the fund. He was responsible for it. If it disappeared 'on his watch,' so to speak, he might very well view it as his fault. He would feel that he was honor-bound to replace the money no matter who took it."

"He wouldn't have turned the matter over to the police?"

"No, I think Mrs. Baker was right in that. He would have wanted to keep the whole matter secret, whoever the culprit was. Avoiding scandal would have been his first priority. An investigation would have made it all public." He sighed. "I wish now I had talked to him about it, that I'd asked him the details."

"I wonder . . ."

Graeme turned to look at her. "What?"

"What if we were to look into it?" As Graeme's eyebrows shot up, Abby went on hastily. "I don't mean bring the authorities into it. I mean us, you and me. Are there any records from that charity?"

"I suppose so. Our family isn't apt to throw things away. There might be some old files—correspondence, maybe even the financial records. But I'm not sure how they would prove anyone else embezzled the money."

"Mr. Baker figured it out somehow. It's possible he did so from working on your father's financial records. And if Mr. Baker knew of it, there might have been others as well. We could talk to some of the other people who were in the organization. I presume you never questioned any of them."

"No. It never occurred to me; I thought Father was the one who had committed the crime. But I doubt anyone's going to confess to it."

"Probably not. But people might have suspicions that they would share with you. You're one of their own, after all."

"It would make no difference now," he said slowly. "I could do nothing because of the scandal."

"But wouldn't you like to know anyway?"

"You're right." Graeme smiled at her. "I would."

Abby settled back against the seat. She realized that in the course of talking, she had forgotten to let go of Graeme's hand. He made no move to pull away. Neither did she.

chapter 18

"Well." Abby cast her eyes around Graeme's study. "Where should we start?"

Graeme leaned against the doorjamb, arms folded, watching her, a faint smile on his lips. Her eyes were sparkling with enthusiasm; clearly, Abigail was a woman who enjoyed a hunt.

How had he not noticed ten years ago the way her eyes lit up? Or how kissable her plump lips were, how lustrous her thick black hair. Could she have changed this much over the years? Had she hidden her emotions before? Her wit? Or had he simply been blinded by his rage? His love for Laura?

Graeme shifted uneasily. He didn't want to think about that. Or about the fact that this time would pass, and things would return to normalcy. It was easier, better, to simply enjoy the moment. He had liked other women through the years, enjoyed their company, taken his pleasure with them. But none had ever filled up his life as Abby did. Suddenly she was everywhere—in his bed, in his house, in his thoughts.

She excited him, intrigued him. Being with her was like watching a storm approach—wind whipping at him, dark clouds rolling, electricity crackling in the air—stirred by it all even though one knew it wasn't safe.

It wasn't just the passion, though God knew that was more bone-deep thrilling than it had been with any other woman. That was part of it, but there was something more that tugged at him. He had tried to analyze it, but, as now, whenever he began to think about Abby, his thoughts devolved into maneuvering to catch her in some deserted hallway or pull her into an alcove and steal a kiss. Better yet, whisking her upstairs to his bed in the middle of the afternoon, as he had the other day.

"Graeme?"

He straightened, realizing that she had asked him something and was waiting for a response. He cast his mind back. "Oh. Well, I'm not sure. When I came into the title, I went through everything here. I don't remember anything about the soldiers' fund. Father ended it after he replaced the money; that was a few years before his death. Perhaps he had discarded the papers by then or packed them away."

He took a key from the top drawer of the desk and unlocked a cabinet. "This is where I keep the account books. It's possible there's one for that fund still on the bottom shelf."

Abby squatted down and began pulling out the logs and peering at the dates. He noticed that she had worn a different sort of dress today, with fewer petticoats and no bustle. More practical attire for stooping and bending and searching through shelves and drawers. Also, he reflected cheerfully, much easier to remove.

He went down on one knee beside her and joined in the search. Unsurprisingly, while there were a few account books dating back more than ten years, there were none pertaining to the Fund for Invalid Soldiers. They moved on to another cabinet, this one made up of a number of shallow drawers, a letter of the alphabet on each.

"I'm certain these are all mine," Graeme said, though he opened each one anyway and riffled through the letters laid flat inside.

Abby turned her attention to the bookshelves. When Graeme finished the letters and turned to her, he found that she was watching him. He felt faintly embarrassed yet also pleased, with a snaking thread of desire running through it all. He thought of taking her into his arms, but the door of the study stood open. He crossed his arms and tried to be sensible.

"I don't know where to look. There's nothing in the desk." He glanced around. The only other pieces of furniture were the armchairs in front of the fireplace.

"What did you do with the things that were here before?"

He leaned against the desk, considering. "Well . . . I remember burning some old papers, and I think I packed a few things away. I'm not sure what happened to that trunk."

"Would it be in the attic? A storeroom?"

"If anyone would remember what happened to it, it would be Norton. Let's ask."

If the dignified butler was surprised by his employer's question, no sign of it crossed his face, though Graeme had known him long enough to recognize the touch of chagrin in Norton's eyes when he could not recall what he had done with the item in question. After some consideration, Norton came to the conclusion that it was most likely to be in the attic, so Graeme and Abigail turned there next.

A narrow set of stairs led from the servants' corridor on the top floor to the attic above. Carrying a lamp, they climbed the stairs and stepped through into the long, narrow room. Windows at the front and back admitted light to add to the glow of their lamp. Graeme glanced over at Abby and smiled.

"You like this, don't you? Searching for it."

"Of course!" She looked surprised. "Why wouldn't I?"

"Well, there is the dust." He pointed to the floor. "The cobwebs. The gloom. Mice?"

"Oh, pooh." She dismissed such things with a wave of her hand. "It's exciting. And mice, I imagine, will run from us, not vice versa."

She walked along the central aisle to the window at the far end, and Graeme followed, trying to imagine any other lady of his acquaintance who would have shrugged aside the dust and spiders. Of course, this was a woman who met strangers at a dockside tavern without a qualm.

He shrugged out of his jacket and hung it on the post of an abandoned headboard, and they started on their task. They opened trunks and peered into corners and shifted aside old umbrella stands, toys, and whatever other detritus of the past had wound up in the attic. Abby was momentarily distracted by a trunk containing ball gowns from a hundred years earlier, carefully unfolding a gown and holding it up to admire the elaborate embroidery.

"Can't you imagine what this must have looked like?" She stood, holding it in front of her.

"Indeed, I can." It was easy to picture her in the vivid blue dress with its stiff bodice pushing her breasts up almost indecently. No doubt her neck would have been draped with sapphires and diamonds, more jewels dangling from her ears and nestled in her hair. It had been an extravagant time, he'd read.

"Of course, it would have been a trifle short." She cast a laughing look down at the skirt, which ended a good six inches above her ankles. "It must have been a tremendous production to get dressed. The powdered wigs. Painting your face and putting on beauty marks. The panniers out to here." She held her arms out. "I wonder how they managed to walk through the doorways."

"You've little room to talk, Countess." He strolled toward her, smiling. "Given your bustles and corsets and countless petticoats."

Abby widened her eyes in mock horror. "Why, Lord Montclair, it's quite shocking for you to be discussing such things."

"Is it?" He stopped very close to her, bracing his hand on one of the attic beams.

"Indeed. I believe gentlemen are supposed to be politely unaware of such feminine items."

"Are they? And yet, I've had a bit of experience with 'such feminine items.' "

"So you have." Abby stepped closer, settling her hands on either side of his waist.

"Yes." He brushed his lips across her cheek. "And they're a damned nuisance."

"Hmm." Abby slid her hand up the front of his waistcoat. "One can only wonder why you continue to deal with them, then."

"Because . . ." He nipped playfully at the lobe of her ear. "The prize is well worth the trouble."

She giggled. "Stop." She looped her arms around his

neck in a way that contradicted her words. "We are supposed to be looking for a trunk."

"Ah, but the trunk will still be here later." He nuzzled into the crook of her neck.

"So shall we," Abby pointed out.

"Yes, and hopefully feeling more relaxed."

"I am feeling quite relaxed now."

"Are you?" His lips traveled up her neck. "Let me see what I can do about that."

She tilted her face to receive his kiss, her body melting against his. He knew how she would taste, how she would feel beneath his hands, and he tightened with anticipation. Abigail was pliant and willing—more than willing, he thought, as he curved his hand around the nape of her neck and felt her skin warm under his touch. She shivered, pressing up into him, and he slid his hands down her back, curving over her, enjoying the feel of her rounded derriere without the obstacle of a bustle.

He dug his fingertips into the fleshy cheeks, lifting her up and into his pelvis. She murmured, rubbing herself against him, and he hardened in response. Her untutored, eager reactions never failed to stir him. Graeme lifted his head and looked back down the length of the attic, considering for an instant the prospect of pulling her down on the dusty floor.

"No. Not here," he decided.

Abigail turned in his arms—and that was a pleasure in itself, for now that rounded bottom was flush against him, and her front was open to his hands' exploration. "It isn't the most comfortable of surroundings," she agreed. "Mmm." She leaned back into him. "Graeme, if we are not to do this here, you must stop." But the hand she placed on his roaming hand was more caressing than restraining.

"Yes. You're right. I'll stop." He bent to kiss the side of her neck. "In just a moment."

She let out a laugh and pulled away, reaching back to take his hand and pull him along with her. "It's not far to my bedroom."

"It seems a very long way at the moment." But he went along amiably, lacing his fingers through hers. It was tantalizing to forestall the pleasure for a bit, to whet his appetite with images of spending the remainder of the afternoon in bed with her.

They left the attic and trotted down the back stairs to the bedroom floor. As they emerged into the corridor, Graeme whisked Abigail into the alcove by the back window, pressing her up against the wall and kissing her thoroughly. She countered by running her nails down his back. He fisted her skirts in his hand, sliding them upward.

"Graeme!" she hissed. "Not here. What if a servant comes out from the back stairs?"

"I'm not sure I care," he murmured.

"So you say now!" She ducked out from under his arm and turned into the main hall, glancing back at him over her shoulder and laughing. He started after her.

"Graeme! There you are!" Lady Eugenia stood halfway down the corridor.

Abigail let out an undignified "Eek!" and halted abruptly. Graeme took a quick step to the side so that he was behind Abby, his lower half concealed.

"Don't you dare move," he murmured, clamping his hand on her waist. His wife began to giggle.

"Where have you been? Siddings has been looking for

you." His grandmother peered at them. "Where is your jacket?"

"What—oh, um, I must have left it in the attic."

"The attic! Why on earth were you in the attic?"

"Well, um . . ."

"I asked to see it," Abigail put in, much to Graeme's relief.

"How odd." Fortunately, his grandmother seemed to feel no explanation of Abigail's oddity was necessary. "Well, it is time for tea. Lady Theresa and Sir James are joining us."

"Who?"

"Your aunt and cousin." Lady Eugenia narrowed her eyes. "Montclair, are you ill?"

"No. Course not. I'm fine."

"You are rather flushed." His grandmother took a step toward them.

"No! No, I am perfectly well, I assure you." He could feel Abigail shaking with laughter, her hand in front of her mouth to hide it, and he pressed his fingertips into her sides, whispering, "Stop that!" But his own lips began to twitch.

Lady Eugenia frowned. "Really, Montclair. You are acting most peculiarly." A quick cut of her eyes toward Abigail revealed where she thought the peculiarity came from. "Do get cleaned up. You look a fright. Your hair is every which way. I'll tell Norton to hold the tea for ten minutes." She walked away.

Abigail turned to him, both hands clasped to her mouth to control her laughter, her eyes dancing above them.

"You will be the death of me." Graeme strove for a stern voice, but the teasing laughter on Abby's face sent the fire in him leaping even higher.

"Oh, dear, we wouldn't want that." She cast him a provocative look from beneath her lashes.

Graeme grabbed her wrist and swept her down the hall, pulling her into his room and locking the door behind them.

"What are you doing? Lady Eugenia's holding tea for us. We haven't time." Abby backed up as he advanced on her.

"What I want won't take much time."

"Graeme!" Abby's eyes lit up. "What are you suggesting?"

"This." He looped an arm around her waist and picked her up, setting her down beside the bed, facing it. As she turned her head to look back at him in surprise, he took her by the wrists and set her hands flat on the bed.

"Graeme . . ." Intrigue turned her voice throaty, and the sound sent shivers through him. "What are you—oh!" She broke off as he shoved up her skirts and reached under to pull down her pantalets. "Oh, my." Abigail stepped out of the undergarments, widening her stance.

He sucked in a breath at the sight of her and ran his hands slowly over her soft white buttocks.

"But I still have on my shoes," she protested.

"I know. I like it." He slid his hand between her legs, finding the heat and the flooding moisture there. He smiled. "I think you like it, too."

He slid his finger over the satiny nub, and the soft moan that escaped Abby ratcheted up his hunger. His own flesh was throbbing, pressing against his trousers, but he clamped down on his desire, continuing to stroke her until she was moving against his hand, her breathing as harsh and ragged as his own. Only then, when he felt as if he might explode from the need knotting within him, did he unbutton his trousers and shove them down.

He buried himself in her with a deep groan of satisfaction, pausing to keep from hurtling to a climax right then and there. Sliding his hands up to cup her breasts, he began to move, reveling in the tight heat that surrounded him. Her body shifted with the power of his thrusts, and he moved one hand to her waist to hold her steady. His other hand slid down to the exquisitely sensitive flesh between her legs, and she moaned again when he found her.

"Graeme . . . Graeme . . ." She repeated his name in a low incantation, and the sound of it stirred him more than he would have thought possible. Then she gasped and shuddered as she reached her peak, tightening around him. With a low cry, Graeme let loose the reins of his own desire, hurtling into deep, dark ecstasy.

chapter 19

Unsurprisingly, they were late to tea. Lady Eugenia frowned in reproof as she rang for Norton to bring in the tea cart. From the amusement in James's eyes, Graeme thought his cousin suspected the reason for their tardiness. Graeme could not find it in himself to care. He politely introduced Abigail to his aunt and cousin, then joined James, standing beside the mantel.

"I see you are adjusting to married life," James murmured, and Graeme shot him a quelling look.

"When did you return to the city, Aunt Tessa?" Graeme asked. It was the surest way to deflect conversation away from himself, for his aunt loved nothing better than to talk about herself. It allowed Graeme to while away the visit watching his wife.

He thought somewhat smugly that Abigail looked the very image of a well-satisfied wife. After their lovemaking, he had had some qualms that she might have been repelled by his raw need and the swift, even animalistic way he had taken her, but the relaxed contentment in her face, the warmth of her gaze when she glanced at him, were enough to dispel that worry.

"I came back yesterday," Tessa said, answering Graeme's question. "One can only ruralize for so long."

"Two weeks, apparently," James added.

His mother flashed a grin at him. "I'm sure my absence wasn't long enough to suit you, dear boy, but I noticed you lasted no longer than two days at Grace Hill." She turned toward the dowager countess and said in an explanatory aside, "James's cousin Maurice was visiting."

"Ah, I see."

"What's wrong with his cousin Maurice?" Abby asked.

Lady Eugenia looked pained at the blunt question, but Tessa turned to Abby, happy to enumerate the man's faults. "It would be easier to ask what is not wrong with him. If he isn't complaining about his headaches, it's his delicate stomach or his earache or one of a hundred other ailments."

"Now, Mother, one can hardly blame the man for being ill," James said mildly. Knowing how James felt about Maurice, Graeme suspected he made the protest solely to goad Aunt Tessa.

"But one *can* blame him for talking about it incessantly. The man's a dead bore."

"Really, Theresa," the dowager countess said. "Must you speak so freely in public?"

"It's hardly public." Tessa lifted her brows. "We're all family here. I quite consider Mrs. Ponsonby one of the family." She directed one of her sparkling smiles at Lady Eugenia's companion.

"Of course she is," Lady Eugenia replied. "George was Reginald's cousin, though I believe he was only a second cousin once removed."

"I think Lady Eugenia was referring to me," Abigail explained to Tessa, looking more amused than annoyed.

"Oh. Well, no use trying to hide the family skeletons," Tessa told her cheerfully. "You're bound to find out someday. Anyway, it isn't as if Maurice is Graeme's relative; he's related to James on his father's side. And he's not really what I would call a skeleton exactly, not like that mad Lady Harlow who was married to Reginald's great-uncle."

"Ah. The tea," Lady Eugenia said in a loud voice. "Why don't you pour, Theresa?"

Tessa accepted the countess's suggestion with good grace, and the next few minutes were occupied with the serving and partaking of tea and cakes.

"Montclair, no doubt you are planning to take Lady Abigail to Lydcombe Hall soon." Lady Eugenia took up the reins of conversation again.

Abby lifted her brows and turned a quizzical gaze on Graeme. "Are you? How interesting."

"Not that I know of," Graeme said flatly and looked over at the dowager countess. "We haven't discussed it, Grandmother."

"Now is the best time to see the estate, when the gardens are so lovely," his grandmother countered.

"Why would she want to go now?" Tessa asked. "The Season is still on."

"I believe Lady Eugenia is thinking more of hiding away an inconvenient American relation than of the Season," Abby told her.

James leaned his head toward Graeme, saying sotto voce, "I smell blood in the water. Perhaps you should introduce a new conversational gambit."

"Grandmother . . ." Graeme jumped in before the dowager countess could marshal her forces and reply to Abigail. "I was thinking about that charity of Father's."

The subject had simply been the first thing in his head, but Graeme was pleased to see that it effectively diverted everyone. Lady Eugenia stared at him. Aunt Tessa looked puzzled. Even Abigail seemed nonplussed.

"What are you talking about?" Lady Eugenia said at last.

"Do you mean that fund for wounded soldiers?" Tessa asked.

"Yes. That's the one. Do you remember it, Grandmother?"

"Of course I do. But why on earth are you thinking about that?"

"It seemed a worthwhile cause. I thought I might take it up myself. It would have pleased Father, don't you think?"

"I suppose," Lady Eugenia agreed doubtfully.

"I didn't know that was still in existence," James offered.

"You know anything about it?" Graeme turned to his cousin, but James only shrugged.

"Nary a thing. It wasn't something Sir Laurence was interested in."

"Oh, your father contributed to it, too," Aunt Tessa assured him.

"Uncle Laurence was involved in it?" Graeme looked at her, surprised.

"No, not in the running of it, as Reginald was," Tessa responded. "But one gave to it, of course. It was simply something one did."

"Who else was involved?" Graeme asked. "In running it, I mean, not just contributing."

"I'm not sure." Tessa looked at Lady Eugenia. "Do you remember?"

"It's been ten years." The old woman looked thoughtful. "There was some military man—who was it? Rogers? Robertson? Rollins. Colonel Rollins. I believe he died a few years ago. Lord Fortenberry, perhaps. There was a vicar, too."

"Our vicar?" Graeme asked.

Lady Eugenia shook her head. "No, the fellow had the living from Lord Fortenberry, as I remember. Reginald got letters from him. Reginald was always corresponding with someone about it or meeting someone. It was my opinion Reginald did it mostly as an excuse to socialize with people when he was at Lydcombe. He always grew bored at the Hall."

"Mr. Ponsonby," Tessa offered. "He was involved with it, wasn't he?"

"Oh, yes." Mrs. Ponsonby spoke up, surprising Graeme, who had forgotten she was there. "Dear George and Montclair were always so close." Her eyes filled with tears.

Lady Eugenia glared at Tessa, then transferred her disfavor to Graeme. "I am sure you can find a worthy charity yourself without digging up painful memories." Having thus declared the subject closed, the dowager countess rang for Norton to clear away tea.

⁂

"Cowardly of us to abandon Lady Montclair to the dowager countess and my mother," James commented, settling back in his chair and accepting a glass of whiskey from Graeme. The two men had escaped to Graeme's study as soon as they politely could, leaving the women of the family in the drawing room.

Graeme laughed. "Trust me. Abigail can take care of herself."

"She didn't seem to be a shrinking violet," James admitted. "She's not the way I remembered her."

"Really?" Graeme sat down across from him, interested. "How do you remember her?"

"I'm not sure." James frowned. "Not shy exactly. But very stiff, reticent. Attractive enough, but she didn't catch one's eye. Truth is, I didn't notice her all that much."

"Neither did I. I'm glad to know I wasn't utterly blind." Graeme idly swirled the amber liquid around in his glass, gazing down into it. "Prescott told me she was intimidated by her father and once away from him, she blossomed."

"That's understandable. *I* was intimidated by her father."

"I doubt that." Graeme glanced up. "Do you mean you had dealings with Thurston Price?"

"I didn't buy that stock, if that's what you mean. Neither did Sir Laurence. Being a cynic has its advantages."

"Then what did you have to do with the man?" Over the years Graeme had learned to read his cousin's inexpressive face, and he did so now. "It was something to do with my situation, wasn't it?"

"I talked to him." James shrugged. "I thought he might be agreeable to a different resolution."

"James. Don't tell me you offered to take my place."

James laughed. "No. I would have if I'd thought it would work—and I wouldn't have made such a muddle of it, either, since I haven't your vexatious romantic ideals. But me getting Miss Price's money would not have helped. Do you really think your father would have allowed me to pay off his debts and fund your estate?"

"No. I'm sure he would not. He would have thought it dishonorable."

"He would have been too proud, you mean. In any case, Price made it clear before I opened my mouth that a lowly baronet would not do for his daughter; his sights were set on an earl. I told him I was seeking a financial arrangement, not marriage, but he would have none of that, either. I knew then there was no hope for you; you had to marry Miss Price."

"So you went to persuade Miss Hinsdale to throw me over."

"To free you from making a ruinous mistake. Yes." There was no hint of apology in the other man's face. "I knew she was more likely to see reason than you."

"And not as likely to hit you."

"True. Though she did make a rather disparaging remark about my character and told me she hoped never to cross my path again."

Graeme's lips quirked up at one corner. "And here I thought Laura was so well-mannered."

"I've found I have a talent for bringing out one's rude side." James was silent for a moment, his eyes on Graeme's face. "What is it that's changed your mind about Lady Montclair's character? Last time we talked, you were sure she was scheming against you. Coercing you into—"

"Yes, well . . ." A faint flush rose in Graeme's cheeks. "I—she—that's not important."

"I take it you haven't found the task too onerous?"

Graeme scowled at him. "That is not what I'm talking about. The other matter—the letters, the secret meetings— wasn't what I thought. It turned out she was trying to help me. The man she met was trying to blackmail her—or give her information, I'm not entirely sure which."

"Blackmail. Are you serious? How did you find this out?"

"I followed her." Graeme related the events leading up to Abigail's arrival in his house.

James listened, his eyebrows soaring upward. "And here I thought you led a dull life."

"Not since Abigail came into it."

"Who shot this man? Why?"

"I've no idea. I presume it must have been some other chap he was pressing for money, and he decided it would be easier to kill him than to pay him. The thing is, the man who was shot was Milton Baker."

"Who? That sounds familiar."

"He was my father's man of business."

"Good Gad, yes, now I remember. But what did he have to blackmail her with— Sorry, I shouldn't ask."

Graeme let out a sigh. "Oh, the devil take it. My father embezzled money from the fund for wounded soldiers."

"So that is why you were asking about that charity today."

Graeme nodded. "He took it to invest in the same stock and of course lost it all."

"Good Lord."

Graeme nodded. "That is how Thurston Price forced me to marry his daughter. It wasn't only the money, though we needed that desperately. Price was a man who believed in insuring the outcome he wanted. He knew what my father had done, and he threatened to reveal it if I didn't marry Abigail."

James gaped at him. Graeme had the dubious satisfaction of seeing that he had managed to shock his cousin. "No wonder you were furious with Price."

"Yes. I believed Abigail knew all about it, that she was a party to the blackmail."

"How do you know she wasn't?"

"By the very fact that she was trying to hide her dealings with Baker from me. If she had been a party to Thurston's blackmail, she would have been well aware that I knew what Reginald had done. But she tried to protect me from learning of it." He gave a wry smile.

"What did she say when you told her about her father's blackmail?"

"I didn't."

"She doesn't know that Thurston forced you into it?"

"She thinks it was just because of my desperate need for money. I started to explain exactly what happened, but then I thought—why put her through that? The man's her father, and she loves him even if he is a scoundrel. It would only hurt her, and she has suffered enough over the years because of him."

"It might help her understand why you were so angry ten years ago."

Graeme shrugged. "I'd rather leave the past in the past. We—things are going smoothly now."

James was silent for a long moment. "Why did you never tell me?"

"I was afraid you would despise Reginald for it."

"Everyone always wanted to spare Reginald."

"No," Graeme said flatly. "Not for his sake. It was for yours. I didn't want you to despise our—your—"

"My uncle?" James quirked a brow. "I don't despise Reginald. How could one? He was unfaithful and foolish with money and generally left his tangles to someone else to clean up, but he was also charming and handsome and warmhearted. He never treated me with aught but affection and kindness, which is more than can be said of Sir

Laurence. Reginald was as he was, just as Sir Laurence was only what he could be. All of us have managed to rub along without creating a terrible scandal. That is all that could be expected."

"I suppose," Graeme said somewhat dubiously.

"Are you certain Reginald embezzled the money?" James said, abandoning the moment of introspection.

Graeme's gaze sharpened. "Why do you ask?"

"Because I find it difficult to believe it of him. You called him honorable and I said proud, but wherever the truth lies in there, he was not the sort of man to put a stain on the family name—not of that sort, anyway. Sleeping with another man's wife was one thing, but common thievery? I wouldn't think so."

"I believed it then. But now I am beginning to wonder. Before he was shot, Baker told Abigail that we hadn't been told the whole story. He asked her for money in return for information that he intimated would throw a different light on the matter."

"Unfortunate that he died before he could tell you."

"Especially for him." Graeme tossed down the whiskey and set his glass aside. "We called on his widow and she said Baker knew my father had not embezzled the money; it was someone else."

"Who?"

"She didn't know."

"Not frightfully helpful."

"The thing is, I believed my father had embezzled the money because *he* was the one who told me it was gone. He said he was to blame. I assumed he meant he had taken the money, but looking back on it, I see that he might have meant that it was his responsibility and he must repay it. That because he was in control of it, he must bear the blame."

"It's the sort of thing he would do." James's tone made clear his words were not admiring. "He would have been more concerned about concealing the scandal than about exposing the culprit."

"Abby—Abigail and I thought we might look into it, see if we could discover what really happened."

"Why? I cannot imagine you opening up that old scandal for the world to see."

"No. It would be just for me." He looked at James. "I would like to know whether my father was really a thief. Perhaps I misjudged him all these years."

"I wouldn't want to delve into that bit of soul-searching if I were you."

"It's better than not knowing the truth."

"Just how do you plan to go about discovering the truth?"

"I am sure Father kept records on the charity, correspondence and such, and I hoped I could find something there—at least the names of those involved in it. But so far we haven't been able to find even a scrap of paper about it. That's why we were late to tea today; we'd been in the attic searching for his old business papers."

"Ah. So that's the reason." James's eyes twinkled.

"Yes." Graeme sent him a flat look.

"I take it you did not find them."

"No. There's more attic to explore, but even if we find the trunk with the papers, I fear we won't find anything about the charity in it. I'm the one who put the papers in the trunk to begin with, and I don't remember any of them pertaining to the charity."

"What's left then? Talking to these chaps Mother remembered?"

"Probably. The ones who are still alive, at least. But something Grandmother said started me thinking. She said it was her opinion Father used the invalid soldiers' fund to relieve his boredom at the estate. And it occurred to me that much of his work with it would have been at Lydcombe Hall—perhaps the bulk of it, if she's right."

"Lady Eugenia is always right."

"Naturally. Anything he did at Lydcombe is likely to still be there. I never used his office. Mother couldn't bear to have it disturbed. There's so much more room at the Hall, I just turned one of the other rooms into my study. If there is anything to find about the charity, I think we'll find it there."

"Then you're going back to Lydcombe Hall?" James quirked an eyebrow. "I didn't get the impression your wife was in favor of visiting the estate."

"Mm. Abigail won't be inclined to accede to Grandmother's wishes." He smiled faintly. "But I think I can persuade her."

chapter 20

Abby drew in her breath as the double lines of pollarded lime trees opened up, revealing a wide green expanse, with Lydcombe Hall at the top, like the jewel in a crown. From the smile on Graeme's face, she thought that for him it probably was.

It was easy to see why he loved the house. Large and symmetrical, it was built of brick that must once have been red and had faded through time into almost a deep rose, outlined along the corners and across the top with white stone cornices. Leading from the drive to the front door were shallow, terraced steps built of the same white stone. On either side stood planters boasting a profusion of pansies in a rainbow of hues. The house managed to appear elegant, gracious, and homey, all at the same time.

Graeme turned to her, smiling, and took her hand. "There she is. What do you think?"

"I think it's wonderful." Any other answer would have been unthinkable in the face of Graeme's obvious pleasure, but in truth, the place was beautiful. She had a vision of her child growing up here, happy and healthy and secure, a dark-haired boy or girl—why not both?—and unexpectedly her eyes welled with tears.

She blinked them away. Better not to dream of things that might not ever come to pass. Right now, she must brace herself to meet his mother.

Abby didn't mind visiting Lydcombe Hall, aside from a brief irritation at the appearance of giving in to Lady Eugenia's wishes. Hopefully they would find papers relating to Lord Reginald's charity here. A longer search of the attic in the London house had turned up nothing. More alluring than that, though, was the prospect of getting out from under the gaze of Graeme's grandmother. The Hall, Graeme assured her, was much larger, and his mother far less intrusive.

Abby remembered Lady Montclair as a sweet-faced, sweet-tempered woman. Though Abby had not spent much time in her company before their wedding, Mirabelle had been pleasant, even kind. Still, no mother could be happy about her son having to marry a woman he did not want. If Graeme had believed Abby was cut from the same cloth as her father, doubtless his mother did as well.

Ten years of Abby's absence would not have made the woman like her any better. No doubt she resented Abby for showing up again, just as Graeme had. Graeme now seemed content with their arrangement, even pleased with it—at least in the bedroom. But there was no reason for his mother to have changed her mind.

Abby's stomach knotted as the carriage rolled to a stop in front of the house. The double front doors opened, framing a rotund man in formal black and white. His face was wreathed in smiles in a most un-butler-like fashion.

"Master Graeme." He hurried down the steps to open the carriage door and put down the step. "Welcome home."

"Master Graeme?" Abigail murmured, her eyes twinkling. "Difficult to maintain one's stature when the man's known me since I was in leading strings," he told her before he left the carriage. "Fletcher. It's good to be home. You're looking well."

"Good of you to say so, sir."

Graeme reached back to give Abigail his hand as she left the carriage. "Allow me to introduce my wife."

"Lady Montclair." Fletcher honored her with a gracious bow. "I hope you will find everything in order."

"Thank you, Fletcher. I am sure I will."

The servants had formed a line to the door, and Abby was introduced to a dizzying array of names and faces, from the housekeeper to the second upstairs maid. Abby hoped that Molly would find herself more at home among this group than she had with the servants in the London house. The housekeeper, Mrs. Sinclair, had a touch of Scottish burr in her tone.

They walked into an enormous entry hall open to the second floor. Abby drew in a breath of admiration at seeing the graceful double staircase. "Graeme. How lovely."

A woman clad in brilliant purple hurried down the stairs toward them. Abby recognized Graeme's mother at once. Slightly plumper, with more gray threaded through her hair and more lines in her face than ten years ago, still she looked much the same. Like her more flamboyant sister Tessa, Lady Montclair had dark hair and gray eyes, and Abby was sure that she had probably had dozens of admirers when she was young.

"It's so wonderful to have you home again!" Mirabelle exclaimed, holding out her arms to Graeme.

"Hello, Mother." Graeme embraced her and bent to kiss her cheek, affection clear upon his face. "You remember Abigail."

"Of course." Graeme's mother turned to her with no diminution of her happy glow. "Welcome to Lydcombe Hall, my dear."

To Abby's surprise, Mirabelle kissed her on the cheek. "Thank you, Lady Montclair. I am happy to see you again."

"Oh, please don't be so formal with me. You must call me Mirabelle, or perhaps Mother, as Graeme does?" She lifted her brows in a hopeful way. "You are, after all, my daughter now. Not, of course, that I would dare to replace your own mother, so I perfectly understand if you don't wish to."

"No, I mean, yes, of course, if you would like it. My own mother died many years ago."

"My dear! I am so sorry. I had forgotten. It must have been hard growing up without a mother."

Clearly, making conversation with Graeme's mother would not be a problem. Abby glanced over at Graeme as Mirabelle continued to chatter, and he smiled and winked. Abby was suddenly filled with warmth. She was going to enjoy it here.

⚬⚭⚬

The next day, they started their search of the previous Lord Montclair's study. The room was large and filled with papers, books, and sundry other items all jumbled together in drawers and shelves and trunks. The place was the complete opposite of Graeme's tidy office, and going through it was a slow process.

Their progress was slowed even more because they often drifted off into conversation and laughter. Each day the amount of time they spent in the study became shorter, taken up by long walks through the garden or rides around the estate.

Lydcombe Hall was set in a large, well-kept park, with wilder woods beckoning beyond that, perfect for a ride or long walk. The gardens were at their glorious best, an array of color and scents, with arbors and fountains and benches where one could sit and enjoy the peace. Where they could be alone together.

In London there had always been social engagements, parties, and callers, and when they were at home, they were rarely alone. With both Lady Eugenia and her companion in the same house, not to mention countless servants, there was little privacy except behind the closed door of their bedroom.

Here, there was no social activity beyond an occasional visit from the vicar and his wife, and the house was larger and emptier. Best of all, Graeme's mother did not push or pry, and, to Abby's amazement, showed not the slightest antipathy toward Abby. Mirabelle tactfully spent most of her time engaged in her usual tasks, giving the married couple ample time alone together.

"Your mother is a jewel," Abigail told Graeme one afternoon as they strolled through the rose garden, coming to stop beneath a latticework arbor.

He had taken her hand as they walked, something she had noticed him doing more and more frequently since they arrived. He smiled as he tugged her down onto the stone bench beside him. "She is that. I'm glad you like her."

"I do. I can see the physical resemblance between her and your aunt, but their personalities are very different." She stopped, realizing that she had not been exactly tactful. "Not that I mean anything bad about your aunt . . ."

Graeme chuckled. "No, you're right, they are very different. Aunt Tessa is charming and beautiful and full of life, but she is best taken in small doses."

"She is not like her son, either. Sir James seems to be a very . . . contained person."

"Yes. He believes in keeping everything under control."

"So do you, but beneath that one can sense the emotions in you, the kindness and depth of feeling. I'm not so sure it's there in your cousin."

Graeme glanced at her, half-amused. "You are so straight-forward. You keep me off-balance."

Abigail shrugged. "I've never been very good at half-truths or polite deceptions. I generally say what I think or I simply hold my tongue."

"As you did when I first met you."

"Yes. I was petrified I would do or say the wrong thing. Everything was so unfamiliar. I didn't belong, and I could tell all the people I met thought the same thing. I would say something, and they would look a certain way, as if they were laughing without really doing so. Then I knew what I said had been gauche. Wrong in some way. But the problem was I didn't know exactly why."

"I am sorry it was difficult for you." He did not look at her, but at her hand cradled in his. Idly he traced the bones of her hands down to her fingertips. "I am sorry I made it more so."

"No need for apologies." She laid her other hand on top of his. "I was naïve; I should have been more aware of what was happening."

"Why did you come here with your father? Why were you willing to marry some pompous British fool?"

Abby chuckled. "You weren't pompous. Or a fool."

"But you seem not to care for a title."

"No."

"Or how far one can trace back one's lineage. Or how blue one's blood is."

"That's true."

Graeme brushed his lips against hers, then settled back against the stone bench, curling his arm around her. "Then why were you agreeable to the marriage? Why did you go along with what he wanted?"

Abby thought for a moment. "There were several reasons. First, because it was what my father wanted. It's hard to swim upstream. He could always out-reason, out-argue any objection. Another part was escaping his dominion. Not having to answer to him or ask him for every single thing I wanted. The money from my grandparents' trust did not come to me, you see, until I was twenty-one *or* married."

"So those were two of the reasons. And the rest?"

She turned her head and looked at him thoughtfully, then said, "I met you."

Graeme's eyes widened fractionally. "I was scarcely charming."

"Oh, but you were. You were elegant and polite, all the things my father was not. You didn't try to flatter or seduce me, as the fortune hunters did."

He chuckled. "So my appeal lay in qualities I did not possess."

"I suppose so. In a way." Abby smiled. She wasn't about to confess that she'd gone weak in the knees when she saw him or that her heart had lifted when he smiled. And she certainly did not want to start examining his reasons for marrying her. She looked out across the view of the house and gardens. "It must have been wonderful growing up here."

"It was. Lonely sometimes, without any siblings. I saw James frequently, but it wasn't the same. He didn't live here."

"I often wished I'd had a sister—lots of sisters. It seemed like such fun—dressing for a party, doing our hair, gossiping and laughing together. I wished I could wake up one morning and magically be one of the Bennet sisters."

"Who were they? Friends?"

Abby laughed. "Of a sort. They were in a book. *Pride and Prejudice*. I used to read it over and over."

"Ah, I see. I had a few of that kind of friends, as well."

"Really?"

"Yes, really." He raised a quizzical eyebrow. "Did you think I didn't read?"

"No. You just seem so . . . I don't know, so *complete* somehow. So sure of who you are and where you belong. You are a part of something—this land, your family, your ancestors."

"I suppose I am. Doesn't mean I didn't long for adventure, though. Sir Walter Scott. *Ivanhoe*. *Waverly*."

"I loved those, too!" Abby beamed. "Alexandre Dumas?"

"Indeed. *The Three Musketeers*."

"*The Count of Monte Cristo*." Abby laughed. "There. So we have something in common."

"We'll have much more than that in common one day: we'll have a child."

"Yes, that's true." A warmth bloomed in her chest. That would be an unending bond between them. "Or, at least, I hope we will." She paused, then said, "It's a little frightening, isn't it, the thought of being a parent? What if I do something wrong?"

He smiled at her. "You needn't worry. I think you'll make an excellent mother."

Abby glanced at him, surprised. Was he serious? Teasing? Graeme crooked his finger under her chin and tilted her head up. He kissed her again, not the light brush of his lips as before, but a firm, confident kiss that stopped just short of passionate invitation. A promise, she thought, and a certainty, to be explored fully later.

He leaned back, holding her in the crook of his arm. She nestled against his shoulder, and they simply sat, gazing in idle contentment at the scene before them. A cloud drifted lazily over the garden, casting a fleeting shadow. Abby could hear the hum of bees visiting the flowers.

She didn't realize she had fallen asleep until she woke up. She blinked, taking in the view and noting that the sun had drifted lower in the sky. "Oh. I'm sorry." Abby sat up, brushing back a strand of hair that had caught on Graeme's jacket. "I didn't mean to fall asleep."

He smiled in that way that lit his eyes while touching only the corner of his mouth, an expression that never failed to stir a vague warmth inside her. "It's all right. I rather enjoyed it, actually."

As she often did, Abby wondered if he meant it. It was difficult to judge the worth of compliments given by such a polite man. She turned aside, tucking the strand of hair behind her ear. "I suppose we should get back to your father's study."

"You don't sound very eager." He grinned, standing up and pulling her up with him.

"I always hate to leave the garden. But I enjoy digging through the things in the study. It satisfies my dreadful curiosity. Though I do rather wonder at his keeping the receipts for all those hats."

Graeme laughed. "My father loved hats. He must have had fifty of them. He was, I fear, a vain man."

"Not surprising." When he sent her a questioning look, she said, "I saw the man, you know. He was terribly handsome."

"I've heard people say so."

"Don't be coy." Abby gave his arm a pinch. "You know perfectly well he was the sort of man women swooned over. I am sure you also know you look a good deal like him."

"Are you saying I'm vain?"

"I'm saying you're handsome." Impulsively, Abby stretched up and kissed him, then broke away, running lightly up the steps to the terrace. Smiling, Graeme followed her.

They spent the rest of the afternoon, as they had many days before, searching for documents related to the Fund for Invalid Soldiers. They had worked their way outward from the central desk, sifting through a jumble of papers. Graeme's father had not been an organized soul. Thinking of her own father's perfectly ordered desk, Abby had to smile. The two men could not have been more different.

"There must be some order to the way he kept his records," she said, gazing around the room. "Though I cannot imagine what it was."

Graeme shrugged. "My father and I didn't think alike, usually."

"Well, where shall we start today? We have cabinets, trunks, bookcases." She swept a hand toward one end of the room they had not yet explored.

Graeme considered the problem for a moment, then

straightened, his face brightening. "You know . . ." He started toward the opposite wall.

"What?" Abby joined him in front of a sturdy chest. It was richly made, with some sort of emblem carved on either side of the fastenings.

"This is a regimental trunk. And that is the way my father might think."

"Wha— Oh!" Her face cleared. "You mean because it was a fund for soldiers. So a regimental trunk."

"We'll see." He bent down to open it and lifted out a shallow tray. Below were stacks of papers, as well as an account book. Graeme reached in and picked up the blue-backed book, opening it. On the inside, in a black, spidery hand, were the words *Benevolent Fund for the Care of Invalid Soldiers*.

"You found it!"

chapter 21

Abby leaned in to peer down at the open book in his hands. "Is that your father's handwriting?"

"I don't believe so. Just a minute." He walked across the room to the desk.

Abby knelt on the floor beside the trunk and began to sort through the papers. "These all appear to be letters to various people."

Graeme came back, carrying another account book, and sat down beside her. Handing her the charity's book, he opened the other one to the title page.

"These are his personal accounts, so I know this is his hand." They looked back and forth between the two.

"They're not the same."

"You're right." He turned the page to the numbers. "Now, the numbers, I'm not so sure about. They are rather similar."

"No, look at this nine." She pointed from one book to another. "They're different." Abby turned another page of the charity's account book. "But, look, these numbers are in a different hand."

"So two different people entered the figures."

She looked at him. "That would indicate that someone else had access to the money, wouldn't it?"

"At least in counting and entering the money they received. If they took small amounts, Father probably wouldn't have noticed."

Abby nodded. "True. But if it was taken to invest in the stock, it wouldn't have been done over time like that. He would have needed a large amount at once. The most likely thing would be taking a sum out of the bank account."

"Or perhaps receiving a large amount and not depositing it." Graeme leaned back against the trunk, staring off into the distance in thought. "I never paid much attention. It was Father's charity, and I never participated. But as I recall, they had events at which they raised money, like church fetes, that sort of thing. And at certain times they'd write around asking for donations."

Abby perused the columns of figures. "Yes, there aren't many entries, even though it covers several years. Several of them are in December in succeeding years. Here's one that says 'St. V.'"

Graeme looked over her shoulder. Unconsciously Abby leaned against him, and he curved his arm around her. "St. V is a church, I'd guess. Maybe they held some sort of money-raising thing there. St. Vincent, maybe?"

"Is that the village church?"

"No, that's All Saints."

"All Saints," Abby repeated, pointing to another notation. "Here. AS." She ran her finger down the lines. "Several initials like that, a couple of other Saints, here's a Lord F."

"Fortenberry. Aunt Tessa mentioned him the other day. I wish I had paid more attention when Father was still alive." He was silent for a moment, thinking, his hand idly stroking up and down her arm. Abby settled against him, enjoying the warmth of his arm around her, the faint scent of his shaving soap, the quiet companionship. This was what she had once hoped for, she thought. She had not known enough about passion to even dream of that, but she had yearned for this sweet feeling of being joined to someone, of belonging.

She wondered how many moments like this she would have. She feared it would change when she became pregnant. As Graeme had pointed out, the child would be a connection between them always. But the arrival of an heir would mean there was no reason to share a bed anymore. However much Graeme appeared to enjoy their lovemaking, she could not help but fear that he would be relieved to be free of the obligation. Tears welled in her eyes, and she hastily blinked them away. She was not about to waste this lovely moment thinking of losing it.

"I remember he used to have a money box for the charity," Graeme mused, obviously unaware of the emotions chasing through Abigail. "I think Father would get payments from donors and keep them in there, but at some point, he would deposit it in the bank."

"So someone could have slipped money out of that box before he took it to the bank. Do you think he knew who it was who had taken it?"

Graeme's lips brushed her hair. "It is kind of you to assume it was someone other than my father. I'm not entirely convinced of that yet."

"Why else would Mr. Baker have told his wife that? He was trying to sell me information. He's bound to have had something more than that vague statement."

"Let's say you're right and it happened that way. I'm unsure how we will discover the culprit. I doubt he left his chit in the box as replacement."

"No, but perhaps Mr. Baker wasn't the only person who knew about it. There might have been suspicions among the members."

"True." Graeme sighed. "Nothing for it, then, but to dig through all this correspondence." Yet he did not move to pull them out of the trunk. "Of course, we could return to it later."

"Indeed?" She drew back, giving him an arch look. "And what would we do instead?"

"I can think of one or two things." He trailed his forefinger down her cheek. "You never did explain what else your 'mentor' taught you about gentlemen's preferences."

"What—" Abby began, puzzled, then her face cleared and she laughed softly. "Oh. *Those* things."

"Yes. Perhaps you'd care to demonstrate some of them to me."

"I might—though some of them I didn't quite understand. Perhaps you would be willing to explain them to me."

"Indeed." He leaned in to murmur in her ear, the touch of his breath on her skin sending a shiver through her. "I would be most willing."

Abby rose lithely to her feet, and he followed, but when they reached the door, to her surprise he merely turned the lock. Another tingle of excitement ran through her, and she looked up into his face. "Here? Now?"

His smile was slow and sensual. "Here. Now." He took her hand, pulling her gently to him. "If that suits you, my lady."

"That suits me very well," Abby said and went into his arms.

◦◦◦

There were, as it turned out, a number of things Abby had been shown, and Graeme's explanation of them was detailed and thorough. As a result, they missed afternoon tea altogether, and their work was abandoned until the following day.

The next afternoon, they sifted through the rest of the trunk. Most of the papers were letters written to Lord Reginald, mixed in with a few receipts. There was nothing to be learned from them other than the names of men who had contributed to the fund, which Abby jotted down.

"Most of these letters are from this Colonel Rollins your grandmother mentioned."

"I think the fund was his idea. Father knew him from his club."

"He seems a likely candidate for the embezzler. He did a lot of work with the society. It seems as if he was the one who determined what soldiers or societies received payments from the fund."

"Mm. He might have had access to the money. On the other hand, several of these letters are recommendations of a worthy recipient, which would indicate that Father was the one who actually handed out the money, based on the colonel's opinion."

"Rollins would be the best person to talk to. He'd be likely to know the most about what went on in the charity."

"Yes, but unfortunately he died two years ago. I asked Mother about him this morning."

"Oh. Well, that's disappointing." Abby leaned over to

dig into the bottom of the trunk. "Ha!" She waved a piece of paper. "Look. The board members are on this letterhead."

Graeme grinned at her and snatched the paper from her hand, settling back against the wall to study the letter. Abigail watched him. He had taken off his jacket and rolled up his sleeves as they worked. His hair fell carelessly down over his forehead, and he looked so relaxed and at ease that it made something in her chest ache. She wished she could hold on to to this small, unimportant moment forever.

"Fortenberry. He's a pompous old fool, but at least he's still alive. Here's Mrs. Ponsonby's husband, George. He was a good friend of Father's, as I remember, but he's dead, as well. Carrington Jones—I don't know him. Sir Laurence—that's James's father."

"I thought your aunt said he wasn't involved in it, just contributed."

"Aunt Tessa's accuracy on matters of business is not something on which one can rely. Now if it was a hat she'd bought or a party she attended ten years ago, I'd take her word."

"But Sir Laurence is dead, too, isn't he?" Abby said. "Were he and your father friends?"

He let out a little huffing laugh. "No, I don't think so . . . Albert Boddington. I think I've met him. Henry Bracewell—Lord, he's passed on, too."

"Graeme . . ." Abby frowned. "Doesn't it seem as if a lot of these men have died? I mean, your father, James's father, Mr. Ponsonby, Bracewell . . ."

"Colonel Rollins." He narrowed his eyes. "Are you suggesting that it had something to do with the charity? The embezzlement?"

"I don't know. But it seems a little odd that so many men connected to it have died."

"I am certain my father's death was unrelated. He died from pneumonia one winter when he got caught out in the rain. Sir Laurence had a heart attack. I don't know about the others. The thing is, they were all of an age with my father. Sir Laurence was older. And I believe Colonel Rollins was a good bit older than either one of them. Perhaps in any group that age, a number of them might die over the course of ten years."

"Someone shot Mr. Baker."

"True." He frowned. "But there might have been any number of reasons someone wanted him dead. It wasn't necessarily about this."

"He was about to tell me the story behind the embezzlement."

Graeme sat up straighter and ran his hands back through his hair. He gazed out the window as if it might hold some answer. "You're saying that someone knew Baker was meeting you there that night, knew what he was going to say, and shot him right at the crucial moment when he was about to tell you? Seems like a tremendous run of luck on the shooter's part."

"He could have followed Baker. Perhaps Mr. Baker approached him also, saying he wouldn't reveal the truth if this other man paid him."

"He could just as easily have followed him for some other reason, or have seen him standing there beneath a streetlamp, an easy target, and decided it was too good an opportunity to pass up."

"So you don't think he was killed because he was going to tell me what happened?" Abby asked.

"I don't know. But if Baker was trying to extort money from you or from this embezzler—who we aren't sure even exists—he was likely to have done the same thing to other people. Perhaps about something more serious than an embezzlement of some charitable funds."

"Especially one that took place ten years ago."

"Precisely." Graeme nodded. "The money was replaced. Who could even prove there had been a crime? There were no rumors, no gossip. As you pointed out, several of the board members aren't even alive now. My father was the only person harmed, and we wouldn't expose the thief because we'd only stir up a scandal."

"Yes. It does seem unlikely to be worth killing anyone over."

"I am beginning to wonder if we'll be able to discover anything. The financial logs were no help; the letters don't tell us anything."

"We found the names of the people involved," Abby pointed out. "We can talk to them; perhaps one of them might have information that would help us."

"We'll have to return to London for that." Graeme did not appear enthused about the idea.

Abby was certain she was not. "Maybe it won't take long, and we can come back home."

"Then you like it here?" His expression sharpened.

"Yes." Abby was surprised at his question. "Of course. Do you not? Do you prefer London?"

"No, Lydcombe Hall is my home."

"You know . . . perhaps we should check some other places here, as well. There might be something stored in the attic, as there was in town."

He smiled slowly. "I believe you're right. We really

ought to check the estate manager's office as well. Father might have put some of the records there. This could take a long time."

∞

Days turned into weeks, and in the end, it was over a month before they took the train back to London.

"Oh. You're here again," Lady Eugenia said when they walked into the drawing room of the London house, her voice tinged with such a lack of enthusiasm that Abby had to choke back a laugh.

"What a nice surprise!" Mrs. Ponsonby bounced to her feet, doing her best to counter the dowager countess's tone. "It hasn't been the same without you."

"True. No one singing in the hallways," Lady Eugenia added drily.

"Well, I shall have to see what I can do to enliven the atmosphere," Abby replied, mischief lurking in her voice.

"No doubt you will." The corner of Lady Eugenia's mouth twitched, almost as if she were about to smile.

"I am overwhelmed by your welcome, Grandmother." Graeme came forward to bow over her hand.

"Don't be impertinent." But Lady Eugenia smiled at him and squeezed his hand, her eyes searching his face. "You're looking well, my boy."

"Thank you. I am feeling well. I would say the same about you."

"You wouldn't if your back was as stiff as mine," she retorted in an amiable tone. "Sit down, sit down, and tell us why you are here. I thought you would stay in the country. Philomena, ring for some tea for the children."

As Mrs. Ponsonby hurried to do her bidding, Graeme dropped onto the sofa beside Abigail, taking her hand.

Abigail noticed that the countess's piercing gaze went to their linked hands, though she said nothing.

"I told you we would be gone for just a few weeks," Graeme pointed out mildly.

"Yes, but I assumed you would change your mind and stay." She turned toward Abigail. "Did you not enjoy Lydcombe Hall?"

"I thought it was lovely, and Graeme's mother is such a gracious, hospitable hostess." Again she saw the sparkle in the older woman's hooded eyes. Abby was never certain whether Lady Eugenia disliked her or simply enjoyed having someone with whom to cross swords. Everyone around the countess was too much in awe of her to do so, and of course sparring with Mrs. Ponsonby would be akin to punching a pillow.

"Yes. Poor Mirabelle has an unfortunate tendency to like everyone."

"There were a few people I need to speak with here," Graeme said. "Is Lord Fortenberry still in the city?"

"I should think so. I would be surprised if that man ever left his club."

"What about Carrington Jones? Do you know him? Or Albert Boddington?"

"Carrington Jones? Of course I know him. He was at Oxford with your father—well, for a year or so. I was surprised he got that far. He married one of the Bracewell girls, you know."

"Henry Bracewell's daughter?"

"His sister. Jones is irredeemably foolish—well, he would have to be, wouldn't he, to marry Madelyn Bracewell? Whatever made you think of him?"

"He was one of the men involved in the fund for wounded soldiers."

"Are you still going on about that? I cannot imagine why you're so interested."

Graeme shrugged. "I thought it might be nice to take it up again. In memory of Father, you see."

"Sounds like nonsense to me."

"Yes, but do you know where Mr. Jones lives? I'd like to call on him. And Mr. Boddington, as well. There are others: Gerard Fitzwilliam, someone named Bangs, W. J. Walters."

"Bangs is Oliver Bangston—odd man; I understand he's become something of a recluse. I imagine he'll see you, though, for Reginald's sake. He used to follow him around like a puppy. If you want to see Fortenberry, you need only go to his club," she assured them. "Mr. Boddington will be at Lady Salwell's soiree on Friday. He is pursuing Mrs. Hargreaves, whose husband finally died and left her a tidy fortune. Mrs. Hargreaves is Lady Salwell's sister. This Gerald Fitzwilliam . . . I don't know him."

"*Gerard* Fitzwilliam," Graeme corrected.

The dowager countess gave him a long look. "Gerald, Gerard—makes no difference. I don't know the man, so he is no one of importance."

Unsurprisingly, the information the dowager countess gave them turned out to be accurate on all counts. Albert Boddington was indeed at Lady Salwell's party, and Lord Fortenberry spent most of his time at his club. Unfortunately, neither of the two men provided any helpful information.

"Fortenberry does well to remember his own name, let alone anything about the soldiers' fund," Graeme told

Abigail in disgust when he returned from quizzing the elderly lord. "He kept calling me 'Reggie' and asking me when I intended to ask for Mirabelle's hand."

"Oh, dear," Abby commiserated. They were seated on the graceful love seat in Abby's chamber, Graeme having managed to sneak up the back stairs when he returned, thus avoiding his grandmother and her guests in the drawing room.

"He looked utterly blank when I asked him about the soldiers' fund. I thought at least he might remember the vicar's name, since Grandmother thought he had the living from Fortenberry, but he could not."

"If we could find out the name of the church it would help. I'm sure they have a record of the vicars' names throughout the years."

"One of the chaps at the club told me that Jones was in Scotland at his fishing lodge. He should be back before long, though, now that autumn's approaching."

"Where do we go next? What about that name your grandmother didn't recognize?"

"Fitzwilliam? Neither Fortenberry nor Boddington could recall him; maybe Bangston or one of the others will have more information about him. I thought I would try Bangston next. If he was as big an admirer of Father's as Grandmother suggested, he might have more knowledge." He glanced at Abby. "If he's as much a recluse as Grandmother claims, I fear I should go there alone."

Abby heaved a sigh. "I suppose, though I must say it's most unfair that I have been excluded from talking to two of these men."

"Mm." He leaned over to kiss her forehead. "Look at it this way: at least you won't have to travel to Sussex."

The truth was, little as she liked the thought of Graeme leaving, even for two days, Abby had little desire to go with him. Her stomach had been queasy for the past few days, and the thought of the sway and rattle of a train ride was enough to make her gorge rise.

Abigail had not told Graeme about her queasiness. She felt guilty about it since she suspected that the reason for the nausea was not illness but pregnancy. She was almost two months overdue, as well. Not to mention the fact that she was frequently tired in the afternoons.

It was early stages yet, she told herself. It would be cruel to get Graeme's hopes up if it turned out that she was wrong. Of course, she knew that was not the real reason behind her reluctance. The truth was that she feared what would happen when he knew. Once she was with child, their bargain would be fulfilled. There would no longer be any reason for him to make love to her.

Indeed, there wouldn't be any reason for him to even stay with her. Graeme could go back to Lydcombe Hall, the place he loved, where he had been living in solitary happiness before she arrived, and leave her here in London. The thought of that happening brought tears to her eyes.

It seemed the cruelest joke that it appeared she was about to have what she had wanted so much . . . and now it filled her with as much dread as joy.

chapter 22

Graeme dawdled about making the trip to Sussex, seemingly as uneager to go as Abby was to have him leave, but finally, a week later, he took the train to see Mr. Bangston. After he left, Abby spent most of her day in the library, some of the time reading, and the rest of the time missing Graeme. She told herself it was ridiculous. She had spent all her life without him, yet now she was restless and lonely and curiously incomplete because Graeme would be gone for a day and a half.

Mrs. Ponsonby took it upon herself to keep her company. Abby felt sorry for the woman—being a penniless relation dependent on others' charity was a hard enough life, but to be constantly at the beck and call of Lady Eugenia seemed especially cruel. So she did her best to smile and chat. But after an afternoon spent this way, her facial muscles hurt and her mind resembled cotton wool, so she pled a headache and retired to her bedroom.

Brushing out her hair and changing into her nightclothes, she settled down on the love seat and opened a book. She made little progress, for her mind kept wandering to Graeme. It was sensible for him to spend the night at an inn in Lewin, near Mr. Bangston's home. He would take an early train and be home tomorrow afternoon. It was silly, really, to wish he had hurried to catch an afternoon train just because she didn't want to sleep alone.

It occurred to her that this would be the first night since Graeme had fished her out of the Thames that she would sleep alone in her bed. Abby smiled to herself. Surely that must indicate more than mere acceptance of their bargain on Graeme's part. Perhaps if she told him she suspected she was pregnant, he would not turn away from her, relieved to be done. Then she could feel an unmitigated joy at the prospect of the life growing inside her. Graeme's child.

The thought melted her, and she spent some time in happy daydreams before doubt crept through her again. If she was wrong about his desire for her, it would be over as soon as she told him. Better to let it go a little longer. She should not tell him until she was absolutely sure.

Molly bustled in with a cup of hot chocolate. Graeme's mother habitually had a cup of hot chocolate each night before retiring, and Abby had begun joining her in it when they were at Lydcombe Hall. After they returned to London, Abby continued the practice. Though the hot chocolate here was not as delicious as that served on the estate (though she would never have admitted it to their London cook), Abby looked forward to it. Recently some familiar foods had started to taste wrong to her, but hot chocolate was, if anything, even more appealing than it had been.

Tonight, however, the first sip left a chalky aftertaste in her mouth. Abby said nothing about it to Molly, however. Her maid would doubtless upbraid the cook for it, and the last thing Abby wanted was to be the cause for discord in the dowager countess's house—or for Molly to be any more antagonistic to the rest of the staff than she already was.

Abby took another couple of sips, then put the cup aside as soon as Molly left the room. Setting her candle on the table beside the bed, she crawled under the covers to continue reading. It was hard to keep her attention on the book; her mind kept wandering to Graeme. Resting the open book on her lap, she leaned back against the pillows behind her, letting her mind wander. Her eyes fluttered closed.

She knelt in front of the fireplace, searching frantically through a pile of papers before her. She had to find it. It was far too hot; she was sweating, and she could feel the heat of the fire upon her cheeks. She should move back, but first she had to find it. Graeme wanted it. The fire crackled in her ear. The air was smoky. Abby coughed, waving away the gray smoke. The flue was closed. She groped toward the fireplace. She had to open it. But she could not find the fireplace, could not even see it. She began to cough and could not stop.

Abby's eyes opened, then closed again. She wanted only to sleep, but she was coughing too hard. She opened her eyes again, still so lost in her dream that she was not surprised to see bright orange flames and smoke drifting through the air. An instant later fear jolted through her. The flames were licking up the drapes at the window.

The stab of terror was enough to send her crawling across the bed away from the fire. Still befogged by sleep, she could not think clearly, and her eyes kept closing. Suddenly she was falling, and she hit the floor with a thud. It was enough to jar her awake again though she lay stunned, staring up at the ceiling as she struggled to pull air back into her lungs.

She saw flames above her, her mind moving so slowly it took a moment to realize that the canopy of her bed was now on fire. "Graeme."

She began to crawl away, her mind so numb she could not think beyond the idea that she had to get to Graeme.

Abby reached the wall and rested her head against it as she gave way to a paroxysm of coughing. Looking up, she saw the bell cord hanging. She reached up and jerked at the cord.

She began to crawl again, keeping her shoulder to the wall, though her body was racked with coughs. She made it to the door into Graeme's room at last, but she could not reach the handle. She was so very sleepy. As she fell into the dark void, she heard a woman screaming.

When Abby awoke again, she was lying on her side, her cheek against the rough wool of a rug, and she was coughing. She could not stop. It didn't help that someone was repeatedly slapping her on the back.

"Stop!" Abby gasped.

"Oh, lovie!" It was Molly's voice, and it was, astonishingly, choked with tears. Abby felt the drops splashing on her cheek. "You're all right!"

Heavy feet pounded past down the hallway, and people shouted. Gradually Abby's cough began to subside. She tried to open her eyes but couldn't, once again drifting into darkness.

"Abby!" An agitated shout cut through the air, and the next thing she knew, Graeme was kneeling on the floor beside her, lifting her and cradling her against him. "Abby, my God! What happened? Are you— Abby, wake up!"

She forced her eyes open. Graeme was leaning over her, his face stark white. A smile curved her lips. "Graeme." She snuggled into his chest and fell asleep again.

The next time Abby awoke, she was lying in a soft bed. She blinked up at the tester, then slowly turned her head. Graeme sat in an armchair beside the bed, his head resting against the chair and his eyes closed.

"Graeme." The word came out more a croak than speech.

His eyes flew open. "Abby! Thank God, you're awake."

"What—" Vague memories of flames and smoke flitted through her mind. She remembered looking through papers in front of the fire—no, that had been a dream. Reality had been the blazing draperies, the smoke clouding the air.

"Your drapes caught on fire. You must have fallen asleep and left a candle burning, and it set fire to the drapes."

Had she? Abby struggled to remember.

"Thank goodness you woke up and managed to ring for the servants. Molly found you by the connecting door to this room." He took her hand, rubbing his thumb over it. "You were very fortunate. By the time Molly got there, the canopy was on fire and falling onto the bed." He tightened his hand around hers. "You would have been burned if you'd still been lying there."

Abby drew in a sharp breath, which set off another paroxysm of coughing. Graeme poured her a glass of water, and she gratefully took a gulp. Her mouth and throat were parched. When the water hit her stomach, it lurched, and for a moment she was afraid that she was about to embarrass herself and toss it all back up. Her stomach settled. She lay back against the pillows. She remembered crawling across the floor, her only thought of finding Graeme, forgetting that he was not home.

Abby frowned. "Why are you here? I thought you were in Sussex."

"I didn't stay. I . . ." He rubbed the back of his neck in an embarrassed manner. "I decided I didn't want to, um, waste an evening there. Fortunately, I was able to catch the evening train back to London."

Abby smiled. He hadn't wanted to spend the evening away. "I'm glad."

"I only wish I'd made it earlier. When I think what could have happened to you . . ."

"I can't believe I fell asleep reading. I never do that." But she remembered how very sleepy she had felt the evening before.

He leaned down, hooking his hand around the nape of her neck, and kissed her forehead. "I'm glad you're safe."

Abby curled her arms around his neck. "And I'm glad you're home."

"So am I." He brushed his lips against hers. "Now go back to sleep. You need the rest."

Reluctantly she let her arms fall away from him. "I will if you'll lie down with me."

"Are you sure? I don't want to disturb you."

She laughed. "I'm sure. I'm not ill or injured . . . just a little fuzzy-headed. I'll sleep better if you're here."

He smiled and stripped off his clothes. Climbing into bed beside her, he took her in his arms. Abby snuggled up against him, relaxing and letting sleep take her. Just as she drifted off, a single thought popped into her brain: how had the candle caught the drapes on fire when it had been sitting in the middle of the table?

∞

Abby was still groggy the next morning when she was awakened by Molly bringing in a breakfast of tea and toast. Molly hugged Abby tightly, then went on to scold her for her carelessness.

"How many times have I told you not to sit in your bed reading?"

"It's beyond count." Abby smiled. She wasn't sure why, but it made her feel better to hear her old nurse's familiar words.

Molly sniffed. "Not that you ever listened."

"I've never fallen asleep before," Abby protested. "A book is more likely to keep me awake than put me to sleep."

"Not this time. And what in heaven's name were you thinking, setting the candle down so close to the drapes?"

"I didn't. I put it down in the middle of the table. I'm certain."

"So you're saying that candlestick walked itself over to the side?" Molly crossed her arms and fixed Abby with a stern gaze that made her feel approximately five years old. "Or maybe the dowager countess goes creeping about the house at night moving folks' candles about?"

"No, of course not." Abby heaved a sigh. "You're right; I must have put it there." No doubt her momentary carelessness, like her sleepiness and the nausea and the occasional swings in her mood, was caused by her pregnancy.

"Well, all I can say is that you best be more careful. It's not only yourself you have to think of now, is it?"

Abby's eyes widened. "What do you—you mean, you know?"

"Of course I know. What kind of gudgeon do you take me for? Do you think I haven't noticed you can't keep down anything but toast in the morning? Or that it's been nigh on two months since your time?"

Of course. She had been foolish to think she could keep anything hidden from Molly. "I'm right, aren't I? It's not just nerves or—" She stopped and sighed again. "I should tell Graeme, shouldn't I?"

The truth was, Abby *wanted* to tell him—indeed, she ached sometimes with the need to share her excitement with him. It would be glorious to see his face light up at the news. They could talk and plan and daydream about their child and their future. More than once, it had been on the tip of her tongue, but always at the last moment, she backed away, an icy fear twisting through her. What if it changed everything?

"Och, well, there's naught wrong in keeping quiet for a while. Many things could happen."

"I wouldn't want to get his hopes up and then be wrong." Abby clutched at the excuse. Indeed, she thought with a sudden chill at the center of her being, what if what had happened last night had hurt the baby? Breathing in smoke, falling out of bed—what if her carelessness had caused irreparable harm?

"Now, don't be getting in a bother about hurting the wee one," Molly said, accurately interpreting the look of panic blossoming on Abby's face. "I'm sure the bairn's fine." She patted Abby's arm. "You just worry about taking care of yourself from now on. Come, now. I've drawn you a bath. You'll feel more yourself once you've gotten that smoke off you."

Molly was right, of course. She did feel much better after she was clean and dressed. As often happened, the queasiness in her stomach subsided, too. Molly had found a dress for her to wear. It has been downstairs in the laundry and was thus uncontaminated by the smoke that had permeated the room. Abby left the room, heading for the stairs, but she stopped outside her chamber door and looked inside. She was suddenly chilled again.

The bed was in ruins, the headboard charred, the canopy hanging in blackened tatters, the mattress charred and strewn with debris from the canopy. The wall beside the window was scorched, as were the draperies (what was left of them). All of it was sodden. The open window had cleared the room of smoke, but the smell still hung in the air. All her clothes would have to be laundered again to get rid of the smell.

"Thank God you awakened in time last night," Graeme said behind her. Abby gave a start, surprised; she had not heard him come up the stairs.

"It's ruined."

"The damage looks worse than it is." Graeme slid his arms around her, and Abby leaned back against his chest. "The structure of the wall is intact; even the bed can be reclaimed. Only the bedding and drapes are complete losses. The fire brigade got here in good time last night, and the servants had managed to keep it mostly confined to the bed."

Abby could not hold back a shiver, and Graeme's arms tightened around her.

"It will soon be good as new." He bent and murmured in her ear, "In the meantime, I'll be happy to share my bed with you."

Abby smiled and slid her hands over his arms as they curled around her. His breath tickled her ear, sending little tingles through her, and he nipped lightly at her earlobe.

"In fact," he went on, "it occurs to me that you really ought to go back to bed and rest after your ordeal."

She laughed and swung away from him, her eyes dancing. "Oh, no, you don't. Not until you've told me what you found out from 'Bangs.'"

He let out a mocking groan. "Don't remind me." But he linked his hand with hers and started toward the stairs. "Mostly I learned that Bangs is a dead bore. He told me—more than once—that Reggie was 'a capital fellow' and that the world was much worse without him. He also related at great length that George Ponsonby was another 'capital fellow,' though not, apparently, as capital as my father, and that he—Ponsonby, that is—accidentally fell off a cliff while walking near his home. In Bangs's opinion, it was Father's grief over his good friend George that made him bring the fund to an end. He clearly didn't know about the embezzlement. Even if he had heard a hint of it, I think he would have refused to believe it. I can well imagine him following my father about like a puppy, as Grandmother said."

"Oh."

"However, the trip wasn't a dead loss. I managed to get a roster of names from him, including that of our elusive vicar. Alistair Cumbrey is the man's name, and the church in question was St. Veronica's in Audley Gate."

"Where is that?"

"In the Cotswolds somewhere, I gather. But Cumbrey is no longer there. Bangston told me the vicar retired a few years ago. Unfortunately, Bangston hasn't the slightest idea where."

"Someone will be bound to know. At least now we can write the church and inquire about him."

"And we have an entirely new complement of people to find and question," Graeme pointed out.

In the weeks that followed, they did just that. Tracking down each name, they maneuvered to run into the men at a party or the theater. Many people had retired to their country estates now that the Season was over, so their progress was spotty.

Abby didn't care. She was more interested in spending the time with Graeme than she was in any actual result. No doubt that said something terrible about her. But, truthfully, Abby didn't care about that, either.

The wall in her bedroom was repainted, the bed and drapes replaced, her clothes thoroughly cleaned and put back in place. Soon it was as if the fire had never happened . . . though Abby made sure each night that every light in the room was extinguished before she went to sleep.

◦◦◦

The ballroom was crowded with people and noise. Tonight was Lady Middleton's farewell ball, for she was spending the winter in Italy, and it seemed as if all of London had come to bid her adieu. Abby, trapped in a conversational circle with Lady Eugenia and her friends, kept a smile on her face as her eyes scanned the room, looking for her husband.

She spotted Graeme at last. She marveled, as she often did, that even in the same formal attire as all the other men he could look so much more handsome than any of them. He was standing, a glass of champagne in one hand, with his gaze fixed on Abby.

When their eyes met, a small, secret smile curved his lips. He raised his glass and sipped at it, watching her across the rim. Abby felt a flush rising in her face. She knew that look in Graeme's eyes. She dropped her gaze demurely, then looked back up at him provocatively from beneath her lashes.

Graeme handed his glass to a passing waiter and started toward her. Abby turned back to the women, trying to suppress a smile of satisfaction. She watched from the corner of her eye as he wound his way through the crowd.

"My dear."

"Why, Montclair," she said, feigning surprise. "I didn't see you."

"Mm. I noticed." His hand rested lightly on her waist, not enough to draw Lady Eugenia's wrath for being unseemly, but enough to establish possession. Enough that Abby felt the heat of his skin through her dress. He greeted the other ladies, flashing a smile guaranteed to charm them. Behind Abby, out of sight, his thumb moved in a circle over her back. "I've come to steal my wife from you. She's promised me a waltz."

Neatly he cut her out from the group, guiding her forward with the faint pressure of his hand on her back. Abby cast a sideways glance up at him. "This isn't the way to the dance floor."

"Is it not?" he asked innocently. "How odd. Perhaps we should take a stroll, then."

They wound through the crowd, emerging from the ballroom into the less noisy corridor.

"Where are we going?" Abby asked.

"I don't know. Anywhere but there." He bent his head to murmur in her ear. "Have I told you how much I like your dress?"

"Yes, but you may tell me again." Her steps slowed, as did his.

"It makes the most delightful noise as you walk."

Abby giggled. "Does it?"

"Yes." She felt his breath against her ear. "I can't think of anything but taking it off you." He nipped her earlobe.

"Graeme . . . someone will see." The warning slid out of her mouth in a purr.

"Shocking." He slid his hand around to the front of her waist, spreading his fingers wide over her stomach. "Perhaps you should not have worn this dress then."

"Would you like for me to take it off?"

Abby felt the surge of heat in his hand. "God, yes."

He glanced around, then whisked her down another hallway. It was smaller and narrower, leading into the back of the house. Graeme pressed her up against the wall, one arm braced beside her head, and nuzzled her neck.

"I've been going mad the past hour, watching you walk, imagining that sound."

"Taffeta."

"Hmm?" His mouth was now occupied with exploring her ear.

"The dress. It's made of taffeta. That's what makes that rustling sound. And I was with you only twenty minutes ago, so it can't have been an hour."

"It felt like an hour. When can we go home?"

"Now, Graeme, you know we can't leave yet." Abby tilted her head to the side so that his lips could more easily roam her neck. She put her hands on his chest and slid them beneath his jacket, gliding up and down his ribs. "It would be rude."

"I find I don't care." His hand curved around her breast, the thumb tracing the outline of her nipple beneath the cloth.

"What would your grandmother say?" Her breath hitched as his teeth grazed the cord of her neck.

"I think I don't care about that, either." He raised his head, gazing down into her face. His eyes were hot, his face flushed and slack. He pressed his body into hers even more firmly. "How the devil do you do this to me? I'm in the most indecent state."

"I know. I can tell." Abby slid her hand down between them, fingernails grazing the hard line beneath his trousers.

He let out a muffled noise and closed his eyes, leaning his forehead against hers. "Abby, I'm a hairbreadth away from shoving up your skirts and taking you right here."

"Well, we can't have that, can we?" She gave him a gentle push; then, pressing a light kiss against his lips, she slipped away.

chapter 23

"Abby, wait." Graeme reached out for her. "What are you doing? Where are you going?"

Abby took his hand, tossing a grin back at him, and led him down the hallway. "Just a wife's duty, dear boy. Seeing to her husband's comfort." She moved quickly down the hall, reaching around the door of first one room and then another. "Ah, here we are." Abby pulled him into the room, turning the gaslight to a dim glow.

"Where?" He glanced around at the space, jammed with tables of various sizes and heights and other pieces of furniture that had obviously been cleared from other rooms. "A storage room?"

"A room with a lock." She reached behind him, closing the door and turning the key.

Heat flared in his eyes. "Abby . . ."

"What?" She looked at him with wide, innocent eyes, her voice lifting in question, "You don't want—"

"Oh, yes." He took her waist in his hands. "I want."

He picked her up and set her down on one of the tables, opening her legs to stand flush against her body. His arms wrapped around her, and he buried his lips in hers. His kiss was hard and urgent, his body radiating heat. Abby wound her arms about his neck and kissed him back, curving her legs around him to press him more tightly against her.

At last he released her, but only to roam his hands over her body. His eyes followed the movement, hot and dark. Abby leaned back, bracing her hands on the table, in unconscious invitation. It stirred something deep and primitive in her to watch as he took his pleasure with her. The taffeta crackled beneath his touch, and he grinned at her.

"This . . ." he said, his fingers sliding over her breasts and delving down beneath her dress to caress the soft flesh. "This is the best party I've ever attended."

Abby began to laugh, and he caught her mouth with his, kissing her until she was almost dizzy. When he pulled away, his eyes were so bright and intense she could not look away. Holding her gaze, Graeme shoved her skirts up and reached beneath them, jerking loose the ribbons of her pantalets and peeling them down and off her legs.

Freeing himself from his trousers, he moved between her legs again and, lifting her a little, plunged deep within her. Abby groaned as he filled her to the utmost, wrapping her legs around his back to take him more fully within her. His thrusts rocked her body, and she dug her hands into his back, unable to muffle the sounds of her satisfaction.

His arms were like steel, holding her to him as he drove harder, faster . . . until at last pleasure exploded in her. Graeme buried his face in her neck, her name an incantation as he shuddered, swept to his own release.

He stood for a long moment, holding her, their breaths panting, flesh damp and trembling from the onslaught of desire. Graeme smoothed his hands over her back and pressed his lips into the soft skin of her neck. "Abby . . ."

"What?"

He raised his head, his eyes filled with sleepy satisfaction. "Nothing." He smoothed a hand over her hair. "I just wanted to say your name."

She stretched up to kiss him, then leaned her head against his chest. "Do you think we could stay here?"

He chuckled. "I think someone might wonder where we'd gone."

"Mm. I wouldn't want to be hunted down by the dowager countess."

"God forbid," Graeme agreed feelingly.

Reluctantly they parted and pulled their clothes back in order.

"I think I'd better go up and check in the mirror." Abby adjusted a hairpin.

"You look beautiful."

Her eyes danced. "I suspect I look like I've just been . . . doing what I've been doing."

"Yes." He smoothed his thumb over her lips. "Beautiful."

She laughed and went to the door to peer out into the hall. It was empty. She looked back at him over her shoulder. Blowing him a kiss, she slipped out the door.

⚮

Abby spent several minutes in the cloakroom. One look in the mirror at her flushed face and disheveled hair convinced her that she must not only make repairs to her appearance but wait some time before it was safe to be seen by anyone. She kept to herself as she repinned her hair and straightened her skirts. She had no desire for company, feeling too soft and dreamy to face anyone.

At last, when her cheeks had finally lost their flush, she left the cloakroom, joining the chattering women making their way down the crowded staircase. Abby looked over the banister as she went down, scanning the hall below for a sign of Graeme. Like the staircase, the hall was filled with people and noise. But she had eyes for only one man.

As Abby took a step down, she felt a sudden shove in the small of her back. She staggered, grabbing frantically at the railing. Though she managed to get her hand around the wooden banister, she feared her momentum would have carried her forward had someone not caught hold of her arm and kept her upright.

Abby clutched the railing. Terror iced her insides as she thought of what could have happened. She turned shakily toward her rescuer. A blond woman had both hands around Abby's arm and was gazing at her with concern.

"Are you all right?"

"Yes. Yes, I'm fine." The truth was, Abby was trembling. What if she had fallen? She could have lost the child, and that thought filled her with terror.

"You look a little pale," the other woman said, taking Abby's arm and guiding her back up the staircase, easing around the women behind them. "Perhaps you should sit down for a moment."

"Yes, perhaps I should." Her rescuer glanced toward the crowded cloakroom, then steered Abby down the hall to an alcove.

There was a plush window seat below the bay window, and Abby sat down on it gratefully. It was quiet here and somewhat shielded from the hall by the heavy draperies hanging on either side of the alcove. Her companion sat down beside her, watching her carefully.

"Better?"

Abby gave her a small smile. "Yes, thank you, it's very kind of you to help me. I'm sorry to be so clumsy."

"What happened?"

"I think someone stumbled into me from behind, and I started to fall. Fortunately you were there and I was able to grab the rail." But it hadn't felt as if someone had lurched into her; it had felt like a push against her back. As it had that time beside the river. But no, that was absurd.

"How rude. They didn't even stop to see if you were all right."

"No. Perhaps they didn't realize."

"Oh, dear, you've torn loose a ruffle on your skirt."

Abby followed her companion's gaze and saw that several inches of ruffle had indeed ripped away and was trailing across the floor. "Perhaps I can find some pins."

"Don't worry." The blonde opened the reticule dangling from her wrist. "I always carry a little sewing kit with me for emergencies."

"You're very prepared."

The woman laughed. "I fear it's more that I am clumsy and quite accustomed to tearing a ruffle or losing a button." Pulling out a small, slim case, she popped it open and extracted a needle and thread.

"How cunning!" Abby leaned forward to examine the compartmented case, where a thimble, two needles, miniature scissors, and a small roll of dark thread were all neatly tucked away.

"Do you like it? I fashioned it myself from a tin of lozenges. It comes in quite handy." She threaded one of the needles. "I'm afraid I've only black thread, but at least it will keep your ruffle off the floor. It would be a shame to tear it further. It's such a lovely dress."

Nimbly, she knelt down in front of Abby and began to tack the ruffle back in place.

"Thank you. You're very kind." Abby watched her new-found friend work, intrigued.

She was slender and small-boned, and though not short, she had a delicate appearance. Her hair was a pale blond mingled with gold and arranged in a tidy knot at the crown of her head. There were women on whom it would have looked severe, but on her it simply revealed to full effect her soft oval face and large expressive blue eyes.

Her gown was simple, even plain, but the sky-blue color favored her classic English coloring and strawberries-and-cream complexion. More friendly and straightforward than most women Abby was accustomed to meeting here, she seemed the sort of woman Abby would like to know.

"I'm sorry, I'm afraid I don't know your name." Abby smiled. "I am Abigail Parr."

The woman's head snapped up. "Lady Montclair."

"One of them, anyway."

The other woman stared at her in silence, then hastily said, "Oh. I beg your pardon. I didn't mean to stare. I am, um, Laura Hinsdale."

"It's nice to meet you, Miss Hinsdale," Abby said lightly. "Obviously you've heard about 'the mad American.'"

"What? Oh." Laura Hinsdale's telltale pale skin could not hide the blush that rose in her cheeks. "No, no, indeed, I haven't heard anything about you. I am not usually in London; I'm visiting one of my cousins for a few weeks." She bent over the ruffle again, her fingers moving swiftly and surely. "I, ah, am acquainted with the Parr family."

"Are you? That's splendid. You know my husband?"

"Yes. That is, somewhat."

"We shall have to find him when you are done. I am sure he would be pleased to see you again."

"I wouldn't want to intrude." She finished the stitch and snipped off the thread. "There. All done. I should look for my cousin. No doubt she is wondering where I've gotten to."

There was the sound of footsteps in the hall. "Abby!" Graeme came into view and stopped. "Ah, there you are. What are you—"

At the sound of his voice, Laura sucked in her breath in a sharp hiss and whirled around. Graeme stopped midsentence. The color drained from his face.

"Laura," he said at last, staring at Abigail's companion. "I . . . I . . ."

Suddenly Abby knew: this was the woman her husband loved. The pretty, helpful Miss Hinsdale, the woman Abby had liked on sight, was the woman Graeme had wanted to marry, the one with whom he had been eager to share his life. And she realized, with a hard, swift stab of pain, that she had been building her life on quicksand.

Breaking the tableau, Abby jumped to her feet and fled from the alcove. She heard Graeme's voice behind her, calling her name, but she didn't stop, didn't even pause. She slipped past the clot of women at the doorway of the cloakroom, and, remembering the second door at the other end of the long, narrow room, she hurried through it and emerged into a side corridor.

She didn't bother to grab her cloak along the way. Her only thought was to get away, to be alone, where there was no one to see her, no one to hear her. Away from Graeme and the pain of seeing that expression on his face.

Abby walked quickly, head down, and took the back staircase to the ground floor. Emerging in the hallway outside the kitchen, she startled a footman carrying out a tray of food. He began to spout apologies, but Abby waved them away.

"Is there another door out? A tradesman's door?"

He nodded, puzzled. "Yes, miss, in the kitchen, but—"

"Thank you." She cut him off and hurried through the door he had just exited. She passed through the kitchen, and though everyone in it stopped what they were doing and stared at her, none moved to stop her. Outside, she found herself in a narrow walkway running down the length of the house.

It was chilly without a wrap, but Abby barely registered the discomfort. She ran to the street and looked up and down, finally spotting the Parr carriage. With relief, she gathered up her skirts and ran to it. The coachman, gossiping with the other drivers, gaped at her, then rushed forward.

"My lady! Is aught the matter? Where is Lord Montclair?" He glanced around.

"He's still inside. I want to go home. I'm, ah, not feeling well."

"Of course, my lady, of course." He hustled over to open the door for her and help her inside. Then, with a last puzzled glance toward the house, he picked up the weight holding the horses and climbed up onto his high seat.

The carriage rumbled off, and Abby fell back against the seat. She realized now that she was shivering, and her heart was racing along as rapidly as her breathing. She felt utterly scattered and jumpy—*scared*—and her cheeks were wet with tears she had not even known she was crying. She struggled to compose herself. The driver had probably decided she was a trifle strange; she didn't want to run through the house like a madwoman, alarming all the servants.

By the time they pulled up in front of Montclair House, Abby had wiped her cheeks dry, tucked away the flying bits of her hair, and pulled her face into some semblance of calm. Stepping down from the carriage, she said, "Please return to the party. Lord Montclair and the dowager countess will need the carriage later."

He tugged at his cap and left without protest. When she opened the door and walked inside, she gave a regal nod to the footman, who had jumped up from the entry bench in surprise. She managed to make it all the way up the stairs before the tears began to leak from her eyes again. How could she be so supremely happy one moment, and only minutes later feel her world collapse around her?

Running down the hall into her bedroom, she yanked at the bell pull. She was desperate to get out of these clothes and into bed, to drag the covers up over her head and cry her heart out. She didn't want to see anyone; she would not have rung for Molly if she had been able to get out of the multitude of fastenings down the back of her dress by herself.

The last person she wanted to see was Graeme. She could not bear it. She didn't consider why, at the same time, it made her heart squeeze with pain to think he might not pursue her. She started to lock the door but realized that Molly would need to get in. She crossed to the connecting door to Graeme's room and turned the key in the lock.

Sitting down before the vanity, Abby pulled the pins from her hair, her fingers clumsy and trembling. She had to stop now and then to wipe the tears from her cheeks—she refused to break down in sobs, but she could not keep the tears from seeping from her eyes.

The door opened, and she whipped around, thinking, *Graeme*. But it was, of course, her maid. And suddenly she could not hold back any longer; she began to cry in earnest.

"Miss Abby!" Molly ran to her and enfolded Abby in her arms. "What happened? It's him, isn't it? And I'd begun to hope he'd—och, I might have known." Molly's eyes flashed.

"No." Abby gulped, doing her best to rein in her sobs. "It isn't him. It's just . . . oh, Molly!" She jumped up, unable to sit still a moment longer, and began to pace aimlessly about the room. "I saw her tonight."

"Who? Who did you see?" Molly followed her.

"Laura Hinsdale."

"Who?"

"The woman he loves." Abby swallowed hard. "I didn't know her name, you see. I knew he loved another woman, but I had no idea who she was. It was easier, not being able to put a name or a face to her. But tonight I met her. She told me her name; she must have thought me a fool when I didn't recognize it. But then . . ." Her breath hitched. "Then he came in and saw her, saw us chatting together—and oh, the look on his face! I knew then. It was she." She began to cry again.

"Here, now, it'll be all right." Molly slipped her arm around Abby and steered her back to the stool in front of the vanity. "We'll get you out of these clothes and brush out your hair, and I'll fetch you your cup of hot chocolate. Then you'll feel better."

"I won't. Oh, Molly, you've no idea what she was like."

Molly snorted. "I can make a good guess. All snooty and

refined." She raised her nose in the air, making a sour face. "Pale as death—blond hair and empty blue eyes."

Abby let out a watery chuckle. "No, no. That is what I had assumed, too. I thought if I ever met her, she would be horrid and insipid or snobbish or maybe all those things." She sighed. "But that wasn't how she is at all. The fact is, I *liked* her. She's pleasant and friendly and kind, not at all the sort who looks down her nose at you. I almost fell, and she grabbed my arm to help me."

"You fell!" Molly frowned. "How did that happen?"

"I stumbled on the stairs. I managed to catch the railing, and Miss Hinsdale was there and kept me upright. That isn't what's important. The important thing is, she was nice. And she's lovely. She *is* blond and blue-eyed, though her eyes aren't empty at all, and she has that wonderful English skin, all pink and white like a porcelain doll."

"I'm sure she doesn't have a thing over you," Molly said stoutly. "You're a beauty, and you know it. There are always men hanging about, trying to get your attention."

"I think it's more the allure of my pocketbook than my face," Abby said drily.

"Anyone who doesn't see the worth in you deserves a good knock on his head, and that includes his lordship." Molly had finished unpinning and brushing out Abby's hair, and now she started on the row of hooks and eyes down the back of the gown. "If he's been dangling after this woman with you at home waiting for him—"

"No," Abby cut her off. "Graeme isn't having an affair with her. I am sure of that." Her mouth twisted. "He told me so himself. He assured me he would never dishonor Miss Hinsdale that way."

Molly mumbled darkly to herself. Abby suspected it

was just as well she couldn't understand what her loyal maid said.

"I'm not worried about him being unfaithful to me, not in that way. Graeme is a gentleman, not just in birth but in his actions, as well. But in his heart, he loves another. I fear he always will. Oh, Molly, I was so foolish. I know you tried to warn me, and I wouldn't listen. I told myself I could remain aloof and . . . and be happy with what I could have."

"Och . . . the man's a stubborn fool, and that's the truth of it."

"Perhaps he is." Abby's lips curved up. "At least a bit. I prefer to think that he's steadfast. Loyal."

"Blind."

"No, sadly, I think he sees quite clearly. He—I think he finds me pleasing enough."

"I should think so, given that he's in your bed every night."

"But that's not the same as loving someone. Cherishing her." And the lovemaking, too, would stop when Abby told him she was with child. Now she was sadly certain of it. His duty would be done, the bargain she had wrung from him paid. "When I saw Miss Hinsdale tonight . . . when Graeme said, 'Laura!' in that way, so shocked and . . . and appalled, I saw how hopeless it was." Unable to sit still, Abby jumped to her feet and began to pace. "She is nothing like me, Molly, not in any way. Her coloring is the very opposite of mine, and she is slender and delicate, like a sylph."

"Well, I don't know what that sylph thing is, but she couldn't be prettier than you."

"It's not just in looks, either. She is so . . . so English.

Well-bred, calm. She was nice and friendly but in a very genteel British way. Exactly the kind of lady that a gentleman would want to marry. I am sure that she would never draw attention to herself by laughing too loudly or talking too freely. No doubt she knows the proper order of precedence for all the titles, as well as their family histories. She would never seat the wrong people next to each other at the table or address someone incorrectly. Most certainly she would not be inappropriate or blunt. Or have to be plucked out of the river."

Abby stopped, finally running down, and came back to the maid. She turned so Molly could finish unhooking the back of her dress.

"Everything will look better in the morning," Molly assured her.

"Will it?" Abby was inclined to think it never would. "Graeme is not fickle. He still loves her, and it won't change. Laura will forever remain a young beauty in his heart and mind. Her hair won't gray; she won't wrinkle. She will never have disagreements with him or habits that irritate him. She will always be perfect. How can I hope to turn his love from that image?"

Stepping out of her dress and petticoats, Abby slipped on the nightgown Molly handed her, but shook her head at the Japanese silk dressing gown. She had worn it that first night with Graeme and the sight of it was too painful. Instead, she wrapped a red velvet robe around her.

"I'll go get you some hot chocolate now," Molly said, gathering up the clothes from the floor.

"I don't want any."

"I'm getting it anyway. Nothing picks up a person's spirits like chocolate."

In the distance there was the sound of a door slamming shut and a startled "My lord!" Abby's head snapped up. Footsteps pounded up the staircase. She could not move, could not speak, could only stare frozen at the doorway as Graeme rushed into the room.

chapter 24

"Abby!" Graeme stopped abruptly just inside the door. His face was flushed, his hair disheveled. "I—I looked for you all over. I couldn't find you. I didn't realize you'd come home."

"I did." Abby was proud her voice came out calmly. She wondered why he found it necessary to explain why it had taken him this long to come after her.

He started forward, and Molly stepped between them, arms still full of the bundle of clothes. Graeme halted, startled, then looked at Abby, raising his brows.

"Molly. Please get that hot chocolate for me," Abby told her maid.

Molly swiveled toward Abby. "Are you sure?"

"Yes. I'm fine."

Giving Graeme a long, dark look, Molly walked around him and out the door. He watched her go and swung back around to face his wife. "Abby . . ." He paused.

"Did you have a pleasant chat with Miss Hinsdale?" Abby had not meant to bring up the subject, had, indeed, been determined to avoid it, but somehow it slipped out anyway. She feared some of her bitterness had oozed out as well.

"No, of course not. I didn't stay to chat; I went look-ing for *you*. You might at least have stayed and given me a chance to explain."

"There's no need to explain."

"No? Then why did you take to your heels?" He stopped, visibly reining in his temper, and went on in a quieter voice. "Abby, I'm sorry. I had no idea Laura would be there. She doesn't live in London; I never dreamed she would be at any party we attended."

"I know. Miss Hinsdale told me she was only visiting— her cousin, I believe." There, that sounded much more in control. Not sad, not tearful, not hurt, just matter-of-fact. But then, like a tongue seeking out a sore tooth, she could not keep from touching on the pain. "She is the one, isn't she? The woman you love."

"Abby . . ." Graeme's face was a study in frustration. He crossed his arms. He glanced down. "Yes; she was the woman I—the one I told you about." He looked back up at her, saying earnestly, "I would not have put you in such an awkward situation. If I had had any idea Laura would be there, I wouldn't have taken you there."

"No, I'm sure not."

"Abby, I don't know what to say. It upset you to see her; I understand. I would change it if I could."

"Of course. There's no need for you to be concerned." Abby paused. "She is not very like me, is she?" Why did she keep poking at this bruise on her heart?

"Laura?" He smiled a little to himself. "No. You're not alike." Graeme started toward her. Abby took a hasty step back, and he stopped.

"I quite liked her." For all her effort, Abby's voice was brittle. "I can see why you love her."

His eyes widened. "Abby! I'm not having an affair with her. Is that what you think? I swear to you, I have not even seen her in years. I'm not. I won't. Ever."

"I know. It would damage Miss Hinsdale's reputation, and you would never do that. You told me so. I believe you."

"Well, of course, but—"

Abby rushed on. "I am just sorry, so sorry, that you had to give up the woman you love." Her throat closed, and she felt traitorous tears welling in her eyes.

"No, don't cry." Graeme's voice was alarmed, and he reached out, wrapping his hand around her arm. "It wasn't your fault. None of this was your fault. I don't want you to be unhappy or to think that I regret it."

"You don't regret it?" She jerked her arm out of his grasp and turned away. "Really, Graeme, there's no need to lie. We both know you didn't want to marry me. You hated the idea. You were in love with Laura, and it's easy to see why. She is perfect for you. She would have made you a wonderful wife. If it were not for my father, you would have married her."

"I couldn't have married her. The estate was desperate for money and she was penniless. I should never have said what I did to you that night. I was just so furious at your father's threat that I—" He stopped abruptly.

"Threat!" Abby stared at him, shaken out of her misery for the moment. "What do you mean? My father threatened you?"

"Well, with, uh . . . bankruptcy. Losing everything. The estate and . . . everything."

"You're lying to me." Her eyes narrowed. "Why? What did he do?"

"Bloody hell," he muttered, raking a hand back through his hair.

"Graeme . . . damn it. I want the truth." Abby's eyes blazed. "Tell me what my father did to you."

"He knew!" Graeme snapped. "There. Are you happy? Thurston told me if I did not marry you, he would reveal my father's embezzlement."

Silence hung in the air between them, as solid as a wall.

"What?" Abby felt as if the air had been knocked out of her. She sank down on the vanity stool.

"Abby, I'm sorry. I didn't want to tell you. I know you love your father."

"No wonder you hated him! And you believed *I* was part of it. That I knew, that I was forcing you—" She let out a choked noise and clapped her hand over her mouth.

"No, please, I—" He stopped, looking torn. "Don't cry."

Abby ached for him to deny it, but he could not, of course. He *had* believed it. He'd told her so.

"No wonder you despise me!" She could no longer hold back her tears. They poured forth, her words coming in sodden, breathless spurts. "I see now why you hated me. Why you shoved me out of your life. I'm surprised you didn't shove me out a window, as well."

"Abby! No." Graeme started forward, his face stamped with concern. "I don't despise you. I—"

"No!" She leapt to her feet, holding out her hand to stop him. "Please, don't be kind. I could not bear that. He ruined your life. *I* ruined your life! I am so, so sorry." She broke down finally, covering her face with her hands, her body racked with sobs.

"Abby, please—" Graeme reached out for her.

Abby whirled away. She would be lost if he touched her. "No! I cannot. Just leave me. Please."

"I can't do that. Abby, I—"

"Leave her alone!" They both whirled at the sound of Molly's voice.

Abby's maid stood in the doorway, a small tray in her hands. She slammed the tray down on the dresser and charged over to Abigail. Wrapping her arms around Abby, Molly glared at Graeme. "Haven't you done enough damage? Go away and let the girl be."

Graeme's eyes sparked. "Don't tell me what to do. She is my wife, and—"

"That doesn't give you license to hurt her."

"What? I have never lifted a finger against Abby. And *you* can bloody well pack your—"

"No! Stop!" Abby wrenched away from Molly and positioned herself between the other two, facing Graeme. "I can't stand this. Graeme, please . . . please, just go."

Graeme started to speak but stopped, clenching his jaw. Letting out an explosive, wordless sound, he strode toward the connecting door to his room. He stopped, his hand on the doorknob, his eyes on the key in the lock. He turned to look at Abby in disbelief. His face smoothed out, and he pivoted, striding through the open door into the hallway.

Abby stood looking after him.

"Here." Molly came to her, sliding her arm around Abby. "Don't fret. What did he say to put you in such a state?"

"It wasn't his fault." Abby pulled away from the older woman. "It was . . . I can't talk about it. Go on to bed, Molly."

"But—"

"No." She shook her head. "I just want to be alone."

Molly hovered, looking doubtful, but finally sighed and said, "You drink your cup, now, and go to bed."

Abby nodded. And, at last, she was alone. Abby glanced around the room. It seemed huge and empty. Mechanically, she sat down, staring into the glowing coals of the fire. She was numb, unable to think, her head aching from the bout of tears and her body drained of emotion.

She had been so happy the past few days, and now her life lay around her in ruins. What a fool she had been to put herself in this situation. She had been so stubbornly, blindly certain she could forge a new life for herself. She had even hoped it would include Graeme as well as a child.

But how could anything good ever come of a marriage built upon distrust, anger, and contempt? Graeme's love for another woman made it unlikely enough, but now that she really understood why Graeme had married then rejected her, she despaired of their union.

It was no wonder he had hated the thought of being shackled to her. She understood why even now, when she returned, he had fought so hard against being her husband. Only her threat of divorce had made him agree to her proposal.

And what did that say about her? Was she any better than her father? She had not intended her offer of divorce to be a threat. Divorce had seemed her only chance at happiness after Graeme turned her down. But that didn't change the impact of her statement. Given Graeme's abhorrence of scandal, divorce had been a very heavy hammer, indeed.

It horrified her, appalled her, to see this glimpse into her nature. No matter what he had said in the face of her tears,

Graeme must despise her. How could he not? Even though she had not been party to her father's blackmail, she was solely responsible for her own coercion. Abby's life lay like a dark abyss in front of her. There was nothing she could do to make up for the wicked things she and her father had done to Graeme. All she could do now was give him his future. She quailed at the thought of giving him up. But, she reminded herself, she had never really had him. It had been a delusion she'd created.

She could not sleep. Abby sat up for hours, wrapped in her thoughts, and when at last she dragged herself to bed, she could not rest. Finally, toward dawn, she fell asleep, only to wake up two hours later, feeling sick, as well as sick at heart.

Molly brought her tea and toast. It was her morning routine to combat Abby's nausea. She peered into the cold cup of chocolate sitting on the dresser and gave a loud sniff of disapproval, then set down the tray beside it and thrust a piece of toast into Abby's hand.

Abby hadn't the will to resist despite the way her stomach roiled at the thought of eating.

"Och, you're looking like death warmed over," Molly told her.

"Thank you so much."

"No doubt you stayed up all night, worrying over that man."

"I wasn't worrying. Just examining my actions. I'm a selfish person, Molly."

"Hmph. And who isn't, might I ask? If you think that that one"—she stabbed her forefinger in the direction of Graeme's room—"doesn't think of himself first and foremost, you're dead wrong."

"I forced him to accept me."

Molly rolled her eyes. "Oh, no doubt you dragged him unwilling into your bed. I'm sure that if you were cross-eyed and bald, he would have done exactly the same."

Abby made a face at her and sat up slowly, relieved when her stomach lurched only once, then calmed. She accepted another piece of toast. Most mornings, after a bit of toast, she went downstairs and joined the others at the breakfast table, her stomach settled enough to face the prospect of food without blanching—even though she ate little of it.

But today the thought of facing Graeme and Lady Eugenia, even the drab Mrs. Ponsonby, was too much for her. She must talk to Graeme, but at least she could do so later, when he was alone in his study. She ate another piece of toast to appease Molly and pulled herself out of bed.

Her hands were icy, her stomach a fierce knot, as she went down the stairs to Graeme's study, relieved not to meet anyone along the way. She paused outside the door. Graeme was sitting at his desk, one elbow on it and his head propped against his hand. There was a paper on the desk in front of him—hopefully nothing important, for he was making aimless circles on it with a pencil, frowning all the while.

Abby drew up her courage and stepped inside, closing the door after her. At the sound, Graeme looked up and popped to his feet. "Abby—Abigail."

When had he started calling her Abby, she wondered. She had not noticed. But clearly he wanted to retreat from that intimacy.

"I wanted to talk to you." She laced her hands in front of her to conceal their trembling.

"Yes. Of course. Sit down." He started around the desk to politely seat her, but she waved him back.

"No, there's no need. This won't take long."

"Very well." He stopped, his expression careful, the wide desk stretched between them.

"I came to apologize for my father."

"No, please, there is no need, I assure you."

"Don't." Abby shook her head. "I don't want English courtesy. It's time for American plain speaking. What my father did was inexcusable. I swear to you that I would never have agreed to the marriage if I had known it. There is nothing I can do to redress the wrong he did you. Neither of us can change the fact that we are married without causing harm to your family's reputation."

Graeme stiffened. "You want to change our marriage?"

"I want to do what I can to make amends to you. Not only for my father's actions, but also for what I—" Abby stopped and swallowed hard, then plowed ahead, determined to get out what she had come to say before tears overcame her. "I deeply regret the wrong that *I* have done you, as well. I was selfish and headstrong. I didn't mean to hurt you, but that doesn't make it right or good. I should not have made the demands I made of you."

She forced herself to meet his eyes. "So . . . I am releasing you from our agreement."

chapter 25

Graeme looked at her blankly. "What? What agreement? What do you m—" Graeme stopped as a blush tinged Abby's too-pale face. "Oh. That."

"Yes, that. We no longer have to live together as man and wife. I will move out of the house and—"

"So that's it?" He went taut as a bowstring, a hot, fierce light flaring in his eyes. "Just like that. You're walking out. First you decide you want to have a real marriage, so you push your way into my life. And now, now when you think it doesn't suit you after all, you'll sail right out again, go running back to New York."

"Don't pretend you ever wanted me here," Abby shot back. "It was all duty to you, nothing more."

"I see. And did I fail in my husbandly duty? Did I mistreat you in any way? Deny you anything? Offer you any disrespect?"

His sarcastic tone galled her. "Oh, no, you were the very soul of courtesy."

"But of course that meant nothing to you."

"Why are you acting like this?" Abby cried out. "Why are you being so difficult about it?"

"Maybe I'm tired of being so bloody easy!" Graeme

turned aside. He took a breath and after a moment, in a flat tone, he went on, "What about this child you said you wanted so much? Have you lost interest in that as well?"

"No." She grasped the back of the chair next to her, fingers digging into it for support. "But there's no longer any need for—I am—I think I'm pregnant."

He whirled back. "What? You're—really?" A smile started on his face, and he took a quick step forward, then stopped. "Oh. Yes. Well, I see." He paused. "I—um, are you certain?"

"Yes, almost positive. I—all the signs are there. So, as you can see, there is no longer any need for us to . . ."

He nodded, once again turning and moving away.

Abby watched him, her eyes filling with tears. She had to leave before she gave way. Swallowing hard, she said, "Good-bye, then."

"No. Wait." Graeme spun back around. "Don't leave. You cannot—you promised you wouldn't take my child away."

"I'm not returning to New York. I meant that I would get a house here in London."

"No, this is where you bel—where my child belongs. He—or she—should be raised in his home, with his family around him."

"It would be rather awkward, don't you think?" How could she bear that? To be around Graeme every day, so close to him and yet so removed, a constant reminder of all that she'd hoped for and could not have.

"I don't see why." His face was as remote, as coolly polite, as when she had first known him. "As you said, we had an agreement. We each got what we wanted. There should be no anger, no recriminations, surely."

"I suppose not." Graeme was right; she had agreed to remain here when they first struck their bargain. The fact that it would be more painful than she had realized did not give her the right to renege on her promises. Most of all, no matter how awful it would be to live with Graeme, the prospect of living without him was worse. "Very well. I'll stay."

He gave her a short, sharp nod. "Good. That's settled then."

They stood for another long, awkward moment. Abby turned and left the room.

∞

Graeme sank down into the chair behind his desk, stunned and disjointed and so tangled in conflicting emotions he could not bring himself into any kind of order. He had been in a state of turmoil ever since seeing Laura last night, unsure of what he felt, what Abby felt. Unsure of everything, really, except that the incident had upset Abby and that he felt somehow guilty and in the wrong—and vaguely resentful, too.

He had gone after Abby to try to explain that he hadn't known Laura would be there, but their conversation had only made it worse. Why had she asked him whether she was like Laura? The question was so absurd he'd almost laughed. Abby was so tall and statuesque, so . . . *healthy*. Raven hair and those bewitching green eyes. Nothing at all like Laura's pale delicacy. God knew, as much as he had loved Laura, he had never felt for her that driving, madness-inducing hunger he had for Abby.

Laura was so British and ladylike. Calm, soft-spoken, careful. There was none of Abby's impetuosity or flaring emotions or lively sense of mischief. Well, perhaps Laura did possess a similar sense of humor, though more understated and sly. And there was their stubbornness—and wouldn't Abby have loved for him to tell her that? Their strength. Courage, steadfastness. Very well, they were alike in some ways.

But that was beside the point. The important thing was that he had said no, she wasn't like Laura, which surely was the right answer. No woman liked to be compared to another woman, especially a former love. Yet his answer had not appeased Abby in the slightest.

Then he feared that Abby had leapt to the conclusion that he was having an affair with Laura, but apparently *that* had caused her no concern—no doubt Abby thought him too dull a fellow to have strayed. Or perhaps she just thought him too enthralled by her own seductive charms for his eye to wander, which was rather maddening even if it was true.

But then why was she so upset? Graeme hadn't the least idea.

He had apologized for putting her in an awkward position. Not that he had really put her in it—he would have avoided the party like the plague if he had known Laura would be there. And, damn it, how was he supposed to have known that, anyway? He didn't ask for a guest list. It wasn't as if he'd planned for Abby to run into Laura. He hadn't made them sit there, mending skirts and chattering away as if they were bosom friends.

And, anyway, despite the fact that he could not see how he was to blame, he had *apologized* for it. Her tears panicked and confused him. He tried to comfort her, but she would have none of it. She turned away from him as if he were a veritable villain. She locked her bloody door against him!

Graeme regretted letting it slip about her father's blackmail. He knew it must have hurt and shamed her that her father had behaved despicably. But Graeme didn't want, didn't need, an apology from her. It was her father who had forced his hand, not Abby. He had long ago told her he didn't believe she had been part of the scheme.

As for Abby wronging him—well, yes, she had maneuvered him into her bed. And he had been furious at her, sure that her talk of divorce was a threat. But how could he resent her for something that brought him such pleasure? He knew her now, was sure she had not acted maliciously. It had torn his soul today to see her tears. He'd wanted to take her in his arms and soothe away her pain and regret, to assure her he was happy, not angry.

Then, in the next breath she told him that she was leaving him. Not only that, she'd had the gall to act as if he was the one at fault. As if *he* had asked for it. Damn it, he hadn't asked for any of it. She was the one who had swooped in and gleefully turned his life upside down. And just when everything was going well, she'd jerked the rug from beneath his feet.

"Don't pretend you ever wanted me," she had said. It had been "all duty" to him—oh, yes, clearly that was nothing but duty that had sent him into her bed all those nights.

And if she was so appalled by her father's actions, if she regretted her own bit of marital coercion, then why the devil was she punishing him by kicking him out of her bed? Where was the logic in that?

While he was reeling under those blows, she had delivered the coup de grâce: she was carrying his child. Sweet heaven . . . his child. A strange warmth blossomed in his chest at the thought, and along with it a rush of anticipation mingled with alarm, even fear. What would it be like to hold his own child in his hands?

He tried to imagine a boy in his image. No, easier by far to see a girl who looked like Abby—black curls tied with pink bows, and a frilly white dress. But how could he possibly manage to be a father? He realized that he hadn't the slightest idea what to do. And what kind of example was he of anything? Worst of all, what if the baby died? What if Abby miscarried? What if she died giving birth to his child?

Graeme leaned on the desk, bracing his head with his hands. What he wanted most at this moment was to hold Abby, to cradle her in his arms and spill out all the joyous, fatuous, horrific things rattling around in his head. He wanted to lay his hand across her abdomen, dreaming about that fragile life inside her, a part of him nestled beneath her heart. He wanted to kiss her and assure her that he would take care of her and her child.

And that was precisely what Abby had denied him. What the devil was the matter with the woman? Why had this warm, willing, generous creature, this smiling green-eyed temptress who was so eager and adventurous in bed, abruptly turned away from him?

The answer to that was obvious, no matter how galling it was to admit it. She had never wanted him. What she had wanted was a child. Graeme had been nothing to her but a means to an end, and now that her goal was accomplished, she had no use for him anymore. Perhaps he had not been wrong in his original assessment of her. Maybe she really was cold and hard as stone.

But no . . . he remembered the hurt that had flashed across her face when she'd realized who Laura was, the sadness in her eyes, brimming with tears, her stark white face, smudged with blue shadows beneath her eyes. He thought of her smile, of the mischief that danced in her eyes, the soft moans that escaped her lips when he made love to her. No, she was not cold.

It could be her condition. Pregnancy caused women to act peculiarly, didn't it? The truth was, he had no experience with pregnant women. He was an only child, not married except in name, and he had been careful to make sure such an instance didn't arise with any mistress he had taken. The married men he knew were not in the habit of discussing their wives, and his grandmother and mother would sooner have swallowed nails than discuss something so indelicate.

Or perhaps it was simply that Abigail was right. They had made an agreement. And this, he knew, was last in his thoughts because it was the one he did not want to examine. But he knew Abby now; she did not lie. With her, there was no subterfuge, no hidden meaning. Their marriage had been a straightforward bargain made between two adults. They both wanted a child and had agreed to conceive one. Now she was pregnant, and their agreement had been fulfilled. There was no longer any need for them to sleep together. No reason to pretend they were a normal couple.

Abigail understood and accepted it. She was simply continuing with their agreement. Only he was foolishly holding on to something that had been form, not substance. He should really be relieved that he could return to the life he'd had before. He should be glad Abby was willing to move forward on her own.

Graeme groped beneath his tumultuous emotions for the resentment he had once held for Abby, the love he had felt for Laura, the independence of living without thought of another person. It must be there underneath all these painful feelings. Surely he could get back to himself. Being with Abby had been fun and pleasurable and easy, shimmering with excitement. But it wasn't a normal life. It wasn't something that lasted. It was only an interlude, too intense to live with always.

There. That made sense. That fit. It was just as it should be. His life would return to the way it had been, the way he liked it. And he was certain, absolutely certain, that soon he would no longer feel this hollowness inside.

⌒

After spending much of the day brooding over the matter in his study, Graeme approached teatime with some trepidation, unsure what to say or how to act around Abby. It was with a curious combination of relief and disappointment that he saw that only his grandmother was taking tea with him.

He watched Lady Eugenia pour. "Um, Abigail is not partaking? Or Mrs. Ponsonby?" he added hastily. It occurred to him that he should tell his grandmother the news; it was, after all, what she had been hoping for this whole time.

"No. Philomena felt it her duty to stay with Abigail when she learned the countess was feeling under the weather. Philomena is always so insistent on doing her part, but I fear she'll grow rather thin if she intends to keep this up the whole nine months."

Graeme refrained from saying that it was more likely Abigail would bar the door against Mrs. Ponsonby after one session of being "entertained" by her. He wondered if the woman had read a section of *Pilgrim's Progress* to Abigail to ease her suffering, as she was apt to do with his mother. It took a moment for the import of his grand-mother's words to sink in. He narrowed his eyes. "Wait. You already knew?"

"About Abigail's delicate condition? Yes, of course." Lady Eugenia offered a rare unrestrained smile.

"She told you?" Abby had confided in his grandmother before him?

"Of course not. Don't be foolish. She didn't have to say anything; I could see the signs. I do have some familiarity with the subject."

"Why didn't you tell me?"

"Really, Montclair." She sent him the sort of look that had always pinned him to his chair. "It's hardly a fit topic for conversation in mixed company."

"I didn't see any signs."

"Of course not, dear, you're a man."

"I should have, shouldn't I?"

"I can't see why." She sipped her tea.

"Because . . . I don't know. Grandmother . . ." He toyed with his spoon. "I don't know what I should do."

"Do? I'll tell you what you should do. Stop all this idiocy about your father's charity, for one thing. I cannot imagine why you feel the need to seek out everyone who ever had any interest in that fund. It can't be good for a woman in Abigail's condition. She should be resting, not digging through trunks or chasing about the city."

"How could talking to a few people or searching through a cabinet or a trunk hurt her? She's not lifting anything or shoving things about."

"I cannot comprehend why you ask me a question if you intend to ignore the answer."

"Grandmother . . ." Graeme realized he was gritting his

teeth and forced himself to relax his jaw. "I certainly don't mean to ignore your answer. But I fail to see how talking to someone about that alms society would be any different from paying a call."

"Paying calls is entirely different. It requires no mental effort."

"I can't disagree with that, but why—"

"You shouldn't disturb a woman in her condition. She should have calm and peace; it does not do to distress her. Although I must say, when it comes to Abigail, it's more likely she is the one distressing others. You, for instance, have not been the same since she arrived. Look at yourself—your cuffs are uneven, your ascot is crooked, and your hair is every which way. You look as if you've been tearing out your hair."

"I *have* been tearing out my hair."

"There you are." She nodded, pleased at having proved her point. "There's no good to be had in what you're doing. If you want to give alms, then pray do so. All this stirring about just muddies the waters."

"What waters?" He leaned forward, intrigued. "Grandmother, do you know something about what Father was doing?"

"Of course not. I found it best not to know what your father was doing. I can't imagine what Reginald could have done with that fund that is so interesting, anyway. You have been asking the most peculiar questions. You're upsetting Philomena."

This statement, he knew, should be interpreted as, "You're annoying me." Gravely he said, "I assure you, I have no desire to upset Mrs. Ponsonby. Though I cannot think why my questions would have done so."

"It reminds her of her husband. George was a bit of a fool, but she was enamored of him. Reginald was fond of him as well; I suppose George must have had hidden qualities."

"What does Mr. Ponsonby have to do with the fund? He was a trustee, I know, but he didn't do anything special, did he? He wouldn't have known anything, would he?"

"Really, Montclair, what is this obsession you have with knowing things? It isn't the fund that upsets Philomena; it's that time. She hates to be reminded of, well, you know . . ."

"No, I don't know. That's why I'm asking you."

She gave him an exasperated look. "That George took his own life."

"He did?" Graeme's eyebrows shot up. "I thought it was an accident. He fell from a cliff."

"Of course that is what we told everyone. We were hardly going to say he *jumped*."

"He did? How do you know? Did someone see it?"

"No. But we all knew he wouldn't just go for a ramble along the cliffs. He was the laziest man who ever lived."

"Why would he commit suicide?"

"Must you phrase things so indelicately? You've spent too much time around your American wife. George was in despair because he lost all his money in that stock scheme. Your father felt quite guilty about it because of course he had encouraged George to invest in it, thinking to help him. Philomena blames herself; she says George believed he'd failed her. Well, he had, of course, but how that silly man thought it would help her for him to die, leaving her penniless, I cannot imagine."

"Mm. Thoughtless of him." Graeme considered what

Abby would make of this news. She would be certain it supported her theory that the deaths of fund members were suspicious. In the next instant, he remembered how things were between Abby and him now. He wondered if he would ever have such conversations with Abby again.

His fears were borne out that evening, when he suffered through a stilted, awkward conversation at the dinner table. He and Abby exchanged nothing but meaningless pleasantries along the paths his grandmother chose to follow. He was glad for the respite of the customary glass of port alone while the women retired to the drawing room. By the time he joined them, Abby had already gone to her room.

"Poor dear. She was quite tired. Of course, that's only to be expected." Mrs. Ponsonby nodded significantly at him. "I fear she wasn't feeling herself this afternoon. So pale."

Graeme thought of Abby's pale face and shadowed eyes. Had that been because of pregnancy? It seemed more sorrow and lack of sleep that he had seen in her face. But why was she unhappy? She had reached her goal, the conception of a child.

Perhaps her unhappiness came from causing him pain. That would be in keeping with her character. She took too much upon herself; look at the way she suffered for her father's deeds. If he went to her, if he told her how much he wanted her . . .

And wasn't that a perfect indication of how low he'd sunk, that he was actually considering trading on her kind nature? He was disgusted with himself.

He wished he could talk to someone about the feelings roiling inside him, but there was no one. He couldn't discuss such things with his mother, even if she were here, and he could well imagine James's scornful reaction to such maunderings. There was only one person to whom he could talk freely. Unfortunately that person was Abby.

Graeme went up to bed early. He saw the light under Abby's door and hesitated, but resolutely passed by. He tried to read but could not. He thought of ringing for his valet, but then he would have to go to bed, and the thought did not appeal. He paced the floor. He flung himself back into his chair.

The sliver of light that came from beneath the door to Abby's room went out. He stood for a long moment, battling with himself. Finally he walked to the door and took the knob in his hand. It would not turn. The pain that pierced him was unexpectedly sharp. Graeme set his jaw. At least he could act like a man about it.

He turned away.

chapter 26

Abigail started down the stairs. She had breakfasted on tea and toast in her room. The pattern of the past few days was that usually the other members of the household had gone their separate ways by the time she emerged from her bedroom. Graeme retired to his study or sometimes left the house on some piece of business or other. Lady Eugenia and her companion spent the morning in the upper sitting room, leaving Abby the peaceful solitude of the library.

The afternoons required her to make an appearance in the drawing room to greet callers or to venture forth with the dowager countess, paying calls. Before teatime, Abby often escaped to her bedroom for a nap—she was uncharacteristically sleepy these days, but it was also a convenient way to escape Mrs. Ponsonby, who had apparently taken it as her mission to keep Abby's spirits up.

After that there was tea and later dinner or an evening out. It was then that she was with Graeme, trapped in a miserable charade of marriage. Gone were the intriguing conversations, the laughter, the kisses stolen in alcoves or hallways. There were no more seductions or teasing anticipations, no sweet lovemaking, no long nights wrapped in his arms.

Now there was only the most prosaic of conversation between them. His only touch was a helpful hand up into the carriage or the formal extension of his arm to her as they walked. Graeme had retreated to his former polite, remote behavior, his smile perfunctory, his laughter nonexistent.

There had been a few times when she glanced up and found his eyes on her, and she had felt the familiar breathless certainty that he wanted her, that at any moment he would sweep her up to his bedroom. But then he would glance away and the moment was over. Sometimes during a conversation with others, they would glance at each other, their eyes alight with laughter, and she would feel the old familiar closeness, the shared amusement. When that happened, she ached for what she had once had, no longer hers.

They did not talk about their investigation. Abby knew that Graeme had gone out a time or two to see someone connected to the fund, but he had not asked her to accompany him. And that, she thought, had hurt more than almost anything. Had their closeness been only an illusion?

She had to think that his show of desire for her had been a pretense, too, given how quickly he had accepted her release from their agreement. Even as she set him free, she had hoped deep inside her that he would not want to be released. That he would take her in his arms and tell her that making love to her had never been a burden, that he desired her as much as she did him.

But he had not.

Abby told herself it didn't matter. She had gotten what she wanted. She had done the right thing, even though it hurt. It was better, really, that it had ended when it did. She had grown perilously close to loving him. Any longer, and she might very well have lost her heart to him. That would have been worse. Surely it would have been worse.

Abby went to the library, as was her custom, but she was unable to settle down to read. She went from shelf to shelf, seeking something that would pull her from her gloom. It was a welcome interruption when Norton announced Mr. Prescott.

"Yes, send him in." Abby knew a twinge of guilt. She had neglected her friend recently.

Norton's disapproval of her receiving visitors in the library was clear, but he merely looked at her with an expression of long-suffering and bowed out of the room, returning a moment later with David Prescott in tow.

"David." Abby extended her hand to him, her spirits lifting. "How good it is to see you again."

"Hello, Abby." He smiled. "Are you well? Is everything all right?"

"Yes, I'm fine. Do I look so awful then?" she asked in a teasing tone.

"No, of course not. You could not be anything but beautiful. But you look a bit . . . thin. The last time I called on you, they said you were indisposed."

"It's nothing to worry about. I have been a bit under the weather lately, but it is due to a 'happy event,' not illness."

"Ah. Of course. Then I am very pleased for you." His face looked more regretful than pleased, but Abby chose to ignore that.

"Thank you. I am, as you must guess, elated."

"Then you must take especial care of yourself," he said.

"I am quite cosseted." Abby saw no reason to add that it was Mrs. Ponsonby and the dowager countess doing most of the cosseting.

"Abby . . ." His tone was serious, and he peered intently into her face as he spoke. "You know that if anything is wrong or you are unhappy or . . . frightened in any way, you need only come to me, and I will help you."

She raised her brows. "Of course. You are a true friend. But I'm fine, I assure you. It takes more than the prospect of a baby's birth to frighten me."

"I wasn't referring to that. I know you are fearless—too much so. A little caution would be healthy for you."

"David . . . whatever are you talking about?"

"The other day, the last time I was here, when I could not see you, I talked to your maid." At Abby's grimace, he went on hastily. "Do not blame Molly; I asked to speak to her. I wanted to be sure you were all right. She's concerned about you. She told me there had been a fire in your room."

"You must not refine too much on what Molly says. She worries about me as if I were still five years old." She turned away, sitting down at the library table. "There was an accident, and the curtain caught on fire. I was not harmed, I assure you. I'm quite well and intend to remain so. Now . . . sit down and tell me what you have been doing. What is the latest news from New York?"

"Very little, I'm afraid." He laid a large envelope on the table and took a seat across from her. "Have you had letters from home?"

"Yes, my aunt and cousin have both written me, but they had very little gossip, as they'd spent much of the summer in Carolina with the Vanderbilts."

They chatted for a few minutes about friends and acquaintances, then Prescott shoved the envelope across the table to her. "I received some reports from various of your investments. I thought you would like to see them."

"Thank you. Has your business gone well here?"

"Yes, I am almost through; I shall be returning to America before long."

"I hope you will not go without letting me know."

"No. Of course not. It is my hope that you will decide to come back with me."

She smiled but shook her head. "No, this is where I must stay."

Conversation fell off after that, and David rose to take his leave. As Abby walked with him into the hall, the front door opened and Graeme stepped in. He stopped, seeing them, then nodded.

"Good afternoon, Abigail. Prescott." Graeme handed his hat to the waiting footman and strolled forward. "Kind of you to keep my wife company."

"Always my pleasure."

Graeme smiled grimly. "Have you come to make your farewells?"

"I haven't decided when I'm leaving London."

"Rather a long time to stay away from your business, isn't it?"

The undertone of Graeme's words was unmistakable: he did not like finding David Prescott in his home. Abby contemplated the possibility that he was jealous. It was terrible of her, she supposed, but she couldn't help but feel a little fillip of pleasure. Perhaps Graeme was not as indifferent to her as he acted.

"Oh, I have business here, I assure you," Prescott said. "Important business."

"Ah. Well, I wish you well with that." The bite in Graeme's voice belied his words. With a terse, formal good-bye, he strode off down the hall.

David turned to Abby, frowning. "Are you sure you're all right here?"

"I'm fine." At the moment she felt almost cheerful. "Really."

"Very well. But remember, if you need me, you have only to send for me."

"I'll remember. You're a good friend, David."

After he left, Abigail glanced down the hall. Graeme had disappeared. She turned and made her way back to the library. There was little chance of a book engaging her interest now, so she opened the envelope David had brought and began to look through the reports of her investments. She picked up a statement from her bank, and started perusing it. She stopped suddenly, an idea forming.

"Graeme!" She jumped up from her chair and hurried down the corridor, her heels clicking on the stone marble floor. Graeme must have heard her approach, for he was already coming around his desk when Abby whipped through the doorway.

"Abby! What is it? What's wrong?" He extended a hand toward her, then let it fall back to his side.

"Nothing. I'm fine. I just had a thought." She waved the paper in her hand. "The bank account. If your father put the money in a bank, he must have received statements from the bank, yet we found none when were at Lydcombe Hall."

"Oh. Well. Yes, I suppose so."

"We must have missed them when we were searching his office. We could compare the bank statements to the ledger your father kept for the fund. There might be useful information in them."

"Actually . . . Father would have done his banking in London. He collected whatever came in at Lydcombe in a strongbox, and when he returned to London, he deposited the money in his bank here. So if those records exist, they would be in this house."

"Oh." Abby felt deflated. "But we've already searched this study."

"I didn't throw away the bank statements. There wouldn't have been a lot of statements for the fund, and they would have been old because it was inactive by that time. I may have just bundled them up with the other banking records."

Graeme opened one of the cabinets and pulled a box from the bottom shelf. He rooted around in it for a few moments, then pulled out a small stack of papers and held it up triumphantly.

"Aha! Here we are." He spread the papers out on the desk.

"You found them?" Abby went to stand beside him, bending over to look at the pages. She was achingly aware of how close she was to him. She could feel the heat of his body, breathe in his scent. It was all she could do not to lean into him.

Graeme's forefinger trembled faintly on the lines of numbers. "I'm not sure that these tell us anything pertinent. Just entries of the sums he deposited and the dates."

"Where's the ledger we brought back from the estate?"

He pulled a blue-backed volume from the bookshelf and handed it to her. "What are you thinking?"

"I want to see if there's anything odd or different, some discrepancy that might be suspicious." She slid her finger down to the bottom of the account book, then returned to the bank statement. "Look. At the end, there is a final large deposit, and afterward the account was closed."

"Yes. That was when Father put back in the money that he—that had been taken from it. Afterward he closed the account, disbursing the money to a few homes for old soldiers."

"Yes, but here . . ." Abby pointed to the account book. He leaned in, his arm brushing hers, and Graeme went very still. Abby cleared her throat and continued, as if all her senses were not tinglingly aware of Graeme next to her. "After March twenty-third, three large sums were entered into the account ledger. St. V, Lord F, and another one that says 'dues.' Add them together, and they're almost three thousand pounds. That's a good bit of money. It is also the exact amount your father put into the bank account before he closed it in May. But on the bank statement, there is no record of those amounts. There are no deposits between February and the date your father put the money back."

"So that's the money that went missing. It was taken in and recorded in the logbook, but not deposited in the bank. Instead it was pocketed."

"I think so. It makes sense," Abby agreed.

"It fits the timing. But this is my father's handwriting." His face was bleak. "It makes it more certain that he was at fault." He tapped the accounts book. "He received it, put in the lockbox, and never deposited it."

"Graeme, no." The sorrow on his face pierced her. Abby reached out, laying her hand on his arm. "Not necessarily. Someone could have stolen that money from the box. You knew where your father kept the money; I imagine other people did as well. Your father could have found that it was missing and felt he was to blame since the money was in his keeping."

"You are kind to say so." He smiled faintly.

"It's the truth." Without thinking, she slid her hand over his arm in a soft, soothing motion. "If we can find someone who was there when this money was taken in—this vicar of St. Veronica's, for instance—he might be able to shed light on it. You mustn't give up hope."

"I won't. Though truthfully, I'm not sure it matters that much to me anymore." He laid his hand over hers. "Abigail . . . do you really—that is, I've been thinking. I miss—I mean, I do not want to be at odds with you."

"Nor I with you." She looked up into his face, beguiled, as she always was, by the sky blue of his eyes, the depth of his gaze. She longed to reach up and trace the arch of his eyebrow with her finger.

He leaned his head toward hers a little more. Her heart picked up its beat.

"Can you—" Graeme broke off at the sound of footsteps approaching in the hall. Stifling a low oath, he straightened and swung toward the door just as the butler entered.

"Beg pardon, sir." Norton carried a small silver tray in one hand.

"Yes, Norton, what is it?"

The butler extended the tray, on which lay a small square of folded white paper. Graeme impatiently picked up the notepaper and an odd look crossed his face. He glanced quickly up at Norton, whose sharp gaze did not match his supremely blank face. Graeme's gaze flickered to Abby, then away. He slid a finger beneath the seal to open the missive and began to read.

Graeme frowned and muttered something under his breath, then turned to the butler. "When did this arrive?"

"Just now, sir," Norton replied. "A boy delivered it to the door."

"I see." Graeme returned to the note, studying it as if it held great wisdom, though Abby could see only a few lines of writing on the paper.

"Graeme? Is something wrong?" Abby moved closer.

"What?" His head shot up, and he shoved the note inside his jacket, groping for the inner pocket. "Oh. Yes, I mean, no, it's nothing. Just, um, a reminder of something I must do this afternoon." He nodded toward the butler, who still hovered in the doorway. "Thank you, Norton."

Thus dismissed, the butler retreated reluctantly. They were both acting peculiarly, Abby thought. She waited, but Graeme made no explanation.

"I must—I have to leave. But I—" He took a step forward. "Abby, may I talk to you? Later, I mean, after I return?"

"Of course." Coolness replaced the former concern in her voice. Graeme was hiding something.

"Good. I'll return soon." He swung around and left the room. Unnoticed, the folded piece of paper slipped out from beneath his jacket and floated to the floor.

Abby stood for a moment, gazing at the square of paper. It was Graeme's; she had no right to read it. She walked over and picked up the note. She should simply put it on his desk and leave; it was wrong to snoop. Normally she would have done just that.

But she thought of the way Graeme had glanced over at her, the odd, almost shifty, look in his eyes when she asked if something was wrong. There was something in that note that concerned her; she was sure of it. Something he didn't want her to know.

Perhaps it was about meeting someone involved in the fund they were investigating, and Graeme wanted to go without her. The idea pierced her.

She had thought for a moment that their old warmth and closeness might return. That Graeme was about to say he wanted to be with her again. But when the note arrived, his demeanor had changed.

Abby looked down at the folded sheet of notepaper. Graeme's name was written across it in a flowing feminine hand. Her heart squeezed within her chest. She knew it was worse than not wanting her to accompany him. She opened the note and read the brief message within:

Graeme,

I must speak to you. Please call on me. It's urgent or I would not have asked.

Yours,
Laura

Graeme had run to the side of the woman he loved. Abby stuffed the letter in her pocket and walked away.

chapter 27

Abby pelted up the stairs and into her room, only barely restraining herself from slamming the door behind her. She wanted to smash something—anything, as long as she could pretend it was Graeme's head.

"Miss Abby! What's wrong?" Molly hurried toward her. "What has that infernal man done now?"

Abby had not meant to tell her; she hated for Molly to dislike Graeme any more than she already did. But talking was better than breaking things.

"He's gone to see Laura." Anger spurted up in her anew. "He received a note from her just now and rushed off."

"The man's a devil. Running off to a tryst with that woman with you right there in front of him!"

"No, I don't think it's a tryst." Somehow her maid's anger calmed her own a bit. "It sounded as if she wanted to talk. She asked him to come and said it was urgent."

"He told you that?"

"No. I read the note. He just told me he was going to meet someone."

"He lied to you."

"Not exactly." Abby sighed. "But, yes, he concealed who it was. Obviously he wouldn't want me to know."

"It's time you left here. We'll go home, and you can have the baby there, among your friends and family."

Abby shook her head. "I promised I would stay in England. That I wouldn't take his child from him."

"Pah! He doesn't deserve your promises."

"No. It's his child, too. His heir, if it's a boy. I couldn't take our son away from his father, his birthright. His heritage."

"He'd be better off growing up as far away from *him* as you could get."

"It's not Graeme's fault that he loves her."

"It is when he loves someone other than his wife."

"He loved Laura before he even met me. And if it's punishment you're after, he's received more than he deserves already. He's saddled with a wife he doesn't want."

"The best wife a man could ask for!"

Abby smiled faintly. "Still, one he did *not* ask for. He'll never be with the woman he truly loves."

"Not as long as you're alive," Molly said darkly.

Abby's head snapped up, and she stared at the other woman. "Molly! What a terrible thing to say!"

Her maid crossed her arms. "Aye, it's terrible. But it's a worse thing for a man to do away with his wife so he can have another."

"That's ridiculous. Molly, you must not say such things. Graeme would never—"

"Would he not?" Molly leaned forward to look straight into Abby's face. "I've held my tongue because I know how you feel about him. I didn't want you to be hurt any more than you already are. But I canna stand aside and say nothing when your life is in danger."

"Molly! Is this what you told David? Is that why he kept asking me if I was all right?"

"Aye, and I won't apologize for it." Molly's chin jutted out. "Someone ought to know what's going on here."

"Nothing's going on here. I cannot imagine why you have—"

"Can you not? That's only because you're blinded by your love for the man."

"I don't love him. I will admit that I could, that I—that I like him very much, that I hoped for—"

"Love, like, hope, whatever you want to call it. The fact is, you refuse to see what's staring you in the face. You've almost died three times since you came here."

"No. What are you talking about? That man pushed me into the river, but it certainly wasn't Graeme. I don't think he even meant to kill me. He was after Mr. Baker, and he ran into me as he was running away."

"What about the fire in your room?"

"Molly!" Abby stared, astonished. "That was an accident. I nodded off while I was reading, and I left a candle burning."

"You find nothing strange in your falling asleep like that? I have never known you to do so."

"It's not usual, but I've been much sleepier lately. You know that."

"So when you sat down to read, you set that candle on the other side of the table from you, right beside the drapes?"

"No, of course not. It must have fallen off and rolled. Even if you were right, and someone set that fire purposely, it couldn't have been Graeme. He wasn't even here."

"Yes, it very conveniently happened on the one night when he had an alibi. A man like that wouldn't have to do his own dirty work. He'd hire someone else to do it and make sure he was somewhere else. And he wasn't anywhere else, anyway. He came in not half an hour later. He could have sneaked in earlier, set it, and left again, coming back when it was all over. He thought he'd come in and play the grieving husband. He didn't count on you waking up and ringing for me."

"And what, pray tell, was the reason he rescued me from the river? Why would he even be there?"

"Maybe he thought he'd play the hero, look like he tried to rescue you, only there were too many people there, and they helped save you."

"Why would he shoot Mr. Baker?"

"Have you thought maybe he wasn't aiming at that man, that he meant to shoot you and missed his mark?"

"No, I haven't. I haven't thought about any of this because it's absurd. If you have to come up with these complicated explanations, it means it's very unlikely. You don't like Graeme; you've never liked him. So you're imagining something wicked where there's nothing."

"I'm not imagining that you've nearly died three times."

"Three? Those are just two—two *accidents*."

"What about your falling on the stairs the other day?"

"At the party? But that's—" She stopped, remembering the push against her back. "Someone merely stumbled into me."

"Three accidents in three months?" Molly quirked an eyebrow. "I've never known you to be so clumsy and careless before."

"Very well. Yes, it's odd. But Graeme wasn't even on the stairs. Are you going to claim he hired one of the other ladies around me to push me down the stairs? All of this is completely out of the question. No matter how Graeme feels about me, he would not harm his heir. He can't kill me without killing his own child as well."

"Maybe it wasn't him. Maybe it was *her*."

"Her? Who—you mean Laura Hinsdale?" Abby gaped at her, then began to laugh, trying to envision the composed, kind, and ladylike woman as an assassin. "If you had met her, you wouldn't think that. She was very nice and friendly. She helped me. Indeed, she is the one who grabbed my arm and kept me from falling."

"You're too trusting; you don't want to believe bad of anyone. She might have gotten tired of waiting for him; she figured she'd make sure his present countess died so she could step into her place. Or maybe she just hates you for taking him away from her and wants to see you dead. Or the two of them are in it together. With you gone, he'd have money, and he could marry whoever he wants. He can have an heir with this Laura."

"Stop! Molly, you're wrong. Graeme would never do anything like this. And I have serious doubts that a proper English lady like Miss Hinsdale is creeping about other people's houses setting fires, or firing guns at people and pushing them into the river."

"But—"

"No!" Abby's eyes flashed. "I mean it, Molly. Stop talking this nonsense . . . to me or anyone. I forbid you to go to David Prescott and fill his ear with these foolish notions. You raised me, and I love you, but I will not keep you with me if you go on spreading poison like this."

Molly gasped, taking a step backward. "Miss Abby! You canna mean—"

"I do."

Molly clenched her teeth, obviously biting back the

words she would like to say. She gave a short nod. "Very well, ma'am. I'll say nothing else. If you need nothing here, I will go back downstairs to clean your shoes."

Abby nodded, flooded with guilt at the woman's formal words. She had always been "Miss Abby" to Molly, no matter her age or married status. Abby steeled herself against the emotion. She could not bear to listen to Molly's delusions.

She walked to the window and gazed out at the graceful row of houses across the street. Three accidents in the space of time she had been here were unusual, even suspicious. Despite her words to Molly, she herself had wondered if she had been targeted.

It was not like her to fall asleep so suddenly and soundly as she had the night of the fire. And why would the candle fall off and roll over to the drapes? It would just melt where it stood.

There had been a second shot that night at the river. Had it been aimed at her? Might it have hit her if she had not quickly knelt beside Baker? The person slamming into her and knocking her into the water had not felt like an accident. It had been hard and direct, not a glancing blow. There had been no sound of the runner stumbling.

She was even more certain that the other night on the stairs she had felt a deliberate hand in her back shoving her forward. If one of the other women had stumbled into her, there would have been some noise, an exclamation of distress. Nor had anyone apologized or asked if she was all right.

The problem, of course, with believing that any or all of these things were attempts to murder her was that there was no reason for anyone to kill her. No one would benefit from her death except her cousins, who were far away in New York, and her favorite charities. And her husband.

To anyone who did not know Graeme, he would appear the logical choice of suspect. If Abby were dead, Graeme would have the freedom to marry again, along with the added benefit of whatever she might have willed to him.

But Abby did know Graeme; she knew him well. She was certain Graeme had not tried to harm her. All the logical reasons meant nothing when measured against his character. Graeme would not commit cold-blooded murder no matter how much he disliked someone. She would stake her life on it.

That left only Laura Hinsdale. But the thought of that lady running about shooting at people or knocking them into the river or down a flight of stairs was laughable. Even more absurd was the idea that she had sneaked into the Parr mansion late at night and crept up the stairs into Abby's bedroom to set her drapes on fire.

Abby liked Laura. Even knowing that she was the woman who held Graeme's heart, Abby could not help but like her. She had been nice, unaffected, and warm. Far nicer and more down to earth than any of the other ladies she'd met in London.

Abby frowned. Now that *was* odd. Laura had not been cool and aloof. She had not acted snobbishly. Though her manner had been perfectly polite and ladylike, she had also been friendly and practical. Her behavior was even stranger when one considered that Abby was the wife of the man Laura herself loved. Abby had not known Laura, but Laura would have realized who Abby was as soon as Abby introduced herself.

At the time, Abby had thought her kind, but perhaps she

was merely deceitful. Surely Laura must resent Abby, who had married the man Laura loved. Worse, she must know that Graeme had been forced into it. Abby and her father had ruined Laura's life.

And wasn't it quite a coincidence that Laura had been at that party, that she'd been right beside Abby on the stairs when she stumbled? Abby frowned, trying to remember exactly how the fall had occurred. She could not remember whether Laura had been next to her the whole time or if she had just suddenly appeared when Abby stumbled. Wasn't it possible that she had given Abby a push as she stepped down onto the stair beside her?

But why then would she have reached out and grabbed Abby's arm to keep her from falling? Abby had grabbed the banister; she probably would not have had a worse fall than stumbling to her knees or lurching into the banister. Perhaps, seeing that her plan hadn't worked, Laura had taken her arm so that Abby would not suspect Laura of being the one who pushed her.

Laura would know that Graeme would turn to her if Abby was out of the way. He still loved Laura—look at the way he had rushed to her today the moment she beckoned. Perhaps the two of them had to discuss their plans.

No. It was impossible. Abby would allow the possibility that Laura might be plotting against her, despite Abby's initial impression of her, but she simply could not accept that Graeme would try to harm her. If she was so wrong about his character, if he hated her that much, then Abby preferred not to know. She would rather just meet her fate.

chapter 28

Graeme strode impatiently up the street. Blast it. This note couldn't have come at a worse time. As he and Abby had looked at the accounts, there had been a few moments of closeness, of normalcy. Hope had swelled in him. He had thought that if he could just talk to Abby, if he told her how much he wished everything was the way it had been between them, how he missed her presence, not only in his bed, but everywhere in his life, that she would listen and understand. Perhaps she wished the same thing. They could bridge this gap between them, have a life together with their child.

But just as he was groping for the right words to say, Norton had come in with that note. The sight of Laura's familiar hand, the stamp she always used on the seal, had astonished him. His first thought had been alarm. Abby would be upset, just like the other night. Worse. He had the uneasy feeling that Abby would find it difficult to believe that he did not routinely receive letters from Laura.

For an instant, he considered ignoring the note. But even as he'd thought it, he knew he could not. The moment had been broken. It would look odd to stick the thing into a drawer without reading it—he remembered quite well what he had thought when Abby did that very thing so many weeks ago. Abby would be bound to ask questions. Besides, no matter how inopportune or annoying it was, Laura would not write to him without an important reason. She had never tried to contact him before.

Once he'd read it, he knew he had to go see her immediately. There must be something very wrong; Laura would not ask him to call on her for something trivial. And it was truly alarming that she had said it was urgent. Laura was one of the steadiest, most composed people he knew.

Torn between worry and frustration, Graeme trotted up the steps of her cousin's house and knocked. It was something of a shock to see a different footman open the door, but at that moment the butler emerged from the hallway.

"Lord Montclair."

"Hello, Boggerty. Good to see you."

"And you, my lord. Miss Hinsdale said you would be arriving. She's in the music room."

"Of course." Graeme smiled. The music room was where he had often found Laura, her blond head bent over a sheet of music, her graceful fingers flying over the keys.

Boggerty ushered him to the door and left quietly. Graeme stood for a moment, watching Laura. He had not talked to her the other night, too busy chasing after his fleeing wife. She looked much the same as ever—light blond hair pinned into a braided coronet, neat and practical, the strawberries-and-cream complexion, the plain gray dress, and the intense concentration on her face as she read the music. The years sat kindly on her face; at twenty-eight, she was still lovely.

His heart warmed to see her. He missed her friendship—her wit, her warmth, her steadiness. Perhaps it would be

possible to be friends again—but no, it would be too upsetting to Abby. It was too bad, he thought. Under different circumstances, Abby and Laura would have liked each
other.

He must have made some noise, for Laura glanced up
and saw him. "Graeme! You came." She popped to her feet
and started toward him.

"Of course. Did you think I would not?" He bowed for-
mally over her hand.

"I hoped you would, but . . ." She shrugged, her cheeks
turning pink. "Well, it's a trifle awkward, isn't it?"

"Yes." Somehow the admission made things less un-
comfortable, and Graeme smiled at her more naturally.
"You're looking well."

"Thank you. So are you. Please, sit down." She gestured
toward a chair and sat down across from him. "I quite liked
your wife. She's a lovely woman. I'm very sorry for the
other night."

"It wasn't your fault."

"I didn't know who she was at first, and when we introduced ourselves, I didn't know what to do. I felt as if I
were deceiving her, but what could I say? I hoped I could
get away without any awkwardness or embarrassment."

"But I came blundering in." He paused, then said, "But
surely this is not why you wrote me."

"No. Oh, no, of course not. I hesitated about sending
you that note; I wouldn't have . . . only . . . Perhaps I am
being foolish, but I was worried, and I—I didn't know what
else to do."

"Do about what? What's the matter? May I assist you
in any way?"

"No, it's not about me. It's about your wife."

"Abigail?" His eyebrows rose. "I don't understand."

"I thought what happened on the stairs was simply an accident, so I really didn't think anything about it at first."

"The stairs? What do you mean? What happened on the stairs?"

"Lady Montclair falling. At the party the other night."

"She fell?" Graeme jumped to his feet. "When? What are you talking about?"

"She didn't tell you?"

"No. She did not." His mouth tightened, and he took his seat again. "Tell me what happened. Was she hurt?"

"No. She didn't fall to the ground; she just stumbled and began to fall. I happened to be walking down the stairs beside her, and I grabbed her arm. She caught the railing."

"That's bad enough." He scowled. "Why the devil didn't she tell me?"

"Perhaps she didn't think it was important."

"Of course it was important. A fall—she could have lost the baby."

Laura's eyes widened. "Oh. You mean she's—"

"Yes." He smiled faintly, feeling pleased, proud, and slightly embarrassed.

"I'm very happy for you. And Lady Montclair." If there was a faint tremor in her voice, it was quickly suppressed. "But that makes me even more concerned. As I said, I put it down to an accident, but this morning, Mrs. Penwyler came to call, along with one of her friends, and one of them mentioned Lady Montclair. Cousin Elizabeth said something about Lady Montclair almost falling—I had told her, you see—and Mrs. Penwyler said Lady Montclair was always stirring things up. She said Montclair's wife was always acting as if something had happened to her—falling in the river and getting trapped in a fire. She intimated that Lady Montclair had set the fire herself, just to attract attention."

"What rubbish."

"Well, you know Mrs. Penwyler; she's a harpy. But the thing is, it didn't sound at all like the woman I met."

"No, of course not. Abby is more likely to pretend nothing happened than to dramatize a situation."

"I also thought it was very peculiar that she had had several 'accidents.' I thought about that 'accident' on the stairs. And it seemed to me, looking back on it, well . . . that she had been pushed rather than that she had stumbled."

"Pushed!" Graeme's heart began to pound in his chest. "Are you sure?"

"No. That's just it. I'm not. The whole thing happened very fast, and I was more intent on catching her arm than anything else. I didn't actually *see* anyone push Lady Montclair. But I didn't see her stumble, either. She lurched forward and to the side very suddenly. It didn't appear that she had caught her toe in her skirts or anything like that. I think I was the one who then stepped on her ruffle and tore it as I jumped to catch her arm. She wasn't hurrying. There were people in front of us, so she couldn't have." Laura stopped, uncertain. "Am I being foolish, Graeme?"

"No. Not at all. I am the one who's been a fool." He shoved a hand back through his hair. "God help me, I've been blind. I thought the danger long past. I thought she was safe with me. I was sure no one could have gotten into the house to set the fire."

"Safe from what? What danger?"

"That's just it. I've no idea. I've been so caught up in my own feelings I've ignored everything else." He stood up. "I have to go. I'm sorry, but I—"

"There's no need to apologize. Of course you must go to her."

Graeme rushed out, in such a hurry that he did not realize until later that he had forgotten his hat. He hailed a hansom this time, unwilling to waste even the time of walking. As he rode, his mind raced, dread, frustration, and anger rising in him. When the carriage pulled up in front of his home, he fairly shot out of it, tossing money at the driver without even asking the amount.

Charging up the steps, he strode through the front door, nearly bowling over a footman. He went first to the less formal sitting room downstairs, but only his grandmother and her companion were there. "Good heavens, Montclair, what is the—"

But he was gone before Lady Eugenia could finish her sentence, pounding up the stairs and into Abby's bedroom. Abby was staring out the window, and she jumped and whirled around at his abrupt entrance.

"Graeme! What are you doing?"

"What am I doing?" he shot back, all the emotions that had been building in him rushing up in a surge of fury. "What the devil are *you* doing? Why didn't you tell me you fell on the stairs? Did you think I didn't deserve to have even that bit of knowledge about you?" She made no reply, only stared at him in astonishment. It served to fuel his anger. "Don't you realize what could have happened?"

"Of course I realize it!" Abby snapped back, breaking out of her momentary paralysis. "It's not as if I set out to stumble on the stairs! I didn't *hide* it from you; I had other things on my mind at the time."

"Yes, I know, you were too busy punishing me because you met Laura."

"What?" Her voice rose, and she practically jumped forward. "How dare you accuse me of *hurting* you! I gave you what you've wanted all along—your freedom. Now you're castigating me because I had an accident? Because I didn't report to you? You don't control me."

"I understand that you don't want me, but, damn it, I am still your husband. You had no right to hide it from me."

"I didn't hide it from you." She held herself rigidly, fists knotted at her side. Her voice was tight, but level. "Clearly it would have done no good if I had. Obviously you have your own sources of information. I would ask who told you about the accident on the stairs, but we both know the answer to that."

A prickle of unease ran through him.

"No, don't bother to lie." Abby's voice was acidic. She dug into her pocket and threw a piece of paper at him. It fell to the floor at his feet. He didn't need to pick it up to see that it was Laura's note. "I know you've been with your . . . *friend*." Abby's mouth twisted bitterly.

"I wasn't going to lie." Graeme's chest was so tight he felt as if he might choke. "And yes, she is my friend. Yours, too, more than you know."

"Mine?" Her eyebrows lifted mockingly.

"Yes, yours. She asked me to call on her because she was worried about you."

"What? Oh, yes, I am certain she was most concerned about me."

"She was. You may not care to acknowledge it, but Laura is a kind person. Fair and honest. She would never wish you ill."

"Yes, yes, I am well aware what a paragon she is."

"Stop being so bloody contemptuous. Laura was worried. She heard about your other accidents. She is afraid you are in danger."

"In danger? Well, she should know."

"*I* should have known—but you didn't see fit to tell me that someone tried to push you down the stairs."

"What could you have done about it? It had already happened."

"What I can do is make sure it doesn't happen again. You're going to Lydcombe Hall."

"I beg your pardon. You intend to pack me off to the estate, like some mad aunt? You think I'll quietly do as you bid and—"

"I am sure you will *not* quietly do as you're bid," he thundered back. "Ever. But, by God, this once I intend to make sure you will be somewhere safe and secure."

"As soon as I get away from here, I'll be safe and secure!"

Graeme's eyes widened. There was a moment of dreadful silence. "You think that I—that I am the one who is trying to kill you?" He felt as if she'd slapped him. "Abby . . ." Unconsciously he took a step back. "You believe I could want to harm you?"

Abby reached out, looking stricken. "No, Graeme . . . I didn't mean that the way it sounded. I'm sorry. I know—I told Molly you wouldn't hurt me."

"Molly? You've thought about it, you've been discussing it—discussing me—with your maid?" Now a saving anger was rising up in him.

"I didn't think *anything*—apparently I am the only one foolish enough to think no one wanted to kill me. But Molly was worried. She thought—"

"That I would murder you. I see. I might have known you would value your maid over your husband." He swung away, then turned back, saying acidly, "You needn't worry. You won't be bothered by my presence at the Hall. I will remain here. I intend to find out who is behind this. But you *will* go to Lydcombe Hall, where I can set men to guard you. And though you don't trust me, you can rest easy, knowing that your maid is there to protect you."

∞

Graeme moved numbly through the next few hours, refusing to think about the fact that Abby believed him capable of killing her. Instead he went methodically through the necessary details, talking to his grandmother and to the footman who would accompany Abby's party to Lydcombe Hall, a quick man both physically and mentally, and one on whom he was sure he could rely. He wrote a letter of instruction to the butler at the Hall, and, finally, he sent one of the maids to bring Molly to his study.

The middle-aged woman entered, jaw set, eyes bright, looking the very image of someone prepared to fight. She stopped in front of his desk and fixed him with a glare, saying, "If you're thinking to let me go, don't bother. Miss Abby's my employer, and I'll not leave her till she says so."

"That is what I would expect, I assure you. I sent for you because I want to impress on you the need to protect my wife."

Her eyebrows shot up. "You think you need to remind me of that! That's what I've done for the last twenty-five years, and I'll do it till my dying breath, and that's a fact."

"Good. I am relying on your loyalty to Lady Montclair. I am aware you think I am to blame. I won't bother to argue the matter with you. But I'm afraid you will assume she's safe because I'm not there and you will relax your guard. You must not."

Molly frowned. "What are you saying?"

"I am saying that I'm not a danger to her. Someone else is trying to harm her."

"Who?"

"I don't know. If I did, I would already have taken care of him. I am staying in London to find out who tried to hurt her. I will alert the servants at the Hall to watch out for strangers, and I'm sending a footman with you, as well." Graeme stood up, leaning forward and bracing his hands on the desk. "But you are the one who is most with her, the one most dedicated to her safety—not to mention one of the most suspicious human beings I have ever had the misfortune to meet. Don't let your dislike of me blind you to other dangers." He had to stop to clear his throat. "Watch over Abby."

"I will." She lifted her chin. "Just like always. *Nobody*'ll hurt her while I'm there." She fixed him with a piercing look.

"I am counting on it."

chapter 29

Graeme was at his cousin's door and about to knock when he heard a single thunderous bark behind him. He turned to see James strolling toward him, his mastiff by his side. The dog apparently recognized Graeme, for his stiff, watchful posture was replaced by a wag, and the animal loped forward to greet him. Graeme braced for a two-hundred-pound welcome, but James's mild "Dem—manners" brought the dog to a halt and he merely planted his massive head against Graeme's hip.

"Walking Dem yourself?" Graeme asked.

James snorted. "All the servants are terrified of him except Hastings, and he wasn't here." He frowned as he drew closer. "What's wrong?"

Normally Graeme would have protested that nothing was wrong, but today he didn't bother. "I've come to ask a favor of you. Will you escort Abigail to Lydcombe Hall?"

"I beg your pardon?" James paused in the process of opening the door.

"I need you to escort her home and after that, to keep an eye on her and the Hall."

James simply looked at him for a long moment, then said, "Best come inside. I suspect this will involve a lengthy explanation." Graeme followed his cousin down the hall, the mastiff padding at their heels. He managed to keep silent until James had closed the door of his study behind them, before he burst out, "Abby is in danger."

"Danger?" James turned to stare at him. "Bloody hell, Graeme, what the devil are you talking about? Why would Lady Montclair be in danger?"

Graeme could not sit down. He paced around the room, the dog following him. "You remember what I told you about Mr. Baker?"

"Your father's agent, the man who was shot."

"Yes. I told you the killer also knocked Abby into the water. I thought at the time that it was probably an accident. But the thing is, a fortnight or so ago, her bedroom drapes caught fire. Fortunately, she woke up and managed to escape, but she could easily have died. I put that down to accident, as well, because . . . well, it seemed absurd to think it was anything but that. But today I discovered that someone tried to push her down the stairs at Lady Middleton's ball."

"If it were anyone but you telling me this, I would be certain you were playing some ludicrous prank."

"I'm not."

"For pity's sake, Graeme, sit down before you drive Dem into a state."

"What?" Graeme glanced down at the dog, who was staring up at him intently and whining. "Oh." He threw himself down in one of the chairs.

"Now." James sat down across from him, reaching out to put a soothing hand on the dog's broad head. "I don't understand. If your wife is in danger, surely you will go with her to Lydcombe?"

"No." The twist of Graeme's lips was more a grimace

than a smile. "You see, I am the one she thinks is trying to kill her."

James's jaw dropped at this statement. "You? She thinks *you* are trying to do away with her?" He began to chuckle.

"I'm serious," Graeme snapped. "She and her Valkyrie of a maid have decided that I want to be free to marry Laura."

"And is the inimitable Miss Hinsdale part of this plot, as well?"

"Joke all you like." Graeme sent him a fulminating glance. "My wife wants nothing to do with me. She's—" The words stuck in his throat. "Abby's frightened of me."

James studied him silently. "Well, it would make sense."

"Thank you for that vote of confidence."

"If one didn't know you, of course. Freedom, an inheritance, the woman you love—it would tempt a number of men."

"Yes, I recall you suggested something similar," Graeme replied acidly.

"To be fair, I said you would be fortunate if she died in childbirth. I didn't actually suggest you do away with her."

"I'm glad I am able to afford you so much amusement."

"I'm sorry, Graeme. I don't find your distress amusing. If you want me to, I'll go, of course."

"Thank you. Abby won't be alone. Mother will be there, and Grandmother and of course Mrs. Ponsonby are going along."

"Egad, you're asking me to escort the dowager countess as well?"

Graeme rolled his eyes. "I imagine you'll be able to bear up."

"I'm not so sure."

Graeme ignored him. "I'm sending an extra footman to help guard the house. And I've written instructions to have a gardener or groom patrolling the grounds night and day."

"Sounds like an armed camp."

"Hopefully whoever is doing this will realize that. Still, I'd feel better knowing you were at least close by and checking on things every now and then."

"I will. But you'll pardon me if this seems rather ludicrous. Why would anyone want to kill Lady Montclair?"

"I think it has to be because of that blasted charity."

"Your father's fund for wounded soldiers?"

"Yes. I told you we've been digging into that."

"What have you found out?"

"Nothing. At least, nothing that indicates anything other than that my father embezzled money from it and repaid it. In fact, I was about ready to give up the project when someone gave Abby a push on the stairs. I have to wonder if we found something and just didn't realize it. Maybe one of the people we've talked to is the culprit, and he's afraid we'll figure it out."

"But why your wife? Why wouldn't they go after you?"

Graeme shook his head. "I don't know. Perhaps because she's an easier target than I? Maybe they think I'll stop looking if something happens to her."

"Or maybe it isn't this embezzlement story at all. What if it's because she saw Baker was shot?"

"The shooter is afraid she could identify him? I suppose it could be, though how she could identify someone at a distance in the dark—and behind her, as well—I cannot imagine. I'll hire a detective to look into Baker's affairs, see if he can find anyone who might have had a reason to kill him. Scotland Yard certainly hasn't seemed to come up with anything." Graeme frowned. "What I wonder is . . . maybe it's someone Abby knows and I don't. He could be worried that at some point she will realize he's to blame."

"Why would she know anyone involved with the fund or Baker? She's been in the States for the past ten years."

"Maybe he's not English." Graeme looked at him intently. "Maybe it's David Prescott."

"Who?" James's blank expression cleared. "You mean the American? The chap who gave you a black eye?"

"He took me by surprise," Graeme muttered. "But yes. That one. Prescott was here ten years ago. I don't remember him, but he told me he worked for Thurston Price. We know the sort of man Thurston was. What if Thurston set up the embezzlement himself? He would know it would give him the leverage to make me do what he wanted. Maybe Thurston had Prescott steal the money and make it look as if Father was to blame. Prescott is in Abby's confidence. She may have told him about Baker, and he realized that Baker could implicate him. So he followed her and shot the man before he could tell her anything."

"But the two of you started investigating anyway, so there was still the possibility he could be exposed."

"Exactly. He could be charged with embezzlement, and even if he were not, it would cause a scandal. Worst of all, Abby would discover the sort of man he is."

"But would he kill your wife? I thought you were certain Prescott was in love with Lady Montclair."

"I'm sure he is. But men have been known to kill the women they love. Prescott was the one who urged Abby to seek a divorce, I'm sure. But she didn't. Instead she came to me. Now she's carrying my child. He's jealous. He'll never have her. He knows Abby's nature; she will remain here, however little feeling she has for me. So he decides that if he can't have her, no one will."

"Seems to me it would be more to the purpose to kill *you.*"

"He might presume it would be more difficult to kill me. Besides, even if he got rid of me, I think he's come to realize Abby isn't going to marry him. She is his friend, but she doesn't love him."

"Graeme . . . are you sure you wouldn't rather be the one to take Lady Montclair to Lydcombe?"

"Of course I—" Graeme started explosively, then cut himself off. In a more even voice, he went on, "It isn't a question of what I would rather. It's what Abigail wishes."

"She wants to be away from you?"

"I think you'll find not many people want to live with someone they think is trying to kill them."

"You can't convince her it's not true?"

"I'm not going to grovel." Graeme folded his arms, glowering. "How could I live with a woman who has so little understanding of me, so little faith, as to think I could try to murder her? Besides, there's no reason any longer for us to be together. She wanted a child and now she's going to have one. Hopefully it will be a boy and I'll have my heir. Everyone is happy."

"Yes, I can see how delighted you are," James agreed drily. "Very well. I'll say nothing more. I am scarcely one to give advice to the lovelorn. I shall escort Lady Montclair— both of them—to Lydcombe. And I will ride over to see them every few days. Though I do trust that at some point my exile will be over."

"It will. Trust me." Graeme's jaw tightened. "I'm going to find who's doing this. And put an end to him."

◦◦◦

When Abby walked out the front door the next day, she was confronted by a tableau of the dowager countess facing down Sir James and an enormous brindle dog. None of them appeared happy. Watching them from the side was Graeme, who merely looked weary. Abby's heart clenched in her chest at the sight of him as Graeme turned to look at her, his face the same remotely polite mask he had worn all yesterday. Not, of course, that she had caught sight of him very often—only at dinner.

She had started more than once to go to him, to try to make him understand that she never believed he had tried to hurt her. But each time, before she'd made it to his door, she had thought of how he had run to Laura when she beckoned, and anger had boiled up in her chest all anew. What did it matter if he thought she misjudged him? That was better than showing him her bruised and battered heart. His anger was preferable to his pity.

"I am not accustomed to sharing a carriage with a beast," Lady Eugenia was saying as Abby came down the steps to the sidewalk.

"He's quite good at warming one's feet," James replied mildly, which earned him a frown from the dowager countess.

"I see no reason for levity," Lady Eugenia snapped. "He can ride in the wagon with the servants and the baggage."

The dog made a noise low in his throat. James laid his fingertips lightly on the animal's head. "Dem . . ." The sound turned into a grunt. The animal sat down, but he and the dowager countess continued to regard each other with disfavor.

"The servants are frightened of him."

"And you think we are not?" Lady Eugenia countered.

"Countess, I don't believe you are frightened of anything."

"Och, for pity's sake," a voice said on the stairs behind them, and they all looked up at Molly, tromping down the steps, a basket on her arm. She snapped her fingers at the mastiff. "Come along with me, you great beast."

The huge animal trotted off beside her, tail wagging and eyes riveted to her basket. The others stared after them, slack-jawed.

"Well, I suppose that settles the matter," James said drily and opened the carriage door.

Graeme handed his grandmother up into the carriage, then turned to Abby. Abby thought she might break down in tears if she stood here another moment looking at him. Averting her face, she put her hand in his and stepped up into the vehicle.

She sat down beside Lady Eugenia and turned to gaze back out the open door. Graeme said nothing, just nodded to her. She could not speak; her throat felt swollen shut, a storm of tears churning in her chest. Abby wanted to reach out to him, but she kept her hands clasped tightly together in her lap. She would not make a scene in front of all these contained Englishmen.

James climbed in after them, taking the seat across from the women, and Graeme closed the door. Abby kept her gaze on her hands, but at the last minute, she could not keep from glancing up. Graeme's face was as smooth and remote as marble. Abby swallowed hard, determined not to cry. She was all too aware of Graeme's cousin watching her with a coolly assessing gaze.

Graeme's grandmother had brought a full quiver of barbed remarks for the journey, though thankfully most of them were directed at Sir James, not at Abby. James, with his cold gray eyes and sardonic expression, seemed well-armored against them. It was almost enough to make Abby miss the company of Mrs. Ponsonby, who, however banal she might be, at least was friendly. But Mrs. Ponsonby had been sent with the servants and luggage, Lady Eugenia having decided that four people in the carriage was entirely too many for her nerves.

Abby was inclined to wish she had gone with the servants as well. The rocking movement of the coach, along with the turns and rises and falls, soon threatened to make her queasy stomach revolt. It had been less than two hours when she had to ask James to stop the carriage.

He took one look at her ashen face and rapped on the roof. They rolled to a stop. Before Lady Eugenia could get out a question, Abby opened the door and scrambled down, hastening away from the carriage.

She drew slow breaths, eyes fixed on the horizon. The cool breeze caressed her cheeks, and gradually her jumping stomach settled. She heard a noise behind her and glanced back. Sir James strolled toward her. "Countess."

"I'm sorry."

He shrugged. "Better to stop than the alternative."

She wondered if the slight movement of his mouth was a smile. "Yes, I suppose it would be."

"Would you like to sit? We could haul one of the trunks down."

"No. I'm fine. I can sit over there on the wall if I need to." She nodded toward a low stone wall with a stile marching over it.

"A mite rustic."

Abby laughed. "I think I can manage it. Right now, I believe a stroll might be best." She started along the dirt path to the stile. To her surprise, James followed. "You needn't come. I'll be fine."

"Montclair would have my head if I let you wander off into the fields alone. I am, after all, here to protect you."

"I doubt anyone is going to attack me in the meadow." Abby climbed up and over the stile, taking a narrow dirt path that led toward a small copse of trees.

"Probably not. But I would be quite red-faced if someone did, now, wouldn't I?" He paused, then went on, "Unless, of course, I'm in on the plot with your husband and plan to do you in once we get out of sight of the carriage."

Abby shot him a sardonic glance. "I am aquake with fear."

"I can see."

"I will admit I could imagine it more of you," she went on in a musing tone, surprising a little crack of laughter from him. "But when you added Graeme to the plot, you lost all hope of convincing me."

"Indeed? I was under the impression you accused him of trying to murder you."

"I was angry. And I didn't accuse him of anything. What I said was that I would be safe as long as I was away from there. That's probably true—*if* someone is trying to kill me. All the 'incidents' have occurred in London. That doesn't mean I think Graeme is behind it."

"Then who do you think is behind it? Aside from myself, of course."

"I don't really know why anyone would be trying to kill me, which is why I find it difficult to believe. All I'm certain of is that it isn't Graeme."

"If that's true, why didn't you tell him so?"

"I told him I didn't mean it, but you can't really 'unsay' things, can you? And he's right; it will be better this way."

"I see. So now that you've gotten what you wanted, you'll toss him aside."

"Toss him aside?" Abby stopped and faced Sir James, a flush of anger staining her cheeks. "I am doing what I can to make up for the wrongs my father and I have done him. He's free to live as he wants now. He can see Miss Hinsdale every blasted day if he chooses. He won't have to lie or pretend to feel what he doesn't. And I won't have to be there to watch him do it."

Tears sprang into her eyes, and she whirled away, embarrassed. "I won't stand here trying to justify myself to you." She turned and stalked back to the carriage, Sir James politely trailing a few steps behind her.

Abby spent most of the rest of the journey with her eyes closed, pretending to sleep and doing her best to keep her stomach under control. That task was helped by the fact that Sir James stopped several times along the way, allowing her to get out and walk around a bit. She was surprised by his thoughtfulness, given his obviously poor opinion of her, but of course, as he had said, stopping was preferable to her being ill inside his luxurious carriage.

They pulled up to Lydcombe Hall late in the afternoon. By the time Abby stepped down from the carriage, the front doors had opened and Graeme's mother was rushing toward them, arms outspread.

"Dearest girl! I am so happy to see you. What wonderful news!" Mirabelle engulfed Abby in a hug. Her mother-in-law was warm and soft and smelled faintly of jasmine.

And, surprising even herself, Abby wrapped her arms around the woman and burst into tears.

"There, now, sweetheart." Mirabelle patted her back, seemingly unperturbed by the sudden storm of tears. "It's going to be fine. Don't you worry about a thing. You're home now."

∞

Strangely enough, Abby did feel as if she was home. Mirabelle swaddled her in such loving care it was impossible not to feel cherished. Abby loved Lydcombe Hall and its gardens, even in the autumn. Her bedroom was lovely and comfortable, the meals delicious. If she expressed a preference for any food, it was on the table the next meal. Her mother-in-law was happy to stay with her or leave her to her own devices, as it suited Abby's mood. Abby was in the best of health, and the baby was as well. Abby knew she should have been walking on air.

Instead, she was lonely and miserable and far too apt to break into tears. Even though she had not yet gained weight, her waist disappeared seemingly overnight. It was wonderfully freeing to give up her corsets, but equally lowering to let out the waists of all her frocks. The nausea began to recede, fortunately, but her moods swung up and down. She found herself snapping at poor Mrs. Ponsonby, whose constant and extreme solicitude grated on Abby's nerves. Abby immediately apologized, of course, but it left her feeling both guilty and annoyed. She had always heard that a pregnant woman's complexion glowed. Hers was pasty. Her hair had lost its sheen.

None of those things would have mattered, she knew, if Graeme had been there. It was his absence that made her ache, that turned her happiness to sorrow. She wanted to talk to him, to share every new and exciting change she was experiencing. Each time she walked through the gardens, she was bombarded by memories of being there with him. She thought of the way his eyes crinkled at the corners when he smiled, the way he turned his head, the heated, heavy-lidded way he looked at her when he was about to take her in his arms.

It seemed almost perverse that she should daydream about him, that her body should ache for his touch, his heat, his kisses. Abby would have presumed—if she had ever thought about it before—that a woman approaching motherhood would have higher thoughts somehow, her physical needs ebbing. But she had found that it was precisely the opposite. Her body betrayed her, yearning for pleasure, and her wayward mind made it worse, returning over and over again to Graeme's lovemaking.

The days dragged by and became weeks. Each day she watched for a letter from him, but there was nothing except a few notes addressed to his mother, in which he always included a terse inquiry as to Lady Abigail's health—she noticed he never called her Abby or his wife. Abby wrote him every day, but tucked each missive away in a growing pile, unsent.

Humiliatingly, she was even reduced to asking Sir James on one of his short, periodic visits if he had heard from Graeme. He glanced at her sharply, but said only, "Yes. A few times. He asks after you."

She nodded. "That is courteous of him." After a moment's silence, unable to stop herself, she went on, "He is well?"

"If he is not, he doesn't say so."

"What does he— I suppose he is quite busy." Abby picked at the monogram on her handkerchief.

"I don't know. His correspondence is more peppered with questions than with details of his life in London. Perhaps, Lady Montclair, if you wished to know what he is doing, you might write him."

"Oh, no, I'm sure he wouldn't . . . he is busy and I, um . . ."

Abby blushed to the roots of her hairline, embarrassed by how much she had revealed of herself. It was clear that Graeme had removed himself from her in every way. She was nothing to him but the carrier of his heir. He did not care about her. He did not desire her. He did not miss her.

And she, who felt all those things for him, was trapped— not by this house or these people or even by the baby inside her, but by her own heart.

chapter 30

Graeme rolled out of bed. He couldn't sleep anymore. Truth was, he rarely slept these days. He just lay awake and churned with feelings. Regret. Lust. Self-pity. Resentment. Pain. All those and a thousand more ran through him, unstoppable, unbearable . . . and utterly *pointless*.

He could not do anything about the situation. James had written him to say Graeme was being a fool, assuring him that Abby had told him she did not suspect Graeme. But Graeme knew that people were apt to tell James what he wanted them to say. And if Abby didn't believe Graeme wanted to do away with her, why the devil didn't she write and tell him that herself?

More than once, Graeme had sat down to pen her a letter, but each time he wound up tangled in a mess of explanations, pleas, and recriminations that would, he was sure, convince no one he was safe or, indeed, even sane. In the end, he would toss the letter into the fire, watching bitterly as the flames took it.

His only hope lay in proving he was not the culprit. To keep Abby safe, to win back her regard—if, indeed, he had ever had it—to make everything *right* again, he must find and punish the man who had tried to harm her.

Punishing him would be no problem. Just thinking about him made Graeme's hands curl into fists, his brain buzz with bloodlust. Finding him, however, had proved rather more difficult.

He had tracked down the other contributors to the soldiers' fund, but with little tangible results. None seemed to have the slightest knowledge of the finances of the charity, nor did any have even a whiff of scandal to relate. Eventually there was no one left to question except the retired vicar of St. Veronica's. Graeme had written the parish asking for the man's current whereabouts, but he had yet to hear from them. And why would Reverend Cumbrey know anything about an embezzlement?

Graeme had been sure the villain was David Prescott. He had hired a detective to investigate Prescott, and Graeme himself talked to every person he could think of who had anything to do with the man. But so far those efforts had proved just as futile as the rest of the investigation. And, really, if he looked at the matter with less heat, he had to agree with Sir James that it made little sense for Prescott to harm Abby. Abby's death would not benefit Prescott. Indeed, it would not benefit anyone—including Graeme himself, for he would be left with only a great gaping hole in his life.

Just as he had been for three weeks now.

With something like a growl, Graeme began to throw on his clothes. Lately he had started getting dressed as soon as he arose, much to the dismay of his valet. But early in the morning, prowling around his room, he felt somehow more vulnerable to all the dark thoughts that plagued him at night. The starched shirt, the layers of waistcoat and jacket, the accoutrements of watch and chain, cuff links, and handkerchief—these things armored him. They were part of his orderly life, the one he'd lived before the whirl-wind of Abigail swept in.

Better to have the binding cuffs, the ascot wound in just the right way and pinned. Far better than the soft glide of a silk dressing gown over his bare skin or the cool caress of sheets against his heated body. They were too-potent re-minders of the sybaritic pleasures he had known and lost, stirring memories that skimmed below the surface, waiting to haunt him.

He cut himself shaving. Twice. He usually left that to Siddings. It was too woeful having to stare into his own eyes. But this morning, he could not stay inside. He had to move, he had to go somewhere. And however far he might have sunk, one could not go out unshaven.

Shrugging into his jacket, he trotted down the stairs to the small anteroom in which he'd taken to dining. Sitting at the formal dining room alone was like living with ghosts. Tea was already waiting on the sideboard there, with Nor-ton standing by. He'd known he would be. It was impossi-ble to arrive before Norton.

Graeme drank a cup of tea and picked at the plate of meats and eggs Norton laid in front of him. It would have taken a trencherman to eat what the butler presented. He and the cook were apparently in a conspiracy to save Graeme with food.

He thought about the small dining room at the Hall. Would Abby be seated there yet? No, far too early; she liked to sleep in. Abby would still be snug in her bed, curled on her side, dark curls tumbled all about her head, soft lips slightly parted.

Graeme's fork clattered to his plate. He shoved back from the table. He could not just sit here. He had to move forward. He had to *do* something. And that something, he decided, would be to confront David Prescott. There was something there. There had to be something there, no matter how little the detective had been able to uncover.

The detective had given him the address of Prescott's office. It was too early for him to be there, but that was all right. Graeme would walk; the chill in the air would help clarify his mind. And he wanted to be waiting when Prescott arrived.

Graeme was lounging against the wall an hour later when Prescott came up the stairs. Prescott saw Graeme as soon as he started down the hall, and there was a momentary pause in his steps before he continued toward him.

"What the hell do you want?" Prescott said without preamble, unlocking the door.

"I want to talk to you."

"I gathered that much." Prescott gestured inside. "Well, come in, then. I'd just as soon not start a shouting match in the hall."

"I have no intention of shouting, Mr. Prescott."

"No? That'd be a switch."

Graeme suppressed his irritation and followed Prescott past a vacant clerk's counter and into an inner office. Prescott nodded toward an uncomfortable-looking wooden chair and went around his desk to sit down behind it. "Now, what do you want to talk to me about?"

"My wife." Graeme ignored the chair and leaned forward, bracing his hands on the desk and fixing his gaze on the other man.

"I would think you'd know more about her than I do, seeing as how you've whisked her away from town and her friends."

"I have 'whisked her away,' as you say, so I can protect her. And I'm not here to find out what you know about her. I'm here to make sure you understand that I will not let you harm her."

"Me?" Prescott's brows shot up. "You're saying *I* would try to harm Abby?"

"Stop calling her that," Graeme ground out. "She is Lady Montclair. And what I'm saying is that you already have tried to harm her. But I won't let it happen again."

"I always thought you must be crazy, but now I know it. Why in the hell would I try to hurt her?"

"Because you're afraid she'll find out you were involved with her father's schemes to blackmail me? The embezzlement?"

David Prescott gaped at him. "I have no idea what you're talking about."

From the man's bewildered expression, Graeme was inclined to think he was telling the truth. "Then maybe it's as simple as this: you covet Abigail. She is married to me; she's carrying my child. You know you'll never have her. And you cannot bear it."

Prescott surged to his feet. "I've known that for ten years." He came around the desk. "I'll tell you this: I've thought a few times about killing *you*. But I never once considered hurting her. There's only one person that would want her dead, and we both know who that is."

"Don't you dare try to turn this back on me." Graeme moved closer to him, fists clenching at his side. "I would never hurt Abby. Never. I am trying to protect her."

"If you're so keen on protecting her, why is she immured in your little castle in the country while you're here in London?"

"Because she's as bloody suspicious as you are!" Graeme swung away. He would have loved to punch something, but he refrained, knowing he'd only look like an even bigger fool than he was.

"You're saying Abby thinks you're trying to kill her?"

"Apparently."

Prescott let out an inelegant snort. "You really don't know a thing about her, do you?" He looked at Graeme for a long moment, then sighed. "Look, I don't like you."

"That doesn't exactly come as a surprise."

Prescott ignored him. "But I'll do you a favor anyway. If I thought Abby would leave with me, I'd take her away from you in a second. But there's no way Abby would go. I know, because I offered."

"What?" Graeme stiffened.

"I told her that I feared for her safety. I offered my help. Abby told me Molly was wrong. It was all nonsense, and you would never hurt her."

"That's a trifle different from what she said to me."

"If Abby was scared of you, why hasn't she fled? She's got money; she's got me; she's got Molly. And she has a father who could slice you up six ways to Sunday and never turn a hair. If she wanted to, Abby would be on the next ship to New York, and I don't care if you're the Earl of Montclair or the King of England, you'd never get her back." Prescott shrugged. "But you go ahead and deceive yourself all you want."

"What is that supposed to mean?"

"I'm not sure if you're a coward or a fool, Montclair. But

it's pretty damn convenient to put the blame on Abby for your desertion."

Rage shot through Graeme. He grabbed Prescott by the lapels and slammed him into the wall behind him. "Damn you! How dare you say— I didn't go with Abby because she didn't want me." Graeme gave him a last little bump into the wall for emphasis and released him.

"Oh, really? Well, if I had a wife and somebody had tried to kill her, I wouldn't be sitting here whining about how she hurt my feelings. I'd damn sure be with her to make certain it didn't happen again. No matter what she told me."

∽

Graeme left Prescott's office in a fury. His mind raging, he strode aimlessly through the streets. He remembered the last night he had walked like this, lost in his thoughts, until he was literally lost as well. That, too, had been about Abby. It seemed he always wound up in a daze over her. If he believed in magic, he'd think she had bewitched him.

Graeme had always tried to conduct himself as a gentleman. He didn't intrude on others, least of all a lady. He wouldn't think of forcing his attentions on her or even importuning her. One treated one's wife with care and respect, and in that area he had fallen woefully short at the very beginning. It seemed the least he could do now was to leave Abigail alone.

It didn't matter that he wanted her so much it hurt or that he was lonely or bored or missed her smile. Her laugh. Her eyes. Except, damn it, he did want her, and he was thoroughly miserable. And, truthfully, he was bloody tired of being polite.

What if Prescott was right? Was he a fool? Or a coward?

Maybe he was both. Sometimes he felt as if he didn't know anything anymore, least of all himself.

What if not imposing on Abby was merely a pretext, a way of holding himself apart, aloof? A way of avoiding the truth. What if it was just that he was frightened? Scared that he might tell her all this—how he felt, what he wanted, how utterly miserable he was without her, and she wouldn't care?

He wound up finally sitting in Hyde Park. He felt adrift, unable to find the guidelines. It was hours before he dragged himself home. He avoided Norton, who sought to press more food on him, and shut the door on Siddings's fussing.

Alone, he opened the door to Abby's room.

The faint scent of her perfume lingered here, as tangible as a caress. His eyes moved around the room, finally stopping on the bed. He turned away from it and crossed the room, trailing his hand along the dresser. There was nothing on it but a lamp and a lace runner, no trace of Abby. The vanity was much the same, the little pots and bottles and cases that had sat there gone.

He thought of watching her brush out her hair or apply her perfume before a party. He remembered the way she would dab it behind her ears, on her wrists, between her breasts. His loins tightened with the familiar, insistent ache.

He opened the wardrobe. She had left a few dresses there, one of them the purple taffeta gown she had worn the night of Lady Middleton's ball. The night their marriage had crashed into ruin. The last time they'd made love.

Graeme slid his hand down the dress, remembering the swish of it as she walked. He bunched the material in his fist. He thought of how he had stood across the ballroom, riveted by the sight of her in this gown, completely unaware of the conversation around him. Abby had turned and looked across at him and she had smiled, lowering her eyes as if she were a blushing maiden, but sending that wicked glance up at him.

The thought was enough to make him harden. He leaned in, resting his forehead against the fabric, cool as water, breathing in the scent of her, remembering the smell of their sex in his nostrils, the bliss of being sheathed in her tight heat, her arms clasped around him as if she would never let go.

He stepped back and closed the door. And he knew: whatever it cost, whatever the pain or fear or right or wrong of it, it didn't matter. He refused to stay away from Abby for a moment longer.

chapter 31

It was too late to take the train, so Graeme rode to Lydcombe. It was almost midnight before he reached Lydcombe Hall, and the windows of the house were dark. He was gratified to see a groom walking around the house, lantern in hand, keeping watch as Graeme had ordered. The man turned at the sound of the horse's hooves and stepped forward to stop Graeme, raising the lantern.

"My lord!" The groom broke into a grin. "Welcome home, sir. Didn't know you was coming in tonight."

"No one did." Graeme dismounted and tossed the man the reins.

"A surprise, eh? The ladies will be happy."

"Let us hope so." Graeme trotted up the steps.

A footman sitting on the bench inside the entry popped up, reaching for the cudgel beside him. "Oh. My lord. Sorry, sir." He set the thick stick back on the bench.

"No, I'm glad to see you're at the ready." He, like the footman, spoke in the hushed tones the darkened house seemed to call for.

"Thank you, sir. I'll get your luggage."

"No need. My valet will bring it with him tomorrow. I came ahead early." Shrugging out of his jacket, he cast a look up the stairs to the darkness above. "Everyone's already in bed, I see."

"Yes, sir, country hours."

"And the countess, is she well? My countess, I mean."

"Yes, sir, in the pink, I'd say. She'll be even better now you're here."

"Mm." Graeme was less sure of that, but he said nothing, just picked up a candle from the nearest table and, throwing his jacket over his arm, started quietly up the stairs. He tugged at his ascot as he went, progressing to unfastening his waistcoat and shirt as he slipped softly down the corridor toward his room. Tired and ready for sleep as he was, still he stopped outside Abby's closed door. He was sorely tempted to go inside.

But it would be unkind to risk awakening her just so he could see her face. And what if she *wasn't* happy to see him? He could not bear that. Graeme continued to his room, his head down, his attention on the cuff links he was removing. He had walked several steps into his bedroom before he looked up. His gaze fell on his bed, and he froze. Abigail was tucked into his bed, sound asleep.

The candlestick trembled faintly in his hand. And the knot that had been sitting inside his chest for so long loosened. She had chosen to sleep in his bed. Graeme set the candlestick on the dresser and sat down to remove his boots. Taking up the candle again, he went over to the bed.

Abby lay on her side, just as he had imagined her yesterday, dark hair spilling over the pillow. Her lips were slightly parted; her lashes shadowed her cheeks. She was the most beautiful thing he'd ever seen. He should, he knew, snuff out the candle so he wouldn't awaken her, but he wanted too much to look at her. It seemed forever since he had seen her, though it had been only three weeks. He knew; he had counted every dragging day.

Putting the candlestick on the table, he sat down on the bed beside her. Abby stirred and edged closer to him, her hand sliding over onto his leg. It lay like a brand on his thigh, and if he had not already been stiff just from the sight of her curled up cozily between his sheets, he certainly was now.

Need throbbed in him. It had been so long. He wanted her so much. He shouldn't awaken her. Graeme curved his hand over her cheek, pushing back the strand of dark hair that had fallen across it.

Abby's eyes fluttered open and she looked up at him, still half-asleep. "Graeme!" A smile blazed across her face and she flung herself up against him, her arms curling around his neck. "You're here."

He wrapped his arms around her, squeezing her to him. God, it was heaven to hold her again, to feel her burrow into him, to hear her murmur his name in breathy little gasps as she pressed her lips against his neck.

Graeme kissed her all across her face, digging his fingers into her hair, and settled finally on her mouth, drinking in her taste, her scent, her feel—all so deliciously familiar, so long untasted. Until this moment, he had not realized the depth of his emptiness, the glacial cold that had settled inside him. He slid his hand over her body, curling over her breast, and his mouth traveled over the tender skin of her throat, wanting her, all of her, at once.

Abby's hands slipped beneath the sides of his open shirt, gliding across his naked skin. He pulled his hands away from her long enough to shrug out of his shirt and waistcoat and throw them blindly behind him. Abby had sat up and was tugging at her nightgown. Graeme reached over to whip it up and off her, sending it to join his clothes on the floor.

He looked at her in the golden glow of the candle, rediscovering each line and curve of her body. Reaching out, he cupped her breasts, teasing the nipples to hardness with his thumbs. "You are so beautiful."

Bending down, he took one breast in his mouth, his tongue stroking, circling, as if nothing existed in the world but this pleasure. Abby made a soft noise, her fingers clutching at his shoulders. Lifting his head, he pressed a soft kiss on the pebbled nipple, then turned his attention to the other breast. The moan that escaped her now was not so soft.

Still tormenting them both with the slow, languid caress of his mouth, he reached down, groping for the sheet and blanket still covering Abby's lower half. He ripped them aside and his hand started a slow glide up her leg.

He left her breast, sitting up now so that he could look at her. The curve of her hips, the dark V between her legs, the shadowy separation of her legs. She filled his vision. He could not get enough of looking at her.

Graeme watched his hand on her satiny white skin as it slid up her leg. His fingers slipped between her thighs, seeking her hot center. A tremor shook him when he found her ready for him, slick and wet and hot.

She whimpered his name as his fingers stroked her. Almost immediately she arched against his hand, her legs clamping around him, and a sharp little cry escaped her lips.

"Abby . . ." he murmured in surprise.

"I'm sorry," she whispered. "I just—"

"No." His voice was laced with satisfaction. "Don't be sorry. Don't ever be sorry. Just let me take you with me now."

He unbuttoned his trousers and shoved them down. He moved between her legs, resting on his forearms. Gazing down into her face, he entered her with aching slowness, his muscles taut with the effort of holding back his desire. Her soft groan as he filled her was his reward, as was the way she moved with him, urging him on. She felt slightly different against his body as he slid over her, and he realized that her abdomen now curved out a little, his seed growing inside her. And that was another delight, as well.

Burying his face in her neck, he struggled to rein in the hunger that raged inside him, prolonging the supreme pleasure of being in her. Her scent, her heat, her softness surrounded him, her ragged breath filled his ears. Her fingertips dug into his back. This was all he wanted. All he needed.

And now, at last, he let go, felt the rush take him, hurtling him into the deep, dark well of passion, and felt, too, the convulsion inside her. He collapsed against her, utterly spent and mind-numbingly sated, unable to move or speak or even think, aware only that he was, completely and finally, home.

∞

Graeme's relaxed body pressed her into the mattress. Abby didn't mind; she loved the feel of his weight on her. She slid her hand lazily over his back, tracing the familiar contours of muscle and bone. It was in these moments that she felt that he belonged to her and she to him. It seemed forever since she had basked in the glow of his satisfaction or felt the blissful languor that flooded her now.

Finally Graeme rolled to the side. Abby hated the loss, but he slid his arm beneath her and pulled her with him, tight against his side. She settled her head into his shoulder and let her hand roam his chest. She could not keep from touching him.

"I've missed you," he murmured, and she felt his lips press against her hair.

"You have?" Abby rose up on her elbow, staring intently into his face.

"Yes. Of course." He lifted his eyebrows. "Why else would I come riding in at this time of night?"

"I don't know."

He sank his fingers into her hair, studying her face. "I was . . . surprised to find you sleeping in my bed."

"Oh. I'm sorry; I, um . . ."

"No, no, don't apologize. I liked it." She could hear the smile in his voice. "I just wondered why."

"Well . . ." She cast about for a reasonable explanation. She could hardly say it was because his scent clung to the pillows or because it made him seem nearer. "Sometimes, when I can't sleep, I come in here. It's . . . I . . ."

He stroked his fingers lightly down her arm. "Are you saying you missed me as well?"

"Yes," she admitted grudgingly.

"Even though you think I tried to murder you?"

"Graeme! I never did." She sat up, glaring at him. "I told you I didn't really think that. I just said the first thing that came into my head." Abby turned away, pulling up her knees, looping her arms around them and laying her head atop them. "I was talking about London, that house; it was only there that I had been in danger." She paused, then admitted, "And I wanted to insult you. I wanted to make you angry, as I was angry." She let out a sigh. "I'm not a lady; I'm not even nice. I realize more all the time that I am becoming like my father."

"Believe me, you are nothing like Thurston Price." He reached out and smoothed back her hair. "It wasn't the insult, Abby. It was knowing you didn't trust me that hurt."

"No." She whipped back around, taking his hand between both hers. "I *did* trust you. I do. I was just so furious."

"Is that why you pushed me away from you?"

"I didn't push you away." Abby frowned. "What are you talking about?"

"You told me my services were no longer required. You'd achieved your goal, and I was no longer necessary."

"I didn't say that!" She stared at him, aghast. "Graeme, I know I did not say that. I released you from our agreement; I gave you your freedom."

"You might have asked me if I wanted my 'freedom.'"

"But—I was trying to make up for forcing you to do something you didn't want."

He reached out, curling his hand around her wrist, and said fiercely, "I didn't do anything I didn't want. Do you think you could have forced me to drag you into bed every chance I got? That I was coerced into turning hard as stone whenever I looked at you? That you compelled me to spend my days weaving lascivious fantasies about you?"

Abby stared at him, heat stirring low in her abdomen. "Graeme—"

"I desired you from the moment I saw you standing in that ballroom in the midst of your innumerable admirers. I wanted them all at the devil and you in my bed. Your offer was temptation, not force. I was angry because I didn't want to give in to you, and I feared I couldn't resist."

"Really?" Abby's smile was impish. She swung her leg over his hips, straddling him, her fingertips straying over his chest. "I'm not sure I believe you."

"No?" A half smile played upon his lips, and his lids grew heavy, his eyes dark and hot with promise. He laid his hands on her legs and ran them slowly up her body. "Then perhaps I ought to show you."

She moved against him, eliciting a low groan as he pulsed and hardened beneath her. "Yes. I think perhaps you should." Abby bent to kiss him.

chapter 32

Abby awoke the next morning feeling a little sore and wonderfully replete. It was a bit of a disappointment to look over and see that Graeme was not there. But it was like him to thoughtfully slip out without awakening her.

She stretched lazily like a cat and folded her arms behind her head, contemplating the delightful turn her life had taken last night. Why had Graeme come? Had it truly been just because he missed her? Her smile spread. She had the feeling she might not ever stop smiling.

She sat up, running her fingers through her hair, then reached for her dressing gown, loving the glide of the satin lining over her sensitized skin. He had not said he loved her, but Abby could live with that. He had been hurt by her offer of freedom, and that was enough. He wanted her, and that, too, was enough.

It would be nice, of course, to hear him say he loved her, only her, and that Laura Hinsdale had no hold on his heart. She yearned to know that he felt for her what she felt for him. But for now, for this moment, she would bask in the glow of his desire, in the knowledge that he had ridden from London just to be with her.

She had enough love for both of them.

Abby swung out of bed and started toward her room, smiling to herself at the sight of their clothes scattered over the floor. She paused to pick them up and toss them onto the bed, then continued to her room.

Her mood was too sunny for even Molly to dampen—and surprisingly, her maid didn't say a sour thing about Graeme arriving last night. Abby sailed downstairs on her cloud of goodwill, so happy that she beamed at Lady Eugenia and Mrs. Ponsonby as well as Mirabelle.

"Abby, darling," Mirabelle trilled. "Isn't it wonderful that Graeme arrived?"

"Yes. I'm very happy." She loaded up her plate, humming beneath her breath.

"Oh, dear, now we're to have singing again?" Lady Eugenia asked.

Abby laughed. "I'm afraid so."

"Don't be so stuffy, Eugenia," Graeme's mother said, surprising them all. "I love to hear Abby sing. It raises my spirits."

"Where *is* Graeme?" Normally Abby would not have exposed herself by asking after him, but this morning she felt too good to care.

His grandmother sniffed. "Off chasing his foolish notions."

"He went to call on Mr. Cumbrey, dear," Mirabelle explained.

"Cumbrey!" Abby stared, her happy certainty beginning to crumble. Was that why Graeme had come home? "He found out the vicar lives nearby?"

"Yes, I told him a few minutes ago," Mirabelle replied. "It was the oddest thing. I asked him what he'd been doing, you know, as one does. He said he'd been talking to all those men who helped Reginald with that charity. Graeme seems to think that it would help keep you safe."

"Poppycock," Lady Eugenia snorted.

"Yes, well, I didn't really understand it, either, but he was obviously feeling at a loss about the whole matter. So I suggested he talk to Cumbrey; the dear man was always so helpful to Reginald. Wasn't he, Philomena?"

"Oh, yes." Mrs. Ponsonby nodded. "He was. He was most fond of Montclair and of George, too." Unsurprisingly, her eyes glinted with tears.

"Anyway," Mirabelle hurried on, "when I said that, Graeme literally jumped up from his chair and exclaimed, 'You know where he is? Why didn't you tell me?' Well, he'd never asked, had he?"

"Oh, my!" Abby began to laugh. Graeme's mother stared at her, which only made her laugh harder. Abby brought her napkin up to her mouth to muffle the sound.

"You're acting just as odd as Graeme did," Mirabelle said in amazement.

"They're both mad as hatters," the dowager countess proclaimed.

"I'm sorry." Abby struggled to control her laughter. "It's just that we have been hunting all over for Mr. Cumbrey."

"But he's right here. Well, not right here, but he's only an hour's ride away. He retired to a little cottage in Lower Brockington. He used to have the living there, you see, before St. Veronica's. That's how Reginald knew him."

"I cannot imagine what Montclair finds so fascinating about the man," Lady Eugenia said. "He's very ordinary."

"However that may be, Graeme went tearing off to see him," Mirabelle assured her. "He left half his breakfast on his plate."

"All this rushing about." Lady Eugenia shook her head dolefully. "It's bad for the digestion. He'll be gone half the day, and he just got here. We've barely seen him. You'd think the boy could have some consideration."

"I know!" Mrs. Ponsonby spoke up, startling them all. "We should go to Tunbridge Wells."

"Whatever for?" Lady Eugenia asked.

"Lord Montclair will be gone. I'm sure Abigail would enjoy having a day out, wouldn't you, dear?"

"I—yes, certainly." Abby had no interest in Tunbridge Wells, but it was so rare that Mrs. Ponsonby spoke up, she hated to turn her down.

"We could go shopping," Mrs. Ponsonby proffered. "It's not far. We could take the train."

"I would like to buy a new hat," Mirabelle agreed.

"Before we come home, we could rest at the Swan," Mrs. Ponsonby suggested. "You know, that inn where you liked their rack of lamb, Lady Eugenia."

The dowager countess looked thoughtful. "Their flummery is rather pleasant, as well."

The famously pleasant pudding was apparently a powerful lure, for in the end the dowager countess agreed that the day's expedition would be nice. Abby would have preferred to be at home when Graeme returned, but the trip would pass the time, and anyway, perhaps she should not seem so patently willing to sit and wait for him. After all, he could have delayed it a bit and taken her with him.

Abby soon found that a shopping trip with the Ladies Montclair left a great deal to be desired. Graeme's mother tended to like everything and his grandmother nothing, which made for an endless morning of bickering, genial on Mirabelle's side and acerbic on the part of Lady Eugenia.

Mrs. Ponsonby, however, was clearly thrilled. She chattered away, pointing out all the sights of Tunbridge Wells to Abby, and even Lady Eugenia's curt admonition to her to be quiet did not throw her into a hurt silence. Looking at the woman's bright eyes and the color in her cheeks, Abby could not be sorry she had agreed to go.

The meal they shared at the private dining room at the inn was too heavy for Abby, and she ate sparingly, ignoring the thick potato soup. After the flummery, Lady Eugenia decreed that they should sit for a moment and "let it settle." The room was very warm, and both Graeme's mother and grandmother soon nodded off.

Mrs. Ponsonby yawned delicately, raising Abby's hopes that the companion, too, would succumb to a nap, freeing Abby to leave the suffocating room for a stroll outside. She had caught a glimpse of an attractive park behind the inn, with a pathway leading across a quaint bridge.

"My, there must be something in the food. I am a trifle drowsy myself. It's rather stuffy in here, isn't it?" Mrs. Ponsonby tittered, covering her mouth. When Abby agreed, she went on, "Shall we take a stroll out back? It's a lovely place, for a common inn."

"Wonderful." While Mrs. Ponsonby would not be her preferred choice of companion, Abby was eager to get out of the overheated room and into the fresh air. Putting on her bonnet, she left her coat and gloves behind. The cool air would feel pleasant, coming from the heat of this room.

It took Mrs. Ponsonby longer to put on her coat, bonnet, and gloves, and she grabbed a parasol as well. Abby wasn't sure why the woman thought she needed both bonnet and parasol in the pale autumn sun, but Abby was by now accustomed to Mrs. Ponsonby's cautious ways.

They strolled out the side door and wound around to the back. Here, away from the noise of the inn and its stable yard, was a pleasant rose garden with a winding path through it and a few benches here and there. At the far end was a small footbridge leading across a rushing stream.

"Are you feeling well?" Mrs. Ponsonby asked anxiously. "Would you care to sit and rest for a bit?"

"No. I'm fine. But you are welcome to sit if you want." Perhaps Mrs. Ponsonby would choose to stay and rest on one of the garden benches, leaving Abby to meander on her own.

"Oh, no, I'm quite well, thank you. But you mustn't tire yourself."

"I enjoy walking."

"Yes, I have seen you in the gardens at the Hall." Mrs. Ponsonby fiddled with her gloves, glancing about. She was always a fluttery creature, but she seemed unusually so today. Abby began to suspect that Lady Eugenia's companion was working up the courage to ask her something, but the other woman merely said, "You shouldn't go out alone, you know. The earl would not like it. He's most concerned about you."

"There are always gardeners around."

Mrs. Ponsonby continued to scan the area, even turning to glance behind them. She had not opened her umbrella, but carried it on the shaft as one would a club. It occurred to Abby that the woman, though several inches shorter and many years older than Abby, considered herself Abby's protector.

"Still, you should take a companion. What if no one was close enough to come to your aid?" Mrs. Ponsonby peered anxiously into Abby's face. "Are you feeling tired? Sleepy? Here is a bench; we could stop to rest."

Abby suppressed her irritation. The woman meant well. "No, I'd like to look at the brook. It's a charming bridge." She pointed to the small humpbacked stone bridge.

"My, yes, of course, so charming. But the wall is rather low, don't you think? You must be careful. Are you sure you wouldn't like to stop and rest first? That's the last bench, and—"

"No." Abby spoke more sharply than she had intended. With an inward sigh, she turned to apologize. Mrs. Ponsonby was clutching the parasol so tightly her knuckles had turned white, and her customary ingratiating smile was more a grimace. Whatever was the matter with her? "Is something wrong?"

"Why aren't you sleepy?" The older woman's voice was thin and high. "You should be sleepy. The others fell asleep."

Abby stared, taken aback by the odd statement. "Well, ah, I—the meal was a trifle heavy, and—Mrs. Ponsonby, are you all right? You're trembling."

"Didn't you eat the soup?"

"No, I didn't care for it." Abby reached out to take the other woman's arm, alarmed by the wild look in her eyes. "Come, you should sit—"

A shriek broke from the woman as she jerked her arm out of Abby's grasp. "You never do what you're supposed to! Why won't you die?"

Mrs. Ponsonby lifted the folded parasol and swung it at Abby's head. Instinctively Abby dodged, and it struck only a glancing blow, knocking Abby's bonnet askew. Still, it was hard enough to make her head ring.

Abby whirled to run, but her heel caught, and she stumbled. She grabbed at a bush as she fell, and though the thorns pierced her skin, she was able to break her fall. *The baby.* She had to protect the baby.

Mrs. Ponsonby was already on her, swinging the parasol from the tip end, so that the heavier handle would strike Abby. All Abby could do was raise her arms to block the blow. As the other woman drew back to hit her again, Abby grabbed the parasol, and they grappled over it. Abby was larger and younger than the other woman, but Mrs. Ponsonby held the better position and she seemed possessed of an insane strength.

She now put all her weight against the shaft, bearing down, and Abby knew she intended to crush it against Abby's throat. Abby locked her arms, exerting all her strength and will.

"Die! You *will* die," the other woman said over and over, almost chanting.

At that moment a voice floated through the garden behind them. "Lady Montclair? Mrs. Ponsonby?"

Abby was flooded with relief. Some servant at the inn must have been sent in search of her. Mrs. Ponsonby would have to stop now that there was a witness.

But she did not. Instead she bore down harder, taking advantage of Abby's momentary relaxation, and the parasol moved several perilous inches closer. Abby turned her head, shouting, "Here!"

A slender woman appeared in the distance, and at the scene before her, she broke into a run. Her bonnet fell back, exposing the sedate knot of blond hair atop her head, and Abby recognized her. Laura Hinsdale.

Despair flooded her. It *had* been Laura Hinsdale behind this. It was not help running toward her, but reinforcements for her enemy.

chapter 33

Graeme dismounted and strode up to the door of the small cottage. He wished he had not jumped up and run out at his mother's news. It would have been far more pleasant to have taken Abby with him. But by the time he thought of it, he was already halfway there. Well, it wasn't as if he was likely to learn anything from the man. He would get this task done, and then he would have as much time with Abigail as he wanted.

He smiled a little to himself, wondering if that was even possible. The door opened to reveal a small, stoop-shouldered man with a fringe of white hair.

"Reverend Cumbrey? Please forgive me for dropping in on you like this. I was hoping for a word with you. I am Lord Montclair, Reginald's son."

"Lord Montclair!" The man's face lit up. "Come in. Come in. It's no trouble, no trouble at all." Cumbrey smiled benignly at him. "Always happy to talk to Montclair's son. Such a good man, your father. You look very like him. I expect you hear that often, though."

"Now and then. But one never objects to such a compliment."

The old man offered him tea and inquired about his

mother and the dowager countess. The social niceties taken care of, he settled back in his chair. "Now, then, lad, what can I do for you?"

"I was interested in the fund my father established, the one for soldiers."

"Ah, yes, wounded and indigent soldiers. Excellent idea. I was always happy to hold a fete or two at St. Veronica's. I was always fond of him . . . and his cousin George, of course."

"Do you recall why my father ended it?"

"I was sorry to see him do so." The old man shook his head dolefully. "But, of course, things were in such a state at the time. I believe he had been adversely affected by a stock that crashed. Ponsonby, too. Then poor Ponsonby had that dreadful accident, you know."

"Yes," Graeme said encouragingly when the vicar paused. "The loss of money had an effect on the fund?"

"On them, of course. I don't believe any of the fund money was invested in it. Your father always kept it in something safe, you see. He was careful like that. I remember he told me once he hadn't a head for business, so he took extra care with the charity's money. No, it was losing his friend like that, I think, that hit him hard." He sighed. "Especially coming right after they'd quarreled."

Graeme went still. "They had a disagreement? My father and Mr. Ponsonby? Do you know why?"

"Oh, well, one doesn't want to speculate. I overheard a bit of it—quite by accident, you understand. It was a while after that last fete; I had come to call on Lord Montclair because I was in London. I was waiting to see him—walking along the hall there, looking at the paintings, you know. The door was closed, but their voices grew rather loud. I didn't want to eavesdrop, so I returned to the bench in the entry."

"Please, sir, it's very important to me. If there is anything you remember . . ."

"Well." The vicar paused, wrinkling his brow in thought. "I don't remember the exact words, but it sounded like Mr. Ponsonby was supposed to do something for your father, and he didn't. Forgot or something, I suppose. I do remember that Lord Montclair said something like, 'How can I trust you now?'" Cumbrey's pale cheeks colored a little. "Sounds a bit dramatic, doesn't it?"

"Yes, but please, go on."

"No doubt it was something minor, but I'd no sooner gone back to that bench than Ponsonby came rushing out. Walked right past me and out the front door without a word. Your father followed, looking like a thundercloud. When he saw me sitting there, Montclair seemed a bit taken aback, but of course I made it clear that I had heard nothing."

"Of course."

"The next time I saw your father was at Ponsonby's funeral, in fact. He was quite shaken, you know. We all were. Such a terrible accident . . . and coming right on the heels of their harsh words."

Except, Graeme thought, it hadn't been an accident. Ponsonby had killed himself.

Cumbrey went on, shaking his head, "I am sure Lord Montclair was most distraught over it. He would have bitterly regretted that his friend had died with hard words still between them. No chance to make things right."

"Tell me, did Mr. Ponsonby help my father a good deal with the charity?"

"What? Oh, well, yes, I imagine he did. As I remember, Ponsonby was apt to run errands and such for him if Lord Montclair needed it. Mr. Bangston, as well." He smiled. "Your father had that effect on people, you know."

"Yes, I remember."

"Not, of course, that he took advantage of anyone," Cumbrey added hastily. "He was just such a pleasant fellow."

"I suppose Mr. Ponsonby dealt with some of the financial matters for the fund—that is the sort of thing he did for Father?"

"Yes, I think so. Your father always dealt with the people; he had such a way with them. But I'm sure he left a number of the details to his friends."

"Like entering the numbers in the accounts book?" Graeme suggested.

"Yes. Exactly." The vicar beamed at his quick understanding. "I remember after that last fete we held, Ponsonby was going to London, so he carried the money to the bank for Lord Montclair."

"I see." There it was, tumbling so innocently, so casually, from the vicar's lips . . . the secret Baker must have known and intended to sell to Abby. It had not been his father who embezzled the money from the charity, but his childhood friend, his cousin. Reginald had entrusted the money to Ponsonby and Ponsonby had instead used it to buy into the same worthless stock that ruined Montclair.

Graeme stayed for a few minutes longer, talking with the vicar, though afterward he had no idea what had been said by either of them. As soon as he could politely take his leave, he did so, mounting his horse and riding for home. He was eager to lay the whole story out in front of Abigail and see if the same conclusions leapt out at her as they had at him.

His father had been happy to leave a mundane task such as depositing the money into the bank to his trusted friend George. It wouldn't have occurred to Reginald to think that it wasn't safe, that the money might prove too much of a temptation for Ponsonby, who was always in financial straits.

Ponsonby had taken the money and foolishly followed Reginald's example by investing in the same stock, with equally disastrous results. No, far more disastrous, for Ponsonby had had no American robber baron waiting in the wings, eager to exchange cash for a British title. Ponsonby must have gone to his friend and confessed, resulting in the quarrel Reverend Cumbrey had overheard. Devastated by Montclair's anger at what he had done, facing the loss of Reginald's friendship and the public disgrace, Ponsonby had gone home and committed suicide.

No wonder his father blamed himself. Reginald had allowed his friend access to the money when he should not have and as a result had lost both the money and his friend. It all made sense—although it threw his speculations about the attempts on Abby's life off course. The danger couldn't have come from the person who had taken the money ten years ago; he was dead. No one would care about the damage to George's reputation if they discovered the truth.

Graeme's hands tightened convulsively on the reins as he realized that there was one person who would care. Philomena Ponsonby, who adored her husband and would hate to see his memory tarnished. The woman who was living in his home, only feet away from Abigail. The woman who was with Abby at this very moment.

Graeme dug his heels into his horse's sides, and the animal leaped forward. He turned off the road, taking a path that cut through fields and trees, an ancient byway used long before the Normans came, probably even before the Romans. It was narrow and in places rougher, with walls and brooks along the way. But his mount was a hunter and could handle the obstacles, and the old path was far shorter.

Even as he rode as fast as he dared on the trail, he told himself he was being foolish. Surely the meek, diminutive woman who was his grandmother's companion was incapable of trying to kill anyone. It was ludicrous to think that she had left their house in London that night and hidden herself at the docks, then shot Mr. Baker.

That thought steadied him, but hard on its heels came another—she would have been in a perfect position to set fire to Abby's room. It was that attempt that had seemed unlikeliest to Graeme, the one that made him wonder if he had merely been starting at shadows. How could a stranger have broken in and gone creeping about the house in the middle of the night without anyone noticing?

But it would have been easy enough for a resident of the house to do it. Mrs. Ponsonby would have known it was Abby's habit to drink a cup of hot chocolate every night. The cook made it and set it out for Molly to carry up to her. No one would have noticed if Mrs. Ponsonby slipped by and poured a bit of laudanum in it. No doubt there was a bottle of the stuff among their medicines; his grandmother often took it when her rheumatism flared up.

Then she would only have had to wait until the household was asleep to finish the deed. No one would have seen Mrs. Ponsonby walking down the hall and if by chance she had run into someone, she could easily have made up an excuse for being there. All it would have taken was entering Abby's room and lighting a candle or taking an already burning one and holding it to the drapes.

Easy, too, for her to mingle with the other women on the staircase at the Middleton ball and give Abby a push. Mrs. Ponsonby was one of those women one never noticed.

She wouldn't have had to shoot Mr. Baker herself. There were people one could hire to do such things—though how a genteel middle-aged woman like Mrs. Ponsonby would know how to go about that was a mystery.

He cursed himself for not having talked to the vicar sooner. He should have made more of a push to find the man. Instead, he had focused all his attention on David Prescott. Hell, all he would have needed to do was ask his mother. Most of all, he should not have sent Abby to the estate. He should have kept her close to him, but he had let himself be ruled by his wounded pride.

His reason reasserted itself somewhat at this point, and he had to chuckle at the idea that he could "send" his wife or "keep" her as he chose. Abigail would go where and when and with whom she pleased.

If he thought about it rationally, he realized, there was no reason to think that Mrs. Ponsonby, if she was indeed the culprit, would attack Abby in broad daylight in the company of his mother and grandmother. The other attempts had been sly and secretive; she would not suddenly turn to an outright assault. They had been here for almost a month, and she had not tried to harm Abby. Indeed, maybe she balked at the idea of killing the Montclair heir. All the attempts had been before Abby announced she was pregnant.

His reassurances could not quell his anxiety, and when he reached Lydcombe, he tossed the reins to a groom and ran into the house. Since the nearest entrance was through the kitchen, he startled the servants. Fletcher immediately popped out of his butler's pantry.

"Lord Montclair. May I help you?"

"Where's Lady Montclair? My wife. I need to speak to her."

"Why, all the ladies have gone into Tunbridge Wells, sir."

"What? Why?" The anxiety he had tried to suppress spurted up in him again at full force.

The butler looked startled at Graeme's reaction but quickly shuttered his expression. "A shopping expedition, and I believe they meant to dine at the inn the dowager countess favors."

A curse escaped Graeme. "What about Mrs. Ponsonby? Did she go, too?"

"Yes, I believe so, sir. Shall I send a maid to see if she is here? Perhaps you'd like to sit down; I'll fetch you a cup of tea."

"No, no. If you say she's gone, I'm sure she is." Graeme turned away, then back. "The Swan? Is that the inn you mean?"

"Yes, I believe so. Also, sir . . . Miss Hinsdale called here earlier."

"Laura?" Graeme gaped at him. "What in the world is she—no, it doesn't matter. I can't see her now. I have to leave; give her my abject apologies and—"

"Oh, she's not here, my lord. When I told her the ladies had gone to Tunbridge Wells, she seemed most agitated. She said she could not stay; she had to find them. I had the carriage brought round for her; I thought you would not—"

Graeme interrupted him. "Are you saying Laura went after them?"

"That was my understanding, sir. She was, well, she was acting in a manner most unlike Miss Hinsdale, if you'll pardon me for . . ."

He trailed off as Graeme whirled and ran back through the kitchen and out the door.

∽

Desperation gave Abby an added burst of strength, and she shoved upward with all her might, twisting as she did so. The sudden move shifted Mrs. Ponsonby off-balance, and with another heave, Abby rolled the small woman off her. Mrs. Ponsonby scrambled to get up, but Abby swung her legs out, cutting the companion's feet out from under her. Mrs. Ponsonby tumbled to the ground.

Abby jumped to her feet, sweeping up the parasol with her. She didn't take the time to look back at Laura. She could hear the woman's running footsteps and knew Laura was altogether too close. Abby would have no chance against the two of them, but her legs were decidedly longer than either of theirs and she was unhampered by a corset. Abby ran away.

Behind her she heard Mrs. Ponsonby's enraged screech, and Abby could not keep from glancing back. The woman had made it to her feet and was turning to pursue Abby, but at that moment, Laura barreled into the woman, knocking her to the ground.

Abby was so shocked she stumbled to a halt, staring at the two women rolling around on the ground. Laura had not come to join Mrs. Ponsonby, Abby realized, but to help Abby. Lifting her skirts, she ran back toward the wrestling women.

Laura, her bonnet torn loose and hanging by its strings down her back, managed to get on top of the other woman, but Mrs. Ponsonby reached out and grasped a branch lying on the ground.

"Laura, watch out!" Abby screamed, but Mrs. Ponsonby was already swinging her hand up, and she hit Laura on the side of her head.

Laura collapsed, blood streaming over her pale hair. Abby knew she should run; her first duty was to protect her unborn child. But she could not run away and leave the woman who had tried to help her lying helpless on the ground. Lifting the parasol, Abby let out a wordless bellow and charged.

Mrs. Ponsonby came up swinging the branch. The parasol and branch clashed together like swords. The branch was stouter than the slender shaft of the sunshade, and it left a dent in the side of the parasol. Abby felt the shudder of the collision all the way up her arm. She barely managed to keep her grip on it.

It was an unfortunate reality that the branch was not only thicker than the stem of the parasol, it was also longer. Its length negated Abby's advantage in reach, making it almost impossible for her to get close enough to hit Mrs. Ponsonby. Mrs. Ponsonby moved forward, sweeping the branch back and forth in front of her, and Abby was forced to retreat, parrying her blows as best she could.

At some point, Abby knew, the branch would break the parasol's staff. Her only hope was to keep the woman occupied long enough that someone would come out and see what was happening.

"Mrs. Ponsonby, stop! Think about this. How will you explain what happened to Laura and me?"

"That silly creature! Why would she try to stop me? Graeme will be free!"

"Perhaps because she's a decent human being who doesn't want to see anyone murdered?" Abby took a quick step backward as the branch whipped across in front of her. As it came back, she blocked it with her own "weapon."

"She doesn't know! She doesn't understand! They think you're nice." Mrs. Ponsonby made a scornful sound. "As if that mattered. You have no name, no lineage. You don't deserve to be married to a Parr. I stopped when I found out you were carrying his baby."

She continued to swing her weapon in a dangerous arc, driving Abby toward the bridge . . . and the water. Abby didn't dare take her eyes from the branch, but she feared that she would eventually step backward, all unknowing, into the stream.

"Of course you did," Abby agreed. "That's why you must stop now. You don't want to hurt Graeme's baby. You can't kill his heir, the future Lord Montclair."

"No, no, I realized!" Mrs. Ponsonby's voice rose in excitement. "Your blood will taint them. You're nothing but a mongrel American. God only knows where your family came from."

"But it's just a baby! You cannot wish to kill a child."

"I wouldn't have had to if Graeme hadn't kept after it! I thought it was over when he sent you away. But now he's here and as besotted with you as ever. He's gone to see the vicar."

"What does that matter? What does the vicar know?"

"I don't know! Nothing. Everything. Eventually Graeme will find out the truth. And I won't let you ruin his name."

"Whose name? Graeme's? How—"

"No!" Enraged, Mrs. Ponsonby slammed the end of the branch against the ground. Abby was pleased to see that the blow snapped off the end. "George! My George—you ruined him, you and your father."

"George? Your husband? *He* was the one who embezzled the funds?" Abby was so startled she dropped her guard. But fortunately Mrs. Ponsonby was too much in the grip of her obsession to take advantage.

"He would have put it back!" she shrieked. "He would never have taken the money if Thurston hadn't dazzled them with all his talk. George thought he would double his money. Triple it. No one would have noticed it had been missing a fortnight or two. It was your fault!" She swung wildly at Abby.

Abby knocked it away, taking another step back. "Me? I had nothing to do with it."

"Yes, you! You were the reason for all of it, so Graeme would have to take you. George lost everything—not only the money, but his good name. And Reggie! They were like brothers and then Montclair looked at him as if he were a worm, just because of that one little mistake. He—he abjured him! George, who had been his best friend his whole life, who'd always done whatever Reggie wanted. George couldn't bear to live anymore. All because of you!"

Eyes lit with fury, the other woman threw herself at Abby, swinging with all her might. Abby jerked to the side, blocking with the parasol, which finally snapped and went spinning away. Mrs. Ponsonby roared with triumph and raised the branch again.

chapter 34

Abby threw up her hands and caught the branch as it came down. The rough bark scraped her palms; the shock of it shot up her arms. But she held Mrs. Ponsonby off. The two women grappled over the stick, not even registering the shouts or the sound of running footsteps.

Suddenly Graeme loomed up behind Mrs. Ponsonby and, clasping his hands together, brought them down hard on the back of her head. The woman crumpled. Abby staggered at the sudden release of pressure on the stick, but Graeme lashed out with one hand and grabbed her arm, keeping her upright.

Abby flung herself into his arms. He squeezed her to him so tightly it took the breath from her; then he took her by the shoulders and set her back, anxiously examining her face and form.

"Are you all right? Did she hurt you?" Before Abby could answer, he wrapped his arms around her again. Cradling her to him, he kissed her hair and face, saying in broken spurts, "I was so worried. And then, when I found Mother and Grandmother . . . I knew she had gone after you. Are you all right? Truly?"

"Yes. Yes." Abby nodded, faintly surprised to find that

tears were running down her cheeks. "Oh, Graeme! I was scared she was going to hurt the baby. But she didn't," she added hastily when his arms tightened around her. "Wait. Laura! She hurt Laura."

"Laura! You're right. I forgot." They turned. Laura lay motionless a few feet away. "I saw her, but I couldn't stop."

They hurried over and knelt beside the blond woman.

"Look at all this blood," Abby gasped. "Is she—"

"No. I saw her fingers twitch. Head wounds bleed a great deal. Do you have a handkerchief?"

"No, it's in my reticule back inside. But no doubt Laura does." She found the pocket of the other woman's skirts and triumphantly pulled out a tidy white square.

Graeme chuckled. "Of course she would." He pressed the square against the cut, and Laura let out a groan. Her eyes fluttered open.

"Graeme?" Her face cleared. "Graeme! Abigail—Mrs.—" She struggled to sit up.

"No, don't worry. I'm fine." Abby put a firm hand on Laura's shoulder. "Just rest. She hit you hard."

Laura winced. "So it seems." She reached up a tentative hand. "I'm going to have a bump."

"Why did you come? I mean, how did you know?" Abby sat back on her heels. "Either one of you? I didn't suspect a thing until Mrs. Ponsonby came after me with that sunshade!"

"After I talked to the vicar, I realized that she was the only person who would care if the news got out." Graeme explained what he had learned that morning.

"I had no idea why she had tried to hurt you," Laura added. "But I was concerned about your fall on the stairs, so I asked around. Mary Littleton told me that she had been talking to Lady Fawley, who told her that she—Lady Fawley—had seen Mrs. Ponsonby push you."

"The idiotic woman." Graeme scowled. "Why didn't she speak up?"

"Lady Fawley rarely sees importance in anything that doesn't involve herself." Laura grimaced. "I was alarmed, of course, and I dared not wait for a letter to get to you, so I decided to simply come see you. When Fletcher told me you were with her, I came straight here. I told myself it was foolish, that she would not try anything with the other ladies around, but I had such an uneasy feeling about it. . . ."

"I'm very glad you did," Abby told her emphatically. "She was about to overcome me when you arrived. She was insanely strong."

"I think perhaps she is. Insane, I mean." Graeme sighed. "I can't believe we never realized. . . . Mrs. Ponsonby always seemed so meek."

"Apparently not when it came to her husband. She kept raving that I had ruined him and that she wouldn't let me destroy his reputation."

"Didn't it occur to her that she would create an even larger scandal by murdering you?" Laura asked.

Abby shrugged. "I suspect she thought that Graeme and his family would cover it up. She believed he would be relieved at getting his freedom once I was gone." Abby stopped, her cheeks filling with color. In her relief and gratitude to Laura, she had momentarily forgotten that Laura was the woman for whom Graeme would want his freedom.

"Abby . . ." Graeme turned to her, frowning.

Abby jumped to her feet. "Look. I think Mrs. Ponsonby is stirring."

Laura and Graeme followed her. Mrs. Ponsonby was indeed conscious, but all the fight had gone out of her. She turned on her side and began to weep, her body shaking with sobs.

Graeme shifted, his expression uneasy. "I've never struck a woman before. It wasn't very gentlemanly."

"Well, I, for one, am very glad you didn't play the gentleman this time."

"As am I." He curled an arm around Abby, pulling her against his side. "I have no regrets." He smiled down into her eyes. "None at all."

∞

It took some time to settle matters. The police were called, and Graeme turned the now-silent Philomena Ponsonby over to them. She seemed surprised to find that Montclair would not conceal what his grandmother's companion had done. No doubt it would be a terrible scandal and the whole wretched story of the embezzlement would come out. But Graeme had no intention of allowing the woman who attacked Abigail to go unpunished.

By the time he had finished explaining the events to the police, including Mrs. Ponsonby's likely guilt regarding an unsolved murder that had occurred in London, and returned to the private assembly room of the inn, Laura and Abby had managed to awaken the two older women. As soon as Graeme walked in the door, he was bombarded by questions.

Raising his hands as if to stop the flow of words, he said, "No, no, I beg you. I promise to answer all your questions when we reach Lydcombe, but right now, I only want to get Abby safely home. She's been through a terrible ordeal, and she must rest. I've ordered the carriage brought round for you. I rode here, so I shall follow you on horseback."

"I'm fine, really," Abby said.

"No use protesting, my love. You might as well resign yourself to being coddled and cosseted the next few days."

"Very well." Abby smiled. "I shall try to take it with good grace."

Laura elected to go back to London by train. Despite Mirabelle's and Abby's assurances that she must spend the night at the Hall with them, she insisted on leaving.

"It's not that long a distance, and fortunately trains run frequently to London. I shall have no trouble catching one."

When Graeme eventually managed to get his family out of the inn and into a carriage, Laura insisted, too, that there was no need to escort her to the train station. "Really, Graeme, I am quite capable of finding the station myself. You should be with your wife."

"I will be, don't worry. And I am aware of how capable you are. However, you must allow me to offer at least this small measure of assistance. I have done little enough today to protect anyone."

"What nonsense." Laura smiled. She had cleaned the cut on her head and wound her hair back up into its usual order. Popping her plain bonnet on her head, she looked once again her neat, practical self.

He could not imagine his own Abby even possessing so plain a hat or dress, let alone wearing it. How was it, Graeme wondered, that he had given his heart to two such different women?

At the train station he bought her ticket home despite her protestations, saying, "Laura, please, it is the least I can do after all you have done for me today." He looked down at her seriously. "You saved my wife. My child. I cannot ever repay you."

"I was happy to do so." Laura reached out and laid her hand on his arm. "You must believe that, Graeme."

"I do." He paused, then went on, "Laura, you know that I care for you. You were long my dearest companion, and you will always have a place in my heart."

"I know. And you in mine." She smiled. "Graeme, dear friend, I know what you are trying to tell me."

"Good, because I'm not entirely sure I do."

"You have fallen in love with your wife," Laura said simply. "That's a good thing. All I want is for you to be happy."

"I am happy." He heard the surprise in his own voice. "I really am."

"I won't pretend I wasn't sad to lose you, or that I haven't missed you many a time over the past years. But that was a long time ago, and we are different people now. We've made other lives for ourselves. I am your friend, and I hope that you are mine as well. But you love Abigail."

"I do." An almost conspiratorial grin flashed across Graeme's face. "I love her more than I ever thought possible."

"And she loves you."

"Do you think so? I—I have made so many mistakes with her."

"I'm sure. Anyone who sees her look at you knows it. And if you've made mistakes, I'm sure she will forgive you. You are an easy man to forgive."

"Like my father." He shrugged.

"You are a far better man than your father, Graeme." Laura patted his arm. "I promise you."

Laura's words were enough to keep his spirits buoyed all the way back to the estate. There he was slowed down by his mother and grandmother, who assured him that Abby was upstairs asleep and that they desperately needed to hear his account of the afternoon's events.

"You know I treasure you, Mother," he said, gently removing her hand from his arm. "And I will tell you everything in the most minute detail later, but right now, I must go to my wife."

Lady Eugenia started to protest, but after her initial surprise, his mother only smiled. "Of course, darling."

He took the stairs two at a time. When he reached the top, he saw that Abby's maid was standing outside his door as if on guard. Little as he looked forward to dealing with the woman, it gave him a spurt of satisfaction to know that Abby had once again chosen to sleep in his bed.

"Molly." He nodded to her and started past, but she shifted so that she was squarely in his way.

"I wanted to thank you, sir." Her words shocked him into speechlessness. "For saving Miss Ab— Lady Montclair. I was wrong about you, and I admit it."

"I am stunned." Graeme grinned.

"Aye, well, you'd best take care of her, that's all I have to say."

"I will."

Graeme stepped around Molly and opened his bedroom door. He looked immediately toward the bed, but Abby was not there. She sat in the easy chair before the fire. Her hands, palms bandaged in strips of white, lay in her lap, and her head was tilted back, her eyes closed. Obviously, she had refused to rest in bed—little surprise there—but exhaustion had caught up with her anyway.

He knew he should leave the room and let her sleep, but he could not turn away just yet. As he stood there, Abby's eyes opened and she saw him. A smile curved her lips. "Graeme."

"Abby." He crossed the floor to her in two quick strides. Sinking down to his knees, he wrapped his arms around her, laying his head against her breast. "My love."

∽

Abby went still. She had fallen asleep waiting for Graeme, and for an instant, she wondered if she was still dreaming. Caressingly, she ran her hand over his hair, letting herself drift in the moment. Finally he lifted his head and sat back on his heels, studying her face.

"I was so frightened. I thought I would lose you, and I—I've never felt like that. So scared and helpless. I rode like a maniac, and then I saw you struggling with her . . ." He shook his head. Graeme picked up one of her hands in his and looked at her palm, his fingers gently sliding over the bandage. "Your hands. I didn't realize you hurt your hands."

"I scraped my palms holding on to that branch." Abby shrugged. "It looks worse than it is. Molly slathered salve on them so enthusiastically she had to wrap bandages around them to keep me from sliding off everything I touched."

"I'm sorry." He raised her palm to his lips and softly kissed it.

"It's not your fault." She smiled at him, reaching out to brush a strand of hair from his forehead.

"Yes. It is. Ultimately it is all laid at my door. I've made a thousand mistakes. More. From the very beginning I was blind and stubborn and so wrapped up in my bitterness,

I didn't even look at you. I assumed a great deal without having any real knowledge. I didn't give you—I didn't give *us* a chance. Worse, I was unfair and unkind to you."

"That's all long ago. You aren't the only one who made mistakes. My pride was hurt, and I ran away. I could have stayed and explained it to you. And before that, I could have discovered what my father was doing; I think I probably didn't want to know. Because I was getting what I wanted. It was selfish of me. I wanted to marry you so much."

"Why?"

Abby chuckled at his astounded tone. "Because the moment I saw you, I wanted you. You were handsome; you were the perfect gentleman. You may not be aware of it, but when you smile, you take a person's breath away. I suspect a large number of girls would have been thrilled to marry you. I know I was. I'm not entirely sure I would have turned you down even if I had known then that you loved another."

"Abby . . ." He did not look at her for a long moment, frowning down at their linked hands. Just when she thought he would say nothing more, he raised his head. "I've known Laura since we were children. Her mother and mine were good friends, and they visited often until her mother died. Even after that, we saw her when we were in London."

"Graeme, you don't need to explain. I understand." Abby tried to tug her hand away, but Graeme held it fast, his eyes intent on hers.

"No, you don't. *I* didn't understand. I did love Laura, but it wasn't the way I love you."

Abby's breath caught in her throat, but she did her best

not to show any reaction, afraid she might stop the flow of his words.

"What I felt for Laura was nice—a quiet thing, a natural progression, I suppose, from the friendship we had always had. I still care for her, but I think it is the way I would feel about a sister. I've never had one; perhaps if I had, I would have recognized it for what it was. It was nothing compared to the way I love you. The passion and fire and depth . . . Oh, the devil, I'm not good at explaining how I feel."

"I think you're doing a stellar job of it. Go on."

"This afternoon, I realized that if I were faced now with having to give you up as I did Laura, I wouldn't do it. No matter what the consequences—scandal, penury, whatever came—I would never have set you aside. It would have been like tearing out my own heart."

"Oh, Graeme!" Abby clapped both hands over her mouth, tears welling in her eyes.

"No, please, don't cry. I realize you probably don't feel the same. But I'm going to do everything I can to change that. I will woo you and win you—you know I am stubborn enough to keep at it and too proud to admit defeat. If we were not already married, I would ask you on bended knee. But as it is, I can only say I want to be with you, to have a real marriage."

"You idiot!" Abby flung her arms around his neck, belying her words. "Of course I love you. I fell in love with you ten years ago, and when I returned a few months ago, I did it all over again."

Graeme surged to his feet, taking her with him, and locked his mouth on hers. When at last he lifted his head, he smiled down into her face, saying, "Then you bartered with me for more than a child?"

"I told myself I would be content with a child, but that was a lie." Abby linked her hands behind his neck. "The truth is, I want it all—marriage, children . . . and most of all you."

"Then, my love, I would say we have a bargain."

"Indeed we do." Abby grinned up at him saucily. "How should we seal it, do you think?"

Graeme swept her up in his arms and carried her to the bed. "I'll show you."

epilogue

Graeme strode from desk to window to fireplace, unable to keep still. "It's taking far too long, don't you think? There must be something wrong."

His cousin, sitting in the comfortable chair before the fire, long legs stretched out to warm his toes, opened an eye and regarded him. "As I said the last three times you asked, I haven't the faintest idea. I've had no more infants than you."

"Clearly not. This is where you're supposed to tell me I've nothing to worry about and that it's all going as it should."

James rolled his eyes. "Why don't you sit down? You're making me dizzy."

Graeme released a long-suffering sigh and threw himself down into the chair across from James.

He immediately popped up again as his mother sailed into the room, beaming. "Is it over?" He hurried toward her. "Is Abby—"

"Mother and daughter are fine."

Graeme stopped, feeling suddenly a little light-headed. "Daughter? It's a girl?"

"Congratulations, Graeme." James arose and followed him.

"Yes—I—thank you. I must go see her." He swung back around to his mother. "Abby's all right? You said she's all right."

"Yes. She's doing very well. The doctor will be down to tell you shortly, but I couldn't wait."

"I don't want to see the doctor. I want to talk to Abby." Graeme strode past her and trotted up the stairs. The doctor was just stepping out of the room, and Graeme nodded at him as the man began to speak. "Yes, just a moment. First, I must . . ."

He bypassed the man, going straight to the bed. "Abby."

Her eyes were closed and her face was pale, which set his heart to racing, but as soon as she heard his voice, Abby opened her eyes and smiled up at him. "Graeme."

"My love." He took her hand and bent to kiss her forehead. "Are you all right? I can't believe . . . Mother said it went fine, but it's been so long. You look tired." He realized that he was babbling and stopped.

"I'm fine." Abby squeezed his hand. "I'm wonderful."

"Yes, you are." He smoothed his hand over her forehead.

"We have a baby girl." She turned her head. "Molly? Where is she?"

"Here we are." Molly bustled forward, smiling broadly. Graeme could not recall seeing such an expression on the maid's face before now. In her arms, she carried a small bundle. She stopped in front of Graeme, holding out the roll of material to him, and he realized that inside the blanket lay a small, red-faced creature.

Before he knew what she was doing, Molly settled the bundle in his arms. "Oh, but I don't . . ." He raised his head to find that Molly had already stepped back.

Graeme looked back down at the tiny face. She was

slightly less red than a tomato, and her eyes were squeezed tightly shut, her mouth wide open, though the sound that came out was more a cranky hiccup than a cry. Tiny black brows curved above her eyes, miniature replicas of Abby's eyebrows, and atop her head was a damp mop of hair the same raven color. Her tiny fists waved spasmodically, and he could see her feet beating against the blanket. With her flying fists and the faint bruising beside one eye, she looked as if she'd been sparring.

"She's . . . beautiful," he breathed, awestruck.

The noise she was making became a wail, and her face grew even redder. Graeme, feeling a bit panicked, jiggled her a bit, and amazingly, she hiccupped to a stop. Cradling her in one arm, he reached out a finger to her hand, amazed at its tiny detail. Her fingers curled around his, and his heart swelled in his chest.

"Abby, she's absolutely perfect."

"I know."

Graeme grinned at his wife, then leaned over the bed to carefully place the baby in the crook of Abby's arm. Watching his wife, her dark head close to her daughter's, Graeme thought that he had never seen anything so beautiful.

Together they watched the baby, exclaiming over the perfection of her many features, from her shell-like ears to her tiny toenails, until she fell asleep and Molly swooped in to take her away. Abby smiled up at him, but he could see the weariness gathering around her eyes.

"You should sleep. You need your rest. She'll be a whirlwind. Just like her mother."

Abby took his hand. "You aren't disappointed, then? That she's not a boy?"

"No. How could I be disappointed? She's beautiful. Again, just like her mother."

"But you don't have your heir."

"I don't care. I'd take ten more just like her."

"Ten!" Abby chuckled, rubbing her thumb over his fingers. "I think not."

"Besides"—Graeme bent down and kissed her forehead—"it'll give us a reason to try again."

"Do you need a reason?"

"No." He smiled into her eyes. "I need no reason but you, my love."

Turn the page for a preview of

A Momentary Marriage

By Candace Camp

Coming soon from Pocket Books

Laura glanced around the cluttered room. She had packed most of her belongings, but she hadn't had the heart to enter her father's study. Now, looking at his books and papers haphazardly stacked and scattered and wedged in wherever they would go, tears clogged her throat anew.

It was so unfair that a good, kind, intelligent man like her father, a man who had spent his life healing others, should be taken away when so many other men far less worthy than he survived. Venal, brutal men like Sid Merton.

She scowled at the thought of their landlord. He would be coming around today, wanting his money in full—no matter that her father had been in his grave less than two weeks. She had been selling everything she could, but few people wanted their multitude of books or their old, well-worn furniture.

As if her thoughts had conjured him up, there was a loud knock at the front door. Laura opened it and faced Sid Merton with all the calm and dignity she could muster. The man started to walk in, but Laura neatly sidestepped him, slipping out of the house and into the yard.

Thwarted, Merton followed, looming over her. Tall and heavily muscled, he was accustomed to intimidating everyone. "I want my rent money."

Laura curled her fingers into her skirts. "It will take time to settle my father's affairs. I'll find a way to pay you what we owe if you will only wait—"

"Oh, I could wait." Merton smiled in a way that sent a shiver of revulsion through her. He wrapped his beefy hand around her wrist, tugging her toward him. "If you were nice."

"Let go of me." Laura tried to pull her arm away, but he jerked her forward. She slammed against his broad chest, and Merton twisted her arm up behind her back.

Behind them someone cleared his throat loudly. "I beg your pardon."

A tall, thin man stood at the edge of the yard beside a carriage. His face was shadowed by a hat, and his pose was studiedly careless, his weight on one leg and a hand resting lightly on the head of a gold-knobbed cane. In a faintly bored voice steeped in aristocratic hauteur, he went on, "It appears your suit is unwelcome to the lady."

"What business is it of yours?" Merton snarled.

"Well, you see, I have come to speak with her father." He swept off his hat and sketched a bow to Laura. "Good afternoon, Miss Hinsdale. I hope I have not arrived at an inopportune time."

"James de Vere." Laura stared. He was the last person she expected to see in her yard. He looked older and thinner—but, of course, it had been eleven years since the day he strode into her parlor to slice her hopes and dreams to ribbons.

Sir James was still as coldly handsome, his tone as supercilious. And though the sight of him awoke a host of bitter feelings, Laura could not help but be glad of his arrival. At least Sir James was a gentleman—and the kind of man who always won.

"If you would be so kind, Miss Hinsdale, I would appreciate a bit of your time," Sir James went on. "If, of course, you are not otherwise occupied."

"I am perfectly free." Laura took another step away

from Merton, yanking her arm as hard as she could. Merton's grip did not loosen.

"You're not going anywhere," Merton growled at her.

James turned a disdainful gaze on him. "You, my good man, are becoming tiresome."

"Tiresome!" Merton gaped at him.

"Yes. I believe it's time you left."

"You're the one that's leaving," Merton said menacingly, his free hand knotting into a fist.

"I think not. For the last time, release Miss Hinsdale."

Merton let out a scornful laugh, making a show of looking the other man up and down. "You think you're going to make me?"

"No." James smiled thinly and snapped his fingers. The largest dog Laura had ever seen jumped out of the open carriage door. "He is."

There was a dead silence as both Laura and Merton eyed the dog. The top of his blocky head was level with James's waist. His muscular body was a mottled combination of black and yellowish tan, but the muzzle and face were entirely black, as if he wore a mask, and it rendered his eyes barely visible, giving him an even more sinister appearance.

James flicked his hand toward Laura and Merton. "Guard."

The dog stalked over—he was even more terrifying at close range—and took up a stance beside Laura, his eyes fixed on Merton. Color drained from the big man's face, and he dropped Laura's arm. Shooting her a vicious look, Merton whirled and strode away, not even glancing in Sir James's direction.

Laura's stunned gaze went to James. Gratitude mingled

awkwardly with her years-old dislike for the man. "I, um, thank you."

He gave a careless shrug and strolled toward her. As he drew close, she could see purplish shadows beneath his eyes. His face was etched with lines of weariness. He looked as if he hadn't slept in weeks. "I could hardly allow the churl to accost you. Graeme would have had my head."

"I doubt Graeme would have ever known." Sir James accepted gratitude as gracelessly as he did everything else.

She looked down at the dog. Her eyes hadn't very far to go. The animal regarded her gravely. His muzzle had a few flecks of gray in it, and the thick wrinkles above his eyes gave him a worried look.

"And thank you," she told the dog. He accepted the compliment better than his master, giving a wag of his tail as he continued to study her. Laura was someone who generally liked dogs, but this one made her a trifle wary. "May I pet him?"

"Yes. He's not likely to bite your hand off." James might look older and more worn, but his voice was still the same, delivering whatever he said in a cool, faintly ironic tone.

"Not likely? That's reassuring." She stroked her hand across his head. The dog allowed her caress without losing any of his dignity—no fawning, rear-end-wiggling, hand-licking response from him. His calm, steady scrutiny was a trifle unnerving. "Trust you to have a pet that terrifies people."

She thought the noise James made was a chuckle. "Trust you not to back away from him."

Had he just given her a compliment? It seemed unlikely. James shifted and cleared his throat. "Miss Hinsdale . . . I came to talk to your father. Is Dr. Hinsdale in?"

Tears suddenly filled Laura's eyes. She had not cried for a few days, but somehow now, at his casual mention of her father's name, she was pierced all anew.

"Papa died two weeks ago," she told him baldly. No need to couch things in a genteel manner with this man.

Despair gazed back at her from his eyes for an instant, before the mask descended once again. "I see. Well, that's that, then." He glanced away. "My condolences." Then, awkwardly, "I am sorry, Laura."

"Thank you." His use of her given name startled her; he had not addressed her so since they were children. Though he was Graeme's cousin, he had never been Laura's friend. But there was a genuineness to the brief statement that unexpectedly touched her. "Would you like to come inside?"

He looked as if he needed to sit down. And he had just rescued her from Merton's unwelcome attentions. Surely that deserved some politeness.

"Oh. Well." James cast a glance around with an uncertainty she had never seen in him. "Yes, thank you."

Both man and dog trailed after her as she led them to the parlor. As soon as they stepped into the room, memories flooded Laura. It had been here that James, in a voice devoid of emotion, had listed Laura's many deficiencies as a bride to the future Earl of Montclair. His cousin Graeme, he told her, must marry an American heiress. Laura would ruin Graeme's life.

She sent him a covert glance. Was James remembering that moment, too? No, in all likelihood, it had been only a minor bit of business for him, barely a bump in the road.

"Would you care for tea?" she asked in a brittle voice.

"Thank you, no," he replied. He seemed lost in thought.

Laura cast about for something to start a conversation, wishing she had not given into courtesy and invited him in.

"Miss Hinsdale . . ."

"Yes?"

"I have a question to ask of you."

"What?" Laura looked at him warily.

"Are you always so suspicious?"

"I have had conversations with you before . . ."

He grimaced. "Well, I'm not here to blight your life this time. I am proposing an arrangement of mutual benefit."

Laura gaped at him, her mind reeling. "Pardon? Are you . . . are you offering me a carte blanche?"

He was the one who stared now. "Good God. No, Miss Hinsdale. I am not trying to lure your nubile body into my bed, lovely as I am sure it is."

Laura crossed her arms over her chest. "Just what *are* you doing?"

"I am asking for your hand in marriage."

His words were so far from anything Laura expected to hear that she could hardly grasp them. "Are you joking?"

"I rarely jest about marriage, I assure you."

"I . . . uh . . . why?"

"I would think the advantages to you are clear." He raised one eyebrow. "I hope it is not too vain of me to point out that you would have a much more agreeable future than the one you are currently facing, which, with your father's demise, offers only penury and the less than alluring prospect of throwing yourself upon your relatives' generosity. On the other hand, I can offer you a gracious home, a generous allowance, and a respectable, dare I say, honored name."

He sounded as if he were offering her employment. "But why would *you* want to? What possible reason could you have for proposing to me?" Long-buried resentment bubbled up in Laura. "If I was not good enough to be Graeme's wife, as you so kindly told me, how could I possibly be acceptable as yours?"

"I never said you were unworthy." It was some balm to her feelings that James looked taken aback. "The only issue was saving the Montclair estate. I can assure you I never questioned your character. In fact, it was precisely your good character I counted on. I was certain that once you understood how ruinous it would be to Graeme to wed you, you would break it off. I knew I could use your sense of honor against you."

"What a cold and calculating man you are." His words were mollifying, at least in regard to his opinion of her, but it amazed her that he would admit it. "It's hard to believe you're related to Graeme."

"It's a wonder, isn't it? But I have never tried to appear otherwise."

"I don't know that it makes it any better." She studied him. "Still, I fail to see any cold calculation in proposing to me."

He gave her a wry look. "I would guess that most women would regard marriage to me a cold thing indeed."

"No doubt. But that's not an explanation."

"My motive doesn't matter."

"It makes a difference to me. It isn't as if you like me. You barely know me. And I am relatively certain I am not the sort of woman whom you would choose."

"You're right," he shot back, temper flaring in his eyes. "You are not the sort of woman I planned to marry. However, at the moment my choices are rather limited."

Her eyes widened. "I can understand why if this is your manner of wooing."

"I have not tried to 'woo' anyone."

"I am your first attempt at a proposal?"

"Yes."

"But why? Why would you choose *me*?"

"I am beginning to wonder that myself." When Laura did not respond, but simply crossed her arms and waited, he continued, "There are many reasons a man would want to marry you."

"I want to know *your* reasons."

"Well . . . you are attractive . . . genteel . . . um . . ." Laura lifted a brow. "Oh, the devil with it. I chose you because I thought you were in such exigent circumstances that you would agree."

"At least you are candid."

"I usually am."

"Then let me be equally straightforward. I may be in exigent circumstances, but I would rather remain in my penniless state, here in my ungracious home, with my un-respectable name, than share your bed."

He let out a dry laugh, surprising her. "Trust me, Miss Hinsdale, the way I feel now, lust is the furthest thing from my mind."

"What about in the future?"

"There won't be any future. I am dying." He delivered his news with a flat calm, almost as if he were discussing someone else.

"Oh." Laura's face softened.

"I don't want your pity." His voice was sharp as a knife. "I am telling you this so that you understand I have no in-tention of robbing you of your virtue. I won't demand my husbandly rights. And you will not have to be my wife long before you are my widow."

Explore the history of desire with bestselling historical romance from Pocket Books!

Pick up or download your copies today!

XOXOAfterDark.com

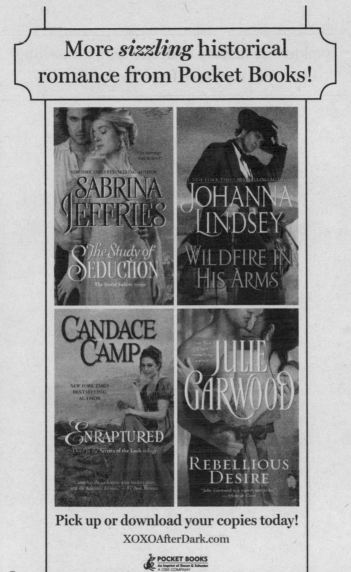